INTO THIN AIR

Also by Caroline Leavitt

Family
Jealousies
Lifelines
Meeting Rozzy Halfway

INTO THIN AIR
CAROLINE LEAVITT

WARNER BOOKS

A Time Warner Company

Warner Books, Inc., 1271 Avenue of the Americas, New York, NY 10020

A Time Warner Company

Printed in the United States of America
First printing: February 1993
10 9 8 7 6 5 4 3 2 1

LIBRARY OF CONGRESS CATALOGING IN PUBLICATION DATA

Leavitt, Caroline.
    Into thin air / Caroline Leavitt.
        p.   cm.
    ISBN 0-446-51704-6
    I. Title.
PS3562.E2617I58   1993
813'.54—dc20   91-51164
                                                         CIP

Book Designed by L. McRee

ACKNOWLEDGMENTS

I would like to thank the New York Foundation of the Arts for financial—and moral—support during the writing of this book. I'd also like to thank my agent, Judith Weber, and everyone else at the agency—Wanda Cuevas, Craig Holden and Andrea Harding—for their committed support, enthusiasm and all-around wonderfulness. And of course, I want to thank my absolutely terrific editor Maureen Egen.

For attentively wading through the earliest drafts, I can't ever thank Linda Corcoran enough. And many thanks, too, to Jeff Tamarkin, Jo Fisher, Anne Edelstein and Jane Praeger.

I'd also like to thank Martha Rhodes, Peter Salzano, Barb Goren, Jerry Gale, Ivan Diamond and especially Nancy A. Lattanzi, for a multitude of kindnesses.

For my mother, Helen Leavitt.

And this book is dedicated, with all my love, to my husband Jeff Tamarkin, for absolutely everything.

INTO THIN AIR

BALTIMORE. A 19-year-old Baltimore woman apparently disappeared from her hospital bed Tuesday morning, only hours after giving birth.

According to officials at Twinbrook Hospital, a nurse entering the private room of Lee Archer, 2134 Eutaw Pl., found her bed empty and no sign of her in the bathroom or on the maternity ward. After finding her clothes in the closet, officials then called police, but there were no signs of foul play, police said yesterday.

The woman's husband was said to be in a state of shock. Hospital officials said Ms. Archer had given birth Tuesday to a healthy daughter after an easy delivery. Nurses said the couple seemed tired but happy.

"We've never had anything like this happen here before," said one hospital official who asked not to be named. "I haven't any idea what happened. I just hope she's okay, wherever she is."

—Baltimore Daily Press, July 6, 1988

MISSING
Lee Archer.
19 years old.
Blond hair, gray eyes, 5'6".
110 lbs.
Small scar on right shoulder.
REWARD.
CONTACT JIM ARCHER, 555-3362
2134 Eutaw Pl., Baltimore

1550 Warwick Avenue
Waltham, MA 02154
July 15, 1988

Dear Mr. Archer:

I think I have seen your wife, but I can't be sure. I think she
had the room next to me at the Best Western just off the
Beltway in Pikesville. She was coming out of the room next to
mine and looked just like the girl on all those flyers I saw
posted all over town, only younger maybe. When I asked her
what her name was, she said it was Beth. I remember because
it was the same as mine. I thought about it all during breakfast. My husband said I was crazy and that it was none of my
business anyway, but the more I thought about it, the surer I
was. I was going to call the police when we got back to her
room, but by then her room was empty. How could I have
stopped her anyway?

I hope this helps you to find her, and I realize I don't get any
reward, but that's all right. At least you know she's alive.

Sincerely,

Beth Brill

Beth Brill (Mrs.)

—1—

Lee was almost two days out of Maryland when she saw the newspaper. She was struggling to eat dinner at the Moon Man, a brightly lit diner just outside of Richmond, hunched over with fever, fighting sleep. The waitress, harshly pretty, dimming into middle age, was dressed in starchy nurse's whites, a black apron cinching her waist. She took one long measuring look at Lee and then glided right over, leaning across the blue counter. "Anything else you need, honey?" she said. "There's hot coffee just brewed."

Lee, sandwich midmouth, saw her over a horizon of grilled cheese. The waitress had a pink plastic Saturn bobbing over her left breast. ADELE, it said in careful curlicued script. She had lavender eyeglasses dangling from a tarnished chain about her neck and stiffly blonded hair pruned and shaped like topiary. She leaned toward Lee with so much cheerful concern, it made Lee nervous. "I don't drink it," Lee said.

"You and my daughter both," Adele said, swabbing down the counter with a dirty red cloth. "A full-grown woman and she lives on that lousy cocoa from a mix." She made graceful parabolas with the cloth. "You kind of remind me of her. Neither one of you knows a single thing about nutrition. Jesus, just look at that plate of yours. Last I heard, grease wasn't exactly one of the four basic food groups. There's such a thing as a nice green salad. You could have ordered our tuna plate and made out just fine," she said. Adele shook her head at Lee's circuitry of french fries and then lifted her cloth, rinsing it in the sink under a spumy stream of water. "You got kids?" she said amiably, wringing out the cloth. Lee flinched.

"Never," she said stiffly, concentrating on the pale circle of skin where her wedding band used to be. She had gotten fifty dollars for it that morning at a jewelry shop right down the street.

"You will," Adele said as if soothing her. "Why, you got plenty of time to change your mind."

She started cleaning farther along the counter, joking with the men sitting there, scooping up tips and trash, stabbing on her glasses to squint out the total on a bill. "You interested in this?" she called, picking up a paper someone had left. "*Washington Post*," she said, sliding it down the counter toward Lee. "Today's too and not a dot of gravy on it."

Unnerved, Lee blinked at the paper in front of her. She hadn't once read a newspaper or heard the news since she had left Baltimore. She had been too rushed, too conscious of the trailing, ominous echo of footsteps, the delicate brush of an arm steeling to grab. It was the *Post*, she told herself, not the *Baltimore Daily Press*; it didn't have to have any news in there about her. She smoothed down the paper with the flat of one hand, but she suddenly felt uneasy, as if she were being watched. She stared back up along the counter, but Adele was pouring long foamy trails of coffee into chipped white cups; two men in faded plaid shirts were passing a crumpled pack of Camel filters behind the back of a third. Everyone under the watery glare of the fluorescent lights looked a strange sallow yellow, but they were living their own lives, not hers; she might have been invisible for all the attention she was getting.

To her left, the front door loomed. Six o'clock and the sun was still beating through the glass, and there she was, the only person here who was so shivery in the artificial cool that she was slouched into a wool plaid jacket half as yellow as her hair. She looked back down at the paper, anticipation muddied with fear.

Lee's focus stumbled across the front page. There were rumors of another nuclear disaster in Russia; garbled reports of possible radioactivity filtering through the drinking supply. The mayor had issued a war on drugs because his son had been shot to death while buying heroin in some back alley. He swore he had never so much as seen his kid take an aspirin, that's how clean the kid was.

She skimmed, past page two, pages five and six, bouncing her focus from picture to picture, catching only the first few words of every headline. There was nothing that even hinted of her. She was on page thirty already, with only two more pages of the paper to go, and then she turned the page, glancing uneasily at a small section, bannered in black, titled "Regional News." And then she saw it. There, sandwiched between one story about a ten-year-old caught joyriding his mother's car in Pikesville and another report of a brutal parking lot murder, was a grainy black-and-white photograph. A girl with voluminous hair and a wobbling grave smile, one arm shielded stiffly across her body.

Lee's hands, in a sudden skip of fear, recoiled from the page. She knew that picture. Jim had taken it the day they had run away from Philadelphia to get married. They had been in a hurry, flushed, overdressed in the bruised June heat. Lee's father and his new wife were probably looking for her; they'd called the police once because of her, they could do it again. Still, Jim had insisted on posing her against the grimy edge of the waiting Greyhound bus. Leaning toward her, he had pushed up the collar of her leather jacket. As soon as he stepped away from her, she flipped it back down. Her green knapsack had bit into her shoulder, weighted with jeans and sweaters and books and half a dozen pieces of the intricately carved silverware her mother had left her. Lee still had a single silver fork, wrapped in disintegrating blue tissue paper, tucked carefully at the bottom of her purse. At night she gently peeled the tissue from the fork, turning it so it caught and broke up the light, studying her reflection in between the tarnish. She was enough of her mother's daughter to have inherited some superstition; sometimes she talked herself into believing the fork had powers. It might be this was a talisman, a protective gift from a mother who might watch more over her in death than she ever had in life. She'd wish on the tines, squinching her eyes shut so tightly that she saw stars of color pulse across her lids.

The photo wavered in front of her, the face of an eerily familiar stranger. Lee tracked it with a ragged edge of nail. She didn't even look like that girl anymore. All that hair was shorn. The lean angularity, the coltish boniness, were softened. That girl's life had nothing to do with hers anymore. That girl had still been in high school, barely seventeen, just a wild betrayed heart who had gotten into trouble once too often, who had had to flee to escape being sent away. A girl so panicky she had actually thought Jim was a temporary solution.

"That's some look on your face, sweetie," Adele said, leaning over to her. "Someone you know die?"

"I changed my mind, I want the coffee," Lee said.

"Now you're being smart," Adele said, pivoting away.

Missing, the newspaper said. Missing. She was suddenly dizzy. The diner seemed to shift in space, disorienting her, and when she looked down at the newspaper again, the words beneath her picture braided together. Abruptly, she closed the paper and stood up, toppling her plate, skidding fries and gravy across the clean counter.

"Oh, bloody hell," Adele said, setting down the pot, reaching for a rag.

"I have to go," Lee said abruptly, glancing at the watch she wore that hadn't worked all week. Every time she looked down at it, it was the wrong time. She clicked open her purse, digging around for loose bills.

She quickly pushed some crumpled dollars toward the waitress, and while Adele's back was turned, she stuffed the newspaper deep within her jacket. She wondered who here might already have seen her picture and made connections. Someone could be casually wandering over to a pay phone right that minute and dialing the police. Lee hadn't been able to read the article; she didn't know if there was any reward out on her. That would be like Jim to do. There were people in Baltimore who did nothing but stare at the Wanted photos in the post office. There was one woman who actually made sketches of the faces, who kept a notebook on possible suspects. There were people who had whole dreams constructed on reward money, on recognizing faces no matter how changed they might be. Lifting herself up from her stool, Lee twisted toward the phone. A woman, her hair in pink sponge rollers, was crying into the phone. "How many times can I say I'm sorry?" she wept.

Adele put a hand on Lee's arm.

"Change," Adele said. She held out a fist full of money, but Lee was already at the door, jerking it open, stepping out into a smothering noose of heat.

She ate hot dusty gulps of air; she was still moving too slowly. Her body felt rusty, but her mind was racing, skimming on the surface of every possible danger, and tormenting her. She had planned on one more night in Richmond, just to get a little stronger, but now she was taking the next train out of here, no matter where it was going.

The bus stop was just another block, an open green wood shelter with a splintered bench inside, and she could already see from here how deserted it was. As soon as she got to the bench, her legs collapsed beneath her. Lee peered down the ribbon of road, bracing her hand against the bench, and then abruptly she pulled the paper out of her jacket and riffled it open to her picture again.

They got most of the details right. Except it wasn't such a mystery. Not to her.

She had planned carefully, packing her hospital suitcase, tucking in a brand-new outfit Jim didn't even know she owned, a sleeveless blue jersey dress she could slide into, a pair of black shoes that wouldn't show the dirt, and an Orioles baseball cap she had bought on the street for just two dollars. There was money, too. Five thousand dollars of Jim's, from a joint savings account. She would have cleaned out the entire account if she hadn't needed Jim's signature in order to do it or if she'd had the slightest talent in forging his name. Instead she'd depleted the account of everything but twenty dollars. The statement wouldn't come for a month, and what money Jim needed, he took from a separate checking account. Lee had kept the money thickly folded up in an envelope, layered under a bag of old clothes in the closet. Every time he even went near the closet, she found some reason to bring him away.

In the hospital she had insisted on a private room, on a door she could keep closed. "Why, there's another mother named Lee, too!" the admitting nurse had gushed, as if Lee might become friends with this other Lee for life. "This is her third, and already she's making plans for a fourth," the nurse had said, patting Lee's arm. "You have any questions, she's the expert." But Lee had no intention of talking to her or to any of the other mothers. She was afraid of all that camaraderie. She didn't want to hear one word about miracles and magic and bonding. She didn't want to know one single thing about what she might end up missing. And most of all she didn't want to see the baby because, then, she might never leave at all. The baby. Oh, God.

She had never intended marrying Jim, never intended winding up terrified and trapped in a suburb, where she had more in common with the kids than with their strongly settled young mothers. She was waitressing, saving money for a train ticket out, edging toward eighteen and freedom. How had escape backfired into prison?

She had had no signs. No clutch of nausea in the morning. No cravings. She didn't feel one thing different until she missed her second period, and then she began waking in the middle of the night, slick with sweat, in a dizzying panic.

"What's wrong?" Jim said. She brushed the air away from her. "My period," she said. "I'm getting it."

She lay spooned beside him. He flung one leg over her hip, pinning her down. Wriggling, she freed herself. "Where you going?" he said. "Drink of water," she told him. Padding in the dark, she went to the kitchen and rummaged for her mother's silver fork; she wished so hard on it, the edges dug into her fingers.

The next morning she went out and bought herself a box of tampons, leaving it on the dresser where Jim would see it, and then, terrified, she called a doctor.

She kept telling herself that the baby was nothing, not big enough to be real. She had even thought of getting rid of it. She had put on a new rose-colored dress. She brushed her hair down her back and had gone all the way into the clinic, giving her name, sitting down on one of the brightly colored plastic chairs. She had one friend who had had an abortion. Her mother had paid for it, had sat outside in the waiting room, crying into a handkerchief. There was nothing wrong with it, she gave her change for the cause, she signed petitions and argued for the rights of women, but when she heard her own name called, something seemed to breathe inside of her. Her bones suddenly filled with fluid. "I—I'll be right back," she stammered. "I forgot something." She cocked her head toward the door and then walked out again, past the protesters who swarmed paper leaflets toward her.

She had tried again, a different clinic this time. Cleaner, more expensive, with a different class of protesters, more tired looking, less vociferous, women in faded fur coats who just looked at Lee sadly. And when she left this clinic, too, she told herself she still had time, that women got abortions later on, it was just more difficult. Her buttery heart was not going to ruin her.

She hated herself for feeling anything toward the baby, for being so weak. If she concentrated, she could get through a whole day sometimes without thinking about the baby at all. But then, there she would be, dipping to fetch a can of corn, turning in bed, and she'd somehow sense the baby inside of her. She swore she felt a presence, and she felt sorry for it. "Oh, now," she'd whisper. "Now, now."

She'd put a hand on her stomach, soothing, murmuring, not seeing Jim waking up beside her, lifting himself up on one elbow to listen, his face baffled. "I'm whispering to you," she said, moving her hand from her stomach to his.

"Are you saying 'I love you'?" he said hopefully. "You never say 'I love you' to me."

She gave him a wan smile.

"I know you do," he told her. "I love you. Forever."

She did this dance. She tried pretending she wasn't pregnant at all, but her body kept betraying her. Mornings, she stumbled to the bathroom, flooding the tub with water so Jim wouldn't hear her throwing up. She couldn't keep breakfast down, so she stopped eating it, complaining to Jim that she was trying to starve off the few extra pounds that even he could see.

She took days off her waitressing job at the Silver Spoon and watched whole lazy afternoons unwind, sitting at one of the local coffee shops sipping a malted and laughing and talking to whoever would come and sit down beside her. And there was always someone, always another pair of eyes in which she might see a future different from her own.

"Sweetie," Jim said one morning, watching her rising carefully from the bed, "maybe we ought to cut out all that ice cream at night." He nodded toward the slope of her belly, and she suddenly sat back down on the bed. "It's just a few pounds," Jim said encouragingly.

"I'm pregnant," Lee said. She was suddenly furious with him. He looked at her, stunned.

"I didn't want to tell you," she said.

Astonished, he blinked at her. "A baby? We're having a family?" Laughing, tumbling, and springing, he flopped on the bed. He pulled her toward him, burying his face in her hair. "But, why wouldn't you want to tell me?" He hoisted himself up on one elbow, studying her. "Why are you looking like that? What's wrong?"

She sank under the covers. He tugged them from her and rested his face on her belly.

"Stop," she said, pushing him out of the way. He looked up at her. "I don't want it," she said.

He sat up, frowning. "You're just scared," he told her finally. He tried to brush back her hair, but she moved away from him.

"It's natural to be scared," he said.

"I'm *nineteen.*"

"My mother had me when she was eighteen. Lots of people have babies young. We may have to prune our expenses a little. Maybe not go out as much."

"When do we go out now?" she said.

"You don't want to go out with a baby anyway," he said. He looked at her solemnly for a moment; his fingers found her mouth. "Don't say you don't want it. You don't mean it. I know you don't." He kissed her still frozen face. "Can you imagine? A little one with *your* face?"

Lee, though, didn't want to imagine anything. She insisted on working longer shifts, telling Jim they would need the money she could earn now. But, really, all she was doing was filling her restless mind with specials and sauces, with anything that might crowd out the idea of a baby. She wore a baggy sweater over her white uniform so no one would notice she was pregnant; she bought crepe sole shoes, and although she knew she should sit as much as possible, she was always the first one up for a new table, always the first one to offer to relieve another girl's shift. It made her popular at the Silver Spoon, it landed her better and better tips because she was always refilling water glasses before they were even half-empty, always putting sauces and condiments on tables before the customers had even thought to ask for them. She came home so tired, she sometimes fell into a deep dreamless sleep right on the couch, waking only when Jim reached up to put her to bed. As soon as she woke up, she made sure there were things she had to rush to do, laundry. Paying bills. Going to a movie. Anything that would keep her from herself.

Jim, though, kept reminding her. When he looked at her, he saw the baby. She could be wearing a brand-new dress, something loose and silky that made her feel pretty and alive and as soon as he came into the house, he would rest his hand along her swollen belly, pulling the fabric tight. He asked her eighteen million times a day how she felt, had the baby kicked, when could he feel it himself? He called her from pay phones after every class just to see how "they" were doing. "I'm doing fine," she told him. When he came home from school, he was always loaded down with presents. He had baby care books and brightly hued plush toys, a thousand and one things he put into the den he now called the baby's room, a room Lee never went near if she could help it.

She began to get bigger. The women in the neighborhood began to reach out and pat her belly, not noticing when Lee pulled back, stunned by her own size. "They're nice people," Jim told Lee. "They just want to get to know you." She saw him talking to some of the families, chatting nights with Maureen, their next-door neighbor, and when he came home with Maureen's old baby books, Lee just hid them in a closet.

She watched Jim change. He began suddenly dressing older, wearing a jacket and tie sometimes, shining his shoes. He came home one day with his hair cut so short that she felt as if she had been dealt a blow. And he began frantically studying the house, readying it for a baby, making a list of the things he thought they needed, things they'd owe money on for years, things with so much weight and substance you might never remove them. A decent couch. A good set of pots and pans. A crib and changing table. "What else?" he said, his face flushed with excitement. "Should we get a new stove in one of those fancy colors?"

She saw him sometimes talking to the men in the neighborhood, but more often he talked to the boys, his voice low and fatherly. "Just practicing," he told her, grinning, but when he saw her jumping rope with the young girls, playing freeze tag on the lawn, he stared at her dumbfounded.

The larger she became, the more she panicked. She began staying away from Jim as much as she could, staying away from the entire neighborhood. She frequented the cafes where you could sit for hours, reading, forgetting, talking to people who actually had lives you might want to lead.

Instead, though, the wrong people always seemed to wander in. She watched two girls, not much older than she was, amble into the cafe. "I'm in love," one girl said. She was thin, with a soft dark fringe of hair. "Again?" said her friend.

Beside Lee, an older man was toasting a young woman in a pastel dress. "To the best daughter a father could ever hope to have," he said.

The only people who sat at her table were women who wanted to tell her about their own pregnancies. "Lord, you can't believe how tired you get," one woman told her. "I'm telling you, you'd better get your lovin' in with your husband now, because as tired as you are now, forget it when the baby comes. And forget going out. You think you can do it all, but I'm telling you, you can't. Only reason I'm out here today is my mother-in-law agreed to sit." She sighed at Lee. "She snoops through the whole house. She hides the outfits she doesn't like, or I'll find them with these sudden mysterious stains and rips on them on places you can't hide. Mustard on white pants. That sort of thing. But you know what, I don't even care. It's worth it just to get out." She had bags under her eyes and her hair was poorly cut, and the next time Lee saw her coming into the cafe, she left.

Lee was nineteen and terrified. She couldn't waitress much longer because the smell of the grill made her sick, the very sight of mayonnaise clouded over tuna would send her reeling to the employees' john, gripping the soap-scummy edge of the sink. Sometimes just the sound of a customer's order would make her stomach clench. "What's in this white sauce here?" a woman asked Lee. "Is it cream or egg yolk or what?" The very thought made Lee so ill that she had to excuse herself and ask Reena, another waitress, to take over. She cut back on her work hours only when the boss told her it was that or get fired. "Customers get queasy with a pregnant waitress," he told Lee. "You come back after the baby's born."

She began spending more and more time at the cafes. She was eating a doughnut one day, dressed in a baggy black mini, her legs in red tights, when a man sitting next to her suddenly looked up and grinned. She recognized what was playing in his smile; she knew that invitation, that promise, and she smiled back. "Good doughnut?" he said, scraping his chair closer to hers. He wasn't much older than Jim, but he was in a suit, and there was a smooth brown leather briefcase at his feet, stamped with gold initials. He shared some of her doughnut, they talked for about twenty minutes, but her body wouldn't let her forget she was pregnant. She had to shift on the chair to ease the pressure on her back; and worse, she had to pee. She kept expecting him to leave, but he lingered over his croissant; he flagged the waitress over, tilting his coffee cup for her to refill. Lee started to tremble. If she didn't get up now, she wouldn't make it. "Excuse me for a minute," she said, trying to be careful how she angled her body as she rose. But she saw his face when he saw her belly pulling against the black fabric of her dress, she saw all the promises folding in. "Look at the time," he said, but he didn't even glance at his watch. He fluttered two dirty bills onto the table by his full coffee cup. He scraped his chair back. "Nice meeting you," he said, and then he was gone.

Lee never went back to that coffee shop again. She stopped going to the cafes at all. She paced the house, caged. She looked at herself in the mirror and burst into tears. She looked through magazines the neighborhood girls had lent her, stacked with stories about girls only a little younger than herself going off to school, having plans, dreaming of falling in love. She thought of her mother, so in love with her father that she had believed nothing could damage their marriage. "You know the right one the second you see him," she used to tell Lee. "You wait. It'll happen to you, too." Lee had thought there was something wrong with her because she had waited and waited, but she hadn't felt one thing toward anyone. And then Claire got sick and stopped talking about the right one at all.

It ate away at Lee, at the future she was supposed to have. It was then that she began to walk along the highway nights, following the headlights as they sped past her to New York, to California, to places where every day might be a second chance. She thought how easy it would be to just jab a thumb out, to be someplace else. Once, a gray sedan slowed for her, a door opened. She froze, trapped in the yellow glare of the headlights. She didn't know what had happened to her muscles, only that she somehow couldn't move. "You need a ride or don't you?" a voice called, and then Lee was moving, running clumsily toward the open door. For one heady moment Lee thought she could just jump in, she could lean back against the seat and just let the car take her someplace. What would it be like to just drive and drive and not think of anybody or anything else but your own heart beating inside of you? A woman not much older than Lee had stopped and was happily peering out at her. She had on a red velour jogging suit, blond permed hair and big gold earrings, and not one ring on her fingers. The radio was blaring a girl group from the sixties. "So when's it due?" she said, pointing at Lee's belly, and Lee stepped back as if she had been slapped. The baby moved inside of her, and she suddenly felt heavy again, oddly cumbersome. Anywhere she went right now, the baby was going to have to go, too. "I thought you were someone I knew," Lee said. "I don't need a ride at all." And then she turned and started the long way back home, keeping her head down, refusing to see the headlights, to let herself be intoxicated for one moment by the steady stream of the cars as they went by.

When she came home, Jim was sprawled in the middle of the living room, surrounded by scraps of paper, his pale face fired with delight. "We can afford it," he announced, waving a sheet of white at her.

"Afford what?" she said.

"A house. Our own, not just a rental."

"A house?" she said. She stood there, her clothes still smelling of the highway, her heart still beating restlessly. She suddenly felt it, Jim's dream house—three small overheated rooms cocooned around her, connected to the outside world only by the car Jim was always using, her own legs cemented in place by a baby endlessly wailing for her. "It takes forever to pay off a mortgage," she said uneasily. "It's not so easy to sell, either. We'll be stuck."

"So what?" he said. "It'll be our home. We don't want to move around with a baby anyway." She nodded numbly at Jim. He was chattering happily, telling her about the house they might find, a family cottage, something with bright red cheery shutters. He stood up. "I can't wait for this baby to be born," he said so vehemently that Lee braced one hand along the wall. "I can't wait to be a *family*."

"What is it?" Jim said. "You look so strange."

"Nothing," she said. "You'll be a great father." He moved to her, draping both arms over her shoulders, rocking her a little. "And you'll be a great mother," he said. She felt suddenly dizzy. "No, I won't," she said.

"Sure you will. Don't you think I worry, too?"

"The baby will love you," Lee said. "Babies aren't selective."

"Why, thanks," he said, grinning. "Thanks a bundle."

"I don't mean anything," she said, shaking free. "I'm just tired, that's all." She couldn't look at him without somehow hating herself. She wandered into the bedroom and lay flat across the bed, wrapping her jacket about her. She kept dreaming about roads and sky and all the cities she had never been to; she thought about women bagging their babies like the week's groceries, leaving them wriggling in brown paper sacks right outside crowded supermarkets, women counting on strangers or the elements or not caring at all. Then she thought about Jim, loving the baby the same way he did her, in a web of false forevers that made her panic to escape, before it all soured, as it always did. She couldn't believe in any kind of forever, but a baby, new enough not to know any better, would. She wondered how long it might take a baby to grow disheartened and give up, how long it might take Jim to hate her for the way her emotions were so dammed up. She thought about Jim alone in his brand-new wonder of a house, carefully cradling a baby in his lap, contentedly whispering some sort of giddy lullaby, and suddenly Lee knew exactly what to do.

She began to see a doctor, to take care, and she marked the days on the calendar until her delivery date. She planned. Jim, walking by, seeing her humming, with a red Magic Marker fisted in her hands, grinned.

She suddenly began slowing down. When she walked now, it was simply around the backyard, one hand trailing among the flowery bushes, disturbing the furred black bees that would angrily circle her fingers. Often as not she would simply lower herself onto a plastic chair and read. If she cooked, she made stews that simmered half the evening.

Lee's daughter, though, would make her rush. The labor started nearly three weeks before the final fiery red X Lee had scribbled into her calendar. Lee's body seemed to be speeding and thrashing ahead of her, careening recklessly toward birth. Mute and cold with fear, she clung to Jim; she let him carry her into a cab because he was too nervous to drive, and as soon as she saw the hospital, she began to weep.

She remembered now, the delivery room, stark and clammy with blue light. She remembered how the woman in the next room had screamed. "Larry," she wailed. "Oh, please, Larry." Her voice slid up a decibel. Lee shifted in her bed, her hands knotted on her belly. She had cried names once, making love in one of the empty houses her father's firm renovated. She remembered the first time she'd made love, with a boy named Tony, a vocational student in love with small engines and not with her, and although going to the house had been her idea, she had stalled at sex. "What's a little penis between friends?" he had joked, giving his an affectionate pat. "Look, it's not like having a baby," he had persisted. But sex had hurt the first time. She remembered bellying against the wood floor, crying his name like a supplicant. And giving birth was unimaginable.

Fiercely she willed the pain away. She panted the way she had read from Jim's books, but all it did was leave her light-headed. She was glazed with sweat, turning into molten liquid. Panicked, she started to get up from bed when Jim came into the room. As soon as he saw her, his smile wavered. She sprang, grabbing his hand. "Don't let this happen," she begged him.

The pain had seemed to breed upon itself. Her mind skittered; she remembered a horror movie she had seen with someone, a woman giving birth to a pulsating yellow larva that promptly ate her alive. Something was ripping deep within her, something with a raw, jagged edge of teeth, and horrified, she bolted upright. Jim moved closer, his features in zoom focus. "The doctor's here," he said.

She would not survive. She shouted at Jim, "Get away!" but he tagged her traveling gurney. She hit at him with weakened fists. "Go away!" she cried. "I don't want you!"

In a white delivery room, somewhere above her, her doctor told her, "Now you can push," but she was hyperventilating, the air swimming past her in a drizzle of light. When she screamed she was sure the pain would stop, the way a nightmare did when sound shattered it. "Push!" a voice ordered, and she bore down.

When the baby was finally born, she burst into tears. "You did just fine," the doctor said, but Lee stretched one hand under the sheet, and every place she touched no longer felt like her. "There, that wasn't so bad, was it?" the nurse said, taking Lee's limp hand, stroking the skin. "Half an hour from now you won't even remember the pain. And now look what a beautiful little girl!"

Lee heard a thin wail. A nurse started bringing the baby toward her, and, panicked, Lee sharply turned her head away. She forced images into her mind: an orange evening sky in Santa Fe, a deserted California beach. The nurse hesitated. "I'll just put her in the nursery, then," she said. She saw Jim only for a moment. He bent down toward her. "Joanna. What about Joanna?" he said. "Or Caitlin. Isn't Caitlin pretty?" She had shut her eyes. "Everything will be okay, now," he had whispered at her insistently, as if it were a secret he didn't want the doctor to hear. "You'll see. We're a family now." She turned her head toward the wall, to a surface that was clean and white and cool-looking. "She's exhausted," Jim announced. He traced a finger along her cheek. "You sleep. I'll be back here before you know it." She heard him walking out of the room, heard the door whoosh shut. She didn't want this baby, didn't want Jim or anybody.

Every time she looked at him she felt as if time had stopped, and if she didn't leave now, she would be cemented forever into this one moment. She would ruin lives. "I know you," Jim kept telling her, making it an endearment. "You're my wife." And yet she could name half a dozen different things he believed about her that were absolutely and completely false. "She needs to get her strength back," she overheard someone say, a voice far away, blurred, as if it were burbled from under water. "Sleep," someone said, and obediently Lee sank, eyes rolling with dreams.

The noise of the hospital woke her. Footsteps. The piercing squeak of carts. So many voices that they all seemed to blend into one sound. In the distance she heard a baby crying; she heard a low murmuring lullaby. She edged herself up, pushing back the cool starchy sheets, her heart clamoring in her chest so loudly that she was sure the nurses must hear it. She was stunned at how tired she still felt, how every bone in her seemed filled with water, dangerously soft, but she had to move fast. She looked at the clock on the dresser. Noontime. She glanced at the chart at the foot of her bed. A nurse had checked her pulse just a half hour ago. She wouldn't be back around for another few hours yet. Jim was taking his finals, coming by the hospital around dinnertime, planning to do nothing but stay with her and the baby until it was time to go home. She got up, bracing herself against the bed with one trembling hand. She forced herself into her clothes, grabbing the packet of money and jamming it into her purse. Her hair was long enough to sit on and so wild and blond and curly it was her one identifying trademark. She tied it up with gold-colored clips, stuffed as much of it as she could under the baseball cap, tugging down the brim, and the whole time she kept one eye on the door. You couldn't just walk out of a hospital anytime you pleased, not with lawsuits and malpractice the way it was, but to let anyone know she was leaving would be the same as clearly marking her trail. If a nurse did come in, she'd say she had thought she'd feel better dressed; she'd say that lying in bed in a nightgown made her feel depressed enough to be afraid of what she might do. She left her suitcase, left her clothes and her sneakers, her bed unmade and still warm. She was moving so slowly, her feet seemed leaden. She pushed open her door and walked out into the hall. It was the beginning of visiting hours, the halls were crowded with people in street clothes, with women in frilly pastel robes and in embroidered pajamas, shuffling in fuzzy slippers. There were nurses striding past, their crepe soles whispering against the linoleum. No one seemed to even notice her. At the front desk, by the elevator, a woman was arguing with a nurse. "Well, I disagree entirely," the woman said. "And frankly, I don't care where you got your training." Lee edged toward the elevators. Lee, she thought she heard, Lee, called to her like a siren song, echoing after her, Lee. She kept her head down; she willed herself to ignore the pull of the cry. If anyone noticed her now, she would say she was going for a walk, that the doctor had told her it was best to get up and moving as soon as possible. She would say she had had a nightmare about the baby, that she was going to the nursery to check to make sure it was still alive. It. As sexless as a ghost; nameless and without substance.

The elevator came almost immediately, but it was so packed, most of the people waiting just stepped back, resigned. "This is just goddamned great," the man standing by Lee said. Lee couldn't wait for another elevator; she didn't think she could make it down a half flight of stairs, let alone four. The elevator door was slowly sliding shut when Lee edged her way in, pushing against a woman who angrily rolled her eyes at Lee, who hissed out a long breath as she stepped farther back into the elevator. "Who do you think you are?" she said. Lee was pinned against the door, nudged forward, and when the door finally opened she was popped out, the other passengers rushing past her. She was sweating, nearly crazy with nerves, and so weak she was sure that any second she would simply collapse to the floor. She kept expecting to see Jim making his way toward her, she imagined nurses, starched and stiff in white, taking her back to bed, staying beside her, holding her hand as firmly as a steel cuff, until it was time to go home. And then she'd be trapped in an overheated house with a baby who'd remind her of everything she was losing, every road she might be traveling on, every heart that might be out there beating for her with a passion so strong and stormy it would make her forget who she was.

She could see the revolving door in front, she could see the taxis just waiting by the curb. But with every step the front door seemed to recede instead of get closer, and for a moment she began to panic. She forced herself to go faster, she lunged forward and gripped the front door and spun through, and as soon as she was outside the hospital, she wanted to lie right down on the tarry sidewalk and sleep. Instead she braced her hand against the railing and then lifted her hand to hail a cab.

It was the middle of the day, and everything hurt. She slid into the cab, letting her head fall back against the back seat, which was taped up with blue vinyl. "Train station," she said, resting both hands on her stomach.

The driver was hunched around the steering wheel. When she glanced up at the rearview mirror she caught his eyes slanting with fury at her. He drove like a crazy person, toppling orange road barriers as he swerved past, dipping and slicing in. She pulled the cap down over her hair; she put on a pair of sunglasses. She watched as the road disappeared behind her. She rummaged in her purse to get the money ready for the fare so she wouldn't waste a second, and when the cab finally pulled into the train station, she stuffed bills into his hand and pushed herself out into the light and noise.

She went to the first ticket window she saw. What did it matter where she went as long as it was miles away? "What's leaving right now?" she asked the ticket clerk, ignoring the way he raised one brow at her. "Come on, what?" she said hoarsely. "Richmond," he told her, taking his time, "five minutes, track two." She fished out her money, grabbed for the ticket, and then she was pushing her way as best she could through the crowd that seemed to shove around her, barring her path. Track two.

There was a throng of people already climbing down the stairs toward the train, kissing good-byes, calling and waving, and Lee blended herself among them. If she cried now, no one would think anything was funny. No one would think anything other than that she was already homesick for someone or something she was leaving behind. She stepped aboard the Richmond train, moving to the very back, by the window, sinking low on her seat, her cap pulled low. "Don't sit beside me, pass by, pass by," Lee murmured to the people threading past and the seat beside her remained empty.

She didn't start to relax until the train pulled out of the station, and then, slowly, slowly, Jim and the baby began to recede, their clamoring, blaming voices growing faint. She tugged off her wedding band and held it up to the light. When she was in high school, they had forced all the girls to take home economics. "This is the most important course you will ever take," her teacher had told the class. "Don't talk to me about science or math. Forget history. You really think it matters who won the War of 1812? Do you know? I'm not one bit ashamed to admit I don't. You think anyone really cares? This class gets you on your way to the only degree there is—the one you girls are born for." She paused dramatically and then scrawled it across the length of the blackboard. "Your M-R-S," she said, underlining each letter triumphantly. Mrs. Haynes, her teacher's name was, and she told them she had gotten her "degree" with her very first boyfriend, which just went to show you how much she knew her stuff. She was only in her twenties and already had three kids and helmet-shaped hair that was dyed a matte black. She used to lecture the class on beauty tips guaranteed to land and keep a husband. Cold cream in white gloves worn to bed every night. Lemon juice rinsed through your hair. "It's good to be a little secretive," she had told the class, "keep up a little mystery." Lee flipped the ring in her hand. She bet she could get some money for it.

She slept all the way to Richmond, deep and dreamless, and by the time the train finally pulled into the station, it was evening. She woke feverish, her dress pasted along her back. By now there must be a bulletin out for her, and she was more than aware that she hadn't had as much leeway as she had wanted. The thing to do was rush and get another ticket, put more distance between her and her past, but as soon as her legs hit pavement, they buckled under her. She didn't know what was going on. She had known about the bleeding, had known that her breasts might leak milk for a while, probably ruining every blouse she had, embarrassing her so much she'd take to wearing blouses three sizes too baggy. But she hadn't expected fever, burning her up so that she was soaked, her vision smearing so she felt she was walking blind. She had cramps, too, thin high wires of pain that doubled her over so badly she thought she might be going into labor again. People were rushing to make connections, flinging themselves into sets of outstretched arms, and it was all Lee could do to sit on a dirty ledge and wait for enough energy to return to carry her to a ticket window. She put her head in her two hands, just for a moment, and as soon as her eyes were covered, she felt a touch. Startled, she turned toward it. A woman in a sleeveless black dress had her head cocked in concern. "Are you all right? Do you need me to get a porter?" the woman said. "I'm fine," Lee said, forcing herself to stand, to walk as if she could go another ten miles without feeling a single cramp. "Well, you don't look fine to me," the woman called after her, vaguely annoyed. When Lee glanced around in back of her, the woman in black was still standing, watching silently, and when she spotted Lee looking at her, she waved energetically. Lee picked up her pace. She couldn't travel if people were going to notice her, and illness was something you'd remember. For a moment she panicked again, and then she thought she could check into a motel, just for a night. She could get some aspirin; she could sleep, and as soon as she felt better she'd be gone.

There was a drugstore right outside the station. She bought a family-size bottle of aspirins, extra-strength; she bought rubbing alcohol and a hot-water bottle. It made her anxious being in a crowded store like this, and she suddenly felt nervous, too, about checking into a motel that was only a state away from Maryland. She was on her way to the checkout counter, making her way up aisle four, when she grabbed up a small pair of sewing scissors, a new pair of dark glasses. Right at the counter was a whole stack of tabloids. WOMAN GIVES BIRTH TO KITTENS, it read. Underneath the headline was a blurred photograph of a woman sitting up in bed, holding something swaddled in blankets. Beside that was a drawing of kitten-faced babies. ARTIST'S DEPICTION, it said.

She ended up at a Holiday Inn in town, prepaying the room so she could leave whenever she wanted. As soon as she walked into the room, she saw the TV, the cabinet so large it took up nearly a quarter of the wall. She didn't have to turn it on, she told herself, she didn't have to think about anything, and then she tumbled across the rose chintz bed and fell asleep, not waking until almost midnight. Her cramps seemed worse. She had this odd feeling that she was being punished, that all the pain was there to keep her from forgetting that back in Baltimore she had given birth to a daughter, that it was meant to work the way a splinter in your foot did, reminding you at every step. Next door she heard a couple arguing; something heavy thudded onto the floor. She heard a burst of applause from someone's TV set. "Why, Mary Avery of Provo, Utah, you just won ten thousand dollars!" someone cried. "What are you going to do with all that cash?" She got up, riffling in her purse for loose bills for dinner later, for the aspirin bottle. Tilting it toward her mouth, she spilled out two pills on her tongue. In the bathroom mirror, her skin looked translucent. She lifted up her hair. "Mood hair," Jim called it, like those cheap rings that turned colors on your finger depending on your frame of mind. It was curlier some days than others, losing an inch with the curl. It seemed to get darker right before her period. He had loved it, had made her promise not to cut it. But the girl who had sat behind her in geometry had disagreed. "Don't you ever comb your hair? We could send you a CARE package. A hairbrush or something. CARE. You need it." Lee leaned over and ran the water in the sink, splashing it onto her face.

It took her a while to get up the nerve to cut her hair. First she just snipped at the ends, a bit at a time. But that didn't really make her hair look much different, and she wanted to feel unfindable. She hesitated for a minute, and then she grabbed her hair up into one heavy tail and simply sheared it off at her fist. Her face in the steamy bathroom mirror looked as pale as a piece of white paper. Her eyes were dull as slate, and her hair looked raggedly cut. She had no idea what to do with the hair; she couldn't just leave it in the bathroom for the maid—a thing like a tail of hair would surely attract attention. She stuffed it into her purse, told herself she'd get rid of it someplace. She stared solemnly at her reflection again, thinking of Samson, his strength clipped short along with his hair; she remembered when she was a little girl, she had once become suddenly fascinated with voodoo. She wouldn't clip her nails or cut her hair because she knew all someone had to do was get hold of a part of her and they could cast spells. "Transformation is inward," her stepmother had once told her when Lee was walking out the door in a skirt so short she was sent home before she even made it through first period French. She touched her ragged hair shyly and went back to sleep.

When she woke the first thing she saw was the TV. It didn't matter that she didn't once turn it on all that morning, that hours when the news was broadcast she tried to be sleeping or out. She swore she could hear the news anyway, she swore she could hear her name, coming through the papered wall from the people next door, mixed in with the game shows they had on, the comedies. Even on "I Love Lucy." "Lucy, I dun't want you or Lee coming to the club," Ricky said, the words clipped and Cuban and so clear they were dazzling. She started, clicking on the set, finding the channel, but now Lucy and Ethel were dressed in a cow suit, lumbering into a makeshift mambo at Ricky's club, while Ricky stared stupefied, and her name wasn't being mentioned at all. Every time there were footsteps outside, she stiffened. When she left the room she imagined the cleaning lady pocketing clues, casually mentioning to someone that the woman in 4D had left so many long blond hairs all over everything that they ought to send her a cleaning bill.

She began to feel better in the evening. She needed to eat something healthy, needed to get herself tough. And she needed to change hotels now. She walked right out past the bored hotel clerk, three blocks away to the Howard Johnson Motor Lodge. "Annie Peters," she signed in, smiling at the clerk because she felt a little livelier, because Jim's voice seemed to be fainter, somehow less alive. The woman at the desk was bored, wanting talk, a history she could pin down. "Where you from?" she said.

"California," said Lee. "Los Angeles."

The woman squinted. "You are not," she said. "Why, you aren't even as tan as I am, and I'm practically Casper the Ghost." She pushed up the sleeve of the red blazer she wore, showing Lee her freckled arm.

Lee reached for the key, again prepaying the room. "Anybody knows the sun is bad for your skin," Lee said.

"Oh, pooh," the woman said. "Only people who can't tan good say malarkey like that."

This room was smaller than the other, with only one large double bed in it instead of two, but the TV was in the far corner and small enough so she could turn it to the wall.

When she went to the Moon Man that night, it was nearly dinnertime. The menu was blue Leatherette and five pages long with unnaturally colored photographs of all the meals she didn't want. Sneezing, she reached into her purse for a tissue and her fingers found her tail of hair. Instantly her hand recoiled.

The ladies' room was in the far corner. The Big Dipper, it said on the door she assumed was the men's. She pushed open the door marked Little Dipper. Inside there were two giggling teenage girls at the mirror, frosting pink shadow on their lids, trading a melted-looking red lipstick back and forth. They were both dressed completely in black, both with small stick-on tattoos on their bare forearms. When Lee walked in their conversation stopped in midsentence, and then one of them stared frankly. "Nice haircut," the girl nearest Lee said finally, and her friend jabbed her, smirking. Lee touched her butchered hair and then went into the farthest stall in the corner. She locked the door, waiting for the giggling to start up again, the cloud of conversation you might be able to move through and be ignored. The stall was fairly clean, but there was graffiti all over the wall. "Paul is my all," someone had written inside a crudely drawn heart, and Lee wondered just how long that had lasted, just whose heart had broken.

She waited a minute, listening to the girls, and then she carefully took out the gold tail of hair and divided it into four clumsy sections. She dropped pieces of it into the toilet, watching how it swam on the surface of the water, covering it completely. She had to flush three times before it went down completely, before the last pale strands had vanished. She continued to flush away her hair, always half expecting the toilet to back up, disgorging hair and water into the restaurant, visibly blaming her. When all her hair was finally gone, when the water was clear, for good measure, for emphasis, she flushed the toilet one last time.

When she walked out of the stall, the girls were gone. There was only one woman by the mirror, a blonde with a French twist, carefully blotting her bright red mouth by kissing the soft fold of a tissue. She took her eyes from her reflection for a moment, crumpling up the tissue, calmly blinking at Lee.

The girls were sitting in a booth by the door, bebopping to music from the minijukebox on the table, and they ignored Lee when she walked past them. Lee sat back down, picking at her cheese sandwich, at the fried potatoes already congealing from grease. Everything tasted funny, as if the grill needed to be cleaned. And then, shortly after that, Adele had given her the newspaper, and then she had seen her own face, from a photograph that had once meant something, peering out at her from a newspaper like a stain. Good-bye, good-bye. Again good-bye.

And now here she was. On the edge of the highway, waiting for a bus to take her somewhere, anywhere else. A sudden glare of headlights made her blink. There was the raw skidding sound of tires.

She fingered the newspaper for a moment. And then she bunched it up carefully and wedged it behind the green wood bench. She tried to shake the headache and the fatigue that were building. Cars whizzed past her, a blur of color, an occasional smearing arc of sound from a radio through an open window, pop songs rising and falling like breath. The bus should be coming soon. She could get on it, sit way in the back where the seats were patched with heavy black vinyl tape, where no one in their right mind wanted to sit, and she'd be left alone. She could ride to the train station or the airport, and then by tomorrow she'd be in another state altogether. And the day after that she could be someplace else. She wasn't anybody's wife anymore. Not anybody's mother. Anybody's daughter. She stood perfectly silent, just wishing under the stars, her image unfolding in the waves of heat and dust, and what she was then was so shimmery she could have been just another mirage.

Lee was almost in Richmond when police discovered that this was not her first disappearance. The detectives began gathering all kinds of stories about her, patching together her past as if such a thing might actually lead them to her present. Lee's father and stepmother were glad enough to talk to the police, and Jim was far too stunned to understand what any of his telling was later going to cost him.

It was Lee's stepmother, Janet, who blamed Lee's behavior totally on Lee's mother, a woman she admitted she had never met. Claire's death, she said, had turned Lee into a piece of bad business—one of those girls who was always arrogantly sucking on a cigarette, a cheap bit of fluff with her skirt hiked too short and her hair in a scramble. Claire, she said, probably never should have been a mother at all. A woman who had never been able to stand still for two moments couldn't be counted on to give a daughter the attention she needed. No, Claire had had moving in her blood, a kind of jittery quality that she passed right along to her daughter.

"That's not how Claire was at all," Frank said to the police. Janet carefully folded one hand over the other.

He admitted Claire was in love with moving, but not the way you might think. When she had met Frank, she had been a gym teacher at Philadelphia High. Every morning she dressed in the same ugly shortall her students wore. It was made of rough cotton the color of boiled salmon, but Claire did what she could to improve the style. She hemmed the clumsy, too wide legs to show off a flash of white thigh;

she stitched the short sleeves into a kind of jaunty submission. She was dazzling back then, with the kind of wild beauty Lee would later grow into. Small and slender with impossibly pale skin, she was almost overpowered by masses of yellow hair she sometimes braided into a moving, glorious spine. Most kids cut gym class, but not Claire's girls. They adored her because she seemed so indifferent to them. "You want to pass this class, you have to work at it," she told her girls sternly, slapping a sharp black pencil against a yellow attendance sheet, but after a few weeks anyone could see that Claire didn't really care at all what you did. She took attendance and then somehow you were on your own. When the class played softball in the muddy field outside, you could slink and hide behind an oak, cringing when Claire walked past, but she never said anything to you. You could edge farther and farther back in line, until it was too late to have to climb the ropes hanging from the ceiling. It made the girls want to be noticed. Some of them hurled themselves after Claire; some of them actually got some praise or a smile or sometimes a brief, bearlike hug, but come the next class, Claire would seem to have forgotten the achievement altogether. The girl would be as much a stranger to her as any of the others. To Frank, who snuck into the school one day to watch Claire's class, it seemed as though she were giving class only to herself, that all the girls were somehow superfluous. "I'm just setting an example," Claire told him later. She would dive into the pool, seallike in a black tank cut high on her hips. She burned her palms climbing the ropes, somersaulting when she reached the top. She ran and batted balls right out of the playing field. Her laughter belled out, reverberating in the gym. At the end of the class she was filmed with sweat, her hair clouded out from its braid. She clapped for the girls, and they for her, the same way it was done in a ballet class she had taken once, and then, as soon as they were gone, she forgot them. It was funny when Frank thought about it, but in all her years of teaching, with all the excited stories she told him, she never really mentioned any one girl more than once. She really never prodded and pushed any girl at all. Not until Lee.

Frank, when he met her, was just starting Franklin Homes, his business. His very livelihood depended on people uprooting their lives. He'd buy the houses they were leaving behind, renovate them, and resell them at a profit. He courted his clients energetically, buying them theater tickets and dinner and sometimes taking the lonelier ones home with him. The clients seemed to love Frank. He made people think he was their best friend; he remembered birthdays and anniversaries and even the dandyish names of their house pets, but he always dropped his clients as soon as he made the sell; his friendliness evaporated as quickly as it had appeared. That was always the pattern, up until the moment he met Claire, and then suddenly everything changed.

He was trying to sell her a house he had renovated, a Cape Cod in a wooded Philadelphia suburb. She was just a slight blonde in running shoes and a boy's white T-shirt, her hair too long, her hands in the pockets of her blue jeans, but something about her took hold of him. He had never seen anyone move so quickly. He couldn't keep her in his sight but instead had to satisfy himself on quicksilvery glimpses of her as she blazed past him. One moment she'd be stretching up to see the top of the built-in bookcases, snapping down again like elastic; the next moment she had whisked into another room to peer suspiciously into the stove. She took the cellar steps five at a time and bounded back up at a clip. "Leaded glass," he said, pointing to a small window over the door, trying to get her to stay still long enough to look. "We have plenty of time," he offered, but she was already in another room. She looked at everything in the house and decided she liked it, and then she decided that she liked Frank, too. She watched the way he stroked the moldings, the tender way he touched a brick wall. It charmed her how in love he was with a thing as basic as a fireplace, as simple as a square of turquoise tile in the bathroom.

She had heard of him before she even called Franklin Homes. People said he had wonderful houses, but women told her how handsome he was, how black and curly his hair was, how blue his eyes. What a charmer, they said. There were women who did nothing but call up Franklin Homes on the pretext of looking at houses just to have time with him, but he always ignored the dinner invitations offered him. The late night phone calls asking for advice were nothing more than that to him. "Confirmed bachelor," women said.

Claire must have known she was having an effect on him because in the dining room they seemed to have switched roles. It was Claire who pointed out the built-in cherrywood hutch, Claire who admired the bay window. In the backyard he forgot to show her the secret passageway, the garden he had landscaped. He stood there, foolishly rocking on his heels, mesmerized by all that energy, by the way she seemed to gleam. "I'll think about the house," Claire told him before she drove off, thinking about him. And that night, alone, while figuring mortgage rates, Frank wrote out her name in a tiny perfect constellation of stars.

They began seeing each other. He courted her with houses, taking her to the ones he was proudest of, surprising her with picnics on polished parquet floors, with an impromptu waltz across a black-and-white-tiled kitchen. He didn't really want her to buy a house, not unless it was with him living in it with her, so he quoted prices she could never quite meet, assuring her he would do what he could to bring them down. And for her, he exercised. He was gangly and tall, a man who tripped on flat surfaces. Unathletic, clumsy even, he struggled to win her. He skied with her in Vermont, breaking his ankle because he was too ashamed to stay on the bunny slope where he belonged. Camping in the mountains, his arms and legs brightly jeweled with mosquito bites, he came down with a poison ivy so virulent, he had to be hospitalized. "Listen, you don't have to do any of that," she told him, and she meant it. She had fallen in love with the way he loved houses, with the smell of his skin in the mornings, not with how high he threw a ball. It was his company she liked, not his prowess, but to please him, she claimed her running time could be cut in half just by his running beside her, shouting to her in breathy gasps that he loved her.

So they married, and a year later Lee was born. "She was her mother's daughter," Frank said. "Born to move." She was a jittery baby who bounced and jumped, a little girl with a fine tumble of blond curls who stomped down the pavement in real pint-size Nike athletics because Claire believed if you were going to do anything, you might as well do it properly. All Claire had to do was look at Lee and she saw herself, and because of that, Lee was the first person Claire really pushed. She wouldn't let her give up. She'd run with Lee, shouting at her to try harder, to do more. She began noticing the girls in her class only so she could compare them with Lee. Claire's favorite sport was tennis, and when Lee said she didn't like it, Claire was hurt. "You don't have to take it personally," Lee told her. "Of course I take it personally," Claire said. "You're my daughter."

There was nothing Claire wouldn't do for Lee. She bought her water skis and cashmere sweaters, and when Lee wanted her ears pierced, Claire insisted on doing it herself, surprising Lee with a pair of sparkling blue studs. The two of them would sit outside after a run, talking like pals, giggling and rolling in the grass.

At thirteen Lee could beat her mother at tennis and water-ski without tangling herself up in the tag line. She played softball summer evenings with a few girlfriends; she roller-skated with a boy down the street. And with Claire, she ran. The two of them often ran without Frank. Streaking effortlessly down the road, Claire would call out to Lee, making her laugh at some silly joke so she wouldn't notice the throbs of pain. When they came home they'd have their arms about each other.

Lee, though, was never as addicted to sports as her mother. She was as dreamy as she was active, sinking into reverie as naturally as breathing. All she had to do was look at the sky and she imagined what it would be like to fly; all she had to do was see a boy she liked, and in her mind she was slow-dancing with him or sharing ice cream or holding his hand. One thing was never less real than another— dreams or dirty dinner dishes, new skates or a new book. She was almost never without a book in her hand, and at first both Frank and Claire encouraged her. Frank built her her own pint-size cherrywood bookshelf; Claire began buying her leather-bound books that might last. "Such a smart girl," Claire said, but then Lee began spending more and more time in her room, devouring books as if she were starved for words. On a balmy spring day Lee would be curled in Frank's armchair, reading one of the books he had brought home for her, *Jane Eyre* or another story by one of those frantic Brontë sisters, or any number of titles Claire remembered wrestling with during her own days at school. She could entertain herself alone for hours; she could ask for nothing. "She's independent, that one," Frank said proudly, but Claire shook her head. "Leave her alone," Frank said, remembering his own reluctant devotion to sports. "She's just fine."

"You're right," Claire said, but still, every time she found Lee just sitting on the kitchen stool, in a kind of trance, her eyes unfocused, her mouth a drowsy, amazed O, Claire would shake her. "Look out that window," Claire advised, making her finger into a fierce point. "You see that day? You could be put in jail for wasting a day like that." If Lee were reading, she would sometimes snatch the book from her hands. "Get some fresh air," she said. "Do something."

"I am doing something," Lee said.

"Circulate your blood," Claire insisted.

Lee, resigned, would dress for running, but inside her sweatshirt she smuggled a copy of *To Kill a Mockingbird*. She'd ambulate lazily on the sunny grass before she stretched, and then she ran, sprinting straight over to the elementary school two blocks away, and then she'd settle on one of the fire escapes and read undisturbed until dusk called her home.

Frank never minded her reading. She read in the car when he drove her to the dentist; she sometimes brought a book to the table. "She's okay," he kept telling Claire. "Just let her alone. She'll stop reading as soon as she discovers boys, and then you'll wish she had never stopped." He was proud of her. He never told Claire it was newly refreshing to be with someone who wasn't always bolting up to sprint three miles or play a fast daring game of tennis even though the temperature was clearing ninety. He introduced Lee to the clients he brought home with him; he sat her on his lap while he talked about window treatments or aluminum siding. "It's educational," Frank insisted when Claire complained their house was becoming a way station. "Look how much Lee gets to learn about the country." What Lee learned was how to twang her speech like that of a businessman from Texas. She picked up cost-of-living figures from couples moving on to Oregon or California. She had a collection of train schedules and colored maps she posted to her wall, sticking colored pushpins into the places she thought she might like to visit. He used to take her with him to the empty houses he loved. "Playing house," he called it, "only we get to do it for real." The two of them bundled in sweaters against an unheated house, scrambling around dark hallways and overgrown backyards in jeans and sneakers. She clung to his waist through the rough wool of his shirt. His ribs expanded when he laughed. He created personalities for each house they wandered through. An open airy colonial was warm and friendly, like a favorite aunt. A split-level was cool and modern like a fashion model. Only in the houses that were not reparable, the disasters with leaky plumbing and a sweet crumbling odor of dry rot, did his enthusiasm flicker. "Juvenile delinquents," he muttered. Fidgety, twisting his fingers through his thicket of dark curls, he'd prod Lee to the door.

Frank sided with Janet about Claire's death ruining Lee. But he said things were wrong before that, that they had started to ruin the year Lee turned thirteen, when Claire's voice suddenly changed. It became husky, scraped raw. She blamed it on the poor acoustics of the gym, the way she had to shout to be heard, but Frank was charmed. "What a sexy, sexy voice," he said. Laughing, Claire started to cough.

"Water," she said. He brought it to her and she tilted back to drink. "I'm fine," she said, rubbing thoughtfully at her damp mouth.

But the cough took up residence. It nagged at her when she was demonstrating a backflip at the pool so that she lost her timing and struck the surface of the water with an alarming slap. At night she dreamed she was choking. Her ribs seemed to shiver and part inside of her. She bolted awake, her lace nightgown pasted to her back, and crept downstairs for tea. She sat up, clearing her throat, nursing cup after cup of Lipton tea, soupy with honey.

Vicks cough syrup suddenly appeared on the white kitchen counter, bolstered with drugstore remedies. She began missing school, dozing restlessly under a burrow of covers. Right before Frank was due home, she would rouse herself, determined to run. "I'll come with you," Lee said, setting down her book, pulling her unwieldy hair into a tail, but Claire shook her head. "Not this time, baby," she said.

Lee and Frank sat out on the front porch waiting for Claire, playing gin with a deck of old cards, the two of them cheating. Lee logged points on a scrap of paper. She was about to get up and make some iced tea when she heard Claire's cough, echoing toward them. In the distance Claire staggered home, her knees buckling beneath her. Her hair was soaked against her skull, her shirt half-mooned with amber rings of sweat, and she couldn't stop coughing. In three steps Frank was off the porch. In another two he had Claire's arm. "You're seeing a doctor," he said. He found her the top internist in Philadelphia. And two weeks later he found out she was dying, of a cancer so virulent even chemotherapy couldn't help her.

They didn't tell Lee. Claire was the kind of woman who wished on stars, who read her horoscope every morning and half believed in it. She actually thought she might get better. "Miracles happen," she said to Frank.

Claire told Lee she had a stubborn bronchitis. Lee knew only that Claire coughed a lot, that she was less active. One day she came home to find Claire energetically frying chicken in the kitchen. The tangy scent of the chicken buoyed Lee, but not half as much as seeing Claire humming over it.

Claire casually pronged a piece of chicken. "I quit my job today," she said cheerfully. Scraping out a kitchen chair, Lee sat. "You love that job," she said.

Claire shrugged. "Loved," she said. "Past tense. The mouths on those girls. Who needs all that lip?" She circled a wooden spoon into a pot, whirlpooling the water. "Anyway, I'm tired of teaching. Always doing the same sports. How many times can you dive into the same stupid pool? I deserve a sabbatical. No one says I can't go back after a while. And for now, I want to spend time with my family." She bent and kissed Lee's hair. "You and me, we'll go to movies. Think of the times we'll have."

But the times they had were Claire fitfully sleeping away entire days, waking to sleepily down a glass of water or pee before getting back into bed. Lee, money folded carefully in her pocket for a shopping trip to Macy's, for a promised movie matinee at the Guild, walked past Claire's closed door, slamming her feet down hard, banging and slapping her hands along the wall, trying to rouse her mother. "Let me sleep!" Claire cried, exasperated. "We'll go tomorrow."

The next day she kept her promise, driving Lee over to the Guild, where a revival of *Casablanca* was playing. They sat in the second row. Lee's sneakered feet sprawled into the aisle; popcorn splintered and cracked into yellow dust beneath her toes. Ingrid Bergman hadn't yet made her appearance when Claire's cough began. Riffling through her purse, she pulled out lemon Life Savers, peeling two of them into her mouth. Her tongue gathered a fine film of sugar, but her throat still felt gritty. "Be right back," she husked to Lee, and got up to water her laboring lungs with some lemonade. In the ladies' room she sat shivering on the lid of a toilet, her head in her hands, willing the spasms to stop. When she sat back down beside Lee, her face was white. "Let's leave," Lee whispered to Claire, but Claire was stubborn. She wouldn't leave until her coughing began to incite some of the rowdier members of the audience. Invisible irritable threats were hissed toward them. A boy in a denim jacket stood up and craned his neck for the source of the sound. Eyes lighting on Claire, he scowled and pulled his fist into a pointing finger. "Why don't you make like a tree and leave?" he said. Stung, Claire abruptly retrieved her coat. "We're going," she told Lee, her face stormy, and they pushed out of the aisle, amid a smattering of applause.

Outside, assaulted by daylight, Lee blinked, trying to focus. Claire forced coat buttons through the holes, misbuttoning, leaving an uneven hem. Her hair looked flat and thin. Her skin was gray in the daylight. Furious, she strode toward the car, Lee keeping pace. "I didn't like that movie anyway," Lee said.

Claire began sleeping days. Nights, sometimes, she could be talked into taking a walk. She tossed on Frank's old aviator jacket, her hair clipped back with a tortoiseshell comb, her face pale and expectant. "Let's go, tiger," she said.

Lee stayed home, nibbling on chocolate bars, swigging flattened Cokes. They never were gone very long, usually twenty minutes at most, and as soon as they came back inside, Claire headed for bed. One fall evening, though, when Lee was studying for a Spanish exam, haphazardly conjugating verbs, she heard Claire coming through the door crying, Frank's voice a dull murmur. Lee crept to the front of the stairs, peering down through the darkness. She could see her mother. Claire seemed to be swimming out of her clothing; her sweater bagged over her, her pants ballooned. Coughing, she clung to Frank. "I'm so sorry," she said.

Even from upstairs Lee could see Frank's face, alive with grief. He lowered her onto the couch, gently pushing a thread of hair back from her buckled brow, and then he settled beside her.

"All those years," Frank said. "I was so afraid you'd leave me."

"You're crazy. I'd never have left you," Claire said.

"You're doing it now," he said. "Isn't life funny."

Frank moved closer to her. His hands lay weighted in his lap. "I'll never forgive you for this," he said. His voice was hard, traveling in the distance. She leaned her head against his shoulder. Lee, terrified, slunk back into her room. She turned on every single light, including the plastic pineapple nightlight she used, and then she reopened her Spanish book and looked at the rivulets of type washing across the page.

Lee had told Jim how Frank had suddenly changed. He couldn't stand Claire's suffering. He retracted like a telescope. When Claire coughed, his shoulders hunched. Every time he looked at her she seemed to be fading from him, so in terror he simply stopped looking. He concentrated on things he could fix, the plumbing he could modernize, the fixtures he could screw in with a twist of just one wrist. And gradually he began going away on the business trips he had always refused to consider.

When he was home, Lee began to catch him with his eyes wet. Furious, he banged dishes in the sink. Fruit-printed juice glasses chipped against stainless-steel pots. Peach stoneware shattered into shards. Claire's discordant cough stayed in the background. Frank switched on the yellow radio to a program called "Melody Makers" and sang along roughly to "Donkey Serenade." Lee, walking by, caught between Claire's cough and her father's odd song, panicked. She fled to her father, wanting comfort. She clung to the ends of the cheery yellow apron he had tied about him. "Is she dying?" Lee cried. Startled, Frank twisted away from her.

"Don't you have homework to do?" he cried. "Don't you have any friends? What's the matter with you, asking a question like that?" He dashed a soapy hand to his eyes, blinking, and, cowering, Lee ran to her room. She bunched herself up on the bed, knees to her chin. Shivering, she bent down and picked up *The Great Gatsby*. She forced herself to read, thumbing page after page, until gradually something let go, and then she wasn't upstairs in a silent house at all, but swimming long cool strokes in Gatsby's pool.

That winter, it hadn't seemed to stop snowing. Storms raged one after another. The snow sifted into drifts scaling the house, smothering the light from the windows. Lee woke to a droning radio voice announcing the school closings and then swiftly fell back to a sleep thick with dreams. She and Claire cocooned in the house, the heat hissing. That was the winter, too, that Claire suddenly fell in love with Lee's books. "Read to me," she pleaded, and Lee would, sitting up beside her as the snow thickened into drifts outside. The two of them went through almost everything Fitzgerald had written; Lee read *The Yearling* to her mother, who wept at the end and made Lee reread the last chapter to her. "Always stop before the end of the chapter," she told Lee. "That way I'll have something to look forward to until tomorrow." One brilliantly sunny day she came downstairs and found Lee reading on the big white wing chair by the window, a pair of skates at her feet. Lee, guilty at wanting to go out, bolted up. "I was thinking about going skating," she said.

"Stay here with me," Claire said. "Read your book."

Lee stayed with Claire a lot, but Frank seemed always to be leaving. "Don't go, the roads are torturous," Claire said. "The planes are delayed." She sat up in bed. "Stay with me," she said.

"It's business," he said. "Otherwise I would." Cheerful, he packed a small leather bag. He was never gone for longer than a few days. He called Claire every night at six, and when he came home he brought presents. Boxes of perfume for Claire, porcelain figurines for Lee, everything from a place called Studley's Gifts in Dallas.

Nights when he was home, he began making late night calls. One night Lee bolted awake from a nightmare. She sprang from bed to turn on her lights. She was almost to the switch when she heard Frank talking, just outside the door. She pushed her door open a bit, letting a sliver of light inside. His back was to her, but his voice was animated. "You know how I feel," he said, so gently it made Lee shiver. She stepped outside, just behind him.

"Who are you talking to?" Lee said. Abruptly he spun toward her, his face torn. His features recomposed, and he put one hand over the receiver as if she might hear who was on the other end. "Client," he said. "Long distance."

She padded to the bathroom. In the mirror her skin looked pasty. Her father's voice blurred from behind the door. What client did you call at midnight? Gently she opened the door. "Oh, God, me too," her father said, and hung up the phone. Lee, silhouetted in the shadowed hall, watched him descending the stairs to his bed on the couch, but this time, she noticed, he was humming. His fingers tapped an invisible beat against his pajamaed thigh.

The calls stopped. But a month later Lee came home to find her parents shouting at each other. Claire, in her blue cotton robe, balled a letter in her hand. Lee reached for the paper and Claire jerked her whole body back, nearly toppling from her chair, but not before Lee saw a careful blue ink, pink flowers sprigged on an edge. "Dearest heart," it said. "Go to the store," Claire told Lee, her voice as tight as a fist. "Take ten dollars out of my purse and get milk at the Top Thrift."

"We have milk," Lee said.

"Go," Frank said.

Lee took Claire's whole purse with her, a soft green leather she slung across her shoulders. She rocketed the four blocks to the market, dashing for the milk, pushing into what seemed the shortest checkout line. Ten items or less. In front of her, a woman wandered one hand through her purse. "I never have what I need," she said apologetically to Lee. Lee, stony-faced, refused to acknowledge her. The girl at the register had to double-check two prices. She stopped once to wink at a boy who was enthusiastically rapping at her from the window outside. "Some people are in a hurry," Lee insisted. The girl finished ringing up the woman in front of Lee and then slid Lee's milk into a bag.

By the time Lee sprinted home, Frank was gone. Claire, eyes swollen and hard, was carefully polishing silverware on the table. The floor was littered with pastel balls of Kleenex tissues; the empty tissue box was on its side. She held up a spoon with an intricate floral design. "Who was the letter from?" Lee asked. Claire ignored her, dipping the polishing cloth into solution. "You never knew your grandmother, but these were her pride and joy," she said. "She gave them to me the day I got married, and I'm going to give them to you." Lee set the milk in front of Claire, but Claire didn't touch it. She scraped out a chair and took up a cloth. "What's going on?" Lee said. Claire picked up a salad fork, flexing it so it caught the kitchen light. "They're worth money," Claire said. "Beauty always is."

"He'll be home," Lee said abruptly.

Claire surveyed her polishing job for a moment. "Who?" she said.

He was home. He rang the front door in the morning, waking Claire with three big pink boxes of Dunkin' Donuts, six of her favorite honey-dipped crullers. The three of them ate breakfast together, tugging restlessly at the doughnuts, balling up the soft dough in their fingers. Frank lingered at the table long enough to miss what he said was an important showing. "I'd better get a move on," he said apologetically, wiping soft white doughnut sugar from his lapels. He bent to kiss Claire's rigid neck; he tousled Lee's hair. "I'll see you all later. Don't eat too many doughnuts or you'll spoil our dinner." He laughed, a nervous hard sputter that was still the first glad sound that entire morning. "Dress for dinner," he told Claire, who was still in her nightgown. "My two beautiful girls." Still laughing, he slapped out the back door; but even after the car peeled out of the drive, Claire still didn't move from the table. She sat there for most of the morning, slowly eating the rest of the doughnuts, then making patterns with the crumbs. Lee was afraid to leave her alone at the table, so she sat there, too, until finally Claire got up. That night Claire did dress for dinner, slipping on a blue flowered dress that she tried to belt into fitting her, spotting her cheeks with rosy blush. "Change out of those jeans," Claire told Lee. "I bet anything he's taking us out tonight." Lee struggled into a button-back dress. She brushed her hair, and the two of them spritzed on some of Claire's perfume. But although they both waited, Frank didn't come home at all that evening. He waltzed back in the next night, as if nothing were wrong. Claire sat in the living room knitting a bright blue ski scarf for Lee, never once looking up at her husband. "Where were you?" Lee said. Frank looked at the window. "Oh, it was business," he said, his voice tired. "Something must have been wrong with the phone. I tried calling and calling, and finally I called the operator and she told me there was some problem." He blinked.

"Yes, it was a terrible night," Claire said.

After that she just seemed to give up. For the first time Claire started talking about cancer, and as soon as she said it, Lee noticed with a shock how thin her mother was, how her skin had grown so translucent you could see the veins webbed beneath. "There are things you can do," Lee said.

Lee began buying medical books from the drugstores. In class, while everyone else was diagraming sentences, Lee read about melanomas. At night she dreamed her own cells were flowering like weeds. She came home with alternatives for Claire. A macrobiotic diet of vegetables and rice had cured cancer in California. Laetrile in Mexico. Psychic healers. Lee and a girlfriend went to one of the gypsy storefronts. Lee, twisting her skirt in her hands, told a bored woman in a red turban about Claire. "Can you help?" she said. Exasperated, the woman nodded. "Of course I can help," she said. Then she told Lee she would make seven white candles from a very special kind of beeswax. Lee would have to light them every night, without fail, and after four days the death curse would be gone. "Poof!" the gypsy said, jointing her hands like wings.

"Seventy dollars."

Lee, stunned, looked at her friend. "I d-don't have that," she stammered. "What about your friend?" the gypsy said, glancing at the other girl, who shrank back.

"Neither one of us has it," Lee said.

"Get it," the gypsy suggested pleasantly.

Sometimes Claire listened to Lee's odd cures. She'd burst out laughing. "Oh, this does me good," she said when Lee told her about the gypsy woman. Sometimes, too, she grew quiet. She would draw Lee to her and hold her for a moment, breathing against Lee's hair. But more and more she simply began shutting off when Lee began to speak. She would reach for the remote control for the TV and click it on, drowning

Lee out. Anytime there was a sports program on, an interview with an athlete, she switched channels immediately. "Anything can happen," Lee insisted. "Yes," Claire said, "and anything usually does."

She lay in bed, talking back to the soap operas. "How can you be so dense!" she cried. "Tomas slept with Aria!" Lee brought her in trays and magazines and the cards that sometimes still came in from her old students, but the cards seemed to depress her. Gradually she just left them unopened on the tray. Lee read aloud to her, articles and recipes, and sometimes just the TV listings, which Claire loved. "It compresses whole lives in a sentence," she said. "You know what's going to be the outcome." Claire leaned across Lee abruptly and reached for the phone. Determinedly, she dialed. "Frank Klantrell," she said, pausing, wrapping one hand about the phone wire. "Well, when can he be reached, then?... I see.... No. It's not necessary.... No. I said no message." She thudded the receiver back into its cradle and turned her head toward the window. Outside, snowy hail pelted the grass. Lee held up a glossy photo of a model twirling in a purple cape. "You like this?" she said hopefully.

Claire, distracted, focused on Lee. "I like sleep."

"I was going to fix chicken for dinner," Lee said. "Chicken's healthy. It has these special enzymes or something. I read it."

Claire hooded covers over her head. "You eat."

"You want me to read to you later?"

Claire, body sloped toward her cave of sheets, stopped her decline with an elbow. "Look at you," she said. "You're my beautiful girl."

Lee, who just that day in school had been compared unfavorably to a beaver, shrugged.

"You know what?" Claire said. "I hope you're going to be a real heartbreaker." She slid under the covers.

Dismissed, Lee went downstairs. She chopped vegetables right on the counter. She was furious with her father for going away, furious with Claire for giving up. Slicing a tomato, she nicked the Formica. She fried the chicken in too much oil and left it in a solidifying bonnet of grease in the pot, her appetite vanished.

She grabbed Frank's aviator jacket, the one that Claire used to wear, and headed for the park in back of the elementary school. It had stopped hailing, but the air snapped around her; her breath was white mist. In the school yard a rusting swing set moved in the wind. Lee sat on one of the swings, the way she had when she was little, when Claire and Frank had both taken her. "Kick toward the stars!" Claire had told her, urging her higher and higher. She said it even on cloudy days, insisting it didn't matter whether you actually saw the stars or not. They were still there, blazing in the firmament, as constant as love. Lee shut her eyes and leaned back on the damp seat. She kicked toward Orion.

Claire would die a month later, the first and only time she had ever been hospitalized in her life. And with her death, Lee's memory slowly began to dissolve. There was no funeral, she believed, no blur of guests in and out of their house, nothing but a dazed kind of emotional hibernation. It was her aunt Teddy who told Lee her life as if it were a story, spinning a beginning, middle, and end: how Lee had been taken out of school, how the two of them had waited for Frank to fly in from Texas. "You couldn't stop crying," Teddy said. "You couldn't pick up a glass without having it shatter in your hand." She had finally taken it upon herself to spike Lee's tea with Valium, culled from her own private stash. Lee listened, but she felt this was all a kind of curious story about someone she didn't know, that really, it had nothing at all to do with her.

There were things she remembered: the stiff, knotted way Frank moved in the house, his refusal to sleep anywhere but the downstairs couch, despite the clean sheets spread on the double bed upstairs, the brand-new comforter Teddy had bought to make things less painfully familiar. She remembered too the Salvation Army truck coming to cart away Claire's things. Stunned, she had watched the house emptying of her mother, until she had spotted the silverware Claire had promised her. "Wait!" she cried, scrambling to the truck, clawing at a pile of blouses and books. A man in gray coveralls stepped back, amused. "Go to it, sister," he said. She pulled out the box. "This stays," she said. "Whatever you say," he told her, tipping an imaginary hat. Upstairs, heart beating helplessly, she carefully layered each piece in newspaper and tucked it at the bottom of her closet.

She and Frank were ghosts. Neighbors sometimes came by, balancing cakes or casseroles in two arms, offering invitations to dinners neither one of them ever attended.

She met Frank at the door mornings. She ate silent takeout pizza or Chinese chow mein with him evenings. After dinner Frank would walk. "Be right back," he told her, but he was often gone for hours, and when he came back his eyes were red and puffy, his face bruised. When they talked it was about Lee's grades or Frank's next business trip or what kind of food to order in. They never mentioned Claire. "You know," Frank told Lee one morning, "all I have to do is tie up a few loose ends and then I'm not traveling anymore." Lee looked up, interested.

She stayed home when he went away, close to the phone, imagining he might call to say hello. Posted on the refrigerator, held in place by a rubber dinosaur magnet, was the number of the Dallas Hilton. She dialed. Eleven at night, his time. "Mr. Klantrell isn't in," the desk clerk told Lee. "Would you care to leave a message?"

"No, that's okay," Lee said, but of course it wasn't.

In the spring Frank came home with a small blue package for Lee, a smile spread across his face. "No more trips," he said.

She peeled away the stiff paper. Inside, a small white box read "Studley's Gift Shop." She lifted the lid; inside sparkled a small, silvery locket. She dangled it from two fingers, delighted.

"I'm getting remarried," Frank said. "Her name is Janet Cooper and she's flying in from Dallas tomorrow."

Gate 707. Ten at night. Lee, dazed, stood away from her father. The whole drive over they had fought, stretching out the same arguments from the night before. He could have told her. She kept asking him questions: Where had he met her? When had they met? How was it possible that he was really in love? He parried her questions. "An eligible bachelor like me," he finally joked lamely, but Lee was unmoved. "Come on, it's for us," he said.

The plane was delayed ten minutes due to fog. Lee zipped and unzipped her leather jacket. She imagined swollen gray mist swallowing the plane whole, disorienting the pilot into a crash landing.

"Flight 707 now arriving," an amplified voice sputtered.

Frank, expectant, moved forward. "Ah," he said, sniffing the air as if it were delicious. People trickled from the gate, heads aloft, eyes drifting from face to face. Frank listed to the left, and then he suddenly sprang forward, pushing past a woman with a baby strapped against her heartbeat, sidestepping a couple and an old man. There, standing perfectly still, her face alive with her smile, was a young woman in a blue silk dress. Her blond hair was cropped close like a boy's, and in each ear she had diamond studs, twin chips of light. Frank blended into her with a kiss so passionate, it startled Lee.

Janet Cooper slowly pulled away from Frank, human honey, and then her blue eyes followed his pointed finger to Lee.

Lee braced herself against the railing, holding on. Janet glided forward, stretching her hands toward Lee, keeping her body at a safe distance. "Call me Janet," she said politely.

The car waited directly outside the door. Lee crunched up in back with the one piece of luggage Janet had brought. "Here we go," Frank said.

Janet talked nonstop. She was faintly southern, drawling out her words, keeping one hand tapping lightly on the back of Frank's neck. Her things would be shipped next week; she'd buy what she needed. Life was just starting. "This man," she said, sighing, turning to Lee. "Let me tell you, he saved my life. There I was working the gift shop in the dead of winter. The heat's on the fritz, I'm wearing three expensive sweaters, one right over the other, and mittens to boot. Not one customer all day." Affectionately she walked her fingers through Frank's hair. "And in this one troops."

"Winter?" Lee said. She remembered Claire solemnly watching a snowy hail bombard the window. "God's bullets," she had pronounced, laughing when the window rattled. "Missed me this time," she had said. Lee looked at Janet quizzically. "But it's winter now," Lee said.

"Almost an anniversary." Janet nodded. "Dear heart," she said fondly to Frank.

Something began to freeze inside Lee. Pushing through the ice, a memory bloomed.

"You carried stationery at your store?" Lee said. "With flowers?"

"Sure we did," Janet said. "Best selection in town."

In the rearview mirror, Frank's eyes avoided Lee's.

"In fact, we carried that heart you're wearing. I told Frank all the girls were wearing them, so it's really a gift from me, too."

Lee felt herself shutting down. The locket, inside her shirt, weighted her back against the vinyl seat.

"That's some hair you have," Janet said. "Isn't it hard to take care of? Especially when they really have so many cute cuts these days."

"I have hair like my mother," Lee said.

In the heavy silence Janet cleared her throat. "I bet I'm going to love Philadelphia," she said.

Lee was mute the rest of the way home. She climbed from the car and went to her room, shutting the door. She could hear them talking downstairs. "She'll come around," Frank said. "It's hard for her." "It's to be expected," Janet said. "It doesn't hurt me." "What about this?" Frank said, laughing. Something rustled and knocked along the wall. "Does this hurt?" "You stop that." Janet giggled.

Lee picked up one of her mother's silver forks; she thought of Claire carefully polishing each piece the day the letter had come. "Dear heart." Janet wrote that. She must have been the one Frank called late nights when Claire was sleeping fitfully. She pronged the fork into the lace doily on her dresser. She heard the voices climbing the stairs, the soft, sipping kisses, just outside her door.

"Good night," Frank called, and Lee reached up and with one hand roughly wrenched the silver locket from her neck.

Frank, telling the police, glossed over details. He said only that Lee had been furious, that she had waited until the next morning, while he was shaving, to accuse him. "*Janet* wrote that letter to Claire, didn't she?" Lee cried. "I know she did."

"No, she didn't," Frank said.

"She did too. Why are you lying?" Defiant, she edged in front of him. Exasperated, he put down his shaving brush.

"The letter was to me," Frank finally said. A bud of foam from his shaving brush settled on the white porcelain. "Look, she made a mistake."

"No, *you* made the mistake," Lee said. "Claire *knew* about Janet," she cried, "and it killed her."

"It did *not* kill her," he told her. "Cancer did."

"How could you have done that to her?" Lee shouted. "How could you do it to me?"

The spigot splashed open. He doused water on his face, then, dripping, turned to face Lee. Droplets sprinkled his face, shimmering. "Baby," he said gently, "no one plans anything. How come you don't know that by now?"

Janet appeared suddenly, blue towels folded across one arm. She was already dressed in a tailored black wool suit. "Why don't you speak a little louder," she said quietly. "I don't think all the neighbors can quite hear yet."

"It's none of your business," Lee cried.

"It *is* my business," Janet said, but Lee shoved past her, past Frank, to the stairs.

Frank and Janet were married by a justice of the peace in a private ceremony Lee refused to acknowledge or attend. There wasn't a honeymoon, not then, but there was a new move, to a larger colonial in a better suburb, with a whole separate attic for Lee. "Starting fresh," was how Frank described it. "Ruining," was what Lee said.

Lee felt banished. Suspiciously she watched the house unfold. Janet's taste, she decided, was trashy. Janet favored framed watercolors of ocean scenes. Black gulls like check marks in the sky. Glazed porcelain cats and gazelles crouched on the washed blue shag carpeting. The furniture was clumsy beige leather that Janet claimed was cool even in the hottest Texan summer. Lee examined the rooms. Playing house, this time solely on her own, she decided the house was dangerously sweet, as calamitous as too much candy.

Lee tried to keep her room exactly the way it had always been. She hung her framed poster of Nike running shoes. She unfolded the silverware she had inherited from Claire and carefully laid a few pieces on the top of her dresser. "Why, isn't that darling," Janet said doubtfully.

"They were my mother's," said Lee.

Janet kept away from Lee. She didn't work, but she didn't stay home, either. She'd wake and breakfast with Frank and then go off shopping for elaborate dinner ingredients or for dresses she hung carefully in her closet. She was the one Frank sometimes took to scout empty houses, not Lee. She wasn't there when Lee got up in the morning; she wasn't there when Lee came home, and when she spoke to Lee it was always in relation to Frank. She wanted to know if Lee would pick up Frank's shirts from the Chinese laundry, if Lee knew whether Frank liked Mexican food. "I like it," Lee said, but that night they had spaghetti.

Upstairs, in her room, Lee wept. She missed Claire, and what was worse, she couldn't help missing Frank. Every time she heard the house creak, she was certain he was coming to find her, to make amends, but instead he seemed more and more removed.

She wandered the neighborhood evenings. She joined the Future

Teachers of America club at school, not because she had any real urge to teach, but because she somehow felt it was a connection to Claire. For two hours every week she sat in a room full of girls in pleated skirts and listened to them talk about motivation and lesson plans until she was so bored that she had to pinch her thigh to keep from sleeping. In groups of ten they trooped to elementary schools to monitor afternoon classes; tirelessly they critiqued their own high school studies. Still, afterward, one of the future teachers would always ask Lee to go shopping or to have a malt. Lee always said yes.

To fill her evenings, she began running. The new neighborhood was dark and heavily wooded, and she had to watch for the more raucous of the dogs, for the occasionally thuggy kid who jettisoned a rock at her moving target. Sometimes, when she was running the hardest, glazed with sweat, she felt Claire right behind her, just out of view. Her breath stitched up. Huh huh huh. She sprinted ahead, faster. She heard whispering, and the more speed she picked up, the clearer the sound. Claire's voice wrapped around her, telling Lee something. Something important. Lee whipped around, panting. The black gleaming road stretched behind her. In the distance a dog barked hysterically. She ran home, her face wet, intently listening. Her shoes slapped on the pavement.

The next evening she came downstairs in black sweats like Claire used to wear, her hair pulled back the way Claire's used to be, fastened with the torn-off ribbing from an old sweat sock. Frank was in the living room, watching a TV movie with Janet, and when he saw her he started. "Want to run with me?" Lee said. Janet arched her feet in high silvery heels.

"I'll let you beat me," Lee said.

He was silent for a moment. Janet rubbed his shoulder. "Tell you what," he said. "You go run, and when you get back, maybe we'll make some popcorn."

Ripping through neighbors' hedges, kicking up flower beds, Lee ran. Moving the anger out, was what Claire used to call it. She cited hospital studies where depressed inmates benefited from a fierce run. Lee ran four miles, tensed for Claire's presence, waiting for her fury to weaken. She looped back around, her face damp, her shirt glued to her body, skimming the lawn to the house.

The driveway was empty. The house silent. The heater clicked on, making the sound of footsteps. "Hello?" Lee called. In the kitchen she gulped water so icy, it tightened her throat. On the table was a note. "Went to get ice cream. Be right back."

She wandered upstairs to their bedroom. Peach wallpaper with a thin silver stripe. A white goosedown comforter on a brass bed. She opened the top drawer of Janet's oak dresser and pulled out a blue chiffon scarf, drifting it around her sweaty neck. On top of the dresser was a crystal falcon of White Shoulders, and she opened that, too, daubing it on the back of her neck. She smelled musty, of sweat and dirt and too much of Janet's perfume. Spreading herself across their bed, she gazed out the window, drinking in the night.

They did come back with ice cream, but not until two hours later. "Chocolate, your favorite," Frank said, but when Lee touched the container, it was warm. She pried open the top. Inside, it was soup. "It'll freeze right up again," Janet said brightly. "Pop it right in the freezer."

"Never mind," Lee said. "I think I'll just go to sleep."

"We'll eat it all," Frank warned.

"That's okay," Lee said. But she noticed that the ice cream stayed in the freezer all that week, finally replaced by a fresher, firmer pint that was eaten away in one hot afternoon.

They began going out more and more, and always without her. She'd come home to notes scattered on the kitchen table. Gone to the movies. Gone to a play. Gone to dinner. And when she asked her father why she couldn't come, he was silent for a minute. "Why, you'd hate the kind of plays we go to see," he told her finally. "A girl like you, you should be out with your own friends, anyway."

Lee's resolve turned steely. She had no intention of letting Frank erase her the way he had Claire. There were other ways of being seen, of getting attention.

At fifteen, Frank said, Lee became beautiful. She dug out the old photographs she had salvaged of Claire and studied them, miming the poses. In front of her oak mirror she smiled the way her mother had. She crooked her arm behind her head, a 1950s pose. When Frank called her to dinner, she sauntered down with her hair in a braided tail down her back, the way Claire had worn it. She smiled at him with Claire's smile. He was still for a moment, and then abruptly he excused himself from the table. "What got him?" Janet said, putting down a steaming plate of green beans. "I think he's seen a ghost," Lee said calmly.

She was in high school then. Philadelphia High, a small middle-class school with a strict dress code Lee made it her business to ignore. She began wearing nothing but black, her skirts so short she couldn't walk down a hallway without a teacher pulling her aside. "Why bother to wear a skirt at all?" a teacher demanded. "It's no bother," said Lee. She disdained the order to go to the sewing room and stitch on an extra hem of cloth and instead walked out the door and home.

She looked for friends. She had dropped out of FTA because the few girls she had befriended had transferred to the Catholic high school a block away and the other girls didn't trust her simply because she was now so different. She spent lunch hours contentedly reading by herself in a corner of the cafeteria; in the girls' room she ignored the girls trading eye shadows and lip glosses; she listened to girls planning on going shopping and pretended she didn't care.

If she couldn't have girlfriends, well, then, she centered on boys. The boys Lee was drawn to, though, were the ones who had somehow become high school legends. There was Dana Lallo, wiry and shaggy looking and bright enough, whose very presence was responsible for intricate love notes carved into numerous desktops and walls, scratched into an occasional gray metal locker. He never stayed with any girl for longer than a week, and it was rumored (though some said Dana himself had started and sustained this particular story) that he had fathered a son in Tennessee.

There was Tony Santa, the first and only punk rocker at Philadelphia High. He sauntered around with his black hair shellacked into stiff fingers. He borrowed safety pins from the sewing teacher to wound his T-shirts with. The endearments he whispered to his fascinated following were the names of New York City subway stops. "Astor Place," he murmured knowingly. "Columbus Circle, Eighth Street." He had a tattered New York City subway map that he studied in class, sometimes passing it to one of his groupies. On Thursdays he drove his motorcycle all the way to the edge of town, to the one newsstand that carried the Village Voice, and even then it was an issue that was a week late.

Lee planned. She scouted Dana in the cafeteria and picked her way through the sour milk–smelling tables, stepping gingerly over the luncheon meat pasted onto the floor, avoiding the slippery pats of yellow butter tossed like Frisbees. Dana ate with an entourage of steadily blonding girls. You could always pick out his latest girlfriend by the whiteness of her hair. Lee sat down at the very next table, reading The Sound and the Fury, feigning a disinterest so mesmerizing,

Dana finally leaned over her table. "That book more interesting than me?" he said. Behind him, four pairs of blue eyes impaled Lee in their gaze. Lee refused his first date, but not his second. They went to a movie. He picked her up at home, and Frank shook his hand, his face pleasant. "Have fun," Janet said. Dana carried two cans of Pepsi, each covered with a thin lip of foil. "I don't like Pepsi," Lee said coolly. "I'll buy myself a Sprite." He grinned at her. "This you'll like," he promised.

They sat in the second row, feet propped on the seats ahead of them. On the screen, aliens demolished a farmhouse. A woman in the audience screamed. Dana handed Lee a can. Tipped against her mouth, skin to metal, she smelled the alcohol. Rum spiked with a little Pepsi. Dana swigged his down. In the flickering light he put one hand on Lee's thigh.

She wouldn't let him touch her. Not then, not two dates more, when he finally got angry. "What are you, a good little Catholic girl?" he said. Instead she let him teach her to smoke cigarettes, and when she felt she had it polished, she dropped him, bored. He didn't read; he didn't talk about anything but himself and the patch of land he was going to buy in Vermont someday. "It's done with," she told him, and when he followed her, moony-eyed, in the school, no one was more astounded than Dana. In the girls' room, Patricia Ryan, head cheerleader, looked at Lee for the first time. "Lend me a mascara," she said, friendly.

After Dana, it was easy enough to get Tony. She loved riding on the back of his Yamaha, her arms clutched about his hips, her head thrown back. They'd pull up to the school, Lee's skirt hiked up, and she could make an entrance. She loved it, too, that he was always ready to leave, always talking about just going to New York City where anything was possible. Her popularity at school soared. Boys began appearing at the front door, asking a startled Frank what time he thought his daughter might be home. The phone rang at night with calls from boy after boy, with dates she turned down simply so she could have some time to herself. "The belle of the ball," Janet said. Frank rubbed Janet's shoulders. "Oh, it's just kids' stuff," he insisted. "Doesn't mean a thing."

The next night, when Tony put his hand on her thigh, she let him, curious. But when he tried gently to push her down into the grass, she resisted. "What's the matter?" he said. "You afraid of something?"

"Who's afraid?" Lee said. "I just don't want to do it on the grass." She stood up, brushing off her skirt. "I know a place we can go to," she said abruptly. "It'll take ten minutes to drive there."

She led him to one of the empty houses Frank loved. It was a small blue ranch in a new development. Only a few of the homes had been sold; even fewer were inhabited. Tony grinned when he saw the Franklin Homes sign pitched into a grassy front lawn. "There's no place like home," he said.

It was easy enough to break in. Frank never believed in spending money on security, because really, who would break into an empty house besides vandals? And if they wanted to wreak havoc, they could do it on the outside as well as in. Lee walked around to the side and squinted at a window. "Give me a boost," she told Tony. He laced fingers into a bridge for her and hoisted her up against the glass. Shoving open the window, she tumbled down onto a smooth wood floor. "You coming?" she said.

Tony pulled himself up, bellying down against the floor, and it was only when he stood up and faced her that Lee realized just how terrified she was. Across the street she could hear blurry strains of music. She could see the house across the street, a white curtain drifting along an open window.

He tugged her to him and began to kiss her, pinning her against him. "Wait a minute," she said, but he was pulling her down against the dusty floor, peeling her clothing from her. She struggled to move away, but his body was shadowing hers, making her moves his own, and then suddenly he was bucking against her, banging her spine into the wood, and when she cried out he kissed her.

He finished fast, unsticking himself from her, rolling into a heap alongside her. "Jesus," he said. Lee, silent beside him, shut her eyes. Outside, a door slapped shut.

"Let's get out of here," Lee said finally.

"Don't you want to hug a little?" Tony said, tracing her face with a finger. "I thought girls liked that. Come on, let's moosh."

"Workmen will be here," Lee said. "We have to go."

She pulled on her clothing, deliberately leaving her blue barrette by the fake fireplace.

She went further and further, trying to feel something. She saw

Tony, and a basketball player named Ted and another boy, Brian, who had his own out-of-tune band, the Grateful Onions. She could walk into the school cafeteria and any table would make room for her. And every once in a while she would bring someone to one of Frank's houses; she would leave a sock crumpled on top of a bathroom sink, a ribbon on the kitchen floor. She waited for Frank to find her things in his houses, but if he did, he never said one thing to her, and she couldn't bring herself to ask.

The next evening she stayed out until three in the morning with Tony. They were just sitting on a hill behind one of Frank's houses, looking at the sky. She was wishing a thousand things that would never happen in a thousand years, trying to dam out Tony's constant talk about New York City. "So go if you're so hot about it," she said.

"Not without you," he said.

He drove her home, squealing the tires in front of the house, and as soon as she got off, the door flew open and there was Frank, his good suit rumpled, his hair askew, and as soon as he saw Lee, his face lit with relief. He couldn't hide his joy as he started his approach to her; he couldn't have been more helpful to her if he had handed her a road map. "How you doing, sir?" said Tony, and Frank suddenly seemed to see Tony, and his face hardened into rage, recaptured back. "It's three A.M.," Frank said, thrusting his watch forward. Lee shivered in the night.

From then on she knew what to do. She began staying out later and later with boy after boy. It didn't matter who. She skipped so many classes at school that Frank had to come and talk the principal out of suspending her. Frank had to talk to her.

Once, she actually was suspended because she had been caught trying to jimmy open a teacher's car door. Frank didn't trust her to stay at home the week of suspension, and Janet declined the responsibility, so he took off work and stayed with her himself. He had her sit with him in the living room, where he could watch her. She bloomed, talking him into games of Scrabble, where she'd delightedly cheat. She made popcorn for the two of them, and they watched a daytime movie. After the fourth day, while she was reading contentedly, he got up. "You've been punished enough," he told her. "Tomorrow you can leave the house if you want."

Lee was astonished at how disappointed she felt.

* * *

Two in the morning. Back from an evening with a boy named Brad Rossy, a vocational student with bad teeth who spent the entire evening talking about pistons and motor valves and spark plugs. He had zoomed off almost as soon as he let her out. She had drunk too much. Her head reeled.

She rang the bell, but the house stayed dark. "Hey," she shouted, pounding at the door. Upstairs, there was a flicker of movement; a curtain fluttered, showing a ruler of light. "It's Lee!" she called. She banged on the door again, and when it opened, Frank, in his robe, strode out to her and struck her abruptly. Stupefied, she stepped back. "Don't you ever make me call the hospitals again, you hear me?" he said. "Don't you ever make me call another police station." He glared at her. "I should just let you stay out all night," he said. "Who were you with this time?" He stepped back from her. "You smell like a swill," he said, and lifted his hand toward her. Lee backed away, and then she was running, across the damp, dewy lawn, out into the street. "Lee!" he called. "Lee," the sound scraping from his throat, but she was gone.

She began walking. There was an all night cafe just off the main road. A trucker's stop called Ketchups. She had enough change for coffee. Maybe one of the waitresses would let her sleep in one of the cots if they were free.

Cars whizzed past. "Hey, baby, how about some fries with that shake of yours!" someone catcalled, and she jabbed up a defiant middle finger. Another carload of boys swerved toward her, making her scuttle to the shoulder, breaking her heel. Limping, she steeled herself not to cry. Be calm, she said. Her stomach roller-coasted.

She was almost to Ketchups. She could see the blue fluorescent lights. Her bladder hurt and burned. A car behind her beeped, and exhausted, she turned.

She knew this one. She knew that face. Jim. Jim Something from biology class. Thin and quiet and serious. No girlfriends. She had sat beside him once in biology the day they had to dissect house cats. In front of him was a small calico. She had seen him absently stroke the cat's fur. He was fine. He was nothing. He didn't count.

"You need a ride?" he said, and she got in, folding her legs under her. Gratefully, she surveyed him. He touched her and she stiffened, suddenly awake. "Seat belt," he said, pointing, and she clipped herself into a bolt of silver.

"Where to?" he said.

She was silent for a moment. "Can't we just drive around?" she said. He rounded a turn. "Yeah, that's okay."

Lee waited, but he never once asked her what she was doing walking the highway alone at night. Instead, he pulled into a 7-Eleven. "Be right back," he said, and when he reemerged he had two cups of coffee fisted into his hands, plumes of steam escaping from the cups. He fitted one into Lee's hands.

"I have insomnia," Jim announced. "That's how come I'm out driving. All I really need is four hours of sleep, anyway, and if I don't get that, I call in sick to school." He sipped at his coffee. "You think I'm crazy?" he said.

"No," said Lee.

He crumpled his empty cup, tossing it in the back. "Let's drive," he said easily.

She didn't burst into tears until they were on the road, and then immediately he pulled over to the shoulder. He didn't touch one part of her except her cheek, and his touch was so delicate, it made her cry even harder. Gallant, he pulled out a none-too-clean napkin from the glove compartment and handed it to her. She took it, lifting it to her face, hiding for a moment. "I was locked out of my house, that's why," she said, and then was instantly sorry she had said it.

He was perfectly silent.

"My father hit me," she said.

"You want to talk about it?" he said.

She shook her head.

"You want to camp at my place? We have a guest room." He turned on the motor. "That's stupid, I guess. You want me to take you home? I'll make sure you're all right."

She folded up the napkin. "All right," she said.

She started to give him directions, but he shook his head. "I know where you live," he said smoothly. She was too tired to question a face that innocent.

He parked in front of the house. "I'll wait," he promised. Lee got out, nearly twisting her ankle on the broken shoe. She was halfway up the walk when the door opened, and Frank, not even glancing toward Jim, took Lee in his arms, leading her inside, saying something low and insistent to her. The door closed, and for a moment Jim just sat there, watching her house and thinking.

* * *

Lee came to school two hours late, two weeks grounded. She took her time walking into French class, and when she entered the teacher lifted a wooden pointer. "Why, how very considerate of you to make an appearance, mademoiselle," she said. Lee, silent, dropped her pass on the teacher's desk. Someone in the back giggled.

All day Lee felt people watching her. She waited for someone to walk up to her and ask if it was true, if her father had really hit her. She was halfway through the day when she finally saw Jim walking toward her. His face filled with his smile. "Everything turn out okay?"

Lee fingered the worn leather of her purse. "About yesterday," she said. "Did you tell anyone?"

He frowned. "Did you want me to?"

"No. No, of course not."

He hesitated for a minute. "Listen," he said. "Would you go to a movie with me Friday?"

She beamed, a little taken aback. "Two weeks from Friday," she said. "I'm grounded until then."

Jim Archer had known where Lee lived because he had once followed her. It was the day he had first fallen in love with her, a stifling summery Wednesday when she had come into his father's supermarket to shoplift fruit. She was in an elasticized bare black minidress and lace-up leather sandals. Her hair was piled on top of her head, looped with a blue silk ribbon. He had never seen anyone so beautiful, or so sloppy a shoplifter. She didn't bother to look around her. Her movements slowed when they should have quickened. She left her purse wide open, walking out with at least ten dollars' worth of kiwi and Chinese plums bobbing in sight. He had been bagging groceries, nearly to the end of his shift, and as soon as she walked out of the automatic door, he untied his apron to trail her. You couldn't accuse shoplifters until they had left the premises; his father had been threatened with a lawsuit once when he had nabbed a woman who had a steak in her blouse. She insisted she was putting it back, that she had just put it there to leave her hands free to gather other groceries. She cried loudly that she'd never shop at the Top Thrift again. She threatened to sue because she claimed she had freezer burn where she had held the steak. Furthermore, she said she'd tell all her influential friends to stay the hell away from a supermarket that treated its clientele so shabbily. "And they buy *lots* of food," she said.

Lee never noticed him following her, but the thing was, he didn't stop her once she was outside. He didn't stop her a block later but continued to shadow her in the hot shiny heat, right up to her front door. He watched her go inside, his heart skimming over each beat. For weeks afterward he took extra shifts bagging, just in case she might come in again.

The Top Thrift was right off of Woodkey Lane, a block or so away from where Lee lived. It was a booming business a less-than-enthusiastic Jim was expected to inherit. His father had started the market up from a small storefront, borrowing the money from his own father. He had dropped out of school at sixteen because the market took so much time, but within two years he had a bigger store and a wife, Gladys, a small pretty Greek girl who helped out on the cash register just to be near him. When Jim was born another two years later, the market had expanded even more, into the Top Thrift Supermarket, bigger, better, and so successful that Gladys retired home.

The Top Thrift *was* one of the nicer markets. It was well lit, well swept, with brilliant blue shelves and shining displays. Jack himself, in starched whites, paraded up and down his aisles, talking to the customers, making sure they had whatever it was they needed. He encouraged people to call him by name.

Afternoons, Jim bagged groceries, dressed in the same blue smock the other boys wore, the name of the store stenciled on the pocket in white. "Bagging's the best education you can get," Jack told him. "You can tell a lot about a person just by what they eat, whether they think enough of themselves to buy the top-quality tuna instead of generic. You see who has food stamps, and how they feel about it, if they don't look you in the eye out of shame or if they act all defiant, like it's your fault the government's supporting them," Jack told him. He talked enthusiastically, but all Jim got out of it was to see firsthand the lousy diets people had. Coke and candy and frozen pot pies. Canned baby food loaded with preservatives. All he learned about human nature was how nasty a woman could be when she couldn't find her coupons. He learned, too, the cruelty of his peers, who wandered into the store in bored wolfpacks. They laughed when they saw him bagging. Deliberately one of the kids would get into his ten-items-or-less line with twelve items, just enough over the limit to be annoying. The whole time Jim bagged, instructions would be barked at him. "Bananas on top, dufus," a voice said. A hand sometimes dumped his work and rebagged it. Sometimes whole groups of guys would watch him, smirking, and then one of them would remember he didn't want a certain item and Jim would have to rebag. "Nice threads," they said. "Do a good job and you could go far." Jim, irritated, dug unseen fingers into new green grapes, squashing as many as he could reach. He packed their eggs on the bottom where they might be crushed. "Come back anytime," he said.

He tried to keep a low profile. Disguising himself, he wore a baseball cap, and once dark shades, until his father embarrassed him further by asking loudly just who he thought he was, James Bond?

He had never been popular. He was thin and serious and so pale and blond, his mother had once been called into the school by a suspicious nurse who wanted to know if Jim ever was allowed outside in the sun. Despite his father's urging, when he bagged he didn't think about the store or displays; instead he dreamed about what he loved—science. He saw bacteria sprouting happily in a petri dish, amoebas swimming on a slide.

He was honest enough, telling Jack as gently as possible that he didn't want to run the business, that his father would be better off handing it down to a cousin or a box boy than to him. Both his parents had been astounded. "It's a good living," his mother insisted. "You want a wife, a family, this is the way to go." Astonished, his father had studied his son. "What is there to do instead?" he said.

"I don't know. Anything. Go to Paris."

"Paris is just like New York City," Jack said. "And nobody in their right mind wants to go to New York City."

"I want to go to school," Jim said.

"School? What for?" Jack said. "I couldn't wait to get out of school when I was your age."

"I want to study chemistry. Be a doctor. Or a pharmacist, maybe," Jim said.

"Listen to me," Jack said. "Waste of time. You got a whole ready-made business here. You just forget it."

Jim didn't forget. He didn't for a moment intend to take over the Top Thrift, and he didn't intend staying in Philadelphia, either. He made friends with Mrs. Fisk, a guidance counselor just out of school, so young and pretty it was rumored the captain of the football team had asked her out himself. She despaired of her job. The kids assigned to her came in grudgingly and only when she called them. They had their minds made up. How the hell could she know what courses were easy enough to sleep your way to an A, what schools might accept anyone who could legibly print their name? She knew they considered the whole guidance department a joke—a job someone who couldn't do anything else took on—and Jim's anxious interest and genuine need touched her deeply. "We have *ways*," she said to Jim conspiratorially. She was the one who found the cheapest and best colleges for him to apply to, the one who had the catalogs sent directly to her so his parents wouldn't find out. She helped him with the financial aid applications, the scholarships. "Tell the truth," she advised. "They know there are parents who don't want kids going to school."

Jim began working longer hours at the Top Thrift, saving every cent he could into a special college account, for a future that didn't include mopping up broken glass in aisle one. Jack beamed. "That's the spirit," he told Jim. "That's what I like to see." He gave Jim a raise.

When he wasn't working and saving, Jim saw Lee. He brought her exotic fruits from the market, mangoes and kiwis. If she were supplied, he reasoned, she wouldn't need to steal.

Lee didn't understand why she kept dating Jim. He never so much as touched her, though she felt him watching her, and the only notoriety she gained from being with him was the disbelief of her peers. "You go out with Jim Archer?" her lab partner asked, shaking her head. "Excuse me for saying this, but I didn't think he *liked* girls."

"He likes this one plenty," Lee said coolly.

She continued to see other boys. Sometimes, on another date, though, she'd spot Jim, blurring past on his white bicycle, his hair dripping wet. The bicycle irritated her. Why couldn't he borrow his father's car? She encouraged Tony to vandalize the bike, but he laughed at her. "Too easy," he said. Sometimes, too, she'd see Jim over at Boon's Burgers, hunched over a Coke and fries, talking animatedly to one of his friends, a boy always as chalky pale and drably dressed as he was, in chinos and some sort of madras shirt. She walked in, in a skirt too tight, a shimmery rayon blouse, hanging on to the arm of some boy, and when she saw him she struggled to make her smile as distant as the rings of Saturn. A flicker of pain crossed his face.

Despite herself, she began to count on him. Nights when she couldn't sleep, nights when Frank and Janet went out to a dinner she wasn't invited to, she would call him. He talked to her calmly. "God, the whole house to yourself, isn't that great?" he said. "No pressure, no tension, you can just be yourself."

"It is nice," Lee said, perking up a little.

He told her stories into the night. About a scientist in the 1870s who thought the moon craters were caused by swarms of lunar insects. He told her he thought time travel was probably possible, and he'd be the first one to volunteer to go into the future. "What about you?" he said. Without hesitating Lee said firmly, "I'd go to the past."

It was ridiculously easy to make him happy. All she had to do was smile at him or thread her fingers into his. She didn't plan on the way he sometimes jammed into her thoughts. She could be doing the dinner dishes and then she'd suddenly think his name, his face would float into her mind. She didn't want to need him; she didn't like the way her stomach folded in upon itself when she couldn't find him at school or when he didn't call. And she didn't like the way he needed her.

She began seeing Tony again, breaking dates with Jim to whiz about town on the back of a motorcycle. "That boy again," Frank said. "What do you mean, that boy?" Lee said. Frank made her come out on the front lawn, where he showed her the tire marks from Tony's bike, greasy black slashes in the green yard.

Lee came home at one and two in the morning; she skipped classes and came to the dinner table with her eyes lined in frosted lilac, her lips streaked with a startling red. On her left arm she had a silver bracelet she had taken from a Woolworth's down the street. She hadn't told Frank she had been warned never to come back there, that a man had grabbed her arm just as she was leaving. All he had had to do was get her to take off her boot, where the bracelet was hidden, but he just made her empty her purse on a table in the back. "Don't come back," he told her. But sometimes Lee did, and always she left with a pair of glass earrings, or a chiffon scarf, or a packet of sewing needles she didn't even want. She'd come home and then make herself baths so hot, she was certain it would burn the restlessness right out of her.

One night Lee stayed out with Tony until three in the morning drinking rum and Cokes from a plaid thermos bottle. "I love you," Tony said, making Lee laugh so much, it angered him. "What, what's the matter?" he said fiercely. "You think that's funny?" He drove her home speechless with fury.

When Jim called to ask her out, when he mentioned how happy he was to be with her, she sniped at him. "Hah, you think that's happy," she said. She planned to talk to him, to let him know he couldn't own her. That night he drove to the lake, the air so clear and cold, it seemed to freeze the light around them. "I have a surprise for you," he said. For one moment she was afraid that he was going to take the clumsy gold ring from his finger and drop it into her palm. She curled her fingers inward, she folded her arms about her. Instead, though, he got out of the car. "Just wait," he said. She pulled down the rearview mirror and blinked at her reflection in the mirror. "Okay," he said, getting back in, holding up a slim glass bottle.

"Champagne," he said. "Château de Top Thrift." He gave her the bottle and opened up the glove compartment and took out two glasses, wrapped in lavender tissue paper. "Waterford crystal," he said, handing one glass to Lee, "courtesy of my mother." He opened the champagne with a pop, ceremoniously pouring her a glass. Gamely Lee took a sip. Metal in her mouth. An edge of tin. "Wait, wait," he said, pouring himself a glass and clinking it against hers. "To us," he said. "Happy days," said Lee.

He kept pouring the two of them wine, and at first he just watched her as she sipped. The champagne tasted flat. She couldn't drink any more of it without feeling ill. Jim poured wine into her empty glass. He was drinking more than she was, downing each glass with a glad, exaggerated sigh.

He listed toward her, touching the side of her face with one finger.

"I see things just as clearly drunk as sober," Lee said. The hand retracted. It moved to the wine; it poured another full glass. Lee stared at the sky through her empty wineglass.

"You want to take a walk?" Lee asked.

Jim studied his glass of wine. "I fell in love with you the first time I saw you." He looked at her, pinning her in his gaze. "I must have because every single moment after that I felt different."

"Don't say that," Lee said. She swung her legs outside and then stood in the night, arms clapped about her.

From a distance she heard Jim's voice. "I never loved anyone before. I never even liked anyone enough to ask them out. My father thinks I'm socially retarded." He laughed and then stopped himself. "I don't go out with anyone else. But you . . . you're always with someone new. Why aren't I enough?"

Lee resettled herself into the car. "You think anybody's ever enough for anybody?" she said. "I've never seen that to be the case."

He took a long miserable swig from his glass. "You're enough for me," he said.

"Hah. You think that now," Lee said.

He poured himself more wine. "I'll always think it."

"It's late. I need to get home."

They drove in silence. The road was flat and gray as slate, and Jim began humming something low and tuneless in his throat, and even though he wasn't looking at her at all, Lee felt him somehow surrounding her, and she shifted uncomfortably on her seat. They were almost home. It wasn't even eleven, wasn't even within an hour of her curfew, when a police car snaked out from around a bend. Red light, a bulb on top of the car flashing, a hand waving them over to the side. "Oh, shit," Jim said.

There were two policemen, both middle-aged, but only one got out, lumbering toward them. Jim sat very straight, eyes focused at a point in the distance.

It was only a broken taillight, but it didn't take the cop long to smell the alcohol on Jim's breath, to lean over and sniff it on Lee, like a kind of rare perfume. "You kids just never learn, do you," he said flatly. "Don't they teach you anything in driver's ed?" He made them get out of the car and blow into a balloon, the whole time shaking his head at them. He scribbled out a ticket and handed it to Jim with the utmost disgust. "Get in the squad car," he said.

The whole way to the station, he lectured the two of them. Drunk driving. Jim could lose his license for a fool stunt like that. He could have lost their lives—or someone else's. You were damn lucky," he said. "Goddamned lucky. I'm sure your parents will have something to say about this. If I were your father, you'd be lucky if I let you on a bicycle."

Lee felt a thrill of fear. "I'll be grounded forever," she said to Jim. "No, you won't," he said, reaching for the hand she had tucked, small and stubborn, into her pocket.

The station was brightly lit and dead quiet. The two cops said something in low voices to the desk sergeant. "Not again," the desk sergeant said wearily, inspecting Jim and Lee. "Sit," he ordered. "I'm calling your folks, not you. It seems to make more of an impression that way."

"Oh, God," Jim said, washing one hand over his face. He looked a little green; his whole body seemed to be crumpling.

"'Oh, God' is right," the desk sergeant said, and Jim promptly vomited on the floor.

They sat on a heavy wood bench, waiting for their parents. Jim was huddled over, his face folded into a damp washcloth. Lee, only a little drunk, put one hand on his shoulder. "Don't touch, I'll be sick again," he said, panicked.

Frank had arrived first, striding in with Janet behind him, pinning Lee in his sights. He whispered something to the cop and then, before he got to Lee, crouched down toward Jim. "Another one I don't know," Frank said. "Where does she get these guys?" Jim lifted the cloth from his face, staring woozily at Frank's stabbing finger. "You go near my daughter again and I'll kill you. You understand that word, kill, or are you too drunk and stupid?" Jim's mouth, fishlike, gaped open. Frank clenched Lee's bare arm and yanked her upward. She tottered on new suede heels, trying to brace herself on Frank's shoulder, but he pulled back, striking her face. Her neck snapped forward; she stumbled. Jim's hands flashed, grabbing for an edge of Lee's shirt, clamping on stale station air. "Honey," Frank said, beckoning Janet.

On the drive home Lee sat in between Frank and Janet. "You reek of cheap wine," Frank said angrily, but after that no one said a single word. The radio remained silent. Frank parked the car in the drive and walked ahead of them, and as soon as he opened the front door, he disappeared into the study, closing the door firmly. Janet put two hands on Lee's shoulders. "You see the state your father's in?" she demanded. "You're going to give him a heart attack."

That night Lee sat up in a thin white nightgown. Something scuttled in her stomach, and she doubled herself over on the bed, head in her hands. She heard the lights clicking shut, the sounds any house made settling, but as much as she strained, she couldn't shape a single murmur coming from Frank and Janet's room, and it somehow scared her.

Morning. Hung over. Her head warring with her stomach, she gingerly dressed for school. In the mirror her face looked as if the features had softened and blurred. Sickened, she smelled eggs frying. Janet, a blue apron around a red dress, a single pink sponge curler in her bangs, nodded at Lee. Frank dunked his toast into his coffee and nodded at his daughter. "Were you sick last night?" he said. "I thought I heard you."

"No, I was okay," she said.

"Lots of vitamin C today," he said.

They were halfway through breakfast. Lee took cautious bites of egg. She suctioned orange juice through a straw.

"You think it's fine, what you did?" Frank said.

Lee put down her glass.

"You think I like to be called into a station by the police? I thought something had happened to you. I could hardly drive straight for thinking it." He dragged the edge of his plate toward him. "We can't live like this," Frank said. "We absolutely can't."

Janet scraped butter from her toast.

"You remember your aunt Bessie? In Ohio?" Frank said. "I think you met her once, when you were really little."

"Didn't she have a cat or something?" Lee said.

Frank nodded. "Well, we want you to go live with her for a while."

"Excuse me?" Lee said.

"She doesn't work, so she could keep an eye on you. The school system there's fairly strict, so there'd be no room for any of your monkey business."

"You can't send me away," Lee said. She looked desperately at Frank, who was calmly buttering his toast.

"What would you do, a daughter running wild? Suspended. Half-drunk. Picked up by the cops with a boy you don't even know?" he said.

"I wouldn't send her away," said Lee.

Janet held up one hand, interrupting. "I know what you think. You think I don't love you, that all of this is my doing, but you're wrong."

"Who cares whether you love me or not?" Lee cried.

Frank touched her arm. "You show us you can be responsible in Ohio, then you can come home."

Lee, furious, flung down her napkin.

"You finish out the year here. But you're grounded. That means you come right home from school," Frank said, "or there's going to be trouble. You don't go out nights unless it's with us. And I catch you talking to that boy and I'll see him jailed." Lee slammed the door. "You hear me?" Frank cried, but she was gone.

Janet was the one who arranged all the details, phoning the high school where Lee would finish up her senior year. She called airport after airport, scratching out departure times on a stubby yellow pad, circling the ones that would have Lee vanished from the house before summer even started to heat up.

Grounded. The phone rang for her, but Frank always said she was out. He never said she'd call back. She was stuck in the house with Janet, who sang and rustled through fabrics and paint chips. She caught Janet standing in her room once, head cocked, and when she saw Lee she smiled.

All that week Jim was absent from school. She tried to call him from the pay phone by the gym, but each time a woman's weary voice answered, and Lee just hung up. She was moody and silent, uninterested in skipping class with Tony to meander in the fields behind the school, refusing to swig brandy from a thermos with another boy. She saw how it was, how they began shying from her, and she couldn't much blame them. She wasn't the good-time girl anymore.

Lee told boy after boy that she had been grounded, that she was being sent away. Tony gamely offered to cut Frank, "just a little over one eye, as a reminder." Another boy, a vocational student studying small engines, wrote Lee notes riddled with broken clichés. "It's always darkest before the afternoon," he scribbled. "Every cloud has a yellow center." One boy, who had been expelled for firing a water pistol filled with tomato juice at a teacher, told Lee that since she was going, they should make up for lost time. His hand gripped a silky spill of Lee's hem, fingers found her thigh. Gradually the boys who used to hum around her began surrounding new conquests, leaving Lee by herself. Girls flashed Lee cold, triumphant grins.

She had fifty dollars in a bank account. She called all the airlines to see how far fifty dollars might get her, but then there was always the problem. Where would she go once she got there, what kind of a job could she get when she got there?

Lee was too much trouble for anyone except for Jim, who had bagged enough cat food and frozen food after school to have accumulated a bankbook two could live on. He had this plan.

He'd always feel that he had been the one to save her. Without him she would have ended up defeated in some little town or dead on the road hitchhiking home. Jim never would have let Lee go. He was making himself half-crazy when Mrs. Fisk told him he had gotten into school. Johns Hopkins. Full scholarship, and suddenly everything gelled.

"We'll leave together," he said. "We'll get married."

"Married—" She stepped back two paces, propelled by a sudden sharp flare of anger. "What kind of a solution is that? Why can't we just leave?"

He flushed, suddenly defiant. "It's the perfect solution," he said. "You think anyone's going to bother with a married couple? It makes things that much harder."

"You're wrong. It makes them crazier," Lee said.

"You never say it, but you love me. I know you do."

Lee dug her hands into the pocket of her skirt, glaring at him. "Why can't we just leave?" she said.

"Because I won't do it," he said. "You think I'm going to get you someplace just so you can leave? I want something in return, and what I'm asking isn't so horrible, is it? I want to get married as soon as we can."

"I'm not eighteen," she said finally. "Neither are you."

"But you will be, when? In January? And I'll be in November. All we have to do is lay low until then."

"How can we get married?" Lee said.

"You just do it. You go see the justice of the peace or a judge and you say 'I do' and that's that." He looked past her, sighting something in the distance. "Who else loves you the way I do? You think that happens every day?"

"Love has nothing to do with anything," she said.

For a moment his face changed. It was the first time she had ever seen him really angry, and it frightened her. His back straightened. "Oh, it doesn't?" he said politely. "You think about it."

When Lee walked back into the house, everything hurt. The phone was ringing, and she plucked it up before Janet could get to it. Startled, she heard Frank's voice. His "Hello" was tired. "I'm not thrilled about this, Frank," a voice said. "You can blame me all you want, but I'm just not. I'm too old for girls."

"Just until she finishes high school, Bess," Frank said. "Come on. You owe me."

"I know it, but I don't have to be thrilled about it. What am I supposed to do with a teenage girl?"

"Nothing," Frank said. "That's the whole idea. Nothing's what'll keep her out of trouble." He sighed. "Just watch her," he said. "That's all I ask."

Lee hung up the phone. She went upstairs to her room. She didn't know how people fell in love. She knew the symptoms, the racing pulse, the way your words tangled up, but they had never happened to her. She dialed Jim's number. She kept telling herself that he loved her. What she was going to do wasn't so terrible, was it? It was what he wanted, and it would be just for a while. Just until she was on her feet. Until she turned eighteen and had some money. And maybe, maybe you could learn to love a person that caring, maybe you could even want to stay. When he answered, she said, "Yes," and then burst into tears.

It was the secrecy Jim loved. He made Mrs. Fisk swear not to tell his parents, promising he would do it himself once he was settled. He didn't tell her about Lee, and he wouldn't tell his parents, either, not until she was his wife.

He planned. He had favorite words. Wife. Marriage. Johns Hopkins. He knew Lee didn't really love him, at least not yet, but he was certain the seeds were there, and that all it would take was some patient nurturing for them to flower. He saw his situation with Lee the same way he looked at a scientific experiment. A scientist didn't give up—you had glimpses of success, a vision of how things could be, and then you just worked your way to fulfill that vision. If he just could figure out the right formula, the right equation, he could make Lee completely happy. He knew it.

He started with finding them a home in Baltimore. He called Johns Hopkins from Mrs. Fisk's office, asking a swarm of questions about student housing, married housing, cheap housing, any housing. He scrawled names and numbers on a piece of paper; he figured budgets. "Trust me," he told Lee. He took a day off school and caught the train to Baltimore to find them an apartment, and all that day Lee wandered from class to class, unable to concentrate, thinking how easy finding a home was for her father but how difficult it might be for a boy like Jim.

In the morning, at school, he told her he had found them a place, a rented house in a real neighborhood.

"A house?" Lee said. "That's a pretty big deal."

"You'll love it," he said, flushing with pleasure.

The secrecy, though, was difficult around his parents. His mother tousled his hair in the morning, and he wanted to fling his arms around her and hug her. He wanted to clap his father on the back and tell him he loved him. "You want the butter? It's right in front of you," Jack said, annoyed when he caught Jim staring at him. In a card store he bought a handsome postcard, a scene of the Kentucky mountains, and wrote on the back: "I'm fine. Cannot explain right now. Will contact you later. Please don't worry. I love you both. Your son, Jim." He stamped it; he'd mail it right before he and Lee left. It didn't seem enough, but he'd rather have his parents furious at his thoughtlessness than worried that he was dead, a smear of chemicals and bone on a highway.

They were going to leave the last day of school, two days before Lee was to be sent to Ohio. Frank had already bought her a shiny pink steamer trunk as a going-away present, leaving it open, encouraging her to pack. "I've started packing already," Lee told Frank, thinking of the green army knapsack she carried her books in, the leather pocketbook she might be able to stuff. "We'll meet right in front of Ratner's Drugstore," Jim told her. They'd hop a Greyhound to Baltimore; they'd get married as soon as Lee turned eighteen, then they'd get her high school records sent up and she could finish school.

The night before they were to leave, Lee packed her knapsack. She put in her favorite blue jersey dress, three black T-shirts, colored bikini underwear, deodorant, face cream, and her favorite pair of blue jeans. In the morning she'd dress in layers. A red T-shirt under a white rayon blouse under a black rib-knit sweater. A black skirt over blue leggings that could double as pants, over tights and socks and parrot green cowboy boots. She'd sling her father's leather jacket over her arm. Seventy degrees or not, Tony had taught her leather was always the material of choice, and it would serve her when the cold weather came. Winterized, she could shed layers on the long bumpy bus ride. She was about to tighten her knapsack when she remembered Claire's silverware spread out and shining on her dresser. She held open the knapsack and, using the flat of her hand like a spatula, swept the silver into her pack. Experimentally she hoisted it onto her shoulder. It was backache weight; a sprain would be a souvenir.

That night she couldn't sleep. She watched the clock track the hours toward morning, and at four she got up to make herself some tea. In the silent kitchen she willed Frank to come downstairs. She imagined him finding her there, how dramatic it would look, just a slight young girl sorrowfully sipping sugary tea. "Stay here," he'd tell her. "I love you." She drank three cups of tea, and as she drained the third she heard Frank's rumbling snore.

In the morning Lee was too nervous to eat. She made two peanut-butter sandwiches, one for Jim, and grabbed two Granny Smith apples. When Frank came into the room she stopped, lifting her face to his, waiting. He looked at her critically. "How you dress," he said.

"All girls her age dress like that," Janet said.

Seven-thirty. She had ten minutes to get to Jim. "Good-bye," she said. She waited until Frank had stood, reaching for the sugar, and then she hugged him, hiding her face in the rough folds of his shirt. Startled, he pulled back, which made it both harder and easier for her to leave.

Jim was waiting for her, his own knapsack slung heavily over his shoulder. His eyes were puffy from lack of sleep; his body jittered from side to side. "Let's go," he said, taking her pack from her. "Jesus, what do you have in here?" he said.

"Things," she told him.

She remembered the Greyhound ride. Squashed in the back of the bus, by the bathrooms. In back of a five-year-old who kept chanting "Old MacDonald Had a Farm," singsonging it until even her own mother slapped her. "Now. I told you to *stop*," she said, flustered. Every time the bus stopped, Lee tensed. At one point a police car pulled the bus over, and she grabbed Jim's hand, but it was only because the bus had been speeding. "It'll be fine," Jim told her, but she saw how unsteady his hands were. She marked time by what she might have been doing. Ten o'clock and struggling valiantly to remember how to conjugate the Latin verbs that had been her homework. Twelve and at a long lazy lunch. Three o'clock and snoozing in study hall. She imagined Frank, showing off a house, stopping to call Janet. "Honey," he'd say. She thought of her aunt in Ohio, waiting, not wanting her, and then she leaned over and took Jim's hand and fell asleep.

Frank would hate Baltimore, Lee decided. Although the roads were sometimes tree-lined and woodsy-smelling, most of the city radiated from the beltway. Their house was a small white clapboard in a wooded suburb. Their lawn was the only lawn untended, sprouted with dandelions.

There was nothing in the house yet but electricity and hot water and the things they had brought with them. Four clean white walls she suddenly ached to vandalize, a polished wood floor she scuffed experimentally. Lee folded her arms across her chest and leaned uneasily against the wall.

"It's late," Jim said. He spread a blanket on the floor. "We'll buy a real bed tomorrow," he said.

She felt queasy. She had never really let Jim touch her, and when he approached her she stepped back. "What?" he said.

"Everyone can see us," she said. Behind her, the picture window looked out on the deserted parking lot.

"No, they can't," he said. "And anyway, it's after midnight. Who's going to see?" Shyly he slid his hand down her side. "You're so pretty," he said, untucking her blouse.

She let him sink her down toward the blanket. She kept remembering a conversation she had overheard in the girls' room at school one day. Two voices from behind two separate gray stalls were discussing whether smart boys were better lovers. "A smart guy may look like a dufus, but at least he knows what to do," one voice said.

"That's shit," said the other girl. "You can know all you want, but if you can't *do*, what good is that?"

Jim nipped kisses along her shoulder. He shaped her shoulders with his palms. She didn't believe he had ever slept with a girl before. His whole body was trembling.

They were out of synch. She rushed toward him, and he drew back, taking his time with her, stretching out his pleasure. She drew herself over him, her hair tented over his face, and he rolled her back down, and the one time she opened her eyes, she saw him watching her, pinning her in his sight. "Shut your eyes," she said, drawing the blanket over her breasts. "No, no, I don't want to miss this," he said. "Okay, okay." His lids flickered and then swam with sight.

In the end she pulled him inside of her; she quickened his pleasure so he couldn't pull back. "Shut your eyes," she repeated, planting kisses on his pulsing lids. His sight glazed, he closed his lids only so she could kiss them. Once she had rendered him sightless, she began to relax and then, to her surprise, she began to turn liquid, greedy with her own pleasure. Her arms stretched out, pinning the edge of the blanket. She rocked against him, and when she cried out, he held her to him.

Outside, a siren whined. Police, she thought. Any moment there might be a knock on the door. Tensed, she waited, half-hopeful, but the sound faded. She was used to just getting up now, putting on her clothes, going home, bringing herself back to herself, but now the only place to go was here. Jim steered her toward him, lacing his fingers into her hair, swabbing her cheek with his tongue. She wanted to get up and make a bed for herself in the bathtub, shut the door, and be alone. She wanted to ask Jim to go out and get her doughnuts and then lock the door behind him, pretending she didn't hear when he came back. She'd never sleep with him lying so close beside her, staking so much claim. This was terrible. "This is wonderful," Jim said, content. "This is the stuff of forever."

Lee, in the dark, opened her eyes.

They bought wedding bands the next day. "Why can't we wait until I'm eighteen?" Lee said. "I'll be legal then."

"It's an act of faith," Jim said.

"We don't have to spend money on rings," she said.

"If you spread the cost out across the years, it's nothing," he said. "Besides, I like the idea of rings."

He chose a band that was so wide and clumsy, he could barely flex his knuckle. She couldn't bear to touch any of the rings. On her finger they felt dishonest. She was sure the gold would stain her finger green, branding her with a mark as telling as a scarlet letter. "Here, let me help," Jim said, sliding a ring on her finger. Hers was the thinnest gold she could find, barely a wire across her finger and almost a half size too big. "You can get that tightened, you know," the salesman told her. "You don't want to lose it."

"It fits fine," Lee said, and when she flexed her fingers, the ring slid toward her nail.

She kept thinking of television drama. Or movies. Her life in Technicolor, spliced into manageable scenes, fast-forwarded when it got messy. Lovely last minute escapes. Dustin Hoffman pounding at the door of a church and stopping Katharine Ross from getting married. A winning lottery ticket found in the pocket of her jeans and toodle-loo, she'd be off to Paris. The police must be looking for her by now. Detectives or maybe Frank himself, showing up to jerk backward through time. "Stay away from my daughter," he had said, but here was Jim about to get as close to her as anyone could, and Frank was nowhere around.

"This might not work out," Lee said abruptly. She would say it to him again, months later, in a freezing February just minutes before they were to be married by a justice of the peace. She grabbed at his arm. She was wearing a long-sleeved white wool dress she had bought at Zayre's for ten dollars. White Leatherette shoes with stiletto heels. "I'm just being honest with you," she said. They were sitting in a dark parlor that smelled of lemon wax and slightly stale flowers. On a desk was a white statue of a grinning Cupid, poised to shoot. The walls were lined with couples, some of them in wedding dress, one in jeans and T-shirts. There was a colored photo of a tropical beach, and across it someone had scribbled in blue ink: "Having a wonderful time, thanks to you! Don't wish you were here! Ha Ha. The Myers." Lee glanced at Jim, who was staring at her, which made her so flustered, she stood up. "You look beautiful," he said.

There was rustling behind the door. Jim stood up, brushing off his suit. "It might not work out with us," Lee repeated. Her breathing was shallow, her skin faintly flushed. "Listen, I'm just being honest with you," she said.

He took her hands, turning the palms up as if he were reading her future. "Everybody knows you can't be honest if you tried," he said.

She had never gotten used to the neighborhood, although Jim had instantly fallen in love with it. It seemed fairly close-knit. People were raising families here, planning to stay. There seemed to be an order that Jim found intoxicatingly adult. Mornings the men got into their cars or waited at the bus stop to go to work. At night they played badminton in each other's backyards. He saw the women moving casually from house to house, sometimes sitting on chaise longues on the lawns, talking. The women watched one another's kids and worked part-time or not at all if their kids were young enough. "It's like our parents' lives," he told Lee, exulting.

"No," she said. "No, it won't be."

Maureen Reardon, a middle-aged schoolteacher who lived next door, came over as soon as Jim and Lee's moving van had left. She brought over her home-baked brownies and a brimming basket of the vegetables her husband, Mel, grew in his backyard garden. She later told Jim that she had had no idea what kind of people this young couple might be, but the truth of it was, no matter what kind of woman the wife was, she sure as hell hoped that the husband wasn't a gardener. She knew how much time Mel spent in the garden he had dug up in the backyard, how much time he and his buddies in the neighborhood spent comparing notes about peat moss and the best way to get rid of woodchucks.

The fights she had with Mel were always about his garden. The last argument had been over forty dollars he had spent sending away for a praying mantis.

She loved Mel, but he could photograph his tomatoes and frame them for all she cared. She hated everything about gardening. There were always too many peaches from the trees. There was just so much broccoli she could sneak into the trash rather than trying to disguise it in another meat loaf, another pot of soup. She walked the aisles of the supermarkets and felt drawn to all the shiny canned vegetables, the frozen peas. She yearned toward the TV dinners with carrots all in one tin compartment.

She rang the bell of Lee and Jim's new house and waited. Lee in bared dirty feet and cutoffs, her hair shored back with a red ribbon, lazily pulled open the door. Her face was scrubbed and open. Maureen glanced back at her uncertainly. Surely she couldn't be this young. "Are you a niece?" she said finally. Lee scrunched up her brow.

"A niece?" she said. She rubbed one bare foot against her calf, scratching a slow circle. Her toenails were painted a chipping lavender. "Do you have the right house?" she said. "I'm Lee Archer. We just moved here."

Maureen switched the basket to her other hip. "Welcome to the neighborhood," she said lamely. Lee smiled. She poked a sudden small hand into the basket, dousing out the sweet crusty brownies, her rough skin handling the smooth, glossy tomatoes that Maureen's husband had once gotten up in the middle of a chilly night to cover lovingly with cheesecloth. "Jim," Lee called in a high, shiny voice, and then Jim had wandered out, looking even paler and younger than Lee had. He had a comma of white paint on his smooth cheek, and his hands were hidden in baggy khaki pockets. His hair was much too long, his face much too innocent, and she looked at his hands, but he was wearing a wedding band, wider than his wife's. She worried for a minute about wild parties, and then Jim picked up a tomato and started genuinely admiring it, and that made her worry even more.

"You garden," she said dully.

Jim shook his head. "My father's in supermarkets," he said. "This is a good one. I can tell."

"Ah," Maureen said, relieved. She waited for an invitation inside. She was curious about how kids so young might furnish a perfectly good house. She tried to peer around Lee, but all she saw were poorly wrapped boxes. "If you need anything, I'm right next door," she said.

She had waited, but neither Lee nor Jim ever came over, though Jim would sometimes wave hello on his rush to class.

A few more neighbors dropped by, especially as more and more of the summer vegetables from their own makeshift gardens came in. Jim was always grateful for the food. It depressed him to shop in supermarkets. He couldn't walk down an aisle or hold a can without thinking of his father and missing him. Every time he saw a grocer in a white coat, his heart bumped and lurched.

There were barbecues that first summer. Someone strung up a badminton net for the adults to bat a birdie back and forth before they sat down to icy gin and tonics, to salads and burgers. Although Jim and Lee were invited, they never showed. Jim was always at class, and Lee kept to herself.

Jim meant to be sociable. He thought about taking up golf, about walking across the street one night and offering to play the winner in the nightly badminton game. But he woke at six, and by the time he got home all he wanted was to be with Lee. He meant to, but he saw the way Lee would sometimes stare at the women chatting in the street nights, watching their kids play, and the one time he saw her in conversation with a woman, she came home vaguely upset. "What's wrong?" he said. Lee gave him a blank stare. "She wanted to know if I wanted to go food shopping with her. She said she had recipes she could give me, too."

"But that's nice," Jim said.

He told her she didn't have to, but almost immediately Lee got a job waitressing at a small cafe called the Silver Spoon. Nights when Lee had to work, he got so lonely for her that he went to where she was. He brought a textbook with him to the restaurant. He could study, knowing she was there, a wisp in the corner of his eye. He loved watching her like that, as if he were seeing for the first time how surprisingly lovely she was, how quickly she moved. Her hair was twisted on the top of her head. At night she would pluck out the pins, complaining that the weight of all the yellow hair gave her headaches. She wore white sneakers and a short white dress starched like paper. He came into the restaurant, happy and embarrassed, but the look Lee sometimes flashed him was not always one of welcome. He settled into a blue vinyl booth, fiddling with the menu, settling his books, and when Lee came by she frowned. "You can't just sit there," she whispered. "You have to order something." So he ordered a steak sandwich he didn't really want, a dessert cake dewy with butter. He cut things up and rearranged them on his plate. He kept ordering, making the time stretch out.

The Silver Spoon filled up gradually. One night he saw people waiting, watching his table with hard angry eyes, and he flagged Lee down, about to order something else, but then she fluttered his bill on the table. "Please go," she said wearily. "It makes me too nervous having you here."

"Nervous, why?" he said.

"Nobody else's boyfriend's waiting on them."

He looked at the three other waitresses. None of them was paying him any attention. One held a length of dirty dishes along one arm. She smiled down at her shoes.

"Am I a boyfriend?" he said.

"Well, you know what I mean," Lee said. "None of them are married, that's why I said that."

He took out some bills. "I'll come get you at closing time," he told her. He scattered two dollars too much for her tip. When he left, one of the people waiting for his table, a young girl in a glittered pink sweatshirt and jeans, hoisted out a haughty hip and glared at him.

Perhaps it was because they were so young themselves, but their connection to the neighborhood would be with the kids. It was Jim the kids noticed first. They watched him. One night a few young boys were sitting on the dusty curb, stamping down on caps, waiting for the sharp lightning pops of electricity, the thread of acrid smoke. They saw Jim come out onto his porch with his telescope.

"You want to take a look here?" Jim called. One of the boys dug a disgusted toe into the dirt, as if Jim had suggested he eat one of the pale translucent worms roiling up the dirt in Mel's vegetable garden. The kids disbanded, disappearing back into the night.

One night, though, Jim saw a boy staring at him. Jim stared back. He had seen this kid before, a small scrappy redhead dressed like a little old man. He swam out of red plaid bermudas, his short-sleeved white shirt was carefully buttoned to the throat, and most curious of all were the tiny wingtips he had on. He couldn't be more than ten. David. That was his name. Jim remembered hearing it one day when some kids on the street were teasing him. David was slower than the other kids. His speech sometimes slurred, and when he ran, his legs tangled him into a heap.

David now had his face tilted toward the porch, and when he saw Jim looking at him, he stepped forward instead of back. "Want to see something wonderful?" Jim said.

"Like what?" David said.

Jim was so happy that one of the kids finally spoke to him that he laughed. "Oh, planets," he said. He gestured at the sky. "Stars."

David shrugged. "I don't care," he said, but he climbed the stairs.

"Okay, you look here," Jim directed, positioning the telescope to David's eye level. "No, just one eye. You close the other one."

David squinted into the lens. He was perfectly still, his breath even. "Well, sometimes it takes time to see anything," Jim said, trying to be kind. "You almost have to train yourself." He moved to take the telescope, to focus on the moon, so inescapable, anyone could see it. He moved his hand, but David's fingers whipped toward Jim's. "It's gorgeous," he breathed, and Jim stepped back. David didn't say a single thing. He didn't move from the telescope until his mother's voice cried out, calling him home. "You come back anytime," Jim told him. "I mean it. Anytime."

David came back the next night, and the night after, and then he began bringing kids with him.

Jim loved the kids. He tried patiently to teach them a little something about the stars. He spread out old star maps on the porch. He gave away paste-on constellations that glowed in the dark. More and more of the kids began hanging out at the Archers' porch. Usually they stayed less than an hour and then they'd return home, waltzing lazily back into their living rooms to announce to their stunned parents that the light from a star was dead light. They mentioned quarks and black holes and white holes. "Well, now," parents said. They didn't like to feel shown up, but it was better having their kids looking at stars and quoting Einstein than ringing doorbells and running.

It was funny. The kids made Jim feel somehow older, more responsible. He credited them with making his voice stronger, his movements more sure; they did something entirely different for Lee. She may not have been comfortable with the other women in the neighborhood, but she was at home with the girls. For the first time since he had known her, she giggled. She sprawled out on the front porch and happily played jacks with the girls. "I did not cheat!" he heard her say, laughing. She had hated the one time he had washed her hair for her. He had thought it would be erotic, but she complained of soap in her eyes. She said his fingers felt like tarantulas crawling over her scalp. She didn't mind the girls doing it for her. She let them roll her wet hair on pink spongy curlers. They fought for the brush.

Jim found it odd how the girls treated Lee. It wasn't with the kind of respect he thought a married woman deserved, but she never seemed to mind. The kids called him "Mr. Archer," but they called Lee "Lee." Girls teased her and called her names and socked her in the arm at the punch line of a joke. It was odder still to come home and find his wife pinwheeling across the front yard in a game of freeze tag. She careened right into him with a sharp surprised intake of breath. Her flowered top fell off one shoulder. Her knees were scabbed and dirty, and her hair was tied into braids. She looked fifteen.

"You ought to get some friends," he told her that evening. "Someone your own age."

"I talk to plenty."

"Who?" he said. "Who do you talk to? The other waitresses? The women on the block? You tell me who."

She looped her arms about his shoulders. "I talk to you," she said finally.

"You need some friends," he said again.

"Oh, is that who needs that?" she said.

He pushed out a breath. He could want more for her all he wanted, but she would always seem to want less.

The boys sometimes trailed Lee, mesmerized. They had never seen anyone who looked like her, who smelled the way she did. When Lee began to get bigger with pregnancy, though, the boys began to avoid her. When they saw her on the porch, her stomach swelling against a cheap cotton shirt, they talked to her feet. They still idled over Jim's telescope, but those were old toys now, and they were all a little bored. Lee was moodier now, and the girls, who were more excited by her now that she was pregnant, began to chafe against her. She crouched under the brush they tried to put to her hair, and then jerked herself free. "My hair hurts," she complained. The smell of nail polish and lipstick now made her so ill that she wouldn't allow the girls to bring any over or to play with hers. She didn't want to play freeze tag anymore. The very sound of the jacks ball hitting the porch seemed to reverberate unpleasantly inside of her. The girls began tightening their circle, three or four of them talking while Lee sat off by herself, cradling her knees. And then, after a while, the girls stopped coming over.

Lee never talked much about how she felt. Once or twice one of the other women would call out to her and ask if the baby had kicked yet. "I guess," Lee said, not realizing how such an answer might shock. And sometimes Jim would see her on the porch, staring out at the street, her back to him, and when he put one hand on her shoulder, meaning to soothe, she jumped back, terrified, as if he had meant to hurt her.

— 3 —

The evening of Lee's disappearance from the hospital, a half hour before the police were contacted, Jim was speeding down the hospital corridor, a red velvet box of chocolates tucked under one arm. It was dinnertime. Candy stripers nudged shiny steel meal carts through the corridors. Faint plumes of steam spiraled from under the covered steel dishes. One of the candy stripers looked frankly at Jim. "Nobody brings *me* no candy," she flirted, but Jim didn't even smile.

He was exhausted, a little stunned from the hard bright heat outside. He hadn't eaten all day, and he was drained from the three hours of exams he had just finished. Thank God, though, school was all out of the way now. He had the whole long lazy summer to spend with Lee and the baby.

He had almost not taken his exams. He kept thinking he shouldn't leave the hospital, that he should be with his wife.

"Come on, she's sleeping," Lee's doctor said.

Lee's doctor's name was Anna Leighton. She had short spiky black hair and red lipstick she kept biting off. Lee had found her by stabbing a finger into the Yellow Pages. Jim had liked her because the whole time of Lee's pregnancy, Anna had made herself available to him. Anna didn't seem to see anything strange about Jim's calling her to find out why Lee's fingers and feet were swelling; why Lee sometimes had nightmares so terrible, she'd refuse to go back to sleep. Anna was warm and calm amid the damp waves of Jim's panic. She never asked to speak to Lee when Jim had phoned her, although she always reminded Jim to tell Lee that Lee could call anytime, that no question was too stupid, and she never seemed to hold it against Lee that Lee didn't.

When Jim had persisted in asking if Lee's deep sleep was normal, Anna became annoyed. In truth she was still a little irritated with him for trying to keep barging into the delivery room after Lee had shouted at him to get out. It just made it harder for Lee, who was panicked enough. Fathers sometimes fainted in delivery rooms; they sometimes were a nuisance. She herself had delivered over a thousand babies that she praised and cuddled and loved for the few minutes she held them, but because of the behavior of a few fathers, she couldn't imagine herself having one.

Jim couldn't wait for Lee to wake. She had been so nerved up during her pregnancy. She didn't want him telling his parents until after the baby was born. "I can't handle visitors right now," she said. "Stop worrying," he had soothed her. "We have enough money. We're going to be fine." He had worked hard trying to show her what a great father he was going to be. He was the one who spent hours mixing shade after shade of yellow, who painstakingly glued glow-in-the-dark silver stars on the ceiling so the baby would look up and wonder over the Milky Way. He went to Baby World himself between classes and bought the small white crib and the changing table; he bought the mobile and the baby dresser with a parade of pastel ducks across it. He'd stand in the center of the room and swear he heard the baby. If he concentrated, he could smell the sweet, sharp tang; he could feel talcum powder sifting through the air. He grasped Lee's arm. "Just come in there and stand with me." But she wouldn't stay for long, and he never understood it. "Don't you like it?" he asked her.

"It's bad luck," she said.

"No, no, it's good," he insisted, but after that he didn't press. She was anxious enough.

He didn't believe in bad luck. None of it had scared or worried him up until the moment Lee went into labor. He couldn't help her—no matter what he did, how he held her or touched her or panted helplessly along with her, none of it made one bit of difference. When she had shouted at him to get out, get out, he had moved closer to her. Lee's nurse had gently taken Jim by the arm and shepherded him to a chair outside.

"Listen," she soothed. She looked to be his mother's age, and it suddenly comforted him. "Hard labor doesn't mean a hard birth. I popped mine out like kittens." He blinked at her. "She'll be fine," she said, patting his hand. "And so will you." She had lied, he thought. He kept twisting himself up, and when Lee was in the delivery room, screaming at him to leave her alone, the nurse had had to eject him forcibly, and even then he stood as close to the door as he could, both palms planted on the door and sliding with sweat. He couldn't stand hearing Lee cry like that; and then suddenly he had heard another cry, an astonishing muddy wail, and this time he had pushed his way back in, and this time no one had stopped him.

He went to Lee first, enveloping her pale hand between his two, stroking back her damp tangle of hair, two shades darker with sweat. She turned her face away from his, but not before he saw a rippling of fear.

A hand touched his shoulder, and he turned. "Don't you want to say hello to your daughter?" Anna said. "A daughter?" Jim said. She laughed at him. Tiny sparklers ignited inside him. The air shimmered past. Anna handed him the baby, and he felt her breath, cool as glass against his hand. Astounded, he began to laugh, hiccuping until Anna clapped him on the back. "Hold your breath," she suggested.

The nurse gently took his daughter from him. Instantly he felt depleted. "They both need their rest now," the nurse said.

"I can't rest," Jim said.

"Jesus, new dads," Anna said.

He floated from the hospital, giddy with excitement. It took him almost twenty minutes to make a five-minute drive to his calculus exam because he kept meandering on the road in reverie.

By the time he got to the examination room, it was practically full. There were fifty people, and not one of them had he ever had the time to become friends with. He took a seat at the back and looked around the room at all the somber faces, the sloped shoulders, the lank despair that came from too much coffee and too little studying. He leaned across the aisle to the girl sitting next to him. She had black hair tied back with a velvet cord. Her jeans were spattered with blue paint, and even though it was ninety degrees that day, she was wearing a velvet jacket. He recognized her, but he had no idea what her name was.

"Guess what?" he said so enthusiastically that she glanced over at him, her eyes hooded with suspicion.

"I'm a dad," he announced, preening.

She lifted up glassy blue eyes to his. "Well," she said finally. "I'm dead, too," she said. "All I can do is pray I can somehow fake it." Frowning, she turned from him.

Jim hummed to himself. He felt invincible, like Superman. Wife and daughter. Baby girl. And then the proctor appeared, and he thought more calmly: calculus.

The exam didn't worry him. His best subject had always been math. His father had seen to that. When Jim had been a toddler, falling out of his striped shirts and bright shorts, his shoelaces always hanging over his shoes, Jack had taught him his sums with an old wooden cash register he kept on an extra table in the house. Every month Jack stocked it with fifty dollars of different denominations, with shiny new coins it would give Jim a shock of pleasure to touch. Jack propped Jim up on the Yellow Pages and let him work the stubby keys with his baby fingers. Sometimes, when the keys stuck, Jack pressed down on Jim's fingers with his own. When it hurt, Jim said nothing. "Okay now," Jack said, pulling out a ten. "I just bought a dozen apples. Green Granny Smiths, at twenty cents a pound. Let's say I have a pound and a half. I give you this ten. Make me some change." He waited patiently while Jim stitched up his brow and figured the math in his head, ringing it up tentatively. "Atta boy," his father said. "Now make me some change." Jim pulled out bills and change, settling it into his father's palm. "That's the way to do it," Jack said. "Put it in dollars and sense and anyone can be a math wiz." Jim loved numbers; he loved the look of money: rusted-looking pennies and bright hard dimes falling across his open, willing palms like buckshot. He loved making towers of dimes and quarters. He spent hours fashioning big-winged origami birds out of new dollar bills until his father walloped him one. "That's not appreciating the value of money," he said. But Jim knew the value. And with a new baby he'd have to know it even more.

The proctor, tall and thin and expressionless, slid a blue book down on Jim's desk. A white edge of exam paper showed. "Begin," the proctor said, and Jim opened the book, glancing at the formulas. Piece of cake. The girl next to him sighed heavily.

He scribbled formulas; he thought about Lee. His parents would embrace her now that they had a granddaughter; they'd maybe embrace him a little more, as well. Jack had never quite forgiven him for running off with Lee, for giving up the family business. The day Lee had turned eighteen, Jim had called his parents, but his father's anxious voice had cooled and hardened when he found out why Jim had disappeared, why he had taken it upon himself to stay silent. "Protecting that girl was hurting us," he said. "Or didn't you see it that way?" Gladys had simply cried, and neither one of them had asked to speak to Lee or referred to her as anything but "that girl." He had told them about his classes, about his scholarship, and his mother had said, "Imagine that," and Jack had told him the supermarket would always be waiting for him, that as far as he was concerned, it was still a father-and-son business, even if Jim had to wait until he was forty to admit it. Jim invited them for Thanksgiving, for Christmas, but neither one would come, although Gladys had sent him a present, a hand-knit red sweater tied in a blue ribbon, and nothing at all for Lee. Lee had cried a little, even after she saw all the presents Jim had bought for her, and the next cold morning she had carefully pulled on his mother's hand-knit sweater and worn it. "It looks pretty on you," he had said.

His parents might be able to resist Lee, but how could they resist a baby? His father couldn't. He'd take his granddaughter up and down the aisles of the store, letting her do all the things he couldn't abide for one moment in anyone else's baby. Jim's daughter could tumble boxes into heaps on the floor. Jim's daughter could have expensive Chinese melons and Australian kiwis as balls. And Gladys would be beside herself, knitting sweaters out of cheap bright yarn, baking enough cookies for half the neighborhood.

"Ten minutes," the proctor announced. Jim wrote a formula. That night they were going to name their daughter. He had all these ideas written down on snatches of paper. Names so beautiful it hurt you just to say them. Deidre. Christine. Annabelle. Lee, he thought. Lee. He thought that that was a name more beautiful than any of them, a name as beautiful as the woman who bore it.

By six-thirty he was back at the hospital. He rounded the corner into Lee's room. The bed was unmade, the white sheets pleated back. Two pillows propped lamely against the headboard. "Sweetie," he said. He peered into the bathroom. Twin white towels were carefully folded over the rungs. In Lee's closet, her faded blue denim jacket was hung up neatly, buttoned to the throat. Her worn black high-tops lay prone, toe to toe, in the closet.

Maybe she was at the nursery. He had wanted to see her first, alone, before he saw his daughter, but as he got closer to the sound of crying babies, something moved deep inside of him. Lee wasn't at the glass, but another man was, older than Jim, in a navy blazer and red leather tie. Frowning, the man stared at the babies; he lifted up his keys and jiggled them. "Hey, pumpkin head, over here," he said. When Jim came and stood beside him, he studied Jim for a moment. "So which one's yours?" he said pleasantly, and in baffled wonder, Jim stepped back. He hadn't a clue. He couldn't remember the same baby he had held in his arms. He scanned the cribs, trying to pin down something familiar, an expression, a shape. "That one," Jim said, pointing to a baby in the corner. "Oh," the man said. "Very nice." And when he lumbered off, Jim immediately beckoned to the nurse. "Archer," he said.

A baby was lifted up. Second row from the glass. The eyes were puckered shut, the mouth barely an underline in the small pale face. Breath caught, Jim trickled fingers at his daughter's closed eyes, her silent face. He still didn't recognize her as anything but a total stranger. He didn't feel any bonding. Maybe he needed to feel her, skin against skin; maybe it was the glass, the hospital environment. Weakly he rapped at the glass. Her daughter stayed motionless, but a baby in front suddenly stiffened and began to wail.

He made his way back to Lee's room, nearly colliding with a candy striper. She blushed hotly when she saw him. She was barely five feet, with shellacked hair shored back with a red plastic headband. He never knew what to make of the candy stripers. They made him feel embarrassed; he always checked his fly when he walked past them. He smoothed his fine, flying hair. He heard them whispering when he walked past.

This one whistled, wheeling in the dinner cart, carefully placing a covered steel dish on Lee's tray. She lifted the cover. "Mmm," she said. "Cafeteria catburger." Jim recognized the green string beans, faded from overcooking, the mealy, muggy-smelling potatoes, but he had no idea what the gray paste was in the center of the plate. "What's the matter with that wife of yours, not being here for food so good?" the candy striper said.

"Where is she?" Jim said.

"Don't know," said the girl, wheeling out the cart.

Jim lifted the cover, poking at one of the potatoes with his index finger, lifting it idly into his mouth. As soon as he tasted the grease and the coarse, grainy coating of salt, he was starving. He scooped up a handful more and chewed. He forked up some of the overcooked beans, which still tasted delicious. The room was so silent. He suddenly felt the way he did when he came home from school to find the house empty, Lee still at work. He felt restless, incomplete, and abruptly he clattered the cover back on Lee's dinner and went to find Lee's doctor.

Anna, when he found her, was leaning against the soft-drink machine, nursing a diet soda. As soon as she saw him, she straightened. "Where's Lee?" Jim said.

"I've been calling you all afternoon," Anna said.

"Calling me?" Jim said. "Why? Where's Lee?"

Anna blinked at him. "She hasn't been with you, then?" she said. "We thought maybe—"

"Been with me?" Jim said, and inside of him something started to freeze. His stomach hurled. He felt suddenly queasy. "She's not here?" he said. "Where is she, then?"

"We don't know," Anna said.

Jim heard something buzzing in the background, a sudden harsh whine of an insect. "Call the police."

"Yes," Anna said. "We intended to."

Jim stood in a corner of Lee's hospital room, crowded by the police and hospital officials and nurses and Anna. The detective wasn't much older than Jim, and he dressed better, in a dark European suit and Italian leather shoes. It unnerved Jim, who was in gray sweats and sneakers, his baby-fine hair threading down into his eyes no matter how many times he swiped it back. Lieutenant Blanwell, he said his name was, and even though he must have known Jim's name, he asked him to say it again, and when Jim did, his own name sounded like that of a stranger in his mouth.

Jim stiffly watched the detective fingering Lee's things, touching her clothing, sitting on the edge of the bed, even examining the bathroom floor. The floor was somehow inexplicably damp, and when the detective stood up Jim saw to his satisfaction that the knees of his pants were wet. Annoyed, the detective tried to slap them dry. He rummaged through Lee's drawer, plucking out the cheap lipsticks and moisturizers. He checked the window. Alongside him, men dusted for prints. One picked up Lee's water glass with gloved hands and slipped it into a plastic sack. Another pried himself under the bed and pulled out a long tail of blue terrycloth. "That's from her bathrobe," Jim said. "The belt." Blanwell studied it for a moment.

"It's from her bathrobe," Jim said again. "Sure, I know," Blanwell said, and nodded at the cop, who put it in a plastic bag. A woman in a rose-flowered bathrobe wandered by, peering in, and the detective shut the door gently. "Well," he said. "It doesn't look like any struggle."

Jim leaned along the wall. The air narrowed. He suddenly remembered the plot of every bad movie he had ever sat through. Lunatics roaming through hospital wards, slicing off hands, injecting deadly drugs.

Blanwell sat on the red Leatherette chair by the bed and stared at Jim. "So would you say you had a happy marriage?" he said abruptly.

"Jesus Christ, we just had a *baby*," Jim said.

"Uh-huh. You have many friends? Who came to visit her beside you?"

"Just me," Jim said. "She wasn't really close to anyone else. Not like the way she was with me." He thought of Lee, giggling and gossiping with all the other waitresses, but not one of them ever calling her.

"Did your wife want this child?" Blanwell asked. "You're pretty young, the two of you. You didn't have to get married, did you?"

"Everything was fine," Jim said.

Lee's nurse crossed her arms. "She had a right to be fresh, in labor like that," she said.

Jim's shirt was pasted along his back. Sweat prickled and beaded. "Why aren't you asking the hospital about security?" he cried. "Anyone could have come up here."

"We aren't a police station," said one of the hospital officials. "We check on everyone who comes in and out of here, we can't tend to a single patient."

"We dusted for prints," the detective said. "We'll see what we got." He looked at Jim. "Anything else you can think of to tell us?"

Jim's mind buckled.

"Well, you said she was happy," Blanwell said to him, and this time Jim thought of Lee walking the highway, the first time he had seen her there. She had always come home, always come back to him. "Sure," he said.

"I'm going to need to talk to you more," Blanwell said. "You go home, get some sleep. Maybe she'll call you. Or maybe someone else will. Or maybe she'll come back here for the baby."

"I'm taking the baby home," Jim said. "You think I trust her here?"

"No," Blanwell said. "You're not. We'll have someone watch her, but until we know a little bit more, everyone is suspect." He tucked his hands into his pockets. "I'm sorry."

"You think *I* did something with my wife?" Jim said, astonished.

"You think I think you did?" Blanwell said. He stood up. The Leatherette chair had an indentation where he had sat. "So I'll call you," he told Jim.

Something had shifted. In cold panic Jim drove back to the house, and the whole time Lee kept slamming up in his mind. She was hidden someplace in the hospital; maybe she had gotten up to take a walk and had ended up fainting in a boiler room no one even thought about anymore. Maybe the hospital had botched something; she was dying on a gurney right now until they could think of a way to cover themselves.

He suddenly thought of this science-fiction magazine Lee had once brought home. Someone had left it at a cafe, and she had picked it up, drawn by the bright lurid cover, an illustration of a blond woman in a torn red dress being sucked into a cavernous black spaceship. *Weird Tales*, it was called, and the date on it was 1952. The pages were stained and crumbling, turning to tissue. The evening she had brought it home, she sat up reading, chewing one thumbnail ragged. There were stories about hauntings and demons and one particular article, reported as fact, about holes in the universe that were responsible for people disappearing. She had read him bits of it. "Scientists say," she had begun to read. "Which scientists?" he wanted to know, but she waved his words away with her hands. There were tears in the fabric of life, the magazine said, invisible holes and pockets in the ground that simply swallowed people up. Fathers didn't drive off and leave families, children weren't kidnapped. It was simply the fault of a blindly cruel universe. Nobody knew where any of these people went, if they were alive in some parallel universe, or crushed by a sudden new force of gravity, or simply in suspended animation. One scientist swore that when he put his ear to the ground, he could hear whispers, but as soon as he started digging there, the sound stopped.

Now, though, he didn't think it was so funny. He couldn't stop thinking of tears in the universe, of Lee's foot poised and arched like a dancer's, pointing toward oblivion.

The house didn't look the same. He had wanted to buy a place, but he had miscalculated his funds, so they had ended up renting a house instead. "It's just an interim step," he had told Lee. It was cheap rent, but it was also a house so in need of repairs that Lee had almost refused to live in it at all.

"We can't raise a baby in an apartment," he insisted. "And we can't afford anything better. Not yet."

He had fallen in love with the house as soon as he saw it. He didn't mind that there was a large wasp nest in the scrubby front yard or that the first two steps on the porch were rotted through. The damp basement didn't bother him or the slapdash look of the neighborhood, the dirty tricycles rusting on the street, the shouts and calls of children. He loved the idea of a house, especially with Lee in it.

The first rainfall there, they had had to put one of the two pans they owned in the center of the kitchen floor to catch the drops where the roof leaked. The sound kept them awake. The landlord fixed the roof; Jim spent two muggy weeks trying to fix the front steps himself before he realized he was just making it worse. His fingers were full of splinters. He gave up and paid someone else to do it. "Nothing's forever," he told Lee.

As soon as he opened the door, he heard her. She was rustling in the bedroom, changing her clothing. He smelled her. Vanilla and Scotch pines.

He paced from one room to another, all the time feeling that she was somehow following him, hiding. Frantic, he began rummaging through her drawers, lifting out the silk shirt he had bought her for her birthday, the string of jet beads she never wore. He pulled out pots and pans and found, wedged in the back of the cabinet, some of the baby books he had bought. He began pulling the house apart, flinging her dresses into a jumble on the floor, upending her dressers. The house piled up around him. The one room he didn't touch was the baby's room, pale yellow with an appliqué of butterflies, eye level to an infant in her crib.

It was nearly four when he stopped. He sat in the middle of the living room, trying to sift things into a kind of order, and then he finally stood, rising up from the mess, and lay across the couch, staring out into the night, terrified. He suddenly wanted to call his parents; he wanted someone else in the house with him, but when he dialed the line rang and rang and didn't catch. He hadn't made any other friends close enough to call. He got up, pacing. He didn't realize just how late it was until he saw that all the other houses were dark, closed off. A big yellow tomcat cried fissures of sound into the stillness. He turned on the couch, then got up abruptly and unlocked the front door. He brought the phone by the couch so he'd hear it as soon as it rang. Come home, he thought. Come home.

He stretched out again, and his eyes rolled into restless sleep. He dreamed. Lee was a nurse, dressed in her waitress uniform, her feet laced into white Keds sneakers. Her yellow hair was smoothed under a starchy cap peaked like a turret. She was carrying a silver tray toward him, moving to some kind of silent beat. She smiled secretively at him. Her thin hips swayed. She nodded, locking her gaze to his. And then she dipped down, lengthening her arms into a stretch to present him with the contents of the tray. And then he saw it. A glossy crimson heart, damp with blood, beating helplessly, making a small, terrified clatter against the polished silver tray.

He bolted awake, tumbling from the couch. Stunned, he peered in the darkness, rearranging shapes into the things he recognized. There was the clock. Over there the bookcase. He stood up and opened the front door, and as he did the neighbor's yellow cat poised on the railing, eyes dilated with the night, then jumped inside. "Hello to you," Jim said. He fetched the cat some milk, but it was so sour and cheesy that the cat wouldn't touch it. In the reflection of the toaster, Jim's eyes were swollen. The cat prowled for a while and then fussed at the door. "Fine, leave me, then," Jim said, opening the door and popping the cat out into the night like a cork.

His eyes burned. He slapped out the front door, leaving it open. Thieves wouldn't get anything worthwhile; a stereo system so terrible he hated to play his albums on it. A TV that flickered and snowed. The same Brownie camera he had taken from Philadelphia the day he and Lee had run away to get married.

He got into the Dodge and began driving, heading for the highway. Four in the morning, and the road was still alive with cars. Where did people go this time of night? He glanced into the cars, but the faces he saw were always unreadable, impassive. He kept glancing alongside the road.

Lee had always been in love with highways. She carried maps in her pocketbook. South Dakota. Wyoming and Tennessee. Sometimes she inked in routes, linking the names of roads she liked with other roads. She had her license, but she told him neither Frank nor Janet trusted her to drive, and she didn't have money for her own car. Some nights he had let her drive, but it had scared him a little. She was so reckless. She weaved in and out of the roads, she speeded and dared.

Nights when he came home late from class or study group, Lee was sometimes sleeping. Sometimes, though, the house was silent. He worried at first. The notes she sometimes left him were cryptic. Went out, they said. But he didn't like being in the house without her.

He didn't know what she was doing at first. Oh, he could imagine all right. Lee drinking Scotch at some seedy bar outside of town. Lee dancing with her head fitted into someone's shoulder. He drove out looking for her. He checked the Silver Spoon, but she wasn't there, and the other waitresses gave him such mocking grins that he pretended he was just picking up some cigarettes from the machine, that he knew perfectly well where his wife was. He checked the record stores, winding up and down the aisles, buying a few tapes to keep him company in the car.

She wasn't at the Dairy Queen or the roller rink; she wasn't at the bookstore, reading the last pages of all the novels she might want to buy. He was exhausted when he decided to drive home. He didn't trust himself on the road when he felt this sleepy; besides, he was sure she was home by now, he was certain he'd find her lying on the couch, reading, half-asleep, smiling up at him drowsily.

That night he had been almost home when he first saw her walking along the shoulder of the road. Amazed, he slowed down. She was in jeans and red sneakers, her father's leather jacket zipped to the throat. She held her head very high, and her hair expanded in the breeze. He got close enough to see her smiling, close enough to beep the horn so that she started, turning toward him, her face white. When she saw him, her smile dissolved. She stood there, the highway lights flickering in a corona about her. He leaned over and opened the door for her. "Get in," he said. She burrowed sulky hands into her pockets. "Please," he said. His voice sounded foreign to him. "Please," he repeated, and then she got in the car and sat beside him. "What's wrong with my just walking?" she said abruptly.

"I'd like to walk with you," he said, and instantly regretted it.

"The highway's dangerous, that's why," he said.

Lee rolled down her window so the wind lashed her hair against the pane. She looked out as the car swallowed the miles toward home. "I won't walk the highways," she said. "I'll walk someplace else."

"The neighborhood's fine," he said. "People know you. They'll watch out. Walk in the neighborhood."

She was silent. He kept waiting for her to say something to him, to burst into tears so he could loop one arm about her, to rage so they could at least connect in a fight. But when he looked over, he saw she was asleep.

He had carried her into the house that night, laying her into the bed, covering her with the yellow quilt. He bent to kiss her. "Sleeping Beauty," he said, but she didn't wake when his lips anointed hers.

She never stopped walking the highways, and he never stopped driving around to find her and bring her back home. He couldn't think of a single thing to do to make her stop walking the highways. He imagined it was the town she was bored with, and sometimes he imagined it was him, that all his studying made him boring. He dressed up and surprised her with reservations just outside of town. He once bought theater tickets in Washington. She had good enough times. She was flushed with pleasure. He felt a rush of desire for her, but when he reached to touch her, she didn't react. She was still traveling.

The night Lee disappeared, Jim drove for two hours. The only person he saw on the road was a young hitchhiker, a girl in a blue dress and white cowboy boots with her thumb jabbed out. He drove past her in a rigid fury because she was another one in love with the road, and then half a mile away he thought of her getting into the wrong car, ending up a smear on the highway, and he swerved the car around to go get her. He'd lecture her; he'd scare her with stories Lee had laughed at. Men who scissored victims in their cars and kept the pieces in mason jars in the trunk. White slavers. The highway, smooth and glossy black, was suddenly so completely empty, it astonished him. He stopped the car, sitting perfectly still, waiting, listening, thinking all the time he would sit there forever, if it would bring Lee back.

By morning Lee was already a news item. While shaving, Jim heard about his wife's disappearance on the news. He stood perfectly still and then slumped onto the edge of the tub. The news announcer didn't mention anything about Jim being suspect, or that he wasn't even allowed to take home his own baby. The authorities are still on the case, the announcer said. And then, in a seamless shift, the story was suddenly about a skirmish in the Far East. Casualties were listed.

He was afraid to get up, afraid to go out into the neighborhood. It was still early, not even seven o'clock.

He had to call Frank, to reach him before the police did. Frank had threatened him once, said he would kill him. Lee had sent him two cards, one when she got married, one when she was pregnant, and he hadn't answered either. Jim's stomach tightened. He dialed.

"Yes?" Frank's voice, anxious, slipped on the line.

"It's Jim," he blurtèd. "It's about Lee."

"You found her?" he said, his voice speeding up. "I've been on long distance with some detective all evening."

"No, I didn't find her," Jim said. "I thought maybe—if she was all right—she'd have called you."

"Me." Frank's voice turned suddenly bitter. "She ran away with you. She'd call you."

"Please, if you hear anything, will you call me?"

There was silence. "Why didn't you call me?" Frank said. "Why didn't you let me know as soon as she was gone? Why do I always have to hear things about my daughter from the police?"

"I'll call you," Jim said.

"Yes," Frank said. "You call me."

When he hung up, he was sweating. His shirt was pasted to his back. He looked at the clock. Nearly eight. If he hurried, he could get out before the neighborhood started waking up and realizing just what had happened. He wasn't due at the police station until nine, but when he stumbled in, it was eight-thirty. Bunched under his arm was a small packet of photographs: Lee when they had first run away, Lee in front of the apartment, Lee sitting on the porch of their house.

There was Lee pregnant in the freak March heat wave, her hair pulled into a ponytail. He had a few letters, too, samples of her handwriting; he had the marriage license he had almost framed, he had been so excited about it.

They had him talk to a new detective this time, a woman with severely cut brown hair and red glass earrings. She nodded sympathetically at the photos before she tucked them gently into a folder. At one point she told him she would do everything she could to help him. "I lost my husband just last year," she said, and Jim, surprised, saw that her eyes were starting to tear. "Heart attack. He got up from the table to get coffee and then—well, that was it." Jim started to reach toward her, to pat her hand in his awkward way, but she suddenly resettled herself on her chair. "Well, it's different here, isn't it?" she said. "What else can you tell us?"

There was something oddly safe about being at the police station, telling story after story about Lee. It was a kind of company, talking to someone, and every detail he revealed about Lee made her somehow more real to him, more there. He didn't tell everything. He didn't tell about Lee's walking the highways; he didn't tell her that he had coerced Lee into marrying him, that he had made it a condition of her freedom. And sometimes he told things that only could have been true. He insisted Lee was crazy to have this baby, that she had even picked out names. He was lost in reverie, he embellished details so lively, he half began to believe they were true. "We were very much in love," he said. "People used to stop us on the street and comment about it."

The detective looked at him. "I see," she said. "Any other person she might have cared for?"

"We loved each other," Jim said stiffly.

He remembered, months before she had gotten pregnant, how he had felt her interest in him rising. She bought him denim shirts and told him he looked handsome in them. She cut his hair and grinned with him into the mirror when she was finished. "Now you look cool," she said. Sometimes she would take his arm when they were walking. Sometimes she would give him a kiss for no reason at all. And sometimes, too, in the middle of the night, he would wake to find her slowly massaging his stomach, kissing his thigh, needing him. And then she got pregnant, and just as abruptly as it had flowered, her interest waned. He told himself it was just because she was preoccupied, just because she was scared. When he put his arm around her, she removed it. "I feel too hot," she said. When he kissed her she pulled away. "What's wrong?" he asked. "Don't make me ask you what's wrong twenty times before you tell me. Save some time and tell me now, why don't you?"

"Nothing's wrong," she said. "Everything's fine." But he saw how her face was crumpling. "Lee," he said. "What's wrong."

"Nothing," she told him.

For the first time, then, dressing better, remade by Lee, he began to notice other women's interest. They smiled when he passed. One woman shyly offered to buy him dinner if he would help her study. And in the library there was his biology lab partner, Linda Lambrose. She was thin and lovely and smart. She smelled of lily of the valley, and she had a mane of curly red hair.

Still, as intoxicated as he was by other women, he had come home for Lee, but the house was empty when he got there. There wasn't even a note on the table, a scribble telling him where she might be. He felt his heart hardening. He got back in the car and began driving, and he wasn't even on the highway when he spotted Lee, bundled in an old red sweater of his, walking purposefully down the road. Her hair whipped behind her, and even from a distance he could tell that she was smiling. Furious, he banged the horn at her. He jerked open the door while she blinked at him, slightly dazed, like something caught.

She was pleasant enough in the car. She told him she had gone miniature golfing by herself that night, that she had done well enough to keep the scorecard. She touched his arm as she talked, but her friendliness suddenly irritated him. The car suddenly smelled faintly of lily of the valley, and if he concentrated, he could imagine Linda sitting beside him, one hand lightly on his shoulder.

The calls began that day. Reporters wanting to talk to him, and at first he would. He kept offering rewards, he kept talking about how much in love he was with his wife, but they always referred to him as suspect. "What would be my motive?" he shouted. "You tell me one reason why I'd do something to her. And what would I do? You think she's buried in the backyard? You think she's in pieces some-where? You go and find her, then." The reporters shrugged. Some looked as if they were considering his requests, and after that he refused to talk to reporters at all.

He thought about not answering the phone at all or about getting a machine, but he kept imagining Lee calling him, hanging up on a machine, and then spinning out into the distance away from him.

That evening his father called. "Why didn't you call and tell us yourself?" he demanded. "I'm your father. Didn't you think I'd want to know I was going to be a grandfather? Didn't you think I'd want to know about all this going on?" His anger coiled across the phone wires. "The police called us," he said. "I didn't tell them one damn thing."

"I called you yesterday," Jim said. "No one was home. And I was going to tell you about the baby." He caught his breath. "Oh, hell, they didn't have to call you," he said.

"Well, they did, and I kept my mouth shut. I acted like I didn't even know Lee."

"You could have said what you wanted," Jim said.

"Not me, I didn't," Jack said.

He wanted to know if Jim was all right, if he needed money. "Your mother wants to know if you want to come home and stay for a while. You know, be in a different place."

"I can't do that," he said. "I have to be here."

"Then we're coming out there," Jack said.

He thought of the police wandering around, the newspapers. He thought of his daughter, still in the hospital because he was considered too dangerous to take her. Between his father and him, the lines hummed.

"We want to see our granddaughter," Jack said. "The police told us we were grandparents. I guess you were too busy to call your own parents."

"Dad—" he said, "I *called*," and his father sighed.

"I know," Jack said. "And believe me, I'm sorry."

Gladys was suddenly on the extension, her voice faded. "Baby," she cried. "What do you need?"

When he started crying, tears across the wires, she made low, soothing sounds in her throat. She waited until he had calmed. "It'll all be all right," she said. "You just listen to me. We're here if you need us. You need money, you need a place to stay, you need one stupid thing, you call us. I don't care what time it is. I don't. And anyway we're coming out there. As soon as I get off the line, I'm calling the airlines. You can't go through this alone. Listen to me, Lee will be fine. They'll find her." She started to cry. "What does my granddaughter look like?" she said suddenly. "Is she pretty? Does she have blue eyes? They do when they're that young, you know."

She stopped crying for a moment. "She looks like you," Jim said.

He waited for his parents, who couldn't get a flight until the next evening. He kept the radio on, listening to the latest about himself. He bought three newspapers, hoping for news no one was really telling him. He hadn't made any real friends here, mostly because of Lee and studying and school, and he did his best to avoid the neighbors, but even so he saw how they looked at him when he walked out of the house. He stopped at the police station to see what they were doing to find his wife and then he went to see his daughter.

Most of the nurses were now a little suspicious of him, but he wasn't so sure he trusted them, either. Any one of them could have been jealous enough to harm Lee. Any one might have accidentally given Lee the wrong medication and then, horrified, tried to cover it up. He stood with the other fathers in front of the glass and hated the nurses because they had more of a right to his baby than he did. It was dangerous. Babies bonded. He didn't want his baby growing up yearning for the scent of hospital antiseptic, falling in love with the color white, forever straining toward the insidious whisper of crepe shoes on linoleum. He watched the couples holding hands, and it made him feel as if his heart were atrophying. He felt like telling them to just forget it, to not make any plans at all. Half of them would probably get divorced. People got cancer. Kids overdosed. Pain was surprising, an endless joke where you were always the punch line.

It made him afraid for his daughter. He made the nurse bring her over so he could hold her. He sang her lullabies, he told her stories until she dozed in his arms, and when he had to hand her back to the head nurse, his heart felt emptied. Eyes wet, he stood outside the glass and looked at her. The head nurse in the nursery slowly began to soften toward him. She let him come into her office and be with his daughter. She shut the door, and once she brought him coffee and a cheese Danish. "She's a good baby," the nurse told him. Her name was Gracie, and she wasn't much older than Jim. She told Jim his daughter slept most of the time, but sometimes she gravely watched what was going on around her. "It's as if she's waiting for something," she told Jim.

"Can't I just take her home?" Jim said. "You could pretend to be in the other room, you could not see."

"They'll put you in jail," she said. "Then you might never see her."

He was silent for a minute. "Listen," she said. "You go home, get some sleep. You come back and you can sit in here with your baby as long as you like."

He went home, and before he even picked up his newspaper on the porch, he knew it would have his picture in it. "Suspect Jim Archer," it said. He bunched it up and chucked it in the trash. When he got inside the phone was ringing. "I know what you did," a voice whispered. "I saw."

Jim slammed down the receiver. He dug out the Yellow Pages from under the counter. He'd find a lawyer. But every name he called had already heard of him, and every name wanted a retainer that would clean out his bank account, his future. He didn't care. He arranged meetings with a few of them and then went to find the bankbook.

He always kept it in the same place. In the bottom of a secret drawer in the rolltop desk. But when he opened the drawer, it wasn't there. He kept flipping open the other drawers, ferreting about loose papers, clips, and staples, and finally gave up and went to the bank.

The teller he spoke to was a young girl with curly dark hair and stiff lacquered lashes. She didn't flinch when she heard his name. Illiterate, he thought with relief. Doesn't watch the news. She disappeared for a moment, and when she came back she blinked at Jim. "Mr. Archer," she said, "this account's only got twenty dollars in it."

"What are you talking about, twenty dollars?" Jim said. Something curled in his stomach.

She shrugged. She showed him the paper with the stamp across it. Five thousand dollars removed, gone as easily as a breath. "I didn't take that much money out," Jim said.

"You did too," she insisted. "Anyway, your wife did. Look, here it is. Here's the date. The signature." Jim stared down at the paper, at Lee's rolling hand.

"Something wrong?" she said.

"Can I get a copy of this?" he said, trying to still the quake in his voice. He waited, impatient, and then gripped the copy from under the glass divider.

He fairly lurched out of the bank, his heart clipping. Out in the bright sunlight, he was suddenly overwhelmed. He kept seeing it—Lee's name, deliberately branded across the page, erasing the account and him, too, along with it.

He could walk to the police station from here. He could smack this on their desk and take his daughter home, and there was no longer any reason anyone would stop him.

4

The next morning Jim went to retrieve his daughter. Gracie, a blue Kleenex tissue petaled about her nose, cried a little when she handed the baby to him. "Allergies," she said, lowering stormy eyes. She plucked at the baby's toes. "It's a terrible thing to say, but I feel like she's mine."

"Don't," Jim said.

Gracie stammered odd bits of advice. Babies liked heartbeats, so Jim might want to buy a recording of the sounds infants heard in the womb. Babies took to water like small spaniels. "Take her into the bathtub with you," she advised. "Hold her in the shower." She told him how to handle the baby's head. What to feed the baby. How to sleep so lightly you might hear colic rumbling in a small, silky stomach. "So what are you going to call this little one?" she said.

For a moment Jim remembered all the names he had inked neatly onto a piece of paper.

"You have to give her a name, for God's sake," Gracie said. "I certainly hope you aren't one of those people who are going to call their child 'Junior.' "

He looked down at the baby. "I'll give her a name."

"Listen," she said, pressing a folded piece of paper into his hand. "The best pediatrician in town," she said. He said good-bye to Gracie and ignored the other nurses. He strode right by the doctors and orderlies. He wished he could parade triumphantly past everyone in the entire hospital, even the patients. Two of the younger candy stripers cupped their heads together. He heard a dry, breathy whisper, like a wind washing dirty sand across a beach.

"We're out of here," he said to the baby, and walked out of the hospital, the same clean way he imagined his wife had when she had taken out their savings as simply as she had taken away his life.

When he pulled into the neighborhood, it was barely ten. His parents wouldn't be arriving until noontime. The streets seemed deserted. Everyone who worked was already gone, the kids at camp or down at the playground. He didn't know what any one of them thought about any of this. No one had called to say "What a shame" or "I knew it would come to this" or "Is there anything I can do?" Not one person had invited him for dinner or said one thing about the baby, and no one mentioned the news reports. Still, he had his suspicions. He walked down the block and swore he saw curtains floating uneasily from the windows, a half-moon of face appearing. He walked by a group of his neighbors, all of them sitting on the curb, sipping sugary lemonade someone's kid had made, and although they boisterously offered him a cup, he could tell something else was going on. The laughter seemed to retract, the conversation to fade. And the other day he had come home to find Henry Sandlovitz, his neighbor from across the street, prowling nervously in Jim's yard. "Lost my golf ball," he said, but when Jim came around to help him look, all they both found were the bright dandelions Jim had never really had the heart to pull. The two men stood silently looking at the flowery yellow heads. "You ought to borrow my power mower," Henry said abruptly. Embarrassed, Jim kicked at the overgrown grass, releasing a wave of grasshoppers that hummed and trembled in the blades.

It was his fate, but the neighborhood somehow seemed to take it on as their own. Threatened by an unseen unease, wives suddenly came out to meet their husbands at the train station. Husbands, too, began bringing home roses in crinkly blue tissue paper or bottles of Spanish wine.

Later, Maureen Reardon, the one neighbor who would befriend Jim, would tell him just how all the women talked about him. As soon as they heard the first reports, everyone said they had known a marriage this young, this strange, would come to this. Lee seemed to be always alone, in those awful faded blue jeans and tattered sneakers, that hair like a wild woman's. They hadn't liked her playing with their girls. They studied Jim's pining silence after Lee had disappeared.

They wondered, too, what it might be like to have someone missing you so much, it robbed them of sleep. The women argued over Lee, too. She was wild. Jim had spoken to some of them, but Lee had never said one word. They would have taken her under their wing. They could have showed her recipes, they could have shared hairdressers and long, lazy talks on hot summer afternoons.

Myths sprang up. When one of the women wanted to threaten their wayward daughters, Lee's name was invoked. "You'll end up a prostitute like Lee!" mothers shouted. "You'll end up dead on the side of the road!" Secretly, though, the daughters, and sometimes even the mothers, might be thrilled. Sometimes they imagined Lee had simply escaped, that she was now in silky red dresses, dining in a restaurant so expensive none of them could even imagine peeking at the menu. They thought of Lee on some older man's arm, diamonds sprinkled across her fingers. Lee not having to be bored and restless at home, waiting for her kids to amble back from school, Lee not having to wake up beside anyone except her own sweet self. Women hung damp, sticking wash onto backyard clotheslines. Their hands chapped. The wood clothespins sometimes splintered and infected in their skin. "Might be nice to be Lee on a day like this," they told one another. "You can bet she's not hanging clothes." Imagine leaving your baby, they said, but still they thought of her when the jammy fingers of their own kids tracked onto the walls, when a colicky baby kept them up one night too many. Could you love something you didn't let yourself know? Was a baby yours if you never claimed it?

Every moment, Jim was aware the baby was his. He had driven his daughter home with one hand laid gently across her. He had driven twenty miles an hour, not caring if the other drivers swore at him. He had brought the baby into the house, and as soon as he opened the door he felt the silence, alive, waiting for him. His throat ached.

The baby erupted in cries. He looked at his daughter, pained, and for a moment he wondered: Who would he rather lose, Lee or the baby? And the answer was always the baby. He let her cry for a moment and then began slowly, stubbornly, rocking her.

A half hour later his parents arrived in a cab. He bundled his daughter and stepped outside. They were loaded down with stiff brown bags and suitcases, and as soon as Gladys saw Jim and the baby, she burst into tears. Jack stood perfectly still, a brown paper bag dangling from one hand.

"I don't know who to hold first," Gladys said. "Oh, that beautiful little angel! Here, let me take her. Please, I know how to hold a baby." She cradled the baby in her arms. "What's this baby's name?"

"I haven't named her yet," Jim said.

Gladys gave him a sharp look. "Well, you had better, don't you think?"

Jim threaded fingers through his hair. "I don't know what's the matter with me, not naming her," he said. "There must be something."

Jack embraced Jim roughly. "Don't you worry," he said. "I've got a feeling about things turning out for the best."

"What feeling?" Jim said, but his father turned and handed him a bag. "New Zealand apples," Jack said. "A little bruised, but you can't get anything like that here, I bet."

"Will you look at this house," Gladys said. "We could have helped you find something nicer than this." Gingerly she stepped inside. "I'll clean," she said.

Jack put away the groceries, eyeing with suspicion the tomatoes in the crisper. "Dyes," he said.

"Wrong," Jim said. "They're from a garden next door."

Jack suddenly lifted up two cucumbers. "You tell me which is garden and which is Top Thrift." He moved his hands up and down like a balancing scale.

"Please," Jim said, but his father waggled his hands again. Jim rolled his hands over the cucumbers. They looked exactly the same to him, so he took his cue from his father's face, from the way his eyes flickered when Jim's hand moved to the cucumber on the right. "That's yours," Jim said.

"What did I tell you, his father's son or not?" Jack said. He slapped the wrong cucumber against his thigh in triumph.

"He gets his intelligence from *me*," Gladys said, cheering a bit. "And we're having both cucumbers in a salad."

For a while it was fine to have his parents in the house. He liked the company, the connection, and his parents took control of the baby. They gave her the loving attention he somehow couldn't, and the baby seemed dazzled. She kept looking around until she caught sight of Gladys or Jack, and then her whole body seemed to relax. She seemed always to be waiting to be pampered. And pampered she was. Every night Gladys would take a bath with the baby, balancing her in her lap. Through the bathroom door Jim would hear his

mother singing, the same lullabies she had sung to him. The two of
them would emerge, skin flushed with pink, Gladys in a blue flannel
robe, the baby swaddled in a fuzzy yellow sleeper. "Bedtime for the
ladies," Gladys said, settling herself onto Lee's rocker, pressing off the
wood floor with one tender toe, lulling the baby before she put her
down. "Little Marilyn," she crooned. "Sweet little Linda." She looked
hopefully at Jim. "Little Amy," she suggested.

Jack, too, was in love with the baby. In the morning Jim would
stumble into the kitchen to find his father seated with the baby,
giving her greedy suck from his finger. When Jack sang to his
granddaughter, he crooned hillbilly tunes about broken hearts and
smashed dreams, sung so cheerfully you couldn't help but think these
lyric tragedies might turn out all right in the end.

Gladys worried. "What are you going to do come September when
you have to go to school? Who'll look after little Andrea?"

"Lee will be back by then," Jim said.

"Honey," Gladys said. "Honey, you got to plan as if she won't."

Gladys began folding and unfolding the baby's things. Tiny T-shirts,
diapers. She started to cry. "This poor little motherless lambie," she
said. "Why don't you come home and let us take care of you both."
She flung up her hands. "Look at you. You don't know how to eat
properly. You don't know how to dress a baby. You have no idea
what's cute."

"I do too," Jim said.

"You could transfer and go to school at home. There's not much
room, but we can manage," Jack said. "And when you're through
with school, the Top Thrift has a pharmacy."

"And a pharmacist, too, I bet," Jim said.

"So I'll fire him when you're done with school," he said. "So maybe
I could use two pharmacists. Something wrong with that?"

"Look, I can't leave," Jim said, a clip of tensions forming at the
bottom of his neck.

"We want you with us," Gladys said. "That's natural enough."

They didn't say another thing, either one of them, but he saw how
Jack scouted the house, silently fixing the sockets he considered
dangerous, shaking his head at the dampness of the cellar, sniffing for
dry rot, peering around for termites. Gladys, the baby cradled in her
lap, told her stories about the house "back home," the flower garden
she would show the baby how to tend when she was older, the dog

she might buy for her. She told her fairy tales about evil mothers who abandoned their babies to wolves so hungry, they might eat swaddling clothes as easily as hamburger, about grandmothers who knitted wings out of magic yarn. It all began to be wearying. Jim felt as if another life were being overlaid over his first and real life with Lee.

His parents refused to talk about Lee at all. The house was inhabited by Lee's photo, her face was in every room, but neither one of them ever commented. Jack, picking up the mail, would sometimes find bills addressed for Lee and stuff them in his back pocket. Jim would find them in the trash, crumpled, unopened, and he'd take them upstairs to his room. He paid her bills. He acted as if it were important to keep up her good credit rating. Gladys, watching, shook her head. "Baby," she said, but stubbornly he kept writing. She brushed fingers along his fingers. "Well," she said, "you do what you like." His anger uncoiled.

He turned toward her, furious. "She's my *wife*," he said. "What exactly is it that you think I *like* to do concerning this? You think she left and that's it, let's just get on with it?"

Gladys studied him for a moment. "I talked to the police, too, you know. They called me. And they told me there was no sign that anyone made her leave the hospital but herself. She left her baby," she said. "She left you."

"How do you know what happened?" Jim said. "Were you there? What do you know about the reasons?"

"What do you know?" Gladys said quietly.

Jim folded inward. "She *married* me, didn't she?" he said. "She *stayed*. And she *had* the baby. You think someone so anxious to leave does that? Maybe she was in trouble and couldn't tell me. Maybe she was forced to leave."

"I never knew anything about that girl," Gladys said. "All I know is now you're unhappy. And don't you think that there's something else here that matters to me, because there isn't." She patted his hand.

His parents might refuse to acknowledge Lee, but she didn't seem to need them to live. She managed to crackle and glint in even the most ordinary events. He couldn't pour the milk for his cereal without seeing her in the shadows of the kitchen. His parents were blind. They ignored the newspaper reports he cut out. They answered his phone as if it were their own, but if the caller had some lead about Lee in California, Gladys's voice would scissor shut. "For you," she said, and then she would walk carefully out of the room. Lee was dead to her, dead to his father. Jim, kissing his daughter good night, fanned his wife's memory. "Good night from Mommy," he whispered.

His parents, too, suddenly began to make him worry more about Lee. He didn't dare go out to the store by himself and leave his parents alone in the house, because what might happen if Lee suddenly showed up and he wasn't here? Gladys, in righteous fury, would drive her away. Jack might lecture her so bitterly, Lee would just leave. They'd bombard her with so many questions, she might think he had hardened toward her as well, and then she couldn't help but flee again. He couldn't risk leaving them alone, but he didn't want them to think he couldn't trust them. Falsely jovial, he suggested outings. "I bet you'd love to see the school," he said. Tense and tired, Jim drove his parents with him to the library. Irritated, he watched Jack browsing through book after book, when all he wanted to do was go home. Gladys, beaming, even started up a conversation with a young woman in the circulating stacks. "You know my son?" she said cheerfully. Before they left Jack insisted Jim check out two books on fishing for him. "We'll have to come back here," Jack said.

Jim felt like a baby-sitter who had to keep watch. When they went to bed early, settling into the spare room, Jim prowled restlessly. He was wary of every noise. He couldn't risk their hearing any sound he himself didn't. He force-fed himself coffee, so black and strong it created a jumpy rhythm in his blood. At night he skimmed on the edge of sleep, and when he woke his face was furrowed.

His parents ended up leaving three weeks later. There was an emergency at Top Thrift. Workers were striking; fruit was rotting on the shelves. "Come home with us," Jack said. "Close up this house for the whole summer. You can always come back here when school starts if that's what you want. I just hate to think of you here alone."

"I can't," Jim said. "What if Lee shows up?"

"I'm staying here, then," Gladys said.

"No, you're not," Jim said. "Both of you have been here for almost a month."

"We'll come back, then," Jack said. "Right this weekend if we can. And I'm mailing you a plane ticket so you and my granddaughter can come home anytime you want."

Gladys placed both hands on the sides of his face. "This isn't your home," she informed him. "No one says you can't be happy." She kissed the baby and then stood back, letting her husband take his turn. Jack was awkward with the baby, but he pulled Jim to him. "I find out you needed anything and you didn't call, there's going to be big trouble." He stepped back. "We understand each other on this," he said.

"Sure we do," Jim said. He watched his parents climbing into the cab, windows rolled down, hands outstretched to grip his, and for the first time he noticed his mother's skin, roughened like a kind of parchment. Stricken, he clutched at her fingers. "I wish you were staying," he blurted.

"Why, honey," Gladys said, "I'll come up every weekend until you tell me to stay put at home. We'll call you every single day to make sure you're okay. And you know I want you home."

He watched them leave, and for a long while he couldn't bring himself to go back inside the house. He sat out on the stoop, rocking the baby, singing something low and tuneless deep in his throat, while behind him the empty house seemed to be alive and moving and dangerously unpredictable.

That night, hours before his own parents would be home, he called Frank. He blurted out three sentences about the baby before Frank cut him off. "What do you want from me?" he said wearily.

"Don't you want to see your granddaughter?"

The wires thickened with silence.

"I want to see Lee," he said finally.

"Well, she looks like Lee," Jim said, although there wasn't one thing in the baby that looked anything like his wife.

"Look," Frank said. "I'd just as soon you didn't call here, you understand? Lee never would have left home if it weren't for you. And every time you call, I remember that."

"But you have a granddaughter," Jim said.

"I used to have a daughter." He was silent for a moment. "I have a whole new life here," he said. "How long am I supposed to keep it on hold for Lee?" And then he hung up in a thread of static. Jim sat, idly cradling the phone, daydreaming, thinking what a lucky thing that might be, to feel as if you had a life.

That night he wasn't hungry at all, but because of his daughter he felt a responsibility to eat. Having a proper dinner suddenly seemed like the mark of being a good father. He tried to remember Jack cooking dinner for him, but all he could remember was one Sunday breakfast when Gladys was sick in bed with the flu and Jack had burned the eggs so badly that the pan had had to soak for a day and a half before anyone would even think about cleaning it. His father was a man who knew everything there was to know about food except how to cook it.

Jim ferreted through the cupboards. Lee had been a terrible cook, as bad as he himself was. They had gotten by on mixes and canned goods and odd combinations of sandwiches. He hadn't minded. He had thought if might only be a problem when the baby was old enough to bring her friends home for a dinner that wouldn't embarrass her.

He pulled out a package of instant Spanish rice. There were three eggs in the refrigerator, half a package of sweating American cheese, and all the vegetables that Jack had filled the freezer with.

He cooked eggs, spattering them with cheese. He made himself a plate, but when he sat down, to his disappointment, his appetite stayed dulled. He ate anyway and then went upstairs and fed the baby a bottle of formula.

He came back downstairs. He felt suddenly uneasy. If he left the front door open, Lee might come back in. He might wake and persuade her to stay. But then, she might come back for his daughter. He got up and locked every door, every window. And then just as he was about to go upstairs, he thought of Lee, a tentative ghost at the front door, shivering, sick, maybe too disoriented to think to ring the bell or to call. He went back to the front door and unlocked it.

His parents kept their promise, calling every other day, keeping him on the phone so long that by the time he hung up he felt swollen with their concern. His ears hurt. Otherwise he kept to himself. He got used to the constant phone calls. The police had advised him to change his number. They themselves got at least twenty crank calls a day. Crazy people claiming they had seen Lee in heaven. A man claimed he had been kidnapped along with Lee, taken up to an alien spacecraft. He didn't want to change the number, didn't want to shut Lee out if she called. Reporters still called, badgering him for stories he no longer would give. Some of the pulpier presses took the few syllables Jim would give them and make headlines out of it. LEAVE ME ALONE, CRIES ANGUISHED SUSPECT. They all thought he did it, cleared by the police or not. He had his own signs posted up all over town. Lee's face staring out from telephone poles, from bus stations. Reward. He never listed any amount because he no longer had much of an amount that he could spare from the money left in the other account, from the loans Jack gave him to live.

People did contact him. "I saw a blonde at the Bestern Diner on Route 3," a man rasped. "Lee is living next door to me," a woman told him. People claimed they had seen Lee in a restaurant, Lee trying on red-haired wigs at Macy's, Lee wheeling a bike down a country road. It didn't matter. He kept a notebook of the calls and the callers, and followed every empty lead he could.

One night he picked up the phone to hear a woman's voice. "Jim?" she said, so friendly he thought for a moment he must know her. "You must be a nervous wreck," she said.

"You could say that," he said, waiting, trying to match a face with the glittering voice.

"I bet you'd love a home-cooked meal."

"Maureen?" he said. He glanced out the window, but Maureen's house was dark, the driveway empty.

"I've been told my steak and zucchini is the best in town," the woman said. "Wouldn't you like that? Some steak? A nice glass of wine?"

"Who is this?" Jim said.

"A good night's sleep," the woman said. "Clean sheets. A warm, comforting body next to you. Doesn't that sound pretty?"

Jim, stunned, was silent. "Well, you think on it," the woman said politely. "No offense taken if you're not up for company yet."

He borrowed money to hire a detective, a man named John Martini, who assured Jim that he would find Lee.

The days had a dangerous edge. He'd go outside and find the buses had changed numbers or a street had suddenly changed names. He suddenly wanted to go to the neighborhood barbecues, to sit on a wicker chair and not think of anything except how much mustard he wanted on his hot dog; but he was no longer invited. He sometimes wheeled his daughter in the cheap pram he had bought with Lee, but no one ever stopped.

When people walked by they averted their eyes. He sometimes thought if he put in a garden, the men at least might be forced into talking to him, and then, if he plowed it over, the women would befriend him. He wasn't working, and school wouldn't start up again for another month. He had the time and money to tide him through the summer, so one day he went outside and tried to dig the yard, but after an hour the bugs bothered him so much that he gave it up entirely.

He didn't know what to do with his daughter. Looking down at her, he felt all his emotions drying. If there were no baby, there might still be Lee. Lee was too young for a child. He was suddenly sure that she had left the baby, not him, and for one blinding moment he saw himself speeding away from the hospital with her, the two of them, outlaws on the road, each holding no other hand but the other's.

His daughter cried, and he picked her up roughly, like one of the brown bags he packed at Jack's supermarket. She stared at him, and he averted his eyes. The phone rang, and a voice told him a blond woman was spotted two hours away at a small bar called Bruntello's. He plucked up the keys and resettled his daughter on his hip, and as soon as he felt how wet she was, she started to cry. He rushed her to the changing table and began prying open diaper pins; he hastily dusted her rosy bottom with powder, and the whole time he imagined the blond woman, his Lee, taking her time, folding her long legs into a strange red convertible and driving away. When the baby cried, recoiling from the prick of the diaper pin, Jim hastily patted her on her shoulder. "Okay," he said, fixing the pin and jerking her up into his arms again.

He drove out with a dry and quiet baby beside him, but when he got to the bar the parking lot was empty. "Up you go," he said, picking up his daughter. Inside, two men sat nursing watery-looking drinks at a leather bar. There were four red vinyl booths, and only one of them was filled, with an older couple silently eating burgers. The bartender looked as young as Jim, and shook his head at the baby. "Isn't she a little young to be boozing?" he said.

"Did you see this woman?" Jim said, pulling out Lee's photo. The bartender blinked. "No, but I wouldn't mind seeing her," he said, grinning.

"Did you see her?" Jim pulled at a waitress's arm. She gave the photo a frank stare. "There was a woman with hair like that," she said. "But I don't know if it was this one." She frowned. "Anyway, she left about ten minutes ago. By herself."

"Fine," Jim said angrily. "Ten minutes. That's just fine."

The whole way home, he ignored the baby. She was quiet until the last half hour of the way home, and then she began to wail angrily. "Yeah, well I'm mad, too," he said, swerving to avoid another car.

"How's my little darling?" his mother kept asking. She insisted he put the phone to the baby's ear so she could warble melodies, so she could tell her granddaughter a bedtime story. "What a good girl," Gladys said, but Jim always felt hollow. He boiled bottles and cleaned diapers and fed his baby, but his heart stayed numb.

The next day he woke at ten. The silence in the house suddenly scared him. Bolting upright, he went into the baby's room. She was completely still, and when he touched her she seemed ravaged with fever. Panicked, he called the pediatrician. Her voice was calm and dry. She kept asking him questions, and when she was finally silent, he shivered. "Wash her with alcohol," the doctor said. "Cool her down. You do that, and if she's not better by tomorrow morning, you take her in." Terrified, he soaked cotton swabs and stroked them on the baby's fevered skin, and this time she started crying. She fretted in his arms. He was sure her cries would fuel whatever rumors were floating around the neighborhood, but he didn't really care. He half hoped someone would come banging at his door, just so he could get some advice out of them.

He needed a baby thermometer, but he was afraid to put her in the car, to take her outside. He sat on the chair and rocked her. He sang every pop song he could remember. Finally he dipped his finger in wine and let her small mouth work at it. He didn't know if alcohol was bad for a baby, but it quieted her down, and when she fell asleep he laid her down on the bed and watched her, balanced on one elbow.

He stayed with her all that night, just watching her, and in the middle of the night he noticed she had cooled. He stroked her forehead, and suddenly he fell dizzyingly in love. The baby clutched his finger.

In the morning he named her. He laid her in her crib and got out a phone book and traced a finger down until he found a name he liked. "Joanna," he said.

He began reading her stories, singing her the songs he remembered Gladys singing. He put her crib in the bedroom with him so he could hear her least sound. Sometimes at night he'd wake up and just stand over the crib, watching her, making sure she was alive.

The evenings started to cool toward fall. He began planning his courses, worrying about getting someone to sit for the baby while he was in class. Someone he could trust. He scribbled plans. The school had already promised him work/study in the library; he could get yet another loan from Jack to help meet expenses until he was on his feet.

He was puzzling over his books one evening when he noticed the woman next door, Maureen, had begun sitting on her porch, too. She was always wearing a short, summery dress, her curly bobbed hair held back by a plastic headband. She couldn't be more than ten years older than he was.

Sometimes, when he looked up, he saw her watching him, and defiantly he stared right back. He wouldn't drop his gaze until she dropped hers. She hadn't said one word to him since Lee had disappeared. Her husband, Mel, nodded to him mornings, though, but since Jim didn't garden, he didn't care.

One cool summer evening Maureen simply walked over with a covered casserole. Jim stood up when he saw her. "I bet you eat terribly," she said. "You tell me where's your oven inside and I'll heat this for you." He nodded her inside, trailing her to the kitchen. She put the casserole in and then turned awkwardly to him.

"That's some baby you've got there," she said. "Can I hold her?"

"Go ahead," he said. Maureen picked her up, soothing the tender skin with one finger.

Maureen ended up staying the evening. She put the baby to bed and then played a long careful game of gin rummy with Jim. "Well, here we are," she said.

"How come you came over?" he said.

She shrugged. "You look harmless enough."

"Is that what the neighbors think these days?"

"I didn't say the neighbors. I said me." She dusted her hands off along her sides. "Listen, who cares what they say. All anyone needs is one friend, anyway, and as far as I'm concerned you got me."

She stretched. "Well, Mel's waiting," she said.

"You can come back anytime," Jim said.

"Then I will," Maureen said.

He didn't expect her back, but two nights later she came, this time with a toy for Joanna and a fresh pack of cards. "Mel's working late," she said. "Lots of nights I just feel stir crazy alone in the house."

She stayed nearly until midnight, until Mel's car pulled into the drive, and as soon as she saw her husband, her face brightened. She put down what she claimed was a winning hand and sprang from the porch to greet him. "I'll see you later, Jim," she called, leaving him to the night.

He told Joanna stories about Lee. She loved the color blue. She never combed her hair so it looked combed. She'd once cracked an egg into her hair because she thought it would make it shiny. The baby, moon-faced, peered up at Jim.

How could someone just disappear? Presto change-o. He wouldn't let her. He left Lee's clothing in the closets. He did what laundry of hers he could find and folded it neatly into her drawers as if she were on nothing more extended than a vacation. Her hairbrush, still sifted through with blond strands, he refused to clean.

Sometimes he talked to her. He was gentle at first, begging her to come home. He promised her they'd move to the country. He told her story after story about their courtship, as if she could hear him, as if his memory were more compelling than her own. "We were so happy," he insisted. Some mornings, though, he shouted at her. He accused her of being selfish, of being so fucking stubborn he'd like to put his two hands about her neck and kill her. "I can't do this without you!" he cried.

He dreaded the nights. Sleep was no escape because Lee was always there, prowling restlessly, eluding him. In the dream he'd go to call her and find that he couldn't remember the one crucial digit. He'd trail her down a street only to have her turn and see him, her face indifferent. Over and over he dreamed she was having a heart attack. He slung her body around him like a coat. He got her to the hospital. "I'll never leave you," she gasped, and then her body would crumple. One night he dreamed Lee was dying. He heard her screaming, and then he began screaming, too. His terror woke him, his scream, and then, there in the night, harmonizing with him, was the baby's scream. Stunned, he got up, kicking off the covers. She was thrashing in her crib, her small face contorted, streaked with red. She didn't calm down; she stiffened when he picked her up, her body quivering in his hands. "Want to compare dreams?" he said. "Who had the worst of it, do you think, you or Daddy?"

He brought her back to his bed and buttressed her in with pillows. "We'll keep each other company," he told her.

He called Lee's old number at the Silver Spoon, half thinking she might answer. He called Information in different cities and asked for listings for Lee Archer. Only once did he get a listing, in Atlanta, and terrified, he dialed. A man answered, his voice heavy with sleep. "Is Lee there?" Jim said, trying to sound casual. If pressed, to get to Lee he'd lie. He could be a job prospect. He could be a relative. "Isn't it awfully late for this?" the man said.

"It's an emergency," Jim said.

The man sighed. "Hold on," he said.

"Hello?" a woman said, a voice as distinctly different from Lee's as his own, and Jim hung up.

One night, when he was most lonely, he cooked Lee's favorite dinner, imagining that this might be the night she'd come home. He fried chicken so crisp and greasy, he had to drain it on four layers of thick paper toweling. He set two places with real linen napkins and silverware and a rose in a water glass. He steamed peas and pale baby carrots from Mel's garden. He arranged Joanna in a plastic crib by the table, and for a while he waited until the food was cold, the chicken congealing. Every time a car door slammed, he told himself it was Lee. Every voice in the distance could be his wife. He waited until the bit of appetite he had had was smothered, and then he left everything on the table, as if somehow the leftovers might still summon his wife home to him.

Every week he went to the international bookstore and bought six different newspapers from all over the country, pruning the pages for stories. Lee could be anywhere. Every body that was found made him terrified because it could be hers. He examined every picture of a crowd, circling faces that might be hers. He felt an odd camaraderie with what he called the "others," the people with missing sons or daughters, with husbands who left. People did show up again, he told himself. Embarrassed, he began buying the tabloids at the supermarkets. He liked *The Planet*, he had a fondness for the *Truth Universal News*. There were stories about people who were thought to be dead who suddenly showed up. There were colorful stories about amnesia. Could that be possible, Lee wandering in Oklahoma, being a clerk in pastel suits, using the name of Delia or Anna or whatever name she might see on the back of a cereal box? He imagined Lee's face flashed across a TV screen.

He went to the Silver Spoon, where Lee had worked, the baby papoosed against him. One of the waitresses knew him and refused to serve him. When forced to by the owner, she smashed his glass of water on the table so hard it chipped. She let his order cool before she slapped it down, and even when he left a tip so large it was embarrassing, she snubbed him. "What is *wrong* with you?" he said.

She jerked her arm away. "I knew Lee, that's what's wrong," she said. "You figure it out."

Memory was stronger than the present. He could see Lee so clearly that it pained him. He walked into a psychic's office once, a storefront with a translucent white palm in the window. A woman in a blue dress gave him a sober, teasing smile. "How can I help?" she said, and he was suddenly so grateful, he burst into tears.

She unfolded a deck of cards. A few fell, sliding onto the dirty floor, but she scooped them up again. "No matter," she said cheerfully. "My wife is missing," he blurted. She glanced sharply at him. "Well now," she said. She pressed the cards back into a pack. "I have something for you." She paused. "Candles. Very special ones only I can make. You burn one every night for seven days and they will bring her back," she said. "You mind, though, if she's dead, they'll only bring her spirit back, and then you'll be in real trouble. You'll need me all over again. One man—he brought his wife back in spirit and she kept hovering over him. In the subways. In a diner. He had to buy more candles to put her spirit at rest." She blinked at Jim. "It's up to you. Twenty dollars a candle."

"Forty for all of them," Jim said.

She sighed. "Did you know the dead take things? You look in your own house. Anything shiny's missing, you'll know who took it. You have electrical appliances? The dead love electricity. When things go on the fritz, that's them."

"Thirty-five," Jim said.

In the end he paid forty dollars for four blue candles. He lit them every night. He sat in the dull blue glow and waited for something different to happen, but in the end it didn't matter one way or another, because he still saw Lee everywhere, he saw her nowhere at all.

5

During that first year of disappearance, Lee felt that every place she drifted through was like another disguise.

She left Richmond for Atlanta, stepping out of a dusty train into a summer so boggy with heat that the people around her seemed to be vaguely stunned. Lee, still sick and chilled with fever, found the heat a comfort. She liked, too, the noise and confusion and the twisting crowds that all somehow seemed to fade her into a background.

Lee let herself be carried by the tide of people, spilling out with them through an open walkway into the simmering morning streets. The crowds siphoned into taxis and waiting cars, into twining, trapping embraces, and she kept walking. She had no idea where she was going, exactly; it only seemed somehow important that she keep moving, one unsteady sneaker after the other. And then, two blocks away, she stopped in front of the Bestways Motor Inn, as if that had been her intended destination all along, unrealized until she had actually arrived and found it right there in front of her.

There was a giant splintered wooden sign, shaped like a hand lifted in a friendly wave. Inside, a young girl slumped at the front desk over a comic book, her fraying black hair in two straggly braids tied with blue mending tape. Lee paid for two weeks up front, signing in as Anna Norfolk, the name of her first-grade teacher, a white-haired woman who gave out brand-new silvery-green rolls of Mist-o-Mint Life Savers for every report card with an A in it. The whole time, the girl at the front desk never looked at Lee.

For nearly the entire two weeks, Lee was cocooned in a cheap single room, emerging only twice to drag herself to the diner next door to buy salted crackers and soda from the vending machine, the only things she seemed to be able to keep down. The days melted together. The small, stifling room claimed her so entirely that sometimes, in the midst of the waves of fever, she thought she didn't exist at all. She'd waft up one of her hands and look at it, waggling her fingers, experimentally touching one thumb against the wavering pulse at her wrist. She'd stare at her sunken face in the bathroom mirror, tracing her nose, her cheekbones, the sudden new hollows around her mouth.

She had bolted the door, keeping the dusty blinds drawn, the window locked closed. She had shucked down to her T-shirt and panties and crawled into bed. She tried to sleep, rolling under a warming burrow of starchy sheets, delirium washing roughly over her. She could hear the rivery roar and hiss of the cars streaming past. The windows shivered from the sound.

Hallucinating, she transformed. She became things. A dark, quivering crow flying desperately into the air. A body without bones. And sometimes, too, she saw things. Rusty iron bars suddenly clanged into place across the window. A small infant's face scowled at her from a dark corner.

One morning she dreamed someone was shooting a hail of bullets at her door. Terrified, she woke. The door was still reverberating with sound. Her feet trembled against the floor, and as she padded toward it, the sound began to soften, to change into knocks. Shaking, she opened the door.

A patchy-haired man in a dark suit nodded at her politely. He introduced himself as the hotel manager. "Is something the problem?" he said quietly.

"No problem," Lee said. He wavered in her focus. "Just a little flu." She blinked. "Why?"

He shrugged. "There were some complaints."

"Complaints?" Lee said, stricken.

"Oh, noise," he said. "Shouting. Perhaps you were just having nightmares. One visitor thought you were being attacked, you were shouting so. That's why we checked."

"What was I saying?" Lee said, dazed.

"If you're sick, if you have trouble sleeping, perhaps I can recommend a good doctor."

"Oh. That would be fine," Lee said. She watched him write something down. She tucked it into a curl of fingers. "Thank you," she said, closing the door slowly.

That evening, in a stupor of fear, she fled the hotel, walking past the desk clerk as if nothing were more wrong with her than the fact that she was out of cigarettes. She walked two blocks back to the train station, stopping only for a package of strong, over-the-counter sleeping pills. She caught the next train out, ending up in Lubbock when she was simply too exhausted to travel farther.

She staggered from the train to a cab to the first hotel she saw, too cloud-headed to think of a different fake name from the last. Two days later her fever finally broke. She woke toward morning on the bare mattress, the sheets and blankets kicked to the floor. Her skin was dry and cool. She got out of bed, and everything in the room stayed where it was supposed to be. The air thinned to normal; colors stopped bleeding from their objects.

Healthier, she could focus enough to be nervous, to keep better watch. At first Lee wouldn't leave her room. She was terrified that as soon as she stepped onto the street, she'd feel this sudden steely grip on her arm and she'd turn around and see the police or a detective, or even Jim. Every blond head of hair might be Jim's. Other times she worried that he was disguised. He could dye his hair as easily as she had. He could be any number of people, biding his time, waiting for the right moment to bring her back to him. He could be here with the baby, a thought that made her slam her mind shut. Don't think about it, she told herself. Don't think, don't think. Panicky, she suddenly picked up the phone to call him, to see if he was really home. "Hello?" he said, and she was startled by the flood of anger she felt at hearing his voice, so soft and sad, so full of need.

She was getting stir crazy in the room. Finally she ventured out, head down, ignoring the desk clerk, an old man idly reading a newspaper. She walked to the local five-and-dime with Jim's money tucked into a wallet she wore under her clothes. She bought a child's white transistor radio. My First Radio, it was called. The whole walk home she felt the radio's presence, like her fortune, waiting to be told.

That evening she listened to the news with her eyes half-hooded, her body poised for flight, and all she kept thinking was that all those news stories were simply layers blanketing her whereabouts, and all someone would have to do would be to peel them away to find her.

When the news was over, she slid the dial to a rock station and lay back on the bed. Sometimes she got up and moved to the music, remembering what it had been like when she had danced on the front porch in a heady bath of gold moonlight, first with Jim, his hands cupped at the bone of her hips, standing so close against her, she could feel his heart trying to beat into her own. Later she had danced with the young girls who had wanted to be her at the very same time she was wanting to be them.

Lee felt so suddenly and vaguely lonely that she stopped in mid-lazy twirl and switched off the radio.

She began going out more and more. She bought maps. She went to three different gas stations to collect what she could and then finally went to a bookstore and bought an atlas, tearing out the pages she was interested in. She began to think about settling in someplace. She tacked the maps up in her room or she kept them in her purse, marking them with the towns she might like to go. Boilerville, Ohio. Porterhouse, Texas. Places where no one thought a thing about a girl so young living on her own, places where girls Lee's age might be leading exactly the kinds of lives that they wanted.

In Lubbock she watched herself transforming. Her voice took on a faint Texas twang. Her walk began to sway and lilt, partly from practice, partly from the red hand-tooled cowboy boots she had bought in a secondhand shop for twelve dollars. She began browning with a tan she couldn't help but collect. At night, when she slid out of her light summer dress, her skin was braced with white where the sun hadn't touched her, as pale as the stretch marks that branded her belly. Her hair turned brassy and red like a gilded penny from the combination of sun and cheap rinse-in drugstore color she had finally persuaded herself to buy. Mountain Peony, the color was called, chosen because it was the one package that didn't seem to have a picture of a woman leaning her dyed head up against the clean pure natural color of a baby for comparison.

She had planned to be here for only a month or so, but then the land began doing something to her. She loved the flat expanse of it, as if the environment had been pared down, simplified. She began falling in love with the way the tumbleweeds skittered across the highway and tangled into one another. They crunched up against the bumpers of the cars, attaching themselves like trophies. When she touched them, they seemed to dry-spark, splintering in bits against her fingers. She found she liked the broad spread of sky, the way it switched on at night into a brilliant spill of stars and planets. She liked the tang in the air, the silence in the early morning, broken by the lashing cry of jaybirds and crows.

She began to get tired of the hotel. She began to want a place that was all her own. People, she told herself, started new lives all the time, and she began to think that this could be a place where she might be able to do that.

She found an apartment almost immediately, a small studio she could sublet three months at a time. The permanent tenant, an art student on his way to try out California and a live-in girlfriend, showed only mild interest when Lee blurted that she was from New York. He didn't ask her a single question but simply took her two months' rent money and folded it calmly into his back pocket.

Lubbock, too, was the first place Lee would try to get a job. Jim's money was shrinking steadily and it made her afraid. She scanned the paper for possibilities. There wasn't much she was qualified for. She applied for jobs as a receptionist and a salesgirl. She took four typing tests, quickening the speed of the three fingers she pecked with, making so many errors that at one place the woman giving the test asked her politely if she were in the right place.

She finally got a job in the fall, at an answering service called Tell It to Us. She had seen an ad, and as soon as she called the number and said she was interested, the owner, a woman named Roxanne Harper, hired her on a trial basis. "Don't you want to meet me?" Lee said, astonished. Roxanne laughed. "Why, you think someone's going to see you?" she said. "You talk to voices, not people. All I need to know is how you sound on the phone, and you got a reasonable enough voice."

Lee gave her a fake name, a fake history. She was Lara Michaels from North Dakota. She started making up a Social Security number when the woman stopped her. "Doll, I pay all my girls under the table," Roxanne said. "It's my business, I can do what I like."

Lee had to take two different buses to get to the Tell It to Us answering service. It took her half an hour each way, but she liked watching the tumbleweeds pinwheeling crazily on the road, liked hearing nothing more than the roll and swagger of the bus, the occasional muted conversation going on in the back. The trees, streaming past, were changing color. The air coming through an open window had bite.

The service was on the top floor of a small brownstone. She rang the buzzer and trudged up five dark flights to a room the size of a bathroom. Three peeling brown Leatherette chairs were rolled up against a narrow long desk, topped by a switchboard. On the far side was one small window with a white paper shade half-drawn. The only thing hanging on the beige wall was a large red clock.

In front of the switchboard were two women. One, much younger than the other, had cropped spiky brown hair, a set of headphones already clamped about her ears. The other, older, woman had dark hair, faintly receded, slicked back from her skull. Both women were wearing jeans and sweatshirts, and Lee, in the one clean dress she had, in heels she couldn't walk in, felt silly. The woman with the dark hair stood up. "Lara, right?" she said. "I'm Roxanne, this here is Dolly."

Lee sat on a small wheeled Leatherette chair, still warm from Roxanne. The chair felt inhabited, somehow alive, and Lee shifted weight.

"Shorton, Rosen, and Latooter Plumbing," Dolly sang with real melody into her headset. She reached for a square of yellow cardboard, punching it into a time clock and then beginning to write something on it. "Yes, *ma'am*," she trilled.

"You got to watch that one," Roxanne said. "They like you to sing the name out."

Lee stared at the buzzing lights Dolly was plugging into. "Dr. Smilberg's office," Dolly said in a bored, tight voice.

"Easy, right?" Roxanne said to Lee. "You watch the board. When a name lights up, you plug into it and speak whatever name is written under the light. Then you take one of these squares of paper and write the message and put it in the drawer under the light. At the end of the day, the people usually call for their messages. Then you toss them."

She touched Lee's shoulder. "We'll try you out for three months. You do good, you got yourself a job." She grinned. "There's your first light. Plug it up, doll. You're on."

By the end of the first three hours, all Lee wanted to do was to go home. Nobody who called ever seemed to believe that she was really the answering service. People wading in flooded basements swore at Lee and asked her just who the hell she thought she was, charging the rates she did for plumbing and then not showing up. "I'm the answering service, it's not my fault," Lee said.

"Don't use that sweet tone with me," the caller said. "So full of sugar I'm surprised you don't have ants. You get over here or I'll sue you for the water damage to my house."

Exasperated, Lee looked over at Dolly, who was idly twirling her phone wire, ignoring Lee altogether.

She started to be privy to these little human disturbances. Bailey Bondsman got about a call an hour. Women, their voices shattered with sobs, always wanted to tell Lee that their husband or boyfriend or son hadn't done whatever he was being jailed for. A man, needing bail for a son who had held up a toy store, spoke with Lee in a voice as cold and hard as smashed pieces of ice.

An actor called every hour to see if he had gotten any messages, making Lee feel so sorry for him, she finally told him someone had called without leaving a name. The worst was an 800 number for people to order an eighteen-piece set of Chinese cooking knives. There were only four hundred sets, and Lee was supposed to have kept count, to stop answering the phone as soon as she had the four hundred, but in her panic she just kept taking orders. Toward four, when Roxanne was sequestered in the back room singing along to an old Rolling Stones song, when Dolly was in the bathroom down the hall, Lee quickly separated four hundred slips from her pile. The switchboard flashed and flickered and buzzed. "Dr. Balmont's office," Lee said loudly, her fingers tripping over the paper. "Yes, I will." She stuffed the rest of the sheets into her purse and plugged into a call, just as Dolly wandered back in, zipping up the fly of her striped pants.

Except for the hour and a half Dolly and Lee were allotted for lunch, Roxanne mostly stayed in the other room off the side, with the door closed. Sometimes Lee could hear country-and-western music. Sometimes she heard ice clinking in the glass. "What does she do in there all day?" Lee asked Dolly, but Dolly just shrugged.

At night, when her replacement came, a sallow thin blonde in a too long plaid dress, Lee yanked off her tight headset, rubbing circulation into her bruised ears. She walked alone to the bus stop, trying to shut off the buzz in her ears.

She found when she lay in bed at night, the voices sometimes didn't stop. She kept hearing the gritty accents, the ringing tones, the pleas and arguments and polite requests, all those momentary contacts, like sparks of static. And all those voices traveling and clamoring toward her made her suddenly hungry for a body, and it was a hunger she didn't know what to do with.

She tried to talk to Dolly. Their lunches were staggered, but once in a while she would bring Dolly a doughnut. "Thanks," Dolly said shortly. She ate the doughnut, but during lulls in the blinking board, when Lee tried to make small talk, Dolly froze her out. "I talk all day," she said. "What do I want more for?" At night Dolly never waited for Lee. She took the stairs four at a time. "Good night," Lee called, down toward the silence.

She tried to talk with the clients when they called in for their messages. "So, busy today?" Lee said, but the voices rushed past her. The doctors wanted their messages with no nonsense; the plumber called her Miss Kate, even though she had told him her name was Lara. The only one who would talk to her at all was the actor. His name was Bobby Estev, and he told her stories so funny that she'd put him on hold so she could take the other calls and get back to him. "This last audition," he said. "They made me quack like a duck. Can you believe it?" He quacked for her, and she laughed so loudly that Dolly flashed her a steely look. "They should have asked me to bark. I do a mean golden retriever." He told her he had a trust fund—"I'm trusted not to blow all of it at once," he said—and contrary to popular belief, he wasn't depressed by the lack of calls. "All it takes is one, right?" he said.

Because of Bobby, Lee slowly began to look forward to work. His conversation gave shape to her days; she could count on calls at noon, at two, and just before she left. It was just enough. It buoyed her spirits; it made the weeks fly. She began, too, to think about him, to imagine him. He sounded blond, she decided. He had longish hair and eyes so black they mirrored yourself back to you. She saw him, but never with her.

They had been talking together for almost three weeks when he asked her out to dinner. "Italian," he said. "This place, they know me, I could make reservations tonight."

She felt an odd flicker of annoyance. "Oh, I can't," she said.

"Why not? You involved?"

"No, I—"

"Look, it's just dinner," he said. "You think you'll ever want dinner?"

"I don't know. Maybe."

"Maybe," he said. "That's the day after tomorrow, right? Let me just write that down in my busy schedule."

He didn't call her for the rest of the day. She kept watching his line, waiting for it to light up. Just talk to me, she thought. Just talk.

That evening she was leaving work when a man took her arm. Startled, she sprang back, her heart racing. "Lara?" he said. "Are you Lara?" He was taller than she was, with a thicket of dark curls. He dressed like a kid, in red high-tops and a blue baseball jacket over a white T-shirt. He grinned at her. "Bobby," he said. "I thought if you saw how cute I was, you couldn't resist." She laughed despite herself. "Come on, what do you say, dinner, that's all, nothing fancy."

He took her for hamburgers. He leaned across the table toward her, his smile so bright and earnest, it unnerved her a little. He kept asking her questions, where had she grown up, what was she like as a little girl. What was it like working at the answering service. "So who are your clients?" he said. "It's not confidential or anything, is it?"

She told him about Dolly's singing lawyer. She told him about her two Dr. Ambroses, one who treated feet, the other who was a dentist. "Waiter," he said. "Two beers."

She kept drinking, kept talking and laughing. She was surprised how relaxed she felt, how good. On her fourth beer the room began to swim. She was woozy enough that when he touched her face, her heart amplified in her chest. She felt a heady pull of desire. "Come home with me," she said.

She woke at four in the morning, and as soon as she felt him beside her, she panicked. He was too close. A voice you could disconnect, you could detach, but here he was, with one arm looped around her belly, his head nuzzled toward her shoulder, making himself at home. All the attraction she had felt was suddenly gone. She jostled him awake. "Listen, you have to go," she said. He pulled the covers over his head. "I have to go late night shift tonight." "I'll come with you," he said. She shook him from the bed. Startled, he staggered for balance. He gave her a soft, sleepy smile. "So how about dinner tomorrow?"

She shook her head. "Bobby," she said. "Listen, Bobby. I can't do this."

"You want to slow it down?" he said. "Anything you want," he said. He pulled on his shirt, stepped into his pants, and put on his sneakers. "You need a lift?"

She floundered, shaking her head. "Dolly's coming for me. She's on the same shift."

"I'll wait, then."

"No, I have to shower, really." She prodded him toward the door. "No, don't kiss me. Morning mouth." She waved her hands. "Please. Go."

He was gone. She locked the door, exhausted. She moved toward the bed, but his body seemed imprinted there. She pulled off the top blanket and made a bed on the couch.

The next morning she still felt invaded. She was late to work because she had to remake the bed with sheets no one had slept on but her. She rushed into the office. Roxanne was covering her board, and when she saw Lee she tapped her wristwatch with annoyance. Lee sat down, plugging immediately into Dr. Ambrose's line, when she heard his voice. "Hey, gorgeous, you working all night?"

"How'd you get this number?" Lee said.

"Hey, you told me the names. I have a great memory. Nice surprise, huh?"

"I thought we were going to slow this down," Lee said.

"I'll pick you up tonight," he told her.

"No," she said, but the connection was gone.

That day he called five times, twice on the Ambrose dentist line, three times on the plumber's line. "Look, I don't want to go to dinner," she said. "Just talk to me a little," he said, but his voice suddenly annoyed her. She didn't take pleasure in his jokes anymore; his stories about auditions were suddenly tedious. She didn't like how he kept telling her about all the things they were going to do together. She left work early, complaining of a cold, wanting to avoid his waiting outside for her at closing time. All that evening she left the phone off the hook, but she couldn't relax. She felt somehow watched.

She began to dread going to work. She was late more and more.

She sometimes left before closing time. She began taking her time plugging in the calls, and once she made the connection, she waited for the caller to speak first. When Dolly pointed it out, Lee snapped at her.

She plugged into Dr. Ambrose's line, told the caller to wait, and quickly took Wayland Plumbing. "I stood outside your house all last night," Bobby's voice stormed on the line. "You didn't go out at all. I slept in my car, and believe me, the weather's getting too nippy to do that."

Lee felt a chill. "You watched me?" she said.

"I can see your window right from the street. I know you. I know things I bet you don't think I know."

"You do not," said Lee, uneasy.

"I know your name is Lee, not Lara, you said it in your sleep the night we were together. I know other things, too." She disconnected him, so violently that a spark of electricity crackled from the board. She plugged into another line. "Why'd you put me on hold! I need Dr. Ambrose! It's an emergency!" a woman sobbed.

"Right away," Lee said. She scribbled the woman's name and number, then she called Dr. Ambrose's secretary with an emergency. She was flustered all day. She took a cab home, and that night she kept getting up to test the windows behind the blinds. She was an hour late for work the next morning, and when she walked into the room Roxanne was sitting on her seat. "I'm late," she said. Roxanne looked at her, her eyes steel.

"It's a real habit with you, isn't it," she said. "You want to come in the back with me for a minute?"

Lee looked at Dolly, who was plugging into a line.

The back wasn't much different from the front. Roxanne had a flowery couch, a minirefrigerator and a stereo. She sat Lee down. "When I hired you, we agreed it was three months' trial basis. Well, the months are over, and I can't say that I think you're answering service material."

"What?" said Lee.

"You got to be quick. You got to remember. I got three complaints this morning. Dr. Ambrose the podiatrist got an emergency call for Dr. Ambrose the dentist. Wayland Plumbing got an emergency call for a fake number."

"I was—I was ill yesterday," Lee said.

Roxanne shook her head. "It isn't just yesterday. Dolly tells me you take your time on the board, that you're getting personal calls here. Is that true?"

"No, not personal," Lee said.

"That's not what I hear. You're always late. You're distracted. Listen, I think we'll both be happier, you work someplace else."

Lee nodded, numb. She got up and got her purse, and as she left she noticed that it was the first time Dolly was really looking at her, her eyes flickering with real interest.

This time leaving wasn't as easy. She was tired of traveling, of being in a different city every month or so. And she had loved Lubbock. She had thought she could stay. She threaded her hair through restless fingers. It felt rough and unbeautiful. Wherever she went next, she wouldn't dye it anymore. She'd let it grow.

It took her two hours to pack her one small bag because she kept stopping to look around her apartment, the first one she had ever had all by herself. It shocked her, how hard it was to go. The phone kept ringing, but she simply watched it dispassionately. She thought about Lubbock and Bobby and the tumbleweeds that Bobby said would soon be decorated in points of ice, and by the time she had finished packing, all that was left was a gray eyeliner in the bottom of one chipping drawer.

She took a cab to the airport. It was early enough so she could take her time deciding where she wanted to go. She craned her neck at the monitors, gravely studying the cities quivering in fluorescent green on the screen, and finally she chose Madison because it seemed so different from Lubbock.

Lee slept the entire flight, not waking until she was on a Wisconsin runway, the windows dusted with snow.

It continued to snow the whole first week she was in Madison. She stayed in a hotel room, drinking complimentary room service cocoa and staring out at the bleached landscape, at the drifts that seemed to be breeding ominously. In the distance, from her window, she could see someone skiing down the road, skidding a network of zigzags. She listened to the weather reports on her transistor radio warning of more snow, droning about school closings, about water freezing in the pipes and old people dying in unheated apartments. In the early morning, when she woke and couldn't sleep, she heard the farm reports. Cattle were freezing in the barns. One farmer brought out so many oil lamps to warm them that he had started a small fire.

When the weather finally cleared, she looked for an apartment, taking the first one she saw, a small bright studio near the university. Resolutely she scribbled a name on the lease. Sara Lee Rider.

She began fixing up the place, determined to stay in it, to make it her own. She bought a bed and a desk and a cheap imitation Oriental rug. She bought dishes and towels. The one thing she wouldn't do was install a phone. She had had enough of voices kindling through the wires.

She thought she'd waitress until she found something better. She walked into the first restaurant she passed, a small cozy-looking place called Valerie's. She was a little dazed to see the waitresses dressed in Hawaiian leis, wearing grass skirt aprons. On the walls were photos of Hawaii, and on each table was a tiny miniature lei made up of plastic beads. Don Ho was piped in over a scratchy intercom. "Hawaiian menu," a woman said. She was only a little older than Lee, wearing a simple black sweater dress, and she had a blue paper hibiscus pinned into the black shaggy braid down her back. She grinned at Lee, lifting up a bright blue menu. "Next week it's Mexican, and you really ought to come back for that. Best salsa in town."

"I'm not here to eat," Lee said. "I've come to apply for the waitressing job."

The woman gave her a long critical look. "Well, let's discuss it over Hawaiian iced tea," she said. "Don't look so scared. It's just tea with a piece of pineapple wedge."

They sat at a small table in the back. "I'm Valerie," the woman said. "I bet you can't believe I own this place." She smiled again and bunched up the sleeves of her dress. "People say I look sixteen," she insisted. "People wonder how I stay so skinny when I'm around food all day."

Valerie didn't really ask Lee much about herself. Lee said her name was Sara Lee Rider, but that everyone called her Lee. She said she had been brought up in Oklahoma, that she had come to Madison to go to school but had decided to take a year off instead.

"Well, good," Valerie said. She leaned on her elbows. "My husband, Roy, gave me this place as a birthday present. You'll meet him. He's a lawyer. It's a real family place. Even my brother eats here." She told Lee the place changed menus every two weeks as a way to entice new clients. "I like that," Lee said. "All those different menus."

"How about you start tomorrow," Valerie said.

She gave Lee a form to fill out. Lee carefully wrote in her name; she made up two restaurants she said had gone out of business shortly after she had left jobs there. She had no idea where the owners were. For a Social Security number, she scribbled in Claire's birthday and her lucky number, nine.

Lee began settling into Madison. She loved the cold, the way the streets emptied out so that she would sometimes be the only person out in them. She bought herself a huge orange fake fur and hat from the Salvation Army and a pair of leather mittens. She put on red rubber boots she had bought from the five-and-dime and walked with nearly every inch and shape of her somehow swaddled and hidden. Exhilarated, she let the wind push her. Sometimes she walked to Lake Mendota, at the side of the university, and watched the wind whisking the water into waves, until she was so cold she couldn't feel her mouth. Her tongue was too numb to let her form a single word. She'd walk home and draw herself a bath, making the water so hot the steam seemed almost solid. Half-dozing, Lee lay back in the claw-foot tub, singing to herself in a low, tuneless voice, one hand trailing against the cool porcelain side of the tub.

She didn't mind her job. Most of the waitresses were students who sometimes lasted only as long as the next menu change. "I don't know why I ask anyone if they're a student or not. They lie anyway," Valerie said.

The clientele was a mix of students and working people, and almost all of them treated Lee with consideration and respect, even when she was wearing a Mexican skirt or an Indian sari tossed roughly over one shoulder.

Lee kept to herself at Valerie's. Valerie never got in until the late afternoon. She carried fresh flowers for the green vase by the door. She prowled around, joking with the waitresses, talking to the regulars, and supervising the cooking. She kept trying to start conversations with Lee, who didn't like the intense way Valerie tried to meet her eyes. "You want to go see a movie?" Valerie would ask her. "Roy's out of town and I'm lonesome." Lee always had some excuse. "Well, another time, then," Valerie said. "You look like the movie type, that's why I asked."

Sometimes when she was eating her lunch in the back room, Valerie would come and sit beside her. "You're so quiet," Valerie said. She'd try to engage Lee in talk, but Lee was so reticent that Valerie finally left her alone.

Every weekend Lee went to the library to look for stories about herself. She told herself it was to make sure no one was on her trail. She rummaged through the papers from every city where she had been, dry panic centering in her stomach. She almost never found anything, and then she'd leave the library feeling queasy and overheated. There was only one time she saw something, a small article in the Philadelphia paper about unsolved cases. They had a picture of a man who found a human skull buried in his backyard garden, but no one knew whose skull it was. They had a picture of a little girl who had been snatched off the street. And they had a small photo of Lee, too, her hair in one long waterfall over her shoulders. It was a picture she had always hated. A small shock of relief shot through her. They had a picture of Jim, too, and underneath it read "Jim Archer, Cleared Suspect." She had to trail the words with her finger, that's how much she was trembling, and when she came to her daughter's name, Joanna Archer, she got up and walked out of the library.

That evening, at the restaurant, she spilled an entire tray of coq au vin dinners. She gave people the wrong change so they had to call her back, she misread orders and forgot to make up bills. "Are you all right?" Valerie asked her. "You look so funny."

"It's the outfit, not me," Lee said weakly, smoothing down the French ruffly black apron.

She stopped going to the libraries; she was more careful listening to the radio. She suddenly didn't want to know anymore; she didn't want to think about Jim as a suspect. The image of a baby girl floated up in her head, the name repeated over and over like a slap.

She kept thinking about it. She couldn't eat. She couldn't sleep, and one morning she woke with fever. She didn't have a phone, but she had to let Valerie know she was ill. She struggled up, bundling her orange coat over her pajamas, and walked through the snow to the pay phone. Coughing, she got Valerie, but she coughed so much it took nearly five minutes to tell her she wouldn't be coming in, and then the operator broke in to ask for another quarter. "Where are you calling from?" Valerie said, suspicious.

"A pay phone," Lee said. "I don't have a phone."

"Everyone has a phone," Valerie said, stunned.

"Everyone except me," Lee said, sneezing.

She managed to get back to her apartment and fell into a deep, almost drugged sleep. That night Lee dreamed that someone was trying to break into her apartment. There was banging on her door, so loud that she woke, her heart wild inside of her. She was in the hazy half state between dream and waking. She still heard the knocking and stumbled up to make sure the door was double-locked, and as soon as she balanced her hand against the wood of the door, she felt the knocking. She imagined Bobby standing there. She imagined Jim or her father. For a moment she imagined a child, and she shrank from the door.

The knocking grew more steady, fine-tuning itself into a pound. "Lee, you're making me scared. You have to open up," a voice called. "It's Valerie." Lee opened the door.

Valerie had two large bags gripped in chapped bare hands. She glowered at Lee and let herself in, dumping the bags on the table. "Are you crazy, not having a phone?" she said.

Lee woozily made her way back to the pullout on the floor and flopped down. "I don't call anyone," she said.

"You called me, didn't you?" Valerie said. "Listen, I'm heating you up some restaurant leftovers. I bet you don't have a thing here to eat, do you?" Experimentally she poked around the cupboards. "Jesus, you have to have more than tea and boxes of macaroni."

She cooked Lee some sort of a fish stew and then sat on the edge of the bed and watched Lee eat it. Then she cleaned the bowl and swept the studio and settled onto a rocker.

"I'm just going to sleep. You don't have to stay here," Lee said.

"Does the door lock when you shut it from the outside?" Valerie said. "Because I think I'll just sit here awhile and read."

"Oh, please, don't do that," said Lee. Exhausted, she pulled the covers up around her. "Please," she said, drifting toward sleep.

When Lee woke up, the studio was spotless. In the refrigerator was a pot of stew and two glass bottles of orange juice. Fresh flowers were in a juice glass on the window ledge, pinning down a note. "Phone company coming tomorrow," it read. "Don't even think about canceling."

* * *

Lee stayed out all that week. Valerie came by every third day, knocking so loudly that one of Lee's neighbors answered the door thinking it was for him. Lee found she liked having Valerie there. She sat up in bed, and the two of them leafed through the magazines Valerie had brought her. When Valerie left Lee felt a little incomplete. She found she missed her.

When Lee came back to work she began eating her lunch with Valerie in the spare back room. "I thought maybe you didn't like me," Valerie told her.

"Want my apple?" said Lee.

"You can't just be alone in a place," Valerie continued. "You know any other people? You got a beau?"

"Nope," Lee said.

"Well, I could fix you up with someone," she said, and when Lee was silent, Valerie asked if she were carrying a torch.

"You think I am?" Lee said.

"Jesus, what love does," Valerie said. with a kind of admiration, and then was silent.

"So, did he hurt you or what?" she said.

Lee pushed back her hair. It was growing longer. Just last night she had seen blond picking through the red.

"He was married," she said finally. "No kids." She tried to find a face, but all she could see was the small hard headache forming behind her temple.

Lee reached for a cigarette from Valerie's pack. "She was Texan," Lee said. "From Dallas. His wife. Short blond hair. She used to run a gift shop."

"What about him, then," Valerie said, but Lee just shook her head. Valerie sighed. "Lots of fish in the Madison sea," she said. "Let me know when you're ready to bait a hook." She laughed, tossing her cigarette, still lighted, right into the sink.

One night Valerie invited Lee to dinner to meet Roy. "You'll love each other," she said.

Valerie's house was large and sunny and filled with green plants. As soon as they walked into the front room, Roy came out to greet them. He was small, fair, and balding, and he lit up when he saw Valerie. "Well, I'm so happy to meet you," he told Lee, but he kept watching his wife.

All that evening he kept following Valerie around, whispering things to her that made her burst into laughter. He flopped her braid between his fingers. "So, Lee, you keeping my Valerie in line, I hope?" he said. He smiled conspiratorially at his wife. Lee felt like an intruder. The two of them made her feel restless. She went into the kitchen for water, and when she came back out, they were kissing, standing in the center of the living room, Roy's hands travelling up and down Valerie's spine. Lee stood perfectly still. She felt a twist of desire so acute it nearly doubled her over, and then she walked carefully back into the kitchen for a moment.

She braced herself against the sink, then got herself another glass of cool water. There were lots of men in Madison. Students, professors, people who worked in the city. Everybody didn't have to be Bobby, she told herself. And everybody didn't have to be Jim. She could be careful. She could be certain not to make the same mistakes.

"Hey, you ready for dessert?" Valerie said. She was leaning in the doorway, beaming, Roy behind her.

"Ready," said Lee.

6

Lee knew who Andy was the moment she set eyes on him. He looked almost exactly like Valerie, mirroring her black curly hair, rangy build, and blue eyes. Valerie introduced Lee to him. "Meet my star brother, finally back from California. He doesn't look like a judge with that gold earring and long hair, does he?"

"I do too," he said, laughing.

"He puts away traffic offenders," Valerie said, smoothing her brother's tablecloth. "He condemns countless couples to matrimony every Wednesday and by appointment."

"It's a living," he said to Lee. He was smiling at her, but as soon as Valerie moved away, his manner changed. His head dipped. He began studying the menu. "Just give me another minute here," he said.

"Take an hour," Lee said, annoyed at being dismissed. Brusquely she began waiting on another table, explaining to a businessman why the lobster that evening was so expensive, and by the time she was finished Andy was already lazily picking at a salad another waitress had delivered.

She began to watch him, at first because he was really the only constant customer in all her working nights. She could gauge time by him. She knew her shift was half-over just by seeing him sit down, always immersed in a book she could never quite catch the title of. And she knew she had only another half hour left when he stood up, fanning bills onto the table. He was always alone, and although he always talked to Valerie, and sometimes even joked with the other waitresses, she could glide past him with a tray of flaming cakes and he'd never lift his head.

Once, Lee noticed he left his book. She was about to call out to him but suddenly found herself crouching down by the table and picking it up, curious about the title. John Cheever. A collection of short stories she hadn't read before. Behind her she heard another waitress reciting the theme desserts. It was midwest week, and everyone was dressed like milkmaids, with broad pocketed white aprons and daintily flowered skirts. "Cheddar cheesecake," the other waitress said. "Apple brown Betty. Chocolate cupcakes." Lee slid the book into the pocket of her apron.

That night she stayed up until one in the morning reading Cheever. She was careful not to crack the spine of the book, not to stain a single page with a sip of the orange juice she had fisted in one hand. She didn't know why, but the pleasure of reading his book was much keener than if she had gone to the bookshop and bought her own. It felt secretive; it felt somehow dangerous.

In the morning she wandered into the kitchen where Valerie was. "Well, look what I found," she said. "Someone'll claim it," Valerie said. "Just leave it by the reservation desk." When Andy ambled in that evening he did, looking pleased and grateful. He leafed through the pages.

She watched him reading other books; she waited for his easy carelessness. It was impossible, but the books he left always seemed to suit her mood somehow. A night when she was sluggish, he left a collection of H. P. Lovecraft that chilled her awake. Once, when she was in need of cheering, he left a dog-eared copy of *Catch-22*.

She began to like him for his books. She began slowly to imprint herself into them. She couldn't bear to hurt the books, but she bent back his paper bookmark or stained it with juice; she replaced it with a matchbook from Bally's Pub down the street. From the kitchen she watched him reclaiming his books, discovering her. He plucked up the matchbook bookmark she had left him and flipped it through his fingers. He frowned at the sudden stains, gazing up into the restaurant, but inevitably he became lost again in the book, reading a few pages until his meal arrived.

"He's cute, isn't he?" Valerie said.

Lee shrugged. "He's all right," she said.

"I keep asking him, so who're you seeing? But all he says is 'Oh, someone.' I think he's lying. I think he's too embarrassed to admit no one loves him but his baby sister."

"Well," Lee said. "You never know."

It was a fairly slow night. There was a blizzard, and most people had stayed home. Valerie, queasy with flu, had Roy come and pick her up, leaving the car for Lee, who didn't once mention that she didn't have a license.

There was something in the air. It was a night when arguments seemed to erupt in the restaurant. Lee saw one woman hurl her fork at her lover and start to storm from the table before he reached out and grabbed her back. A businessman in a pinstripe gray suit, sitting alone by the window, wept quietly into his napkin.

Even Andy seemed somehow different. Bookless, he hunched over his meal, staring dreamily around the restaurant, and for the first time he seemed to be watching her. When Lee passed by him, he suddenly smiled. "You want something else?" she said.

"Nope," he said.

Gradually the restaurant thinned out. Andy was finishing ice cream. Lee wished he had brought a book to forget; she could use something to read. "I'll close up," one of the other waitresses said to Lee. "You get going."

Outside, the snow kept powdering the ground; the streets were nearly deserted, and the same ominous heaviness hung in the air. There were bits of faded yellow light coming from some of the windows she passed. It began to hurt to breathe. She tried tugging up the collar of her sweater and breathing through it; she put one mittened hand in front of her mouth.

She was almost to the car when she heard labored footsteps behind her. Twisting around, she peered into the blur of snow. She couldn't tell whether the person behind her was a male or female, but it had suddenly stopped. The entire body was swaddled in a long bright blue down coat, the puffy hood cinched tight over a face hidden by a wrapping of black scarf. Uneasy, Lee began walking again, and there behind her was the quickening crunch of boots. Lee ran.

Tensed, she began digging for the keys in her purse. There it was. A red car at the end of the street. She was afraid to turn around again, and now all she could hear was her own terrified pant.

"Hey!" someone called, and she stiffened.

A figure was coming toward her, dots of black and red in a blurred matrix through the white.

Lee found the keys, jamming them into the lock.

"It's Andy," he called. Straightening, she turned toward him. The huge down-coated figure was nowhere in sight. Andy swiped snow from his face. "It's not a night to be out alone," he said. "I saw that guy following you."

She studied him. "Thanks," she said.

"You taking Val's car?" he said cheerfully.

"She gave me her keys," Lee said. She gave the door a rough juggle, and it sprang open.

"Well, my car's just down the road," he said. "Will you be all right driving in this? You want me to drive you?"

She hesitated.

"Well, you'll be all right," he said abruptly. "The main roads still look okay." He squinted at her. "Didn't your mother ever tell you about wearing a hat when it's cold?" Her hands fluttered to her snow-soaked hair.

"Well, listen," he said. "Don't get any traffic tickets because I won't fix them for you." He laughed. There was a frosting of snow on his lashes. "Lee," he said. "Have dinner with me tomorrow night."

"You know my name," she said. "You act like you don't know me in the restaurant."

"Well, I don't," he said. "Not yet."

She hesitated. "Dinner's okay," she said, getting into the car. She fit the key into the ignition. The car jerked backward. Agitatedly she rolled down her window a little. "Look, I can do this," she called. "You don't have to watch."

He cupped hands toward himself. "Just back up a little bit more," he said. "You're doing fine."

The car eased out into the road. She clicked the automatic into drive and looked back at him through her rearview mirror. He was standing there, waving at her. She was sure he was shouting something, and she rolled down the window, letting in another clip of chilly air. "What?" she shouted, but he was already turning down a street, vanishing into the frozen white landscape.

Andy always thought that love was this season that had somehow passed without his knowing it.

In college he remembered being in love numerous times. There was easy romance, pledges of undying love, all lasting until the moment when another caught his eye, and then his heart unstuck and reattached as easily as Velcro.

As he got older, though, he began to think about marriage, and with this new seriousness, it suddenly became more difficult to fall in love. He had plenty of dates, but he somehow could no longer muster anything stronger than a vague fondness, and it began to terrify him.

Valerie told him he just wasn't choosing well. "I got myself a great husband, maybe I can help find you a great wife," she said. She began inviting him over. Sometimes one of her friends would be there, a woman pretty enough, pleasant enough, and sometimes he would get her phone number and go out with her a few times, before he grew distant, before the friend called Valerie in tears or in anger to complain, as if his sister could do one thing about him. Finally he just refused Valerie's setups, not wanting to disappoint her, the woman, or himself again.

"Don't you want to be happy?" Valerie demanded. "You've got to give things a chance."

He hadn't given one thought to chance until he had first seen Lee. She had been walking on the street, bundled in some fake furry coat that was a size too big for her, her thin pale face flushed in the cold, her blond hair flashing, and as soon as he saw her something deep hurt inside of him. He had followed her to Valerie's restaurant, imagining how he'd casually sit down at whatever table she was sitting at, how he'd start up a conversation, dazzling her with repartee. He rehearsed a few opening lines in his mind, and then she took off the coat and went into the back room and changed and she became a waitress.

It startled him for a moment, but then he told himself she must be something more. Writers were waitresses. Students bussed tables. Awkwardly he settled into a table in the back. All that night he searched for clues to another life she might be burning up with. She seemed to know some of the regulars, but when she talked with them all he overheard was suggestions about the specials or, once, a comment about a movie she had seen. On breaks she leaned dreamy-eyed along the far wall or talked to Valerie. Her seeming content-ment bothered him. Why wasn't she in a rush to get someplace else—an acting class, a graduate course? He pretended disinterest. He thought about asking Valerie, but he was superstitious. Her participation before had been no help; he didn't want to risk it now, so instead he asked Annie, another waitress he knew. "Oh, that one," Annie said when he gestured at Lee. "She's the only full-time one here. She hardly talks."

Annie didn't know everything, he told himself. He kept studying Lee when she wasn't looking and sometimes when she was. He ate at Valerie's so many nights, even Valerie noticed. "Can't I give my sister some business?" he said.

He tried to be cautious, but every time she passed he felt a change in the atmosphere, a charge. It was ridiculous. He could come up with a thousand reasons why he didn't want Lee. He needed someone bright and accomplished—a kind of kindred spirit—and she seemed to be just a waitress. She was beautiful, but there was a roughness to her beauty. He'd still be embarrassed to be seen with her. Her hair was torn. Her eyes were ringed in black. And the way she dressed—Jesus—bowling shirts with names like Madge or Hanna embroidered on the back in orange stitching, odd pastel skirts that looked as if they came from Goodwill. She wore earrings in the shapes of teapots or fish. He watched her sashaying among the tables, following an edge of her hip, frowning anxiously at the tips before she pocketed them. He looked at her, and he couldn't imagine kissing her, not those chapped, ragged-looking lips. No, he couldn't imagine it, at least not until he had left the restaurant—and her—not until he was back at home and thinking about her, wanting her so much he felt his will draining from him.

When he discovered she was reading his books, his heart began to buoy. That was a good sign. He had started back one evening to retrieve one and had seen her pick it up, avidly read a few pages, and pocket it. Once, she kept his favorite book, *Crime and Punishment*, for over two weeks. When he got it back he placed his hands on the page, where he imagined hers had been. Heat shot up through his fingers; two days later, in the middle of a blinding snowstorm, he asked her out.

He didn't know who was more amazed when they started seeing each other, Lee or himself. He kept himself calm, thinking that any moment he could detach from her, but when he saw that same willingness in Lee, it made him afraid. He was used to women wanting to stretch the nights with him into mornings and afternoons, women who called him every day to remind him they existed, and here was Lee, leaping out of bed so fast that he sometimes woke to find her gone. Lee, who not only never called, but sometimes didn't even answer her phone when she was home. When they walked she didn't cling to his arm. When he tried to take her arm, she sometimes simply removed it.

She was secretive. Their first date, to amuse her, he took her bowling. He scribbled down fake names on the scoring sheet. He was Ward. She was June. She wore a really short red skirt and red lace socks, her hair cinched up into a ponytail. "Whoops," she said as her ball raced toward the gutter. He was an even worse bowler, and in between games he tried to talk to her. He loved the way she listened, her whole body angled toward him, intent. She herself talked only about Madison, about settling in and saving money. She told him she hadn't finished school, that maybe she would do that. "That's a good idea," he said. "The university here's really good."

She gave him a funny look. "High school," she said.

He blinked at her. His smile wavered. High school. "Why'd you drop out?" he said.

She fretted two fingers in the bowling ball. "I just did," she said flatly. She looked at him. "I'm not stupid," she said.

"Of course you're not." He hated his voice. It sounded oily, as if he were speaking more out of politeness than belief. With a rush of air, he asked her about her family.

"I don't have any family," she said. She clenched her fingers about the bowling ball. "How about your first boyfriend?" he said, touching her elbow. "You're the first," Lee said, so seriously he felt his heart breaking.

When he took her home that night, he didn't expect one single thing from her. She sat in his kitchen, warming by the stove, pronging marshmallows onto forks, toasting them on the gas flame. She ate four of them silently, and then, her mouth sticky with sugar, she leaned over and kissed him.

There, in his brightly lighted kitchen, she took everything off except a pair of red lace socks. She leaned against him, weighting him to the floor, bumping his spine against the linoleum. She rolled him toward the braided rug Valerie had made for him. He couldn't get over her; the way her neck curved into her shoulder, the way her skin was so pale and seamless, as if she were all cut from one piece. She kept moving from him, pulling him along the floor with her. She knocked over a chair; she broke a small vase. She kept making these sounds that made him lean nearer to her. "What?" he whispered. "What?" but she only rolled from him. She arched her back. Her closed lids fluttered, and when he kissed them, she gave a small cry.

When they were finished he lay prone on his kitchen floor, perfectly content, but when he turned to her he caught her near tears. "What is it?" he said, trying to smooth her hair from her face so he could see her eyes. "Would you like more?" he said anxiously, but she just shook her head. "I don't feel well," she said, leveraging up onto his thigh. "I have to go home." Her body was shaking, but he didn't touch her. She didn't move. He stretched out alongside her, an inch distance from her. In the corner of the kitchen he saw a jagged bit of cracker he must have missed in his careless mopping. It took him a few minutes to realize she was sleeping, and then he slept, too, and when he woke in the morning, she was still there.

They began to have a routine. He picked her up every other night from Valerie's. He took her ice-skating on the frozen part of the lake and discovered she was as good a skater as she was a poor bowler. He took her to triple features at the Duplex Cinema downtown, and he found he was turning to look at her more than he was looking at the movie. "So, you still like me?" he asked her. "No," she said, taking his hand. "Not at all."

He hadn't counted on feeling so strongly. He couldn't stop thinking about her. He saw her everywhere. In his courtroom. On the streets. And, more telling, when he performed his weekly weddings inside his chambers.

He tried to convince her to come to a wedding. "How can you not like weddings?" he said, aghast. "They're all about hope."

"Sometimes," said Lee.

"Always," Andy said. "Even if they don't turn out. And I can tell who's going to make it just by how they act in the wedding," he insisted. Lee gave him a slow, steady gaze. "Come on," he said. "Please. It'll be a blast."

He took her to his chambers first, showing off the office he himself had painted a soft, reassuring green, his collection of what he called "honeymoon histories." He had postcards from Bermuda or Virginia

Beach, and one from Japan. HAVING A WONDERFUL TIME, the cards said. LOVE BEING MARRIED. He had photos that couples had sent him of their first children, none of them, to his great disappointment, ever named Andy.

He had her wait outside while he got ready. "It adds a little drama," he told her. She sat on the bench with the other couples, waiting for him, the only single person there. Most of the brides just wore street clothes, but the girl next to Lee was in a full-length white satin gown, a long white veil drooping over her face. "Would you mind being our witness?" the girl said to Lee. Her breath smelled like Juicy Fruit gum. Lee glanced at the groom, a boy so young he suddenly reminded her of Jim. "Oh, you don't want me," Lee said. The girl shrugged. She turned to another person, a woman in jeans and cowboy boots, and asked her.

Andy called in the first couple, both probably in their seventies, both in suits and polished shoes. Lee followed them in, standing by the wall, silent. He couldn't understand it, why she looked so tense and uncomfortable, why during the whole ceremony he felt Lee watching only him, ignoring the bride in her pink bow blouse, the groom in his red silk bow tie. As soon as the couple left, he turned to her. "Why weren't you watching the bride and groom?"

"You looked happier than they did," she finally said.

He didn't understand some things about her. Why she was so stingy with her past. BW, Before Wisconsin, he began to call the time she wouldn't talk about. He didn't understand why he'd sometimes see her brooding and unhappy, and when he asked her why, wanting only to get her smiling again, she told him only that it would pass. She was a secret, and he dealt with secrets all day. All of law had to do with secrets. Defendants lied. Police lied. Even evidence sometimes lied. But he had always thought that part of the mystery and beauty of the law was unraveling it all, finding the truth and trying to set things right. He loved the law, and to his absolute amazement, he was beginning to love Lee.

Lee knew Andy wasn't Bobby, but sometimes she thought he was even more dangerous simply because of how much she liked him. Setting up roots, creating a new life didn't scare her half as much as a relationship. In a relationship people wanted things. They couldn't help but lay claim to your present, and your future, and then, inevitably, the past you had tried to bury.

What would you do if you knew about me? she kept thinking. What kind of price would he think she should pay for a crime like hers? "Everyone lies in the courtroom," he had once told her angrily, and it had made her uneasy.

She didn't want to feel anything for him. It made her confused, on edge. Every time he brought her flowers, every time he told her calmly that it was perfectly fine that she wanted an evening to herself and didn't call or disturb her or make her feel one bit guilty, it made her angry. She snapped at him as if it were his fault that she cared for him. "You think you know me," she said contemptuously.

"So tell me what I don't know," Andy said. They were sitting on her couch, watching an old Bette Davis movie.

Lee was silent. "I want you to go home," she said.

"What, are we breaking up again?" he said, amused. He didn't start to get angry until Lee brought him his leather jacket, his thick red woolen gloves.

"Just go," she said. She watched him from her window. He got into his car and drove, and fifteen minutes later she missed him so much, she called him.

Oh, God. Maybe if he wasn't a judge. If he wasn't so in love with the law. Sometimes she would wake at night to find him reading a casebook for the pure pleasure of it. Every time someone on the street said "Good morning, Judge" or "How are you doing, Judge?" —every time a cop or another lawyer stopped to shake Andy's hand, he seemed lit from within.

She came to his courtroom only once, out of a perverse, demanding curiosity. He was draped in a black robe. She could see the top of the bright red tie she had bought him. She sat in the back of his courtroom. She heard only one case. A ten-year-old boy claimed a man had butchered his basketball with a carving knife because his play was so noisy. He carried the ball as evidence, and when he brought it up for Andy to examine, the entire courtroom was tittering except for Andy, who studied the ball seriously.

The law followed him on the street; it came home with him, and it entered the night. She jolted awake once. Andy's side of the bed was empty. The other room was dimly lit. She heard voices. And then she saw a patch of blue, a glint of silver, and a cop came into view, suddenly peering into the dark room at Lee. Lee jumped up and the cop disappeared, but from the other room she could hear him speaking, his voice blurring. She heard Andy. "I don't like to do this," he said. The footsteps amplified. A door opened and closed. She was fully clothed in sneakers and jeans and her red sweater when Andy came into the room, his face terrible, and as soon as she saw him, she wanted to fling herself against him.

"Cops were here," he said simply. He blinked at her. "Something wrong?" he said.

"What did they want?" she said. Her heart traveled inside of her, banging against her ribs.

"Commitment papers. I told them to go to a higher court. I'm not signing away a sixteen-year-old girl."

"Oh," she said. She felt suddenly weak, boneless beneath her skin. She rested her head against his shoulder. "You know something?" she said. "You have a good heart." He lifted one hand and stroked her head. "Sometimes I really like second chances," he said.

"Sometimes I really like you," said Lee.

"All the times," he said. He cupped her head in his hands, just long enough for her to feel the warmth, and then he drew his hands back down and left her alone.

She began dreaming about him nights, and in her dreams she told him everything. But sometimes, too, she would dream about Jim, about the nights when he had been sweet to her, about the nights when she had thought she might almost want to be with him.

She'd wake, surprised, shivering. She'd have to get up and walk around her apartment, reminding herself that these were her rooms, this was her life now. A whole year had passed, a whole new life had finally started, and in its context, her old one with Jim had never even existed.

7

The year anniversary of Lee's disappearance from the hospital, the very first birthday of their daughter, Joanna, Jim jolted awake at five in the morning. He surfaced in watery panic, as if he had been drowning with the weight of his dreams. His blue cotton pajamas were drenched; his heart hammered staccato rhythms, and for one wild moment he thought that all he had to do was turn around and Lee would be sleeping in the crescent of blankets at the hip of the bed. He smelled her vanilla scent wafting lazily into the room, riding over the hazy morning light. Resting on an elbow, he listened for her, but the house was silent, and after a while all he could smell was his own feverish sweat, the sour tangle of sheets.

The baby wouldn't be up for another hour. He could go back to sleep if he were a normal person, waking on a normal day. Instead he shifted out of bed with a rough arc of legs. His feet, planted in front of him, looked dirty and untended. Well, he'd tend to Joanna. It would be a good game, wouldn't it, waking his daughter before she could wake him with her impatient wails, his face rising before her like a cold moon.

He was busy enough. Caught in the middle of the summer term at school. Tied up with loans and baby-sitting deals and a work/study job at the library. Ten hours each week checking out other people's books. He had studying to do. He had to drop Joanna off at Maureen's and then pick her up again. She sat for Joanna four days a week, a few hours each day, but she charged him nothing, accepting only the meals he'd cook for her when Mel was out of town. "Hell, the baby's company for me," she said.

Company. He loved his daughter, but he didn't feel she was company. Rousing himself now, he stumbled into the baby's room and peered down into her crib. "You don't have a clue, do you, Joanna?" he said to his daughter. "Well, you get that from your mother." He stroked her small back. She struggled to pull herself up, and he picked her up, settling her against his shoulder, where she soggily mouthed his pajama top. He had no classes that day, no work, but he still had no intention of making any sort of celebration out of a day that made him feel like dying. His parents had already sent Joanna a four-foot-high white stuffed panda. Inside the birthday card, his father had tucked a check made out to Jim. "For *our* baby," he scribbled. He had set the bear in the crib with Joanna; he had called them and managed to thank them profusely without ever once mentioning the occasion.

Tomorrow he'd celebrate. He'd buy her a set of blocks, give her a sugary cake. He'd do the same every July 6 until Lee was back with them.

He dressed her and spooned strained peaches into her, getting abstract splotches of it on his pajama top. And then, after he had showered and dressed himself, at nine o'clock in the morning, he left Joanna with Maureen, telling her he would just be a few hours. She was still in a red gingham robe, her hair matted about her head. She watched him with a frown. "You all right?" she said.

"Sure I am," he said.

As soon as he got in the car, he felt guilty. He drove immediately toward three different toy stores, and then almost immediately he veered past them. He headed instead to Fuller's Tavern downtown, a place he knew only from passing it every day on his way to school. He parked the car immediately in front and walked into the bar. Fuller's was all shades of brown inside. Deep tan paneled walls, cracking muddy-colored leather booths, brown Formica tabletops. Even the sunlight seemed beige to him here. He was the first and only customer there, and it made him feel somehow defiant. He sat in a dark back booth and ordered three beers. "Bring them all at the same time," he said. The waiter, pad poised at his hip, brown apron tied tightly about his waist, nodded vaguely. Jim didn't know who he was fooling. He had no tolerance for alcohol at all. The very first time he had ever gotten drunk had been the night he and Lee had gotten arrested, the night he had told her he loved her, the night he had thrown up all over a police station floor. The beer came, three icy glasses that seemed to be breathing mist. He cupped two hands about one glass and swallowed as much as he could. Metallic and uncomfortable. He swigged another portion. He wasn't enjoying this, but his vision gradually dimmed, his head felt happily swimmy. The room splashed before him. He tilted his glass in a toast. "Happy anniversary," he rasped. He shut his eyes for a moment and thought of her, so hard and deeply he was sure his thoughts might travel, electromagnetic impulses rocketing toward Lee, cornering her in some town he didn't even know the name of, bringing her home.

He drank some more, polishing off one glass, then starting in on another. He still hurt, only now all the pain didn't seem to be happening to him so much as to someone else. He was more of an innocent bystander, a stranger sympathizing with this poor shaggy blond in a none-too-clean summer white shirt, a man who stumbled to his feet, who missed his wife so much that everything that wasn't her seemed to be disappearing. His blood ached. His eyes felt dirty. Fisting bills in one hand, he reeled toward the register.

He paid the bill and then stumbled out into the sharpening heat. Everyone outside looked like Lee. The small pale woman in a pink dress, a baby on one hip. The teenager in pink plaid stretch pants and white plastic flip-flops. Panicked, he looked away. He blinked and walked a little down the street. Lee followed him and approached him, all at once. There she was, whisking into the dry cleaners. Again he spotted her, jamming dimes into the parking meter, wearing a green checkered kerchief about her head. "Lee!" he called, but no one turned around.

There was a jewelry store on the corner, opening for the day, and abruptly Jim went in. Glittering in the cases, like shattered bits of stars, were all the jewels he had never bought Lee. He leaned against a glass case, ignoring the "Please Don't Lean" sign, and painstakingly stared down into a black velvet case of diamond stud earrings.

The clerk, a young woman in a yellow flowered dress, smiled at him gravely. "What can I help you with?" Find my wife, Jim thought, but instead he stubbed a finger against the glass. "Those," he said. She nodded, looking at him curiously. He stepped back a bit. "It's an anniversary present," he explained, picking up the smallest pair. "Those. I'll take those."

"What a wonderful choice," the clerk told Jim. She leaned toward him happily. The sting of alcohol assaulted her, and she pulled back abruptly. She tried to size him up. "Cash or charge?" she said suspiciously, and when he pulled out a Visa card, she relaxed a little. "You'll make some woman very, very happy," she said.

"You think?" Jim said. "My wife says all I have to do is bring her wildflowers and she's mine for life."

"Ah, a romantic girl," the clerk said. "You're lucky, then. It doesn't take much to please a woman like that."

She held up the earrings, pivoting them until they caught fiery light. "I'll gift-wrap them for you," she said.

She fussed with pale pink layers of tissue paper. He borrowed a fountain pen and scratched a message on the white gift card. He couldn't bear to see it, her name on the paper. Lee. To my wife with heart and soul. I love you always, Jim. As soon as he stopped writing, he felt sickened. Beer crashed in spumy waves against the walls of his stomach. He let the card flop on top of the gift box.

"You let me know how she likes those earrings," the clerk said, touching her own ears, which were ringed with small brass hoops freckled with tarnish.

He felt the weight of the box in his pocket. He waited until he was outside and then he carefully peeled away the rose-colored wrapping paper; he opened the box and held up the earrings. Carefully, tenderly, he placed them in his breast pocket, the shirt fabric so worn and thin he could feel the earrings against his skin.

Maureen, if she knew, would forgive him. She loved the baby, and sometimes, too, he thought she loved him a little. He noticed she had started wearing perfume, a dark woodsy kind of scent that reminded him of Mel's garden. She began to pin a shining rhinestone barrette in her tumult of black curls. She never came over with Mel but arrived on his porch nights when Mel was working late or bowling. She found her empty house as disturbing as he did his. She filled up the spaces with sound. Her laugh belled out; she knew jokes that weren't all that funny and bits of neighborhood gossip about people he didn't really know or care about. But it didn't matter. It never failed to cheer him. And Joanna needed people who adored her.

His parents came when they could, but Lee's father stayed distant.

Jim hadn't given up. He kept sending Polaroids of the baby. Once he sent a lock of hair, but he never got a response. He imagined Frank sitting on the edge of a bed that might once have been Lee's, holding that frail piece of hair and wondering over it, remembering and yearning. Sometimes, too, he imagined Frank ripping up the photos, burning the hair. Frank never contacted Jim, but he never sent any of the things back, either.

That anniversary, with the air so damp and muggy he could have taken off his shirt and wrung it out, he told Maureen he'd be home later. He was not so drunk anymore. His head had cleared some. She knew him well enough not to question. She said she'd bring the baby to her place, that Joanna could have dinner with her and Jim could pick her up on his way home.

That night, to commemorate his wife's disappearance, he wanted to drive and drive the ropes of highway Lee had loved. He wanted to find her, bedraggled, her face dirty, looking at him with eyes filled with grief and love. He didn't care why she had left anymore. He could blindly forgive everything if she would only let him.

He was only half an hour out of town and certainly not driving that fast. Not fast enough for a ticket, not murderous enough to do damage. He was about to turn onto an exit, circling toward a new route he was sure Lee might be on, when in the car beside him he saw a woman's blond head, tilted back. A gesture, fingers fanned out the way Lee used to. He sped up a little, he swerved to see, and then his car skipped and slammed into the other lane and into a sudden, narrowing black.

Lila Gleason started her nursing workweek the day after Jim had been brought into the hospital. Generally she was pretty. Right now exhaustion and loneliness faded her. Her pale skin looked smudged. Her hair, usually one shiny short sheet of brilliant red, was now diluted to russet.

Lila was slumped in the lounge on a break, swiping a wreath of bangs out of her eyes, when the other nurses began talking about Jim. He was a twenty-year-old man who had been peeled from a burning car crash over on I-91. He had had only a small amount of alcohol in him, and he had a pair of diamond earrings in his pocket and a wedding band. His wallet, loose in the pocket of his jacket, was nearly empty. A lip of it was charred, but still they'd managed to find a card with his home number scribbled across it, with his name. And in the space for the name to call in an emergency, he had printed only WIFE. The hospital kept phoning his home number, sometimes letting it ring nearly fifteen times, but no wife ever answered. No woman ever showed up, flustered in a hasty cotton dress, a run laddering along one stocking, her eyes stumbling.

"Broken ribs. Stitches in his head like they were needlepoint," one nurse said to Lila. "He's so medicated, it's a wonder he even has energy to breathe."

"Where the hell is his family?" said Lila. She was tired and cranky and wanted nothing more than coffee enough to jitter some energy into her, and since the new patient's room was right near the one working coffee machine on the floor, she offered to check on him.

She pushed open the door and glanced in. He was sleeping, lying on his back in a confusion of starchy sheets. His eyes were purpled and nearly swollen shut, but even then she could tell how handsome he was and how young. His ribs were bandaged. His head, too, was wrapped in gauze, showing a soft, silky spill of blond hair. She was about to walk past when she heard something, so low and hushed it took her a moment to realize he was crying. She walked in quietly and stood beside the bed. She crouched down toward him.

"You all right?" she said. His face was filmed with sweat; his lids, tearing, still rolled in dreams. "It's all right," she whispered, lifting his hand to take his pulse, but as soon as she touched him, his fingers circled back and clasped her wrist, so strongly that she flinched. "Please," he cried. His eyes were still closed; he was still dreaming. She couldn't get a pulse with him gripping her like that. She lifted her hand as gently as she could. His eyelids quivered. His mouth moved in spasm. He reached for Lila's startled fingers. As soon as he grasped her, he seemed to relax.

She lowered the hand he held down against his chest. His heart beat up against her captive palm, and even as her hand was held there, she could feel the beat evening, becoming less rapid. She waited, and then his breathing calmed, his features relaxed; but his grip held. She stood there for another few minutes and then carefully peeled her hand free. He grabbed at air, and then his hand dropped back onto his own chest. "My God," she said. Her hand was completely asleep, prickling with sudden sparks of circulation. She massaged her palm. She flexed and unflexed her fingers, all the time watching him thoughtfully. When she finally left his room, she left his door open, the way you might do with a child who feared the dark.

All that evening she kept absently rubbing her palm against the bone of her hip, trying to get it back to normal. No matter what she did, she could still feel his heart, impossibly strong, beating up through her skin; she could still feel his hand, twined determinedly in hers.

She was used to people saying all sorts of things in delirium, in drugged, dreamy sleep. People called to the dead. Women sometimes saw Jesus. One young girl, floating on fever, thought Lila was Madame Curie and asked for help on her physics exam the next week. "Please," he'd said. She walked past his room, checking to see if his wife had finally come, if she were seated in the orange Leatherette chair beside the bed, claiming the hand Lila had held for her. The empty chair began to make her angry. She felt pained for him. Why wasn't his wife with him? She wished she could get her hands on his wallet and find a photo of her. Lila bet she was pretty, with a fringe of black lashes and thick black hair cut into a magazine style. She bet Jim's wife would waltz in here in red shorts and high heels, complaining of the heat, insisting no one had called her. "Please," he had said.

She went out to the front desk. The night nurse, a middle-aged woman named Debby who had gone into nursing the day her husband had gone to Club Med to find a younger woman, smiled at Lila. "I feel so sorry for ten A," Lila said.

"He's in bad shape all right," Debby said. Idly she twined a fuzzy curl of hair about her hand. "I heard the car is worse," she said.

"I hate it when the families don't show up," Lila said. "Where do you think his wife is?"

"Who knows," Debby said, flipping through a sheaf of papers. "Where all the husbands and wives are, I suppose. Maybe she's at a Club Med somewhere with my ex-husband."

"Don't be silly," Lila said.

Before she went home she checked on Jim one more time, standing in his doorway, silently watching him toss in the stiff sheets, his face full of storms. It wasn't until the night nurse came by to check on him that Lila realized she had been standing there for almost twenty minutes.

Restless, Lila lay in bed, watching the clock tick toward dawn. She kept thinking about Jim, about the diamond earrings, about his wife.

She knew about love. The nurse in her could categorize all the externals—the wild pulse, the almost audible flushing, the blush like a stain of blood splashed up under the skin. She had had her share of symptoms. She had been in love with a medical student who later took a job in South Dakota. She fell in love once with a hairdresser who had wandered into the hospital looking for a pay phone. His name was Tom, and although they spent an entire year together, every time he caressed her hair Lila thought he was making a comment on the fact that she didn't use cream rinse. "Why do you have to do everything so inappropriately?" Lila's mother asked her when Lila called, crying because her latest lover, Todd, a skating instructor she had met at a party two years ago, had taken a job in a small touring ice show in California and had neither plans to take her with him nor plans to return. "A skater, for heaven's sake," her mother said. "How can you miss him! You miss doctors and architects, not skating instructors." But all Lila could think about was how he had scratched her name into the ice with just a bare tip of his blade, how he had spun her around with a snap and twist of his wrists. Todd had left over six months ago, but she still missed him so much that even putting ice in her drinks wounded her. He had teased her over and over because she was a nurse. Nurses were easy, he had told her. But there had never been anything easy about loving him. And there was nothing easy about pain.

As soon as she got to the hospital in the morning, she headed for Jim's room. Astonished, she saw that the bed had been propped up, that he lay slanted upward, blinking dully in the light. He had on pajamas, new blue-and-white-striped ones with the crease still cut into them. His face had some color. "Well, hello," she said, delighted, and it wasn't until she was halfway in the room that she saw the woman and the baby seated by the far window, and she stopped abruptly. The woman was older than Jim, older than Lila, and was dressed carefully in a sleeveless turquoise dress and blue heels, a rope of pearls about her slender neck, a wedding band ringed about her finger. She was settling the baby beside Jim, who lifted one hand toward the squirming yellow booties.

"Is that yours?" Lila said, walking into the room.

The woman beamed at Lila. "That's Joanna," she said.

Jim looked up at Lila. "Everything hurts," he said dully. "You aren't going to make me eat anything, are you?"

"Of course I am," Lila said. He grinned, and she suddenly thought how interesting his face might look when it was less banged up, when he could really open his eyes. He'd have bruises about them for weeks, she thought. They'd fade, watercolor on parchment. She looked at his hands, relaxed, on the covers. He was wearing a wedding band now. She looked at Maureen's dimpled ears.

She smelled perfume. Something faint and flowery. Tea rose, maybe. Or lilac. Her own skin never smelled of anything stronger than Ivory soap and baby powder. "Ninety-nine and ninety-nine one-hundredths pure," Todd had called her, but she hadn't thought until after he left that maybe he wasn't giving her a compliment.

"Well," she said. "The nurses were all kind of worried about you."

"Worried!" Maureen said. "I didn't know where he was! He didn't call me until this morning."

"Could I get some juice, do you think?" Jim said.

He was cloud-headed. He tentatively touched the bandage on his head. She brought him juice he vaguely sipped at, aspirins he had difficulty swallowing. She didn't want to leave. She adjusted the light; she fiddled with the bed, smoothing the covers, cranking it up until Jim, baffled, lifted his hand for her to stop.

"If you need anything..." Lila's voice trailed away.

"You know, I think this baby could use some milk," Maureen said, resettling Joanna on her lap. Lila hesitated. "Could you fill her bottle, do you think?" She flexed her body toward a heavy brown leather bag in the corner, then turned back to Jim. "You like the doctor?" she asked him. "You think she's good?"

"Maureen, she's fine," Jim said.

Lila stooped, dipping her hands into the bag, fumbling over keys and a stash of tissues before she pulled out the bottle.

She brought back heated formula, fitting it into Maureen's willing hands. "Well, you ring if you need anything," she said.

All that afternoon she sat with a twenty-year-old coma victim. She massaged her arms and legs; she told her hospital gossip. Even though there was a photograph of a young man on the bed stand, Lila was the only person in the room that day.

It was just dinnertime in the hospital. Lila stepped out into halls crowded with visitors and dinner carts and evening medication. She went to get Jim's medication.

When she got to his room Maureen was outside, squinting in at Jim's sleeping form. "I'll come back," she said. "I could use a cup of coffee anyway." Lila didn't mention that she was about to wake Jim for his medicine. Instead she nodded, then waited until Maureen was on the elevator before she reentered his room and roused him gently. He looked faintly shocked, resurfacing from sleep.

"Your wife's getting coffee," she said cheerfully.

He bolted up from the bed, his face bleaching. "Hey!" Lila said, staying him with one grab of her hand. Wincing, he fell back against the bed.

"*Where?*" he said. "Where is she?"

Lila studied him. "Maureen said she'd be right back."

"Maureen?" he said. He drew himself up against the pillow, stiffening. "Maureen's not my wife."

"Oh." Lila rolled the ridged paper cup of pills in her hand. He seemed to be in a kind of trance, moving away from her, and suddenly Lila didn't want to be invisible. She took his hand, peeling apart the fingers and positioning a single blue pill in the center. He frowned down at it and then up at her. "I'll pour you some water," she said, reaching for the pitcher.

Lila knew Maureen was in the room before she saw her. There was that murmur of cloth, that strange faint perfume.

"Look what I stole," Maureen said, holding up a flopping stack of glossy magazines. "I took them from the waiting room downstairs," she said cheerfully. "No one saw a thing."

Lila began to watch Maureen. When she arrived it was always alone, never with a husband or a friend or anyone except for Joanna. But she never kissed more than Jim's cheek or held more than the baby on her lap. Lila watched Jim, but she didn't know how to ask him again where his wife was then, or an even more interesting question: Was Maureen his married older girlfriend?

She didn't know whom to ask. Certainly not Jim's doctor, a woman named Addie Phearson, who considered families annoying satellites around her patients and who refused to gossip.

Lila leaned thoughtfully along the front desk. Debby was sorting files. "You think Maureen's his girlfriend?" Lila said. Debby burst out laughing. "She's got a few years on him, don't you think? And anyway, what do you care?" she wanted to know. "I'm just curious, that's all," Lila said. But it had been a mistake to ask Debby anything. "You like them like that, with their heads like bruised fruits?" Debby said. From then on, when Lila walked toward Jim's room, Debby called out, "So how's Romeo?" Another nurse, leaning along the wall, snorted. "Romeo who?" said Lila.

She pretended she wasn't interested. One morning she even got on the same elevator Maureen did and rode all the way up to the fourth floor with her, and the only conversation they had was about Jim's stitches. It wasn't until Maureen was veering toward Jim's room that Lila suddenly tapped her. "Is Mrs. Archer coming?" she said. Maureen's face tightened. She seemed to be thinking about something. "Oh, I doubt that," she said slowly, and then turned into Jim's room.

Jim's wife continued not to show, and after the first week even Maureen began coming a little less. Joanna had a cold. She had caught it, and now the two of them were suffering in a cacophony of sneezes and snuffles and hard, tearing coughs. Lila began bringing Jim the magazines Maureen used to. She sat by his bed when she could and tried to talk about everything except how she felt.

He seemed happy to see her. The TV was on, background noise. "Company," he said. "Just talk to me for a minute. Come on, sit down."

He held up a copy of a tabloid. "Look, a human skeleton was found on the moon," he said.

"Uh-huh," Lila said.

"They have dead celebrities in here giving advice," he told her. "They try to match you up with the right celebrity. Like if you're a musician and you want to know if you should kick out the drummer, they hook you up with Elvis."

"Elvis was last spotted living on a horse farm in Arkansas," Lila said. "He's not one to give advice." She sat down beside him.

She glanced at the TV. Godzilla was stomping on a building, and idly she began to watch. He thought she was being kind, that was all, sitting with him watching some meteor-headed monster chewing snakes and flinging humans like a happy game of pickup sticks into the air. He drifted asleep, and when he woke, startled, there was a buzz of sound. He saw the TV in a haze of sleep. Mothra rose in front of him in the dark, fluttering dusty wings, and then, beside him, he noticed Lila. She was hunched forward, her mouth slightly open, her hair falling into the collar of her uniform. He laughed, and abruptly she straightened, embarrassed. "You love this stuff, don't you," he said.

"I like being scared."

He scavenged around the night table for his watch. "You didn't have to stay with me," he said. "I know how busy it is here."

She shrugged, laughing. "Well, the thing is," she said, "my shift was over a half hour ago. I just figured by the time I got home, the movie would be over." She riffled her hands through her hair. "And you did look semiawake."

He began to look forward to her visits. He kept telling her stories, nothing substantial, just the barest edges of his life, the things that didn't hurt. He told her about the Top Thrift. He told her about mixing chemicals in his Mr. Science set when he was a kid, and how that's kind of what he was doing now, studying pharmacology. He talked a lot about his daughter. She could recognize her own toes, he said. Wasn't that amazing? She knew the color blue. He asked her a million questions about her life. Where did she live? Did she like nursing? Did she ever feel like just giving it all up and taking off somewhere?

"Where would I go?" Lila said.

"I don't know, anywhere," Jim said, but Lila just laughed.

He was silent for a moment. His mood seemed to shift. He lowered himself into the thicket of sheets and blankets. He looked at Lila for a moment, so still and miserable it started to make her afraid. "Hey," she said, and suddenly he looked back at her and smiled.

"You've known Maureen a long time?" she said.

"Sure," he said. "Sure I have."

"She's nice."

"Oh, she's great."

She looked at her watch. She was off shift in ten minutes. "Is your wife coming to see you?" she said.

He picked up one of the tabloids.

"Is she?" said Lila.

Jim looked up from the newspaper. "Eventually," he said.

The next morning Maureen was back with Joanna, the two of them with chapped pink noses. Jim looked at Maureen with a smile so pure and dazzled that it hurt Lila to see it.

She felt edgy all that day. She brought him his juice and watched him pour a little into a paper cup and hand it to Maureen. She walked out of the room just as if he were an ordinary patient, a man she could never see again and not care about. All that day she had wanted to check back with Jim, but a boy in 4C threw up all that afternoon from chemotherapy, and by the time she was able to get back to his room, Jim was asleep. She sat by the bed for a while.

She spent one whole afternoon lunch hour at the cosmetics counter of Bloomingdale's trying on different scents, letting the saleswoman talk her into a quarter ounce of a scent called Unforgetta-ble. Anyone would want to look prettier. Anyone would like the scent of lilacs behind their knees, in the shadowy slope of an arm.

A crush. That's what it was. Silly and unsubstantial and totally without reason. Inappropriate, her mother would scorn. Your heart didn't flutter over a man who had a wife, a man who seemed to have a girlfriend. She was just on the rebound, going from one ridiculous man to another.

She knew all about cures. She began spending more time with her other patients, reading the TV listings to Mrs. Ames, the woman with a broken hip, who never once switched on the TV. She massaged the coma patient's legs and spoon-fed lime Jell-O to a man in traction.

Lila got through the days, but at night she became uncomfortable, she couldn't eat. Nights she paced her apartment. The rooms seemed too small to contain her.

Lila was in the emergency room covering for another nurse the morning Jim was released. She was fitting an IV into an asthma patient. "How long do I have to be on this thing?" the patient, a young woman with long frizzy black curls, said impatiently, rationing her words with labored slow wheezes of breath. "I have a right to know. I need to tell my boyfriend. He's out there watching *Mutiny on the Bounty* on the TV in the waiting room, and he hated it the first time he saw it. How long?"

"As long as it takes," Lila said, irritated. The woman's eyes flashed, and she started to say something when a bout of coughing silenced her. Lila helped her to sit, thinking all the time of Jim leaning on Maureen's arm, shuffling out of bed.

She was relieved in less than two hours. It would have been enough time for her to get to the room and say good-bye, for her to slip her card into his pocket. "If you need a home nurse," she might say. Instead, though, she leaned along the cool white expanse of wall and imagined Jim being driven home, crowded on the front seat with Maureen and his daughter.

It didn't matter. She began working double shifts; she dated a clerk from the bookstore downtown who brought her hardbacks the way other men brought roses, and after a while, like any fever, her feelings toward Jim began to burn themselves out, dwindling nearly to ash, not igniting again until nearly a year later.

All that year Jim continued to look for Lee, but after the accident he began looking a little less. The car wreck had arced his feelings toward her closer to anger. She had left him. He had almost been killed looking for her. He had a daughter who might have been orphaned, and to his great wonder she was a daughter he was more and more in love with.

It terrified him, the way he could love her. In the morning she toddled into his bed and sang gibberish into his ear. She lifted her arms in small perfect parabolas for him to pluck her up and hold her. She made him pay attention to his life. When he caught her rolling in the dust in the kitchen, webs of it filmed along her corduroy overalls, he mopped her off and then did the floors. When she cried he remembered dinner. He had to sleep because he had to be awake enough in the morning to tend to her. He had to exercise because he had to stay well.

It unnerved him a little, seeing her grow, watching her become less dependent upon him. He watched her struggling to walk away from him, tottering from foot to foot, and, hating himself, he scooped her up and pinned her against his lap. "Stay," he said the way you might to a recalcitrant dog. He saw danger everywhere. He hated to buy milk because of the pictures of missing children printed on the side panels. He'd buy milk only in clear glass bottles. Every time a car passed the street, he went to look for his daughter. The only person he had ever trusted to baby-sit was Maureen, and even then he had his doubts. Maureen was the one who walked right up to the lost cars that strayed into the neighborhood to ask cheerfully if they needed directions. If she liked the people doing the asking, she might even let them inside her house to use the phone instead of offering to make the calls for them herself, the way you were supposed to. She might end up serving them a slice of homemade coffee cake and a cup of decaf to wash it down. He couldn't help himself from checking up on her. Once, when he was at school, he called to check on her so many times that Maureen, disgustedly trying to make a peach pie, finally just unplugged the phone. "Anything happens, you'll be the first to know," she promised. He made them both crazy with his imaginings. He wouldn't let Joanna alone for two minutes. Maureen came over one day to talk to him to find Joanna leashed into a bright blue baby harness that was wrapped about Jim's hand. "New pet?" she said acidly, watching the baby struggle. "For heaven's sake, take that thing off. You want to give her a complex?"

"I thought it was a good idea," he said lamely, but Maureen roughly took it off the baby. "Maybe you should have named her Fido," she said.

It astonished Jim how much she grew, how much she didn't look like her mother at all. When she turned two the blond hair she had inherited from Lee had turned pale walnut, and her eyes were flat black stones. Of course she didn't look at all like him, either, although he searched for similarities, as if sharing a nose might bind them together. The only hint of Lee was a kind of frightening dreamy quality. "Entering the zone," he called it when he saw her staring out into space. What did a toddler have to daydream about? How much life was there for her to start reimagining it? He tried to get her active. He took her to parks and zoos, and still he would see her dreaming.

She was in love with stories. She'd sit curled in his lap, her small face intent while he rambled on about Snow White or Little Red Riding Hood. She sat for hours, rocking her dolls, whispering secrets he couldn't hear.

One day Maureen gave her a red toy truck. For the first time that he could remember, Joanna became animated. He was delighted at first, but then, watching her, he became uneasy. She was suddenly playing with furious determination, so intently she didn't notice him crouching down beside her. She furrowed roadways into her sandbox. She zoomed the truck toward a destination. "Where's that road go to?" he asked her. She noticed him. "Everywhere," she said calmly, and he suddenly imagined Joanna at fourteen, slamming out a rusty door with the same dangerous aplomb her mother had had, taking off in the dirty back of a Greyhound bus, her pockets full of maps.

He began reading child care books, carrying Dr. Spock with him on top of his pharmacology texts. He began to be even more overprotective, warning her of cut glass in the puddles she wanted to jump, of bees in the backyard hedges she was tunneling through. She frowned, worried; she retracted her small hand from the hedge and put it behind her back. "Stay with Daddy," he said. He saw with satisfaction that his overprotectiveness began to work; it began to make her shy. He saw Maureen one day coaxing Joanna to leap across a furrow in the dirt. "I'll fall," Joanna said. "You big silly," said Maureen, urging her with a wiggle of fingers, until Joanna began to cry. Jim strode across the lawn. "Let's go inside," he soothed. "Jim..." said Maureen, but he ignored the way she was planting her hands on her hips, the way she was shaking her head in disbelief. He led his daughter to the house.

Every week he showed his daughter the photo albums, pointing out Lee to her. "Mama," he said, repeating it over and over, and after a while Joanna could point and recognize the face she had never seen. He kept taking pictures of his daughter, too, putting them in an album and labeling them, imagining presenting them to Lee. Other times he imagined hiding them from her because she didn't deserve to see pictures.

He hated the way time moved on. He hated the change of seasons he had once loved, hated even listening to the evening news because Lee was no longer on it. He hated it, too, when clothes he had bought when Lee was with him began to fray. He couldn't bear getting rid of them; it seemed almost as though he were getting rid of Lee. He wore the same green sweater he had worn on the Greyhound bus with Lee, the time they had run away to get married. The yarn was bitten through with age, his cotton shirt showed through the holes. Joanna, too, was getting older. He couldn't keep her from having friends, from going to school. She might not always need him.

She slept through the nights now. He sat on his porch and listened restlessly to the night. Maureen was over less and less these days. She was learning to play tennis with Mel; she said it was better for her marriage to be a sport with Mel than to sit out on Jim's porch with him so often.

Jim understood it. He didn't blame her. He began to want to be central in the life of someone other than a child. He wanted someone of his own. He was suddenly, violently angry with Lee. He had a right to a life; he had a right to fill the endless time she had left him with some comfort.

Idly he began to look around. The women around there knew his reputation. He saw the way women looked at him at school, how all he had to do was walk by and the whispering would start. The only women who seemed to want him were the crazy ones, the ones who handwrote him letters telling him that all he needed was a little understanding, the ones who sent him smashed apple pies that he always threw out, because his detective had told him you never knew what might be in there.

The evening Jim would run into Lila again was one when he was looking for Lee. He had driven an hour away from his home to follow up a lead a phone caller had whispered to him. "A blondie is singing at the Sky Bar and Grill," the voice rasped, so low he couldn't tell if it was male or female. "I saw the pictures, I know who's who. If I'm right, I want the reward."

"Who is this?" Jim said.

"What's that got to do with anything?" the voice said, surprised, and then hung up.

Jim had driven to the Sky Bar. The worst moment for him was always right before he opened any door, that second when anything might be possible, when miracles could happen. He pushed at the door with the flat of his hand. The bar was brightly lit and half-empty, and in one corner a young woman with a long blond braid in a tight red sparkly dress was standing by a piano, a microphone in her hand, singing "Blue Bayou." She belted it out, but no matter how she kept speeding her words, she was always a bar or two behind the man who was playing the piano, a lanky blond who kept glowering at her. She fanned long red fingernails into the air for emphasis, and she ignored Jim as much as she ignored the piano player and every other customer there, and finally he got up and left, swinging the door behind him. He had been too depressed to go right home, so he stopped at a Thrift-T-Mart to pick up some groceries, to wander the aisles a bit. He remembered when such a thing had made him miss his father, but now he found it a comfort.

He was buying baby food and cheese. He picked up three kinds of chocolate cookies and a packaged apple pie. He probably wouldn't eat half the things he had bought for himself, but he liked having them in the house. It made it seem as though he were living. He felt tired, worn out. He rounded the aisle and saw a man in a blue denim shirt tilting a woman's face up to his, kissing her over a loaf of family-size rye. She held out a can of cat food to one side. Jim's stomach plummeted with longing. Swiveling his cart, he went down another aisle, past a young woman singsonging her grocery list to her toddler riding in the cart. At the far end two women were laughing. Both, Jim thought, were beautiful. One had a very long blond ponytail that reminded him of Lee. She was small and thin, and she looked up and saw Jim, and her gaze became suddenly hostile. Jim suddenly felt as if he were in a foreign land. He turned down another aisle. He thought about going back to an empty house, studying for an exam he already knew cold. He had three numbers posted by the phone that he could call, and only one of them belonged to anyone he could consider a friend. He thought how nice it would be just to share a burger with someone, to go to a movie and forget everything but what you wanted on your popcorn.

He was rounding the corner toward the frozen pot pies when he felt someone staring at him. For a moment there was that dazzling second of hope. He was stunned in place, certain he'd turn and find Lee. He sipped a breath and then turned. A woman with straight red hair grazing her small chin, a sheath of bangs nearly hiding her eyes, dressed in baggy white painter's pants and a white T-shirt, stood staring at him. She had a cabbage poised in one hand, and she smiled at him uncertainly. She nodded. He felt himself deflating. He was used to stares. Women used to follow him, wanting the danger they were sure he had in him, wanting to be the one who would right whatever wrong was in him. Disgusted, he started to turn, but the woman walked toward him. "What?" he said, annoyed.

"Lila Gleason, remember?" she said. "I was one of your nurses. Last year."

"The nurse," he said, a memory flickering.

"You look all healed," she said.

"You look all different," he told her.

"I know, I know, the red threw you off," she said, pointing to her bright sneakers.

There was a moment of silence. A woman in a blue silk dress bumped her cart into Lila. "I'd like to get to the cauliflower," she said politely. Lila sidestepped.

"How's your baby?" Lila said politely.

Jim beamed. "Joanna? She's great," he said.

"How's your wife?" He still wore a wedding band.

"My wife?" Jim said.

"Uh, how's Maureen," Lila said quickly.

Jim started. "Maureen's fine," he said, surprised.

Lila glanced at the bruised-looking melons. "Please," he had cried. "Well," she said, embarrassed. She picked up a melon, rolling it in her hands.

Something moved in Jim's face. He remembered her in the hospital, a slim flash of white through his room. He remembered waking to Mothra on his TV screen, waking to her sitting beside him quietly even though her shift was already over. He watched her rocking on her sneakered heels, her red hair sweeping toward her face. She was wearing these earrings, small silvery-and-blue Saturns dangling from sparkling chains, like stars you might wish upon. "So listen," he said. "Have you had dinner?"

---8---

Lila told herself that she was having dinner with Jim the way she would with any friend she hadn't seen in a long time. If her palms were prickling, if her face seemed flushed, it was probably just the over-air-conditioned supermarket or the fact that she had skipped lunch again.

She told herself no one was fooling anyone. Anyone could see the gold band Jim wore, so large it nearly covered his knuckle. Anyone could see how any light in his eyes stayed dimmed, how his gaze danced around. And anyone could see just how little he could offer.

They ended up walking to a cafe five blocks away from the market. They sat in a brightly lighted red booth and ordered burgers and shared a basket of fries. Lila sifted salt across her share of fries, stopping only when she saw Jim watching her.

"That your favorite food?" Jim grinned.

"No, sugar is," Lila said. She pronged a fry with her fork. "You must be almost finished with pharmacy school," she said. "Are you going to practice around here?"

Someone glided past the table, and Jim looked up, his face intent. Lila, baffled, followed his gaze until he refocused on her. "Yup," he said.

"How come you didn't choose to be a doctor?"

"How come you didn't?" Jim said.

"Hey, I *like* nursing."

"Hey, I *like* pharmacy."

She beamed at him. "What a pair," she said.

A couple walked past them. The woman in a red chiffon skirt

scowled. "Because I don't want to, that's why," the woman said. The man beside her shook his head. "You always got to argue, don't you," he said. Jim looked over at him.

"I'll go to the ladies' room if you like, then you can scope out the room all you like," Lila suggested.

"I'm sorry," Jim said. "I don't know what to tell you except I just can't help it." Lila sighed. Jim looked uncomfortable. "I keep thinking I might see my wife."

Startled, Lila pushed the fries away from her. "Is she supposed to be here?" she said.

"She's not here," he said. "I mean, I don't know where she is." He looked at the table miserably. "Look," he said. He laced his fingers into a kind of fist and lightly bumped it against the Formica tabletop. "She disappeared."

"Disappeared?" said Lila.

"Two years ago." He unthreaded his fingers and stretched them on the table, studying the nails. "It was in all the papers," he said. "You must have read about it."

Lila studied him thoughtfully. "No, I didn't."

"You didn't?" He looked at her askance. "You must have. It got a lot of coverage. It was terrible."

"Maybe I did," she said slowly. "I don't know. There's lots of terrible stories in the news."

"How could you not remember? There were all these pictures. There was my picture." He drummed his fingers across the Formica.

She stared at him. "Look, I said I didn't know," she said finally. "You don't have to look at me like that." She ringed her hands about her frosty glass. "So what happened?" she said quietly.

He spoke so quickly, she had to lean forward to hear him. He didn't use past tenses when he spoke but told the story in the present. He didn't seem to be remembering; his stories about Lee were as immediate as Lila was. His pain seemed so newly minted, it almost hurt her to hear it.

Lila pleated the top of her straw uneasily. She sucked at the Coke, which was flat and syrupy. Once, he dipped his head, and she was abruptly struck by the curve of his neck.

She didn't venture her opinions. She didn't know any more than Jim did why his wife might have vanished. Fascinated, she tried to imagine a young woman on the road, her thumb out, but all she saw was herself, sudden and new in that old scene, and Jim was racing after her. She didn't think Lee was coming back. A woman that young, alone on the road, without any skills, didn't stand a chance. And if Lee wasn't dead, then how else could you explain a two-year silence other than a clear indication of disinterest?

The more he spoke of his love for Lee, the more lost and confused she felt. She couldn't figure out what it was Jim wanted with her, and it made her uncomfortable. She didn't much like this. He talked in a rush; he didn't see her.

Finally he slumped back against the red vinyl booth. He put two awkward hands flat on the counter. "I shouldn't have told you," he said.

"Oh—" She shrugged.

"I tell myself, You're not going to talk about Lee, I'm determined, and then before I know it, it just spills out." He retracted both hands into his lap. "I just can't figure out why I can't find her," he said helplessly. He looked suddenly less vivid to her.

"You're falling asleep," she said.

"No, no, I'm fine," he said. He squinted myopically at his watch, a black face on a sturdy brown leather band. "But maybe we should just get the check."

He walked her back to the market in a silence so complete, she felt smothered by it. By the time they reached the parking lot, she was exhausted from the lack of sound. The air around her seemed to be vibrating. "Well, I'll see you," she said, trying to sound airy.

He looked at her, surprised. "Don't be silly," he said. "I'll walk you to your car."

They wound in and out of lanes of bright Chevys and sedans, edging past mothers juggling kids and groceries, men loaded down with bags. "My car," he pointed out, and Lila stared at a rusting sedan in such terrible shape that she was surprised someone hadn't towed it away. She peered in. The seats were peeling beige vinyl, although his was covered with some sort of fake beige fur that was much too hot for the summer. In the back was a red baby seat. She told herself it was just as well they wouldn't see each other again, that it was foolishness to expect even as simple a thing as friendship from a man who couldn't seem to properly groom the car he depended on.

"There I am," she said, pointing to a little white coupe.

He laughed. "Of course your car would be white."

"Pure accident," she said.

He shifted weight from one black sneaker to another. He listed in the thick stubborn heat, and then he moved toward her, smoothing her collar flat, making her start from his touch. Awkwardly he stepped back. "So thanks for sharing dinner with me," he said.

"Thanks yourself," she said. She turned, opening up her clean car, and scooted inside. She could watch him through the window. He was hunched over, hands hooked into the belt loops of his jeans. No one had said anything about anyone seeing anyone again, including her. She pushed the car into reverse. He didn't move when she backed it out of the spot.

She turned toward the exit, her mood plummeting. She got to the exit sign and pressed her foot on the gas, speeding through the exit back onto the highway.

Lila might have felt nothing was possible between them, but Jim knew he was going to call her. It pleased him a little that he could suddenly be in control over some aspect of his life. Lila was bright and funny and pretty, and he liked it that they shared at least a little history. She had seen him bruised and dull in the hospital; she had neither recoiled nor showed the kind of yearning interest other dates had when he told them about Lee.

Telling her had been a release. Sometimes he thought if he told the story of Lee's disappearance enough times, if he made it real enough, he might be able to script a different ending. While he was talking about Lee to Lila, he tried to lock eyes with her, to gauge what she was thinking. He couldn't really tell, but it was strange how there were moments in the conversation when he saw how her eyes were flecked with chinks of green light, how her freckles were the color of the honey he sometimes spooned into his tea.

That night, when he slept, he dreamed about her. He was in a strange city, looking for Lee. Suddenly, walking toward him, was Lila. Her hair was so red, it looked like crayon. Her skin was so white, it was nearly blinding. She looked almost like a cartoon. She came right up to him, wearing her starchy nurse's uniform. "We're almost there," she said, and her voice was so soothing, he took the hand she gave him. She led him down a side street, over a rocky ground. "This way," she said cheerfully. "See it?" She pointed to something shimmering in the distance. "Look closer," she suggested, and then, abruptly, he woke up.

His heart wasn't hammering. His breathing was even. He felt calm, as if someone had been holding him close, rocking him gently all night long. He sat up and reached for the phone.

"I don't know if this is such a good idea," Lila told him. She leaned along the cool white of her kitchen wall, holding on to the phone, trying to still her jumpy pulse.

"We'll have a good time," he promised.

She looked across her empty kitchen. She had a frozen lamb chop she could eat. She had a book about physics, written for the layperson, that she wanted to read. Quasars, she thought. Quarks and nanoseconds.

"Come on, come on, come on," he said. "What the hell."

"Lucky for you I love restaurants," she said finally.

This time dinner was different. She was surprised to see he was wearing a jacket and that he had slicked back his fine blond hair and put on some kind of lime-smelling after-shave. He looked hopeful and friendly, and he took her arm and helped her into his car. She was startled too at just how nice the restaurant he chose was. It was called Island and was quietly decorated all in deep blues and greens, with violet nets stretched across the walls. As soon as Lila walked in, she wished she had worn her blue dress instead of an old skirt. She wished she had put on her lavender-and-silver earrings. They sat at a small table in the corner, with a single gold candle glowing shadows across the white tablecloth.

She braced herself, but he didn't mention Lee at all. She suspected, though, that Lee was there in the way he clenched his hands about the soup spoon, that Lee was there in the stiff way he held his head, as if any moment it would start swiveling around like radar, searching for his wife.

He told her about the supermarket where he had learned how to tell the difference between a sweet melon and a sour one, where he had learned to bag so expertly that he still did his own in the markets. "I annoy all the baggers," he said proudly. He showed her pictures of Joanna and asked her about nursing.

He insisted she order dessert, though she had eaten so much she felt vaguely ill. "No, have the chocolate mud pie," he said, waving over the waiter. The cake, as black as tar, with clouds of cream on either side, sat in the center of the table. She made delicate pinpoints in the frosting with her fork. "Eat some," he said, and she lifted a spoonful, sticky and sweet, to her mouth.

He didn't seem to want the evening to end. He let his coffee get cool, and then he ordered another and let it cool off, too. He ordered a walnut liqueur he barely touched, and then he ordered one for her, too. And when the check finally came, he took so long paying it that the waiter came meaningfully over. "Anything else, sir?" he said, dipping faintly toward the table.

"No, we're fine," Jim said.

He sat talking to her for another half hour, and then, finally, he stretched. "Well," he said. "I guess we should go."

He drove her home. He was about to turn down her street when suddenly he slowed the car. "Would you like to see Joanna?" he said.

She looked at him.

"She never goes to sleep when I go out." He flexed the rearview mirror. "She's really beautiful."

"I remember she was a pretty baby," Lila said. "Sure. All right."

"Good," he said. He didn't say much to her while he was driving, and then suddenly he was swerving into a drive and the front door was suddenly opening. Maureen. Lila recognized her from the hospital, only now Maureen was in blue jeans and a black sweater, and her hair was longer, tied back in a sloppy braid.

"Well, hello," Maureen called. She left the front door open and came out onto the steps. "I know you, don't I?"

"Think white," Lila said, stepping out of the car. Maureen furrowed her brow in concentration. "Think thermometers," said Lila, and then Maureen laughed. "Of course. The little nurse."

"Not so little," said Lila.

"Joanna's asleep," Maureen said. "We played six games of throw the playing cards up in the air and two games of hide the spoon. Then she was finally pooped."

Maureen might have been talking to Jim, but the whole time Lila felt she was looking at her. Lila slicked her hair from her face. She shifted from one foot to another and noticed how scuffed her pumps were, how her blouse had a faint chocolate stain from dinner.

"Thanks, Maureen," Jim said.

"Thanks yourself. I love Joanna. Though I could do without hide the spoon." She glanced next door. "Well, I better tend to my own garden now." She smiled at Lila. "Nice to see you out of a hospital," she said.

"Come in anyway," Jim said to Lila. "You can look at Joanna asleep." He smiled at her uncertainly.

She didn't know why, but she half expected that the inside of Jim's house might be a kind of shrine to Lee, with photographs of her lining the walls. Instead there were only a few framed photographs. On the mantel was a small picture of Lee and Jim. She tried not to peer too closely. She pretended she was admiring a Chinese vase perched on the edge of the mantel. She could see how young they both looked. They were both in blue jeans, both in jeans jackets and boots, posed like outlaws in mean rangy stances, their hips jutting out. Jim was looking at Lee in a kind of dizzy rapture. Somehow that one photo upset her more than if the whole mantel had been crammed with them. She glanced over at Jim, but he was leaning along the far wall, studying her.

"What?" she said, but he just shrugged and smiled.

He gave her a slow, careful tour. He showed her Joanna sleeping. He squired her through his too small, too clean kitchen, his tiny bath and messy dining room, crammed with books and newspapers. His bedroom had nothing in it but a large double bed with a blue chenille bedspread across it. The alarm clock was on the floor, and beside the bed was a colored photograph of Lee, her hair blown across her face. She was staring into the camera, half smiling and mysterious, and as soon as Lila saw that smile, she felt ill. This time Jim followed her stare. "Lee," he said. He picked up the photograph, carefully fingering the surface as if he were reading it like braille. "She's pretty, isn't she," he said.

"Could I have some water?" Lila said. The cake she had eaten was now making her queasy. He led her to the kitchen, where he fitted a cold cup of water into her hand.

"I should get going," she said, putting down the glass, but before she had turned he had bent and gently kissed her. Startled, she flinched back.

He started to reach for her again. He had his fingers threaded through her hair, tilting her face toward a kiss.

She pulled back a bit. "All those drugs you work with," she said. "Can't you concoct one to take care of this?" She laid her head in the crook of his neck.

"This?" he said, suddenly swaying her into a dance. "Why would you want a drug to stop this?"

"No, not this," she said awkwardly.

"No, what?" he said.

"Oh, you know." She blinked at him. "Just last week you were scoping out every person in the diner thinking they might be Lee."

"Did I do that tonight?"

"No. Not tonight."

"She's my wife," he said finally.

She stepped back from Jim. "I guess I don't know what to do with that."

He was silent for a moment. "I guess I don't, either," he said. He rolled her from one arm to the other. "Look, just stay. Talk to me. If you like, you can just sleep here. We don't have to do anything."

"I can't just sleep."

He looked at her, his face uncertain. "I have sleeping pills," he said abruptly.

She started to laugh. "Sleeping pills?" she said. "Are we having a double suicide here?"

He laughed. "Over the counter. Safe as aspirin."

"No, I don't want them," she said.

"Let me put a movie on, then," he said. "If you want to go home afterward, you can."

He started for the living room. "I have forties' melodramas, I have science fiction, I have classics," he said. She trailed after him. He was on the floor, pulling out tapes from a shelf under the TV, scattering them on the floor. "Come on," he said. "Please. Don't go."

"All right, a movie," she said.

He put on a horror film, *Mars Needs Women*. She couldn't concentrate on it. She was too aware of Jim sitting beside her, his arms crossed across his chest. He had set aside three different movies, as if he expected they might watch all three. He kept changing positions, always with the edge of his body touching hers, connecting with a kind of warmth. They didn't talk much during the film, and the last scene Lila remembered, before she fell asleep beside him, there was a woman dressed in a gleaming black space suit, climbing a ladder into a shivering silver ship pointed toward the very middle of the sky.

When he woke in the morning, his head clouded, she was gone, and he felt a cold surge of fear. The TV was gray static fizz. He didn't remember falling asleep in his clothes, and he didn't remember her leaving. He felt the couch beside him as if there might be some of her warmth left there. He couldn't remember what he had dreamed, couldn't remember anything except that he had slept more deeply on his hardwood floor than he had ever slept on his Serta mattress. Six o'clock. Joanna wouldn't be up for another half hour. When he stood up, his back cramped.

He hadn't really expected to bring Lila back to the house with him. He had just wanted a nice dinner and some good conversation, and yet once she was inside the house, he was somehow afraid to let her leave. He kept making these lame excuses why she should stay. The worst was when he suggested sleeping pills. Jesus, what a fool. He shouldn't call her; he should just leave her alone, but instead he reached for the phone and called her home, and when she answered, his heart calmed. "I was worried," he said.

"About what?" she said.

"There was no note. I just woke up and you were gone."

"Oh. Well. Sorry," she said.

There was silence. "Let's have dinner tonight," he said.

She pushed out a breath. "I don't know," she said.

He was quiet for a moment. "What about a movie?"

He swore he could hear her breathing through the wires.

"All right," she said finally. "But I get to pick it."

Every time Jim was with Lila, he felt somehow calmer, but Lila felt that she was going insane. She didn't quite trust the way she felt about him. The whole situation confounded her. When she wasn't with him, she worried the situation like an animal with a scrap bone. Was it having an affair with a married man if his wife had disappeared? Was it courting pain to know that all Lee had to do was reappear and Lila would be as invisible to him as if she were the one who had vanished? Reluctantly she'd agree to see him again, and then there she'd be, sitting beside him watching some stupid movie she didn't even care about, and then his scent would be so pervasive, she felt she couldn't breathe the air. She was dizzy from wanting him, dizzier from resisting.

The first time he made love to her, he seemed to do it as if from a distance. Afterward, he helped her up from the bed, but he didn't look at her. He was distracted. She kept moving in front of him. She began making noise, scraping her feet, banging a chair, until Joanna woke up with small bleating cries. "Oh, Lord," Jim said. His face looked lined with exhaustion. A pang went through her.

He went into Joanna's room, coming out with her balanced sleepily on his hip. When she saw Lila, her damp mouth opened. "Look who's here," he said to each of them. Joanna gave a groggy stare. Lila lifted her hand weakly. "Hi," she said.

That morning Joanna was a kind of buffer. Jim talked to his daughter or about her all during breakfast, never quite making eye contact with Lila. He planted too many kisses on Joanna's downy cheeks. When Lila got up to get water, he gave her too wide a berth. He hummed and whistled to his daughter. He snapped jauntily about the sunny kitchen, all the time with Joanna balanced on his hip, and Lila suddenly knew that making love had been a mistake. She was never going to see him again.

She took up her routine again, working extra shifts, working out at the gym so hard that it was all she could do not to collapse back at home. Her feelings for Jim had passed before; they would pass again. She convinced herself her desire was growing fainter and fainter, and then one week later Jim called, shy and happy and so oblivious of her distress that she thought she might have dreamed it.

They didn't do much that night. They walked around the city, saw a movie, ate hot dogs from a vendor, and then he took her back to her place. When they began to make love, he started off just as distant as before. It was the oddest sensation. She was usually calmer in lovemaking, but with Jim she suddenly began to make herself known. She bit the hands he stroked across her. She repeated his name like an incantation. Her left leg was crushed beneath his, but she fought to make him somehow see her. She kept sitting up, changing position and shape, forcing him to follow her. She trailed her hair across his shoulders, into his face, making him see and feel how straight it was, how unlike Lee's frizzled tangle. She was taller than Lee, so she stretched her legs against his, drawing him face to face. She forced him to interact. "Tell me what you want," she said. "You like this? You like that?"

Afterward, they were both vaguely startled. "Are you all right?" he said. He pointed to the bruises along her arm. "Jesus. I'm a marked woman," she said.

She was happy sometimes. He became suddenly affectionate, always holding her hand, stroking her back, sometimes just lifting up a strand of hair. He sat with her out in his backyard until three in the morning, the two of them talking about everything except Lee. Sometimes she reminded herself that she was with a man who still wore his wedding band. If Lee came back, she would be gone. She told herself to take things for what they were. She played party games with herself. If she knew for certain Lee would be back within the year, would she give any of this up? And the answer, no matter how bruised and bottomless her despair that day, was always no.

She refused to call him her boyfriend, refused to consider she might be falling in love. Not when he was still looking for Lee. It didn't happen all the time, it didn't even happen all that often, but every once in a while he seemed triggered. He'd get jitters in his legs. He couldn't sit still or concentrate on what she was saying, and instantly she knew he was going to go out looking. He never asked her if she'd come along with him when he looked for Lee. He was smart enough not to. He never even mentioned the times he went out looking, but she always knew. He'd get suddenly preoccupied. He'd remember things she had said she needed to do, things she had to do alone. Or he'd tell her he was just running out for an errand, and would she wait. Usually she wouldn't. She'd make him call Maureen. She wouldn't be an accessory to an event she considered a kind of crime.

Sometimes, when she felt most blue, she dated other men. She let the other nurses fix her up; she accepted invitations from strange men in the hospital cafeteria. But all they had to do was one thing, and she became irritated. This one annoyed her because he hadn't read her favorite book. This one made her harden because he tipped the waiter only eight percent instead of twenty. She once refused a second date with a man simply because she didn't like the way he combed his hair. No one seemed to need her as much as Jim. No one ever looked at her with such astonished delight. He never saw any other woman, but she let him know she saw other men. She left the cards on the flowers she received. She turned up her answering machine so he could hear male voices. When he invited her places, she sometimes said "I can't," and she saw the way his face tightened. And sometimes, too, when he called her in the morning, she told him in a sleep-drugged voice that she couldn't talk right now. He didn't have the right to tell her not to see anyone but him, so he called her four times that day. And that evening he drove over with a handful of daisies. She always kept herself a little aloof, and sometimes she thought it was that aloofness that drew him to her, as if he thought she were in danger of disappearing, too.

One evening they were supposed to go to a night game of baseball. She wasn't much on sports, but the idea of sitting out under the stars with Jim appealed to her.

He was half an hour late, and when the phone rang she knew instinctively it was him. She tried to plan her first line, but what came out was, "You're late."

The connection was fizzy with static. She could hardly hear him. "I'm in D.C.," he said. He was panting so hard, he couldn't get the words out.

"We have a game to go to," she said, twisting her body toward the phone. Outside, she heard a bluejay.

"Listen, I got this *lead*," he said. "Someone called me out of the blue. Said there was this new woman that had moved in below him. Really young. Wouldn't talk." He gave a short laugh. "He wants a reward."

"Jim," she said.

"What do you want me to do?" he said quietly.

She went to the game herself. There was Jim's empty seat to her right, but on her left was a man with shaggy blond hair and a black sweater and jeans. He smiled cheerfully when he saw her and gallantly dusted her wooden seat. She let him flirt and buy her popcorn, and when she burst into tears toward the last inning, he turned to her. "Aw, honey, they lose all the time," he soothed, patting her arm, and she turned toward him and wept on his shoulder.

She couldn't help herself. She didn't answer her phone that day or the next, but she began missing him so much, she finally picked up the phone and called him herself, and all the while her life was spinning out of control.

She began not to depend on plans they might have because he was always breaking them. "Hire a detective, then," she said, but he told her he didn't trust them, that they were lazy, and anyhow he *had* hired one, and it hadn't done one thing except deplete his savings account.

She tried to keep control. She refused to watch the news with him because he kept trying to find Lee in a crowd scene, because every mysteriously murdered body made him go right to the phone to call the police. She didn't like long drives because he always ended up checking out a lead he had forgotten to tell her about.

She couldn't help herself. She kept asking him questions, but she couldn't bear to hear the answers. They were in the kitchen, peering into the open refrigerator for something to eat. "What would you do if all of a sudden Lee was in the kitchen buttering toast?" she said. Recoiling, Jim stared at her. "What would you do if one morning we were making love, and all of a sudden you opened your eyes and there was Lee in your arms?" She watched the color blanch from his face. He shut the refrigerator door. "Stop," he said. "Please."

She couldn't seem to stop herself. The next night, while they were walking to the car after a bad movie, holding hands, Lila blurted, "What if Lee was walking right toward us, right now? What would you do?"

"Don't," he said roughly. He let go of her hand.

"What would you do if in the movies—"

"I said *don't*," he said. He stopped walking and faced her angrily. "What do you expect me to say?"

"I think about it all the time," Lila said miserably. "Don't you? Think about it all the time?"

"I'll drive you home," he said wearily.

He wanted to know everything about her. Lila would regale him with exaggerated stories about her childhood, making each one more and more outrageous. There was the time she set fire to the doghouse with kitchen matches. The time she was trapped overnight in the dinosaur room at the museum. "More, more, I love it," he said. She told him every single story she could think of except for the one that had to do with her loving him. She wanted to tell him, to blurt it out like a hiccup, but it always seemed like the wrong moment. She watched him, reconsidering the hungry way he looked at her, the way he listened when she talked. Maybe he was falling in love with her.

The more she saw him, the happier he seemed with her and the more reasons she had not to break it off with him. And to her surprise, one of the reasons began to be Joanna. She had always loved babies. She used to like to walk through the maternity ward on her breaks, admiring the newborns, stopping to talk to the mothers. She herself couldn't have kids. Her first year of college she had been fitted for an IUD that gave her an infection so virulent her ovaries were left scarred. The doctor at the school infirmary had watched how still and serious Lila was and patted her weakly on the shoulder. "Nothing's ever for certain," he told her, but all Lila kept thinking of was the boy she had fitted herself with an IUD for and how suddenly she didn't even like him much anymore. It was funny how as simple a thing as pain could ruin things.

She got used to loving other people's kids—her friends' babies, the babies on the ward. And although she had expected to love Joanna, she hadn't expected how much.

She liked to take walks with Joanna on the street. Sometimes people told Lila how much Joanna looked like her, which always astonished and pleased her, though it certainly wasn't true. She bought a stethoscope for Joanna, a doctor's toy kit much like the one she herself had had as a little girl. "Listen," she whispered, sitting Joanna on her lap and positioning the stethoscope in the child's ear. "That's your heart," she said. They listened to each other's hearts, and once while she was in the kitchen getting a glass of juice, she overheard Joanna telling Jim that his heart sounded funny. "That's because it broke," he said. Lila poured her juice back into the jar.

She was easier with Joanna than Jim was. When he was with the child, he wouldn't let her let go of his hand. If she went down the slide, he would have to stand right beside it. When Joanna turned four he refused to put her into preschool. He said he intended to keep her out of kindergarten until she was six. "She doesn't have to grow up so fast," he said.

"For heaven's sake," Lila said.

Jim might have kept Joanna back physically, but he made up for it intellectually. Every other day he brought home a book for her or a thick yellow pad he helped her make her letters on. She had a toy cash register and all the shiny pennies and dimes he could collect for her, and every time he saw her staring dreamily into space, he clinked the change in his pockets, recapturing her attention. "Money for my honey," he told her, holding out his jangling handfuls.

Joanna never had one idea of anything she might be missing. She had books and new paints and a shower of coins. She had an adoring father and Lila and one whole album of a blond woman Jim told her was her mother. Some nights she'd romp into the living room and her father would just be sitting by the window, the album open, and when he saw her he'd beckon her over. He'd tell her about the pictures. How this one, of a woman with hair as long and as blond as Rapunzel's in her book, was her mother running off to Philadelphia to marry her daddy. How this woman, with her face all scared and tight, was her mother pregnant with her. Your mother loves you, her father told her. Your mother's far away on business and can't come home yet, he said, she can't even call. Joanna believed him. Every birthday she had a card from her mother, and Jim would hang it on the mantel for her. Lila always got angry, but she wouldn't say why, and anyway it wasn't at Joanna.

Jim kept telling her stories about Lee, and Joanna got Lee mixed up in her mind with the other stories Jim told her, stories about wild ducks and grandmothers who hid from wolves. Lee was as real to her as that. She drew pictures of Little Red Riding Hood, and one afternoon Jim came home to find she had put Lee's picture on her pillow, the covers pulled halfway up over the image. She was tilting a glass of lemonade to Lee's pictured lips. "My mother's tired and thirsty," Joanna said. "Her job away from us is hard."

He didn't stop her from sleeping with the picture beside her. He said nothing when she carried on conversations with it. It was only when she lost interest, when he found photos in the backyard rosebushes or on the damp floor of the bathroom, that he would admonish her. "That's not how you treat photographs," he told her. "They're irreplaceable," he said. "They're of your mother."

Joanna didn't feel the loss. And then when she turned five Lila began staying over more and more, and her mother's photograph album was put up in the closet, much too high for her to reach even if she had wanted to.

Lila began to be friends with Maureen. Summers, when she wasn't on her shift, and while Jim was working, the two women would sit outside on balding yellow plastic chaise longues, watching Joanna and talking.

"I like having you here," Maureen said.

Lila looked up, interested. "You do? Really?"

"Why wouldn't I?" Maureen said. "My husband's fine, Jim's more than fine, but what I need is female companionship."

"When I first met you, I thought you were Jim's lover," Lila said.

Maureen laughed, scooping her hair from her face. "There's a lot of strange things going on, but that wasn't one of them, honey." She stretched out her legs to brown them in the sun. "Why'd you think that?"

"The way you were together, I guess. You seemed like a couple."

"A couple of nuts," Maureen said.

"Do you miss Lee?" Lila said abruptly.

Maureen started. "Lee?" she said. "Not that one, I don't." She glanced over at Joanna, who was reading a book under the trees. She turned back to Lila. "Are you surprised?" she said. "I gave her the benefit of the doubt at first. What with the two of them being so bloody *young*. And then when she got pregnant, I used to hear her crying inside the house, and I felt so terrible I'd go and ring the door under some stupid pretense. Did she want to go shopping with me? Did she want a ride downtown? But she always just got stony-faced. Her face was so dry you'd never know she had cried." Maureen shrugged. "I always liked Jim," she said. "I thought liking Lee might just make everything easier."

"Mo!" cried Joanna. "What's this word!"

"Five years old and reading already! Smart as a whip, that one," said Maureen.

"Then why does he love her?" Lila said.

"Why does anyone love anyone?" Maureen said, and then lifted herself up to go to Joanna.

Jim told himself that any moment his new life was going to start. He finished school and got a job at Bateman's Pharmacy, just three blocks from the house. It was an old pharmacy, with a fountain and customers who told him how they had known the old pharmacist as a good friend and hoped to do the same with him.

He tried his best to let go. He had work he loved, he had a woman he loved, and still he was unhappy. Finally he went to a psychologist, a Dr. Gardener he had picked out of the Yellow Pages. The doctor wasn't much older than Jim, but he was carefully dressed in a suit. During the first session, Jim had barely settled onto the padded leather chair when the doctor began to talk.

"What you need to do is think of yourself as an alcoholic," the doctor finally said. "An alcoholic doesn't want to give up alcohol, the same way you don't want to give up your wife. But when he does, he sees he has a new life." Jim looked blank. "I'm *depressed*," he said.

The doctor shrugged. "I'm depressed, too," he admitted. "Do you honestly think that if there were a miracle pill to take for depression, I wouldn't be the first one in line?" He stood up, careful of the crease in his pants. "Get out there and *live*," the doctor suggested. "That's what I would do."

By the time the fifty minutes were up, Jim felt as if he were drowning. He had stopped listening to the doctor altogether but instead concentrated on the details of his dress. The doctor had a tiny brass sailboat tie tack. He wore jade cuff links and cashmere socks. When Jim handed him a check, the doctor placed it under a cut-glass paperweight.

Sometimes he felt like a bigamist. He was beginning to love Lila, but his love for Lee was so unresolved. Every time there was a report about Lee, he was off looking. He didn't think about Lila or Joanna or anyone. Not until the moment he found out it wasn't Lee at all, and then they would all come crashing down around him, and he would miss Lila. He would need his daughter.

Lila, furious, would sometimes refuse to see him. She threatened to leave him.

"That's it, I'm moving to Bermuda," she sputtered once in the fray of an argument.

"Bermuda? Pink roofs and too much sun?"

"There's nothing to keep me here. They need nurses in Bermuda."

"Don't go," he said. "You'll fry and blister in the sun."

"Well, then behave," she said.

She kept telling him she was going to Bermuda. "Ha, ha, big joke," he said, but every time she was angry with him, she furiously taped up a ripped magazine page about Bermuda. Or sometimes not Bermuda at all. Any kind of beach scene would do, and once, in a pinch, she had used a newspaper sale ad on swimsuits from Macy's. He could tell when she was less angry, because then she'd take down the clippings, but what worried him was the fact that she never threw them out, just kept them in a shoebox in her closet. "Hoarding ammunition?" he said.

"I just like some of the pictures," she said.

She had the trip planned out; she knew where she'd stay, how she'd live. She had enough savings. "You'd come back," he said. "You'd miss Baltimore."

She gave him a thoughtful look. "I might come back," she said. "But I wouldn't come back to you."

He didn't really mean to stand her up. He hadn't even been the one to do the seeking. The detective he had once hired years ago had called him, saying he had word about a woman who might be Lee, just twenty minutes away.

"Guess I wasn't the asshole you thought I was," he said.

Jim drove all the way over there to look at some blurred photographs of a woman coming out of a grocery store. She had a kerchief tied about her head, and long blond hair, but even in the blurred photo he could tell it wasn't Lee.

"How do you know?" the detective said. "I found out something. This one goes by the initials L.A. She works as a typist in a typing pool."

"It's not Lee," he said. He was suddenly exhausted. There were lots of women with strange identities wandering around the planet, endless leads that frayed and tangled and led to nowhere. Lee could be alive or she could be dead, but in any case, for the first time, he had this sudden feeling that she was really gone. He thought of the long drive home. The air in the detective's hotel room was stale with cigarettes, and there was an old Danish crumbling away in an ashtray.

"She has no Social Security number."

"I don't care. It isn't Lee." He got up, and when he noticed the clock, he realized he was three hours late for the play he had bought tickets to, and Lila couldn't even go by herself because the tickets were in his breast pocket.

The detective let him use the phone, but Lila wasn't there.

"So?" the detective said.

"I'll be in touch," Jim said, and let himself out. The whole drive home he thought of Lila waiting for the tickets and him. He kept stopping at rest stops to call her, but the line kept ringing and never seemed to catch.

He went to find her at work the next day. She was wheeling a patient to X-ray, and she nodded at him the way she might acknowledge a total stranger. "Listen," he said, but she shook her head, cutting him off.

"I waited for three hours. I thought you were dead."

"I'll get new tickets. We'll go next week."

"I don't want to see that play anymore."

She angled the patient toward the elevator. "You followed a lead, didn't you."

He shrugged.

"I can't do this anymore," she said suddenly. "I really am leaving. I'm going to Bermuda."

He smiled at her, relieved.

"No," she said. "You don't understand. I really am."

She punched for the elevator. "Think where you'd like to go to dinner this Friday," he said. Her head dipped down. "I bet the X-rays show gold," she said to the patient, and then the doors closed silently.

All that week he didn't really see her. She was on the graveyard shift, just when he was getting off, and his lunchtimes were crazy. It was allergy season. He tried to get her on the phone a few times. He left her a message. Friday we'll go camping, he said.

He tried to call her on Thursday and there was no answer. He tried on Friday, and her line rang and rang. He drove to a pay phone and called the hospital, trying to gauge her next shift. She couldn't push him away at work. But when he got through, the head nurse told him Lila had left early. She wasn't coming in again today at all. In fact, she wasn't due back for another two months. "You're joking," Jim said, hunched into the phone.

"Oh, we never joke about leaves of absence here," the head nurse said. "We don't have enough nurses to do that."

"Where's she going?" he said.

"Um," the nurse said. "What did she tell me? Bermuda. No, wait—California."

Jim felt suddenly weak. His legs seemed to fill with water. "When did she leave?"

"Listen, I can't keep track of everything. About a half hour ago, I suppose."

He dropped the receiver and got into his car. Without traffic he could make it to her apartment in half an hour. He wove in and out of traffic. He honked the horn and cursed the drivers, and at one point, rather than be stalled in traffic, he drove along the rim of the road, ignoring the frank stares of the other drivers. The whole drive there all he could think of was that she might come back from California, but she wouldn't come back the same.

When he got to her apartment, he bolted from his running car and stabbed his finger onto her buzzer. He let it ring so loudly that the woman who lived next door to Lila came clomping down the stairs to complain.

He ran outside again and dashed down the block. There was a group of boys bebopping to someone's boom box, trading cigarettes. They were sitting on the stoop, in ragged jeans and sneakers, and if Jim hadn't walked the two extra steps to see past them, he might have missed Lila, struggling to pull a suitcase into her car.

He strode past the boys. "Yo, man," one of them said, and the music suddenly surged. He lunged for Lila, and as soon as he touched her she whipped around, her white purse flailing to the ground.

"I give up!" Lila cried.

"Don't go," he panted.

"Why not?" she said. "Why shouldn't I go wherever I bloody well please? You do. What difference does it make where I go? It only matters where she is."

"Lila, I'm sorry. I just—it was stupid, it was just—I just had to see about a lead."

"It all boils down to the same thing in the end, doesn't it. It doesn't matter where you were, as long as she might have been there."

She thrashed from him. "I thought you were dead," she spat. "I even called the police."

"Lila, listen—" He tried to take her arm, but she jerked from him.

"I'm tired of being second best!" she cried. She began moving back from him. "I'm tired of you!"

"What are you doing? Why didn't you tell me you were planning this?"

"I did tell you!" she cried. She made a mighty effort and swung the suitcase into the car. "Lila," he said. She was already dressed in a summery white cotton dress. Her arms were bare, and she looked so lovely that the air around her seemed brighter. "Don't go," he pleaded. The music seemed to be getting louder. He turned around.

Lila moved forward, closer to the car. "Lila, I love you," he cried, and this time, when she turned around, she was crying.

"No. You love Lee."

"I love you."

"How do you know that?" she cried. "How do you? It's easy to say you love me when I'm leaving."

"So stay," Jim said. "Stay and I'll say it."

"I have a ticket."

"I love you." The boom box suddenly stopped. Jim looked up. The boys were watching the scene with mild interest.

Lila took a step forward, and Jim pulled her back.

"You were out looking for Lee."

"I was out looking for you." His face crumpled. "Please," he said.

"Where are you going to go looking for Lee next time? Paris?"

He was still for a moment. "Lee's gone," he said finally.

He draped both arms about her, burrowing his face against the long cool line of her shoulder. "I told you she was gone," he said. "Tell me what you want, so I can do it."

She slumped, suddenly exhausted. He kept stroking her face, following the line of her shoulders with his hands, but she didn't move. "I'm a fool, and everyone here knows it," she said, but she stooped to recollect her purse, and then she took his arm and let him lead her home.

She moved in with him that month. She kept suggesting they move to another place, a place that would be a fresh start for both of them, but every time she suggested it Jim seemed to contract. "You're still waiting for her," Lila said flatly.

She felt she was in Lee's house. Sometimes she could be doing a thing as simple as washing the dinner dishes and the air would suddenly feel warm, as if someone were breathing down her back. "Go away," she whispered, "you didn't want this," and continued to wash. At night she flung one arm protectively over Jim. She got up and watched Joanna sleeping, and when Joanna woke and saw her, she would stretch up out of bed for a hug.

She tried to make the house her own. She painted it, pale yellow except for Joanna's room, which Joanna wanted blue. She bought new rugs and shelving and threw out every sheet she thought Lee might have slept on. She rearranged things so Jim stumbled, but he never told her to stop, and she noticed how pleased and stunned he seemed when he saw the painted walls.

It was easier with Joanna. Lila didn't even know what Lee's leaving had done to Joanna when she was a baby. Lila kept trying to make it up to her. She cradled her. She sang her lusty out-of-tune songs. She sometimes lay beside Joanna while she was taking her naps just so she wouldn't feel alone. Lila was there when Joanna had chicken pox, there when she wanted to play tag. She taught the child how to fingerpaint and how to blow bubbles from a paper cone. And she convinced Jim that Joanna was much too bright to be kept back from kindergarten, and she herself would walk her to school and pick her up if he was so worried. She could squire Joanna and one of her friends to the movies, just like any other suburban mother.

When Joanna entered first grade, she was already better educated than all the kids there. She read the whole reader in one afternoon. She could write compositions in a clumsy hand while everyone else was printing awkwardly. When the teacher, an elderly woman named Mrs. Kale, called for a conference, Lila came along with Jim. "You're hindering her by teaching her at home," she told them sternly. "And you're hindering me."

"Ha," said Jim. "Education never hindered anyone."

Both he and Lila refused to listen to Mrs. Kale. They read with Joanna nights, all three of them on a porch swing Jim had bought from Kmart, and when Joanna fell asleep in their laps, Jim continued to read softly to Lila. "She'll hear the rest by osmosis," he said. They helped her form her letters. Joanna's best friend, a girl named Denny Wilson, came over every Wednesday afternoon, and when the two girls played school Joanna always insisted Denny be the teacher because it was more fun for her to learn. "Thank you, Mrs. Archer," Denny always said when Lila drove her home, and Lila never did one single thing to correct her.

Joanna might have been only two when Lila began seeing Jim, but children aren't the easy lovers most people think they are. During her training Lila had treated enough unpacifiable kids, enough angry babies, to know how suspect affection can be. Lila knew only that such attentions had been somehow miraculously earned.

Gradually, gradually, Lee faded. Jim could watch the news at night with Lila and not feel sick every time he saw a blonde. He could hear the doorbell or the phone and not jump in tension. And now, instead of worrying about Lee never coming back, he worried more about Lila's staying. On the street now, it was the flash of red hair, the glimpse of white uniform, that stirred him. And he suddenly knew that living with Lila every day just wasn't enough. He wanted to marry her.

He had planned to propose to Lila at dinner at a fancy restaurant, to have the waiter bring the ring in a clamshell to her, but in the end he couldn't wait the two days for the dinner reservation. Dizzy with excitement, he proposed to Lila in the middle of the night, waking her up from a deep sleep. Groggy, she blinked at him. "Marry me," he whispered. She blinked again, beaming. "If you think I need to be half-asleep to say yes, you're mistaken," she told him.

But there were things he had to take care of first, things that had to do with Lee. He was still legally married, legally tied to a past that no longer existed. He hired a lawyer to take care of it, a woman Lila had once nursed through minor surgery. The lawyer told Jim it was a simple thing. Lee could be declared dead; the marriage could be dissolved.

"Dead," he said.

"Well, the legal death," she said. "Seven years missing isn't a bad indication, is it? Most alive people make some effort to contact family or friends."

Jim stiffened.

"I'll handle everything," the lawyer told him. "I'll file the papers. I'll need to contact her parents."

"All I want to know is when it's done," he said.

And when it was, he was surprised at how he grieved, at how suddenly new the loss of her was. A legal technicality and suddenly the house seemed completely empty of her. He could talk to Lee for a thousand hours and he wouldn't once feel a vague contact. He could pick up objects of hers that she had left—a porcelain vase, a cheap brass bell—and not feel one single tremor. He had an attack of loneliness, a melancholy so complete that he suddenly couldn't move past slow motion. He slept through his morning alarm. At work it took him so long to fill a prescription that sometimes people complained. His skin broke out in an adolescent garden of pimples. To his astonishment, the air seemed somehow to have grayed. Everyone seemed to have a pallor.

Joanna was seven and in the second grade, and so bright her teacher was suggesting she be skipped ahead a grade. She had been excited about that. She and Denny had been plotting ways for Denny to be skipped as well, but now Jim's sadness made her wary. She wouldn't go near him but stared dreamily out the window or searched out Lila. He finally told her, sitting out back under the willow. "How did she die?" Joanna asked him, her face grave.

"I don't know," he said.

She stood up, brushing off a caterpillar. Her hair was even longer than Lee's had ever been, her clothing as helplessly disarrayed.

Sometimes, despite himself, he thought he was reraising Lee. He told himself he might be giving his daughter the things Lee had missed, the things that might make Joanna stay. "Do you think it was fire?" Joanna asked suddenly. He had caught her with matches that morning, trying to toast marshmallow puffs.

"No," he said. "I don't think so."

He waited for her to ask more questions. She frowned. "But Lila's going to stay, isn't she?" she said, and then he knew she'd be all right.

"I'm going to marry Lila," he told her. "She'll live with us forever."

Lila never once asked him what was wrong. Instead she put new blue pansies on the supper table. She daubed vanilla scent behind her ears because she knew it amused Jim that she was the only woman he knew who would choose to smell like a bakery. At night she spooned her body against his and soothed the tight muscles in his back with her fingers. She took her time, and then gradually Lee receded as she herself came to his forefront. And then he felt Lila's presence, immediate and real, rising up before him like a sun.

He told Lila they could move, they could look for a new house. In the interim his house, empty of Lee, became Lila's. He wasn't sure when that had happened. He could drift his hand across the kitchen table and feel Lila.

It was Lila who finally said that as crazy as it sounded, it just didn't matter anymore, that she would just as soon forgo moving as not. "Besides, I like it here," she said. She liked having Maureen around, and she had even made friends with Maureen's ghostly husband, who had been charmed enough to help her start a small vegetable garden in the backyard. "How could you!" Maureen said to Lila. "Don't you know there are strict quotas on gardeners on this block?" Lila was a good gardener. Already her tomatoes were coming up and green beans and wild raspberries she ate idly from the bushes. There was also a good school for Joanna. Besides, she believed in continuity for children. Even for one as little as Joanna. You couldn't just wrench a child up and expect her to believe in forever after doing a thing like that. And forever was a thing she herself was beginning to believe in.

They were married in September for no other reason than it was Lila's favorite month. "A real wedding," Jim insisted, remembering the cranky justice of the peace who had married him and Lee.

They rented a small white Unitarian church and a rock and roll band. They invited fifty of their friends, and Denny so Joanna would have someone to play with, and all the family they could think of.

Both Joanna and Lila were in bright red dresses. "I wear white all day long," she said, and instead went shopping with Maureen and came home with a flaming red silk dress. "Red!" Lila's mother cried to Jim. She was newly chummy with him now and insisted that he call her Joyce. "I was hoping you might be able to do something about the way Lila dresses in general," she said. "Lila sent me a picture of you, and you were in a very nice dark green sweater and a very nice pair of chino pants. I remember that." She admitted to Jim that she hadn't trusted him at first, not with that Lee business, but everyone deserved a second chance in life, and now her only regret was that Lila's great-aunt Teddy wasn't alive to see her walk down the aisle. "March is more like it," Jim said. Lila's father insisted he wanted to talk to Jim, but he immediately became so tongue-tied, his wife had to take up the conversation. "He's just excited," she said. Jim's parents were elated. "I never liked that living in sin business," his mother said. His father, though, was more practical. "If you had come to me sooner, I could have supplied the food," he said. "This is my home," Jim said. "I took care of it."

So there it was, seven years after Lee had disappeared, Jim, in a tuxedo he had insisted on buying rather than renting, was watching Lila sail down the aisle toward him, suspended on her father's arm. She was in a shimmer of long red silk, her face flushed from her nervous breakfast of three glasses of wine and six supermarket powdered doughnuts. She had about six more steps before she got to him. Her father was whispering something to her, making her nod impatiently, and then she caught Jim's eye, giving him a smile of such pure happy surprise that he bolted toward her, taking her by the hand, pulling her from her father. "In a rush, are we?" Lila's father said, grinning. He laughed. Serenely, deliberately unrushed now, Jim stepped back into his designated place, his hand clasped about Lila's, and for the first time in a long while, he felt completely and absolutely safe.

Lee had been in Madison for almost two years, and still she couldn't relax. Every night she made lists of what she had. A place of her own that she liked. A job. A boyfriend. She kept telling herself over and over, I have these things, I have them, but no matter how many times she said that, she still felt that any second she might not.

She couldn't understand how people got through their lives, how they were able to trust. Andy told her every terrible thing he had ever done in an attempt to get her to open up to him. Valerie confided how the week before she had married Roy she had gotten cold feet so badly that she had slept with the dishwasher she had just hired. She looked at Lee, so expectant that Lee finally made up a story about finding out her old boyfriend was secretly in love with her best friend.

"I've got another secret for you," Valerie said one day. They were both in the kitchen of the restaurant, chopping up greens for salad. "And you're the very first to know it."

Lee put carrot curls into a wood bowl. She had this terrible feeling that she was going to have to think of something to tell Valerie in return. The odd thing was, she had told so many stories, so many times, that sometimes she couldn't remember anymore what had really happened and what hadn't.

"Roy and I," said Valerie. "We're adopting a baby."

Lee put down her paring knife. "A baby?"

Valerie leaned against the sink. "I can't have kids," she said simply.

"We tried everything and, well, when you have a good relationship, kids just seem the way to deepen it, don't they? Anyway, we got this lawyer. We were going to wait for a newborn, and then this little girl popped up. Four years old. Mother died in a motorcycle accident. Lord knows who the father is."

She dug into her back pocket and pulled out a photo. A little girl in overalls and a plaid shirt stared out at the camera. Her hair was very straight and very black and barely scraped her chin. "Isn't she adorable?" Valerie said. "Her name's Karen. It's been final a long time, but we don't get her for another month."

"Four years old," Lee repeated uneasily.

"You like kids?" Valerie said. "You ever want them?"

"Oh, I can't imagine it," Lee said.

Valerie laughed. "Sure you can. And you'll change your mind. Everyone does." She gave Lee a sly look. "You'd be a *great* mother. And Andy *loves* babies."

"It's not for me," Lee said brusquely. She whisked toward the other room. "I hear customers," she said.

The "Montana Kid" was what Valerie called the girl. Given to a home when her mother died while drunkenly driving her motorcycle. She had been just twenty. No one knew who the father was. No one could even pinpoint a friend. "The Montana mom," said Valerie.

Nights, just before closing, when not one single customer except maybe Andy was there, Valerie would sit around the restaurant and swap stories with the waitresses about who they thought the Montana mom had been. "She adored her baby and wouldn't give her up when she got pregnant. She was drunk that day only because she was coming home from a date gone wrong."

"Wrong," said Addie, a waitress who had just started that day. "Her name was JoLeen, pronounced the same way as the mustache bleach. And she was drunk because she discovered she was pregnant again." She yawned. "You know what? All this talk makes me want a baby," she said. "I'm gonna have to have me a mighty *serious* talk with that boyfriend of mine."

Lee silently stacked clean glasses.

"The Montana mom couldn't drive by a red light without thinking it meant 'speed,'" said Andy.

"The Montana mom never ate in good restaurants. She and her kid ate Cheez Doodles all day long," said Addie.

Lee stretched up to put a row of glasses onto the shelf. She made herself nod and smile, then backed casually into the front room until the voices receded, blurring into a backdrop. She started swabbing down the front tables, upending the chairs back onto the tables. Then she reached for her coat, hugging it about her.

She went back to the doorway and stood there, waiting for Andy to look up and see her. He was excited about becoming an uncle. "Home," she mouthed.

She didn't want him to say one word about Valerie's adoption. She didn't want to think about babies or abandonment or anything other than how lucky Karen might be to have loving, ready-made parents. She needed him to fuss over her, to soothe her, and when he came toward her she reached for his arm and wrapped it about her shoulders. "Here's my baby," he said, kissing her. Quietly she gripped the front door and then led him out into the freezing night.

Karen became theirs in the spring. Roy made all the arrangements, paying for a first-class flight for her, making sure a social worker was beside her right up until the second Karen was relinquished at the gate in Madison.

His wife's nerves were all on the surface. The morning they were going to get Karen, she paced the den they had made into a child's room. She fluffed up the yellow duck-printed curtains she had sewn up herself. She took the stuffed animals from the bed to the bureau and then back again. He sloped against the wall, watching her, thinking how very beautiful she was, how all he had to do was reach out one arm and he could touch her. All Valerie could think or talk about was Karen, but all he could think about was Valerie and how this child might change her. He loved his wife. He wouldn't have cared whether they ever had any kids at all—the only reason he consented to adoption at all was that she was desperate to have a child.

"*Relax*," he soothed her.

She whisked past him to the hall phone. "Where's Andy?" she said, dialing. She had impulsively asked him and Lee along for moral support. Roy had shrugged his okay when she had asked him, but really he wanted Valerie to himself for as long as possible, right up to the moment the child took one of their hands and made them a trio.

Wearily Valerie hung up the phone. "Great," she said. "They can't come. Lee's sick and Andy doesn't want her to be alone."

He lowered his head against her shoulder. "Now that's a shame," he said, and kissed the soft curve of her neck.

Lee had all these excuses why she couldn't go to see the child. She felt fever brewing. She said she had to go to the doctor, that's how bad she felt. She told Andy to send Valerie her best, to tell Valerie she was too woozy to call and she wanted to see the child as soon as she could.

It took her an entire week. She encouraged Andy to come visit her, but she wouldn't let him say one word about the child. As soon as she saw he was about to open his mouth, she would interrupt to ask for some tea, to ask for aspirin or a cool cloth she didn't really need. Sometimes all she had to do was unbutton a few buttons on her shirt, and on his, and then there wasn't room for either one of them to think of one single thing except each other.

She needn't have worried about Andy. His first flush of unclehood didn't last very long. He had been going to visit Karen almost every day, stopping by on his way to court. But things weren't going the way he had planned. She wouldn't come near him, wouldn't touch the toy gavel he had bought for her. She tore angrily around the house. She cried for no reason. Karen seemed either frozen in silence or wild almost every time he visited. She wasn't adjusting, and his sister looked so drained that it began to worry him.

"I don't know about this kid," he managed to tell Lee. "She's pretty ornery." He dug his hands into the pockets of his jeans. "Valerie keeps asking when you're coming over."

Lee pulled on a sweater. She laced up her sneakers.

"We could go Saturday. Spend just an hour and then leave. I can't say I really want to spend more."

Lee, crouched over her sneakers, was silent for a moment.

"Well?" he said. "Just a few hours? A quick dinner?"

"Sure," she said finally. "All right."

They drove up on a Saturday, the blond doll they had bought for Karen cradled in Lee's lap. "You feel okay?" Andy asked Lee. "You don't look so chipper. You want to postpone this?" Lee glanced at her watch. In a few hours it would be nine and they'd be leaving. "I'm fine," she said.

When they pulled up, Valerie and Roy were racing across the front lawn. Andy punched on the horn, skittering Valerie to a stop. She shaded her eyes, frowning. And then, behind her, was a maelstrom of red and yellow and blue, blurring into shape, freeze-framing into a little girl. She stared at the car, her face expressionless. She was so small and thin that she startled Lee. Pale as white paper, with scrubby black hair and eyes like a piece of hard blue sky. Valerie reached to grab Karen, who pinwheeled across the lawn with a shriek.

Andy led Lee over to his sister. "She *does* know how to stay still," Valerie said lamely. "It must just be a bad habit coming out. You know. Speed. Motorcycles. From her mother." Bewildered, she looked at Roy.

"She's just getting used to us, that's all," Roy said.

"Sure she is," Valerie said.

Lee took Andy's hand and folded it between her own. Valerie seemed to see Lee for the first time. Brightening, she draped an arm about her, leading her toward the house. "It's amazing, isn't it?" Valerie said as if she were surprised. "One minute I don't have a daughter, the next minute I do. Next fall she'll even be in kindergarten." She turned toward Roy. "Can you get her?"

They all settled into the living room. "Mom called," Valerie said to Andy. "You know, I don't know what's wrong with her. She gets hysterical. She keeps calling me up with these articles about mass murderers. 'It's in the genes,' she says. Do you believe this woman offered me money to hire a detective to find out about Karen's mother?"

Andy grinned. "Aren't you curious?" he said.

"The woman's dead," Valerie said.

Karen sprang into the room, arms and legs like elastic. Her dress had a damp grassy stain spread across the front. Roy trailed behind her. "Look what Lee and Uncle Andy brought you," Valerie said, lifting up the doll. "No," said Karen, veering violently, crashing into Lee.

Instantly Lee recoiled. Karen surveyed her with stony eyes. "Baby, this is Lee," Valerie said. Lee didn't move. Karen swayed on her sneakers, started for Lee, and then pivoted abruptly, storming from the room.

Valerie pushed out a breath. "Don't worry," she told Lee. "It just takes her time to take to people."

Lee slowly unfurled on the chair.

"I'll put her to bed, then we can have dinner. Potluck, I'm afraid," Valerie said.

"It's hard to be a chef with a child," Roy explained.

Karen slept through dinner. Every five minutes or so Valerie would disappear and come back, eyes bright. The next time she got up, though, Roy gripped her arm, lowering her back onto her seat. "This chicken's delicious," he said.

Valerie kept yawning. By the time Roy served peach pie, she was propped up by her elbows, fighting sleep. "I'm sorry, I don't get much rest these days," she said.

"We have to get going anyway," Andy said.

"So soon?" Valerie said.

"Just let me wash my hands," Lee said.

On her way back, she passed Karen's room. The door was open. A Donald Duck night-light shone through the shadows of the room. Cautiously Lee looked in. Karen was lying in the kind of ruffly canopy bed any child would adore. Her eyes suddenly flashed open, locking with Lee's. Karen didn't move, didn't break her gaze. Unnerved, Lee stepped back. For a moment she felt caught in place, like a specimen pinned against an examining board. Abruptly she jerked free, striding into the living room. As soon as he saw her, Andy smiled. "Now, I take *my* baby home," he said.

The whole first week Karen spent with Valerie and Roy, she acted as if she didn't know them, as if she had been somehow kidnapped and placed into the wrong life. She seemed dazed. She kept planting herself on whatever spot Valerie led her to, or sometimes she would tear fiercely around the house, screaming, striking Valerie if she tried to stop her.

Valerie had done her best to be soothing, to be patient and understanding. "I know you're scared, but you're going to love it here," she said. Karen stiffened under her touch. Her eyes seemed liquid pools of grief.

"What is it?" Valerie whispered. She crouched down to Karen's level. "Can't you tell me?" She gently tilted Karen's small chin so that Karen was looking at her.

"Does my mother know I'm here?" Karen said finally.

Valerie hesitated. She believed in telling children the truth, but on the other hand, she believed in comfort. She half wished she herself could believe in heaven, then maybe she could see all this as a trial that would merit her a just reward in the afterlife. Straightening, she stroked Karen. "Honey, I'm sure she does. I bet she's happy you found such a good home."

Karen blinked. "Is it easy to get here?" she said.

Valerie frowned. "I guess it's easy enough," she said. She smiled uncertainly. "Why, you expecting company?"

Karen jerked from her grip. Valerie tugged her back, a little roughly, but Karen pulled free again.

Valerie didn't understand it. She had thought Karen would be delighted to be in a real home, that she couldn't help but warm to two parents as loving as she and Roy, but Karen stayed remote. She ignored Valerie's offers of paints or crayons or brownie mix. She made her body a board if you so much as looked at her. But she could spend hours staring out the windows, nose to the glass, breathing clouds of mist onto Valerie's clean windows. She gazed outside until Valerie finally opened the front door. "You want to go out, scoot," she said, irritated. Cautiously Karen peeled herself from the window. She followed Valerie out onto the front lawn, and then, almost immediately, she went to the edge of the lawn and stopped, staring at the street, straining right and left. "There's nothing *out* there," Valerie said.

If Karen wasn't staring at the roads, she was at the phone, frantically dialing numbers. "You want me to call someone for you?" Valerie coaxed. Karen slumped and then burst into tears. Astonished, Valerie drew her to her. She stroked her rough hair; for a moment Valerie thought this might be the proverbial breakthrough. She was actually holding Karen and Karen was allowing it; Karen was holding her back. "Oh, doesn't this feel good," Valerie said, but Karen suddenly tore from her, staring at Valerie as if she hated her. "What?" Valerie said, but Karen was gone.

The more she tried to calm her, the wilder Karen became. She screamed in tantrums; she ran around the house. At night she fought going to bed. When Valerie went to check on her, Karen was fully clothed, stunned, staring out the window.

When Karen finally slept, it was with the uneasy sleep of an adult. She twisted under the coverlet, flinging her pillow to the ground. She moaned and sweated and tumbled among the bedclothes. Sometimes, too, in the middle of the night, she screamed, frightening Valerie into a kind of dizzy paralysis. She lay planted and terrified against the bedclothes, waiting until Roy got up and went to the child. In Karen's woozy half-sleep, she never recognized him. She kicked and scratched at him. He had to hold her against the bed, gasping the loveliest lullabies he knew until gradually she grew interested in his effort. He let go, continuing to sing hoarsely until he saw her drowsing. When Valerie came into the room, he wouldn't meet her eyes.

Karen always woke at six, running to the front door, banging on it until Valerie and Roy woke up. They'd stumble toward Karen, who, alarmed, would race into the kitchen. "Don't play with the door," Roy called after her. Valerie would try to make some semblance of breakfast. She'd try to talk with Roy, but usually she ended up mopping up the juice Karen had spilled deliberately, grabbing Karen's hands before she could topple her juice. "*Stop*," she said, a little harder than she had intended. Karen drew back abruptly.

She spent most of her day feeling like the meanest person alive. She tried to be nice, to be understanding, and then Karen would scream or run, and before she could stop herself, she would have slapped her. When Roy called, she was tense. He wanted to make plans for that evening. "I'm beat," she said. "How can I possibly go out?"

That evening when Roy came home, he brought her wildflowers in a pink paper cone. "Oh, how lovely," she said.

"Where's Karen?" he said.

"I got her to go to sleep," she said. He swayed her body against his. "You must be hungry," she said.

"Yeah, I am," he said, touching her hip, swaying her toward him. "Come on," he said, dipping her to the floor. She was too tired to enjoy this. She sleepily catalogued twin scratches on his collarbone, a span of freckles along one shoulder. He slid his body against hers, he pulled at her buttons, and only when his hands were on her bare skin did she feel a prickling of desire. She lifted her face to his. "Roy," she said, and then, at the moment she kissed him, Karen screamed.

"Shit," Valerie said. "No, I'll go," Roy said, staying her. She stumbled after him. Karen was standing in bed, crying. "You just had a dream," Roy said, but Karen kicked at him, toppling herself into the bed. Roy lowered himself onto the bed and carefully stroked Karen's trembling back. "It's just a dream," he said, and when Karen took his finger, he looked up at Valerie with relief.

They both stayed by Karen until she fell asleep, and by then they were exhausted. It took Valerie longer to get into bed than Roy, and when she lifted the covers, his eyes were shut. She rested her face against his.

"What does she have, radar?" he said, his eyes still shut. "What can she possibly have against us?"

"Come on," Valerie said. "You just made real contact. It's more than I've done." He rolled away from her.

"Maybe the Montana mom gave her tranquilizers," Valerie said dully, into the steady new silence of the night.

It didn't last. The next evening, when Roy came home and tried to sweep Karen into a hug, she bit him. He kept trying, but only Valerie loved him for it. She tried, too. She tried one more week, and then another, and the only emotion she could summon up toward her daughter was a kind of draining despair, a feeling that somehow a mistake had been made and she was responsible for it.

An "institutional child" was the phrase that always came to Valerie's mind when she looked at her daughter. She scrubbed her and put her in a gingham dress, and still there was something rough about her, something that smacked of trailer parks and motorcycles. She took her to the playground, to measure her against other kids. She was sure they must be as rowdy as her own, and also that maybe what Karen needed, simply, was friends of her own age. She wasn't in the park for five minutes when Karen roughly pushed a little boy off a swing, tumbling him into the dirt. Stunned, he scuttled away from her. "Hey, hey!" a woman called. She was small and lean and dressed in a sleeveless flowered jumpsuit. She didn't look tired at all, Valerie noticed. The woman scooped up her son, brushing him off, and then marched up to Valerie and Karen. "We don't *hit*," she said sternly to Karen, but she was looking at Valerie. "That's right," Valerie said to Karen, who was stubbornly standing by the swing, chewing on her grimy fist. Valerie felt like a fool. She felt as if she were the one being chastised because she couldn't control Karen. She felt like blurting out that Karen was adopted.

She was crying when Roy came home that night. He rocked her against him. "We have to do something," Roy said finally. "We have to get her checked out."

"She's not a car."

"Come on. A child psychologist." Miserably he dug his hands into his pockets. "I mean, maybe it's us. Wouldn't you want to know that?" She gave him a grudging shrug. She thought queasily of the times she had hit Karen. Innocent times. She had never meant real harm. "I have some names," he said at last.

"We're just going to meet a friend of Daddy's," Valerie told Karen. She smoothed down Karen's red dress.

She and Roy had driven twenty miles to a small office in a shopping complex, a waiting room with four dog-eared copies of *Psychology Today* and *Highlights for Children*, two blue leather couches, and no other people at all.

"Well," Valerie said doubtfully. She riffled through the *Highlights*. There was a puzzle, a maze inviting the reader to find the rabbit hidden somewhere on a page crowded with trains and trees and people. "Karen, look, want to find the rabbit?" she said, and when Karen glumly looked at her shoes, Valerie turned to Roy. "You want to find it?" she said helplessly.

"There," he said, kissing her nose. "There's the rabbit."

The door opened and a woman suddenly strode out, in a bright yellow dress with matching glasses, and as soon as she spotted Karen, she smiled. "Well, who have we here?" she said encouragingly. Karen stood up.

"I'm Doctor Wymon," the woman said, thrusting out a hand to Roy, who shook it limply and then passed it on to his wife. "We'll just have ourselves a chat without the parents present," she said. She looked down at Karen. "I have a puppy in my office. You want to see?"

She had led Karen into the waiting room, ushering her in to see the doctor by herself. And when Karen came out, barely half an hour later, sullen, dark, Valerie's heart sank. Karen sat with Roy while Valerie went in to talk to the doctor, who said her daughter was acting normally, considering the circumstances. "There's been some trauma. Having her mother die. Being in a home. But she's young and resilient. I wouldn't do anything until I saw how she handles kindergarten. With enough children around her, she'll learn to socialize.

She'll start to accept that her mother's gone." The doctor smiled. "These things take time," she said. She leaned forward and handed Valerie a folded bill for two hundred dollars.

Life had to have spaces in it. Roy left every morning; some part of the weekend he went to the solace of his office. She resented his cheerful exits, the easy way he could extricate himself from Karen and sometimes from her as well. She missed the evenings of just lying in bed with him, talking, making love. She was exhausted and he was tense. The one time they managed to go out to dinner, Valerie had fallen asleep at the table, and he had been furious with her.

She tried to forge some sort of path for herself, some escape. She searched for a sitter, using the local high school girls, but none of them ever wanted to sit twice. She went to the restaurant when she could.

"We missed you," Lee told her.

"Motherhood agrees with you," said Nellie, the newest waitress. Valerie colored. She knew what she looked like, with her hair bunched into a flowered band, her haphazard dressing. Her tights had ladders, her shoes scuffs. "Bring the kid in so we can spoil her rotten," said Nellie.

"Soon," Valerie said. She looked toward the kitchen.

"What's she like?" asked Nellie.

"Wonderful," Valerie said. She pulled on an apron, knotting it tightly. She sniffed the air. "Creole shrimp," she said.

It was Lee who found Valerie crying outside in the back of the restaurant, tearfully smoking a cigarette. When she saw Lee she continued crying, but her face was defiant. "I'm getting my period," she said. "You know how I get." Lee nodded and then very gently placed both arms about Valerie. She rocked her for a moment. "Are you and Andy getting married?" Valerie said, swiping tears from her face. "Do you want to have children?" she cried. Lee's hands contracted and for one second time seemed to separate like a seam.

"Every woman wants babies. It's perfectly natural to want your own," Valerie cried. "You probably can have them. You look like the kind who can have dozens. You're so *lucky*."

"Let's go inside," said Lee.

One night Valerie showed up at Lee's with Karen in tow. Andy had night court and Lee was reading *Tom Jones* in the kitchen, her feet propped on the table. She had melted a whole chocolate bar in a copper saucepan, thinning it with milk, and was now sipping it luxuriously. When the bell rang she ignored it, polishing off the chocolate. She didn't do anything until she heard knocking, too, and then she was only going to peer out the curtain and see whom she could blame for disturbing her. She pulled the curtain and saw Valerie, with Karen in tow. Valerie's eyes were swollen, but when Lee answered the door, she kept a bright smile on her face. "We came to visit," she said, looking down at Lee's book. "You weren't busy, were you?" she said. "We won't stay long. This one has to get to bed, and I'm tired myself." She gestured at Karen. Her hair was newly shorn. She was wearing one of Valerie's red clip-on earrings.

Lee looked at Karen doubtfully, who was staring at Lee's long braid with such intensity, it made Lee step back.

"Uh, you like long hair?" Lee said to Karen.

"It's the blond, not the length," Valerie said wearily, following Lee into the living room. "Yesterday on the bus, she stood so close to a blond girl that the girl tripped getting past her. The girl was mad, too, but at *me*."

Karen settled nervously onto the pink velvet rocker Lee had found in a thrift shop. She petted the chair the way she would a cat, carefully grooming the armrests.

Valerie yawned. "You don't have any aspirin, do you? It's been such a bad day. The sink at the restaurant started flooding the kitchen, and I had to hassle with the plumber, and even now the sink still doesn't seem fixed to me."

"Bathroom," Lee said. As soon as Valerie was out of the room, Lee felt uncomfortable. She glanced uneasily at Karen, who was sitting on the velvet chair, watching her angrily. "*What?*" Lee said, then picked up *Tom Jones* again. The words braided together, but she kept the book up and pretended to read.

Almost immediately Karen began running to every window in Lee's house, slapping her hands against it. "Hey," Lee said, following her, but as soon as Lee was within a foot of Karen, she took off for another window.

"Valerie," Lee called, exasperated. "Valerie." She looked at Karen, who was standing in the center of the room, poised for flight. "You wait here," Lee told her. She found Valerie sleeping on the bed, an opened bottle of Bayer aspirin in her hand. Aspirin flaked across the coverlet. "Hey," Lee said, shaking her gently. Valerie reached for Lee's hand and wrapped it about her shoulder, cozying into it. Lee pulled her hand away. "Valerie," she said. "Valerie." Valerie rolled away.

Lee walked into the living room to find Karen spread on the rug, eyes drooping with sleep. "Come on," she said. "Don't lie on the rug. You can sleep on the couch." She patted the couch. She bent to take Karen's arm, and instantly Karen whipped it from her.

Lee lifted her hands. "Fine with me. Sleep on the rug." She went back to her chair and picked up her book.

Lee flipped pages. She forced a look at Karen, and suddenly, in the shadows, Karen's hair looked the same yellow as her own. If she turned so Lee could see her, her eyes might be the same deep, bottomless black. Unnerved, she bolted from her chair. She was sweating. Something was surfacing in her, something she didn't want. She was suddenly furious with Valerie. "Come on," she said. Karen looked out the window, searching. "In the bedroom," Lee said, pulling Karen up and releasing her hold so abruptly that Karen stumbled.

"Come on, let's wake her up," Lee said, rustling covers about Valerie. Karen tugged at the sheet and Valerie's eyes stuttered open. "What time is it?" she said, bolting up, blinking at the two of them. "Jesus, I'm sorry. I was just so tired." She swung her legs over the bed. "What do you say we go home?" she said to Karen.

On the way out she chattered at Lee. "Look, I'm sorry. I really did want to visit with you."

"It's okay," Lee said. "Just call the next time."

"Sure," Valerie said. "Sure, I'll call."

The apartment was empty, but Lee still felt a child in it. Disturbed, she wandered the rooms, checking the closets, and then, in the middle of the bedroom, she felt so suddenly overwhelmed with loneliness that she had to sit down. She leaned across for the phone and called Andy. "Come over," she said.

He laughed. "I'm beat. I'm falling asleep as we speak."

"I'll come there, then," she said. "I'll take a cab."

"You all right?" he said. "You sound funny."

"I'll be there in five minutes," she said.

He was half-asleep by the time she got there. She didn't care. She led him back into bed and tucked him in, and then shucked off her clothes and slid in beside him. She was wide awake. In her own apartment she would have been prowling the rooms, memory stalking her like a dangerous intruder. Beside her, Andy sighed in sleep and then his breath bottomed out. Lee spooned her body about his. She lifted one of his arms and looped it about her. She wasn't such a bad person that someone didn't love her. She did good things for people. She had someone. She had a life. She was not orbiting endlessly. She wasn't that Lee anymore.

Two days later Valerie showed up with Karen again. "I know," Valerie said. "I didn't call."

Lee dug hands into her jeans pockets. "I was thinking about going out," she said.

"We won't stay long," Valerie promised. "Roy's out of town and I just wanted some adult companionship." She tugged at the tag end of her braid.

"What makes you think I'm an adult?" Lee said.

Valerie bustled Karen inside. Karen, in red sweater, red pants, and red sneakers, headed for the one red chair in Lee's apartment, the one chair where Lee had been. She sat on Lee's book. "Hey," Lee said, pulling the book from under Karen, who glared at her. Valerie shucked off her jacket and slumped on the sofa. "So," she said. "Here we are."

"Why do I feel like eating cookies all the time?" Valerie said. "You got any?" She looked at Karen. "I eat more than she does. She doesn't even seem to like sugar, just salts away those potato chips." She rubbed at the sleeve of her sweater. There was a small dark stain on the elbow. The yarn unraveled at the hem.

Karen pulled silently at the tufts in the chair.

Valerie wandered into the kitchen. Lee heard her opening the refrigerator, pulling something out, probably the black forest cupcakes she had bought that morning. "I'm just going to call the restaurant and check on that bloody sink," Valerie called.

"Fine," Lee said. She was uncomfortable sitting there, with Karen staring at her, so she got up and went into the kitchen. Valerie was hunched over the phone, frowning.

"What?" Lee said.

"I'll be right there," Valerie said, and then hung up. She leaned along the counter, annoyed. "Listen, I have to get to the restaurant. The kitchen's flooded again, and the plumber told Nellie he can't get there for another hour. Everyone's panicking." She stroked back her hair. "Do you believe this?" she said. "Why can't this get taken care of without me?"

"I'll go," Lee said, but Valerie raised her hand. "Look, can you just watch Karen? I won't be long," she said.

"We could all go," Lee said, but Valerie was pulling on her jacket, shaking her head. "Please. This one splashing in water, no, thank you. I'll be right back. I'm just going to mop what I can and threaten the plumber with lawsuits."

Valerie whisked into the living room. When Karen saw Valerie's jacket, she stiffened. "I'll be right back," Valerie said. "God, I hate this," she told Lee, but Lee noticed that when she left her step seemed progressively lighter.

Lee couldn't control Karen. As soon as Valerie had left, Karen started racing around Lee's apartment, arms whirling propellers. At first Lee tried to ignore her. Karen would wear herself out running; exhaustion would push her into an early, bottomless sleep. Lee sat on the couch with a magazine in her lap, and she counted ten times Karen rampaged past her, ten times she didn't turn one single page of the magazine. The eleventh time, screaming, Karen rounded the corner, knocking over a vase full of daisies, shattering it across the floor. She leaped over the puddle and dying flowers and kept running, arms still beating stiffly, careening toward the hall, and this time something in Lee snapped. "Stop!" Lee shouted, furious. This time, when Karen came back around, Lee grabbed her. "Okay," she said roughly. She dragged Karen over to the closet and tugged her jacket from the hanger. She pried Karen's arms into her jacket, zipping it up tight. Karen, terrified, made her body rigid.

"Out," she said, jerking Karen outside, into the backyard. The night was spilled with stars. Lee pushed Karen. "You want to run, run then," she said angrily. Karen stood there baffled. And then Lee herself started running in the dark, around in circles, passing Karen. She felt as if she were cutting a swath through the thick, sticky air, as if she were cooling herself with motion. "Move," she said, giving Karen a shove, grabbing her by the hand and making her run, too. She led her out of the backyard and into the street, slowing herself down so Karen could keep up, running until her own anger had burned out of her, until she had calmed, and then she slowed her pace and tended to Karen.

Karen's face was flushed. Her eyes flashed. But she was worn out, panting. "Okay," Lee gasped. Her side stitched up. Her white sneakers were muddied, but she wasn't angry anymore. "Now we can go back."

They walked. Karen kept looking at all the houses they passed, her head switching roughly left to right. They passed someone's red Yamaha motorcycle parked on the front lawn, and Karen came to a dead stop. "Go," Lee prodded, and then she saw where Karen was looking. Lee didn't say anything. She just let her stand there in the deepening night, not moving, just staring at the red motorcycle. Finally Karen walked toward it, tentatively touching the seat, laying her head against it. Something inside of Lee dissolved. She crouched down. Karen was suddenly crying, burrowed against Lee, pushing open her legs so she was pinned there. "Oh," Lee said, wrapping her arms about Karen, "I know." She let her cry until her shirt felt damp against her skin, and then she scooped her up and carried her the rest of the way home in silence.

Inside the house, they stayed silent. Lee called the restaurant, but the line rang and rang and didn't catch at all. Karen stretched out on the rug and Lee draped a yellow coverlet over her and watched her thoughtfully.

Valerie arrived in less than an hour. Her jeans were rolled up and stained, and she had a smear of dirt across one cheek. "I'm sorry I'm so late," Valerie said. "The goddamned plumber took his sweet time getting there." She swabbed at her face with her hands. She looked exhausted and happy.

They stepped inside. "Oh, no," Valerie said, seeing Karen asleep on the floor. "Did she give you a terrible time?"

"Not terrible," said Lee. She thought about the Yamaha. She remembered seeing a high school kid zooming around on it, laughing, his body loose and boneless on the bike.

"I'll carry her to the car for you," Lee said abruptly. She bent down. Karen's heated breath rose and fell against Lee's hand. Lee lifted her up, and in midmotion one of Karen's hands fluttered about Lee's shoulder, holding on.

Valerie began bringing Karen over more and more. Sometimes she called first, sometimes she simply showed up, and she always stayed along with Karen. And then once she called weeping, begging Lee to sit. "Please. It's an emergency," Valerie said.

"What emergency?"

"My emergency. My life. I have to have a few hours alone with Roy. I can't find anyone else to sit."

"Valerie, I can't," Lee said. She heard the fissures in Valerie's voice, and then she remembered Karen, crying in the moonlight, and something caught at her.

"Just tonight," Valerie promised.

"Just tonight," Lee repeated doubtfully.

"One night. Three hours," Valerie said.

That one time, that evening Valerie spent with her husband, she lit dozens of white candles all over the apartment. Roy brought her a dozen tiger lilies and a small glittering bottle of a French perfume she had never heard of. There was Chinese food heating in the kitchen, recipes she had never tried out before on anyone. In the living room Gene Pitney wailed about a town without pity, and the door to Karen's bedroom was closed so tightly, someone might think no one had ever lived there at all.

Lee didn't really know why, but she began to sit for Karen more and more. "You can say no," Andy said, though the truth of it was he liked it when Lee sat. Evenings after Karen had left, Lee couldn't seem to get enough of him. She trailed him from room to room. All he had to do was move two steps closer to her and she would reach out for a kiss.

Lee watched Karen with increasing confusion. She dreaded having her come over, as much as she felt compelled to see her. Sometimes she thought she brought Karen out into the night just to be back in her own element, just to add distance between the two of them, but then Karen would take the same deep pleasure from the darkness that Lee did, confusing her even further.

Lee kept trying to vary the route. It was Karen who wanted to walk all the way home, who liked standing outside in front of her own house and watching the dimly lighted windows. "Want to call out?" Lee asked. "We could wave at them from out here."

"No," said Karen, but she wanted to stand out there a while longer.

Every night, too, eventually, Karen kept piloting them toward the house with the motorcycle. Every time she saw it, she would end up crying, a sound so desperate it made Lee feel undone. Karen never wanted to leave the bike. "Wait," she said. She kept staring out into the night, her body tensed. Light flickered on from the house. She fluttered her small fingers over the chrome, over the soft leather seat, the smooth red paint. The door opened and Karen lifted her face, expectant. A teenage boy came out, in black pointy-toed boots and a white T-shirt. He was smoking a cigarette, taking deep, angry draws. "Hey, get away from there," he said. "That's private property." Lee straightened. She reached for Karen's hand, but then Karen suddenly grabbed back at the motorcycle, swaying it. "Hey!" the boy called. "Get your friggin' kid off my bike!" Karen ran into the street. "And stay away!" the boy called.

It took Lee half a block to reach Karen, and even while she contained her in her arms, Karen was trying to escape. Her small body heaved. "It's okay," Lee said, and suddenly all she could think of were those nights after Claire had died, when she had run and run through the neighborhood, half certain she heard Claire's breath just behind her.

When she got Karen home, Karen fell asleep in her lap. Lee, half dozing, glanced down, and for one moment the child in her lap wasn't Karen at all. All she saw was a sudden flutter of lids, a pair of eyes as luminous as her own, and deeply blaming, before the lids shut again.

Sometimes, when Karen was the stormiest, when she was flailing her arms, racing toward no destination at all, Lee felt the most moved. She recognized loneliness like that. It didn't matter if it inhabited a child or her own self. She knew how dangerous it made every bit of life, how much energy it took to steel yourself against it.

She knew something about how to deal with such a thing. She tried to treat Karen the way she had wanted to be treated. She tried never to touch Karen, and when Karen touched her, she kept herself slightly aloof. She wouldn't punish Karen's rages but instead burned them out with long tearing walks in the night. And she treated Karen just as if she were another adult. She didn't lie to her about anything. When Karen woke screaming from nightmares, Lee didn't turn on the lights and tell Karen there was nothing in the darkness that wasn't in the light. She never said there was no such thing as monsters. Instead she sat in the dark with her, with the moonlight creating shadows on the bed. She didn't touch her, but in a low calm voice she asked her about the nightmare. "What do you dream about?"

"Motorcycles," whispered Karen.

Lee was silent for a minute. "And what do they do?"

"They chase me," Karen said. Alarmed, she sat up. "Sometimes a ghost comes to my room."

"A ghost?" Lee said quietly. "What ghost?"

"I don't know. I'm afraid to really look."

"You talk to it?"

Karen's mouth trembled. "It always leaves too fast," she said, falling against Lee. Lee didn't move, although her arm had fallen asleep. She settled against Karen and thought about ghosts, about all the voices you might hear whispering toward you, all the meaning you might miss.

The way Lee was suddenly taking to Karen surprised Andy. He loved kids. He wanted at least two, but he knew Lee wasn't crazy about them. He had seen how short she was with kids at the restaurant. He wasn't that crazy about Karen, but he had taken Lee's affection as a good sign. He liked it that he could come into her apartment and find her sprawled on the floor with a child. And he liked it even better that when Karen left she would keep close to him. She would seem to need him.

He didn't know what happened, when Lee began to change toward him. He came over one evening and she was coloring a map of Chile with Karen, the two of them not saying one word, not even to each other. He sat watching, reading a Time magazine that was two weeks old, and when he got up to leave, Lee looked at him as if she had just noticed he was there.

She began to cancel plans with him. Oddly protective, she sometimes wouldn't let him come to the house when Karen was there. "It disturbs her," she said. But really it did something to the whole momentum. When Andy was there, things seemed to go wrong. The fuses blew. The apartment was much too hot or much too cold. And Karen seemed somehow more distant, as if Andy had put space between them.

"I'll come by later, then," he said.

"Yes, please," she said. So he showed up late those nights, and although the house was clean and empty of Karen, although she seemed glad to see him, she fell asleep against him almost instantly. Karen, he thought, and felt a vague flicker of anger toward her.

Karen knew everybody was mad at her. Valerie walked by her so fast, she seemed to create a wind. Roy stumbled over a chunk of her Erector set and kicked it violently against a wall. It didn't matter. No matter what Valerie kept telling her about this being her home, she knew that it wasn't. She was only going to be here for as long as it took her mother to find her. Roy told her he was her father now. Valerie called herself "Mother." She had told her that her mother was gone, gone for good, but Karen didn't believe her for one minute. In Montana Karen had spent a lot of time at the next-door neighbor's because sometimes her mother didn't come home at night or even the next day, but eventually she showed up. How was anyone to know that this was different?

She watched the roads. She waited. She tried to dial on the heavy black phone that Valerie had placed too far for her to reach because Valerie didn't want her going anyplace, especially back to her mother. She could call so many numbers one of them would be her mother's. Every house she saw outside could be one with her mother in it. Every car could be her mother's. But every time she strained to look, Valerie would get angry. She'd hit her, tugging her away, keeping her prisoner. "Please behave now," she said.

Sometimes, though, she could feel her mother near her. A presence, closing in. The smell of leather, the beat of her boots on the floor. Sometimes, too, at night, she could hear her whispering through the walls, calling Karen, Karen, and when she looked up there was a faint white mist, a ghost, terrifying her so that she'd tighten herself away, pulling the covers over her head so only her nose poked out. It isn't real, she told herself. It isn't my mother.

She remembered her mother. Cropped blond hair and long earrings Karen's hands were slapped away from. She remembered riding in front of her mother on the red motorcycle, a small hard helmet wrapped about her head with scarves. She couldn't see anything of her mother but her hands on the handlebars, but she could hear her breathy laughter. Sometimes, too, when the bike was parked out in the front, her mother would perch her on it alone, teaching her to drive.

She didn't remember a father. There were no pictures, no stories, and whenever she asked her mother, her mother just laughed. For a time, too, Karen remembered Jack, her mother's boyfriend. He had a ponytail and a leather jacket he sometimes draped about her shoulders, but not in a friendly way, and when he smiled at her she thought of wolves' teeth. Her mother shut the door of her bedroom the nights Jack was there. Karen was supposed to be in bed, but she always got up, prowling the dark living room until she found Jack's cigarettes. She played games with them, arranging them like dominos, breaking the tips and scattering tobacco like dandelion heads. Sometimes her mother would come out and put her to bed, sometimes Karen would just fall asleep on the rug. And in the morning Jack always looked at the cigarettes and shook his head admiringly. "Jesus. I musta really tied one on last night." He shuffled fingers through Karen's hair and then left. Her mother, swollen-faced, surveyed Karen. "Okay, dirty puss, into the bath for the both of us," she said.

The day her mother died, Karen had been at the neighbor's house. The woman's name was Tina. She lived alone, addressing envelopes at home for a living, and she had been happy to feed Karen noodles with butter and ice-cold Coke in a coffee mug. "There's your mum, I bet," she had said when the phone rang. She wasn't on it two minutes when her face turned white. "You poor little piece of sugar," she said to Karen, and then burst into tears.

Karen didn't believe for a moment that her mother was gone. She didn't believe it when Jack showed up, his face swollen, his eyes like spilled pools of ink. When he tried to hold her, she pulled away. She kept thinking there was a way to get back to her mother. If she was good.

She was silent when a policeman took her over to a big white house filled with children. Silent when she was brought into an office to talk to a woman who said she only wanted to help Karen. She was there only a little while, but in that time she was polite. She kept to herself, ignoring the other kids. She ate everything on her plate, even the oatmeal that made her want to throw up. Every time the door opened, she looked up. Then she was called back into the office and told how lucky she was, how some children waited for years for what was going to happen to her now. She was going to be adopted, but all she thought was that now her mother would never find her.

Every time Roy and Valerie acted like her parents, it made her furious. Every time Valerie hugged her, she felt like she couldn't breathe. Valerie's kisses felt wrong, like brands. Every word Valerie and Roy told her—mother, father, home—felt like the biggest lies she had ever heard. Who were they to lie to her, to pretend nothing had happened? She had to run and run around the house, whirling up a wind, just to roughly breeze those kisses off her. She had to scatter the house with screams to blot out all the lies. She had to move and shriek and break everything she could get her hands on to keep them seeing how she didn't belong there, to stop them from trying to swallow her whole.

Only once did she feel any hope, the night when Lee swung her into the night and the wind pushed against her back, the way her mother's hand might, the night Lee led her right past a motorcycle almost like her mother's. The way Lee had held her. Lee had hair the same yellow as her mother. Lee always acted as if she knew Karen belonged to someone else. "Where's Mommy?" she asked Lee, but Lee didn't say "Right here" or "Home with Roy." Lee's face showed a brisk flicker of pain, and then Lee just looked at her as if she knew the answer and just wasn't telling yet.

---**10**---

Valerie didn't know when she started to mind Karen's new devotion to Lee. She should have been happy about how easy it was now to deposit Karen with Lee, how easy to take up her own life again, to work at the restaurant, to be with her husband. To forget. Instead she noticed how Lee smiled at Karen in a way Valerie had never seen before, how Karen calmed almost as soon as she touched Lee but grew rigid again if Valerie brushed by.

"I don't understand you," Roy told her. "You should be glad she's willing to stay with Lee. And anyway, I thought you wanted time to yourself. Time for you and me."

"I do," she insisted. "Of course I do."

Didn't she always have special plans on the nights Lee agreed to take Karen? Things you'd never dream of taking a child to. She and Roy dressed up because time to themselves seemed an occasion as special as any anniversary. They saw plays and concerts. They sat in movie theaters so blessedly quiet, she sometimes fell asleep in them. She'd go and meet Roy in some fancy four-star restaurant that discouraged children, and the whole time he was toasting her with the most expensive wine on the menu, she couldn't help wondering what Karen was doing with Lee. "Earth to Valerie," said Roy, and she plucked up her wineglass. "To us," she said, fixing her smile. She'd drink wine throughout the evening. She'd go home and make love to her husband as long as she wanted and there wouldn't be anyone else there to stop her.

"Thank God for Lee," Roy said. He stroked the line of her face. Valerie fit herself deeper against his cupped palm and shut her eyes.

"Tell the truth, do you slip her a Mickey?" Valerie asked Lee. If she had once thought the problem was simply that she wasn't Karen's natural mother, she didn't think that anymore. Not when she saw Lee with Karen. She watched Lee, but she couldn't for the life of her see Lee doing one single thing differently.

What the hell did they do when she *wasn't* there? Lee just laughed when Valerie asked her. "We go for walks. We read. We play cards," she said.

"You go for walks at night?"

"I'm with her."

When she asked Karen, Karen was silent for a moment. "We go for walks," she said. "Once we even walked here. We rang the bell, but you weren't home."

"Well, of course I'm not home," Valerie said. "That's why I bring you to Lee's." She studied Karen. "I don't want you walking to the house," she said. "It's too far and the roads are crazy." She didn't mention that the real reason she didn't want Karen walking to the house was that sometimes she really *was* home. She'd pull the blinds and close the doors and just bask in the quiet disarray of her own house. And when she went to pick up Karen in the car, she always told her stories about where she had been. Helping Roy who was working late. Visiting a sick friend.

Sometimes with her daughter in the car with her, she would stroke Karen's hair and her fingers would snag against something prickly. "Come here," she said, and groomed Karen's hair, pulling out a burr. "Where did this come from?" she said.

"The sky," Karen said, reaching for the burr.

"The where?" said Valerie.

"The bonny deep blue sea." Karen held up the burr, smiling. Where did a child get an expression like "bonny"? Karen was about to position the burr back into her hair when Valerie plucked it free, sailing it out the car window. It bounced on the highway, disappearing under the wheels of a car. "Oh, pooh," said Karen.

"Don't say 'pooh,'" Valerie said. Wild, she thought. Her daughter looked like a ragamuffin. The new jersey she bought her was somehow already stretched out of shape. Her sneakers were habitually untied, and her hair was trailing from the red poodle barrette she had thought would look so cute.

Going through Karen's pockets, she found things. She found an earthworm, a butterfly, and once a torn piece of brightly colored map. She squinted at it. Texas. Her daughter was carrying around Texas in her pocket.

"Five years old and already she wants to leave us," Valerie told Roy, handing him the map scrap.

He tore the paper in his fingers, grinning. "Not without her map, she won't," he said.

One day Valerie had left Karen in the backyard for two minutes, and when she came back outside Karen was gone. Frantic, she dashed around to the front of the house, calling out for Karen like a madwoman. She sprinted into the road, and then, two blocks away, she saw Karen's small figure walking determinedly. It was easy enough to catch up with her. Panting, Valerie grabbed at Karen's arm. "You scared the dickens out of me!" she cried. "You know you're supposed to stay in the yard. Where were you going?"

"I'm going to Lee's," said Karen.

"Oh, no, you aren't," said Valerie. She gripped Karen's hand so hard that Karen yelped. "We're going *home*," she said. "Home, where you belong."

She began to keep a closer watch and then, in the fall, Karen started kindergarten. Valerie herself would walk Karen to the school and pick her up, and in between she'd have five blessed hours all to herself. She'd have a silence so rare and bountiful she could wrap it around her like a quilt. Northeast Elementary. Depending on how things went, maybe she'd donate some cakes to the bake sale. Or a dinner for two at the restaurant. That might be nice.

Even though Valerie knew the other kids would probably be in jeans and sneakers, she dressed Karen carefully, in a violet cotton dress with a lace collar. She brushed her black hair and tied a red silk ribbon around it. Her daughter looked beautiful, like the kind of little girl who would play with dolls rather than butcher their Dynel hair with scissors, a girl who accepted hugs as willingly as she might give them.

"I'll pick you up after school," Valerie said. She was going to the restaurant today, as soon as she dropped Karen off. She was going to lose herself in crab soup and thick sauces and in the comforting cadences of adult speech.

She brought Karen into the class, a large bright room with painted yellow floors. "Look, a hamster," Valerie said. She pointed to a small clean cage by the window. The hamster was running around and around an exercise circle. "Let's go find the teacher."

The teacher's name was Mrs. DeCamp, and as soon as she saw Valerie with Karen, she came over. "I recognize you from your wonderful restaurant," she said to Valerie. "I had a feast there." She looked down at Karen. "Well, and who's this?" she said brightly. Karen looked up at Valerie as if Valerie were betraying her. "I'll see you at one," Valerie told Karen. She wasn't going to make a fool of herself bending for a kiss Karen would only wipe off. "Would you like to see our kinder garden?" Mrs. DeCamp said, pointing to a small row of pots. "Everyone is going to grow their own bean plant."

"I don't know," said Karen. Baffled, she turned toward the row of cooking pots. "Like mother like daughter," the teacher said, and in that moment Valerie left quietly.

All that morning Valerie expected a phone call from the school. When she went to get Karen she expected Mrs. DeCamp to be standing there, hands on her hips, insisting Valerie keep Karen back another year. But Karen bounded out smiling, a crepe-paper flower in one hand. She seemed to like her first day. "Mrs. DeCamp said I could take the hamster home one weekend," she said. "The whole class gets to."

"Isn't that nice," said Valerie.

Every morning Karen willingly set off for school. She almost always had something in her hand when she returned. Clumsy letters on a sheet of blue-lined paper. A crepe-paper flower. Sometimes, though, she brought home drawings that Valerie couldn't bring herself to tack up on the refrigerator because they were always of a woman she didn't know, a woman with short blond hair and a black jacket and high black boots, standing beside a motorcycle.

"Would you like to invite any friends home?" Valerie asked Karen one night at dinner.

Karen shook her head. "Lee," she said.

Valerie calmly pulled apart a minibaguette. That morning in the restaurant Lee had leaned against the stove and asked a million insistent questions about Karen. Did she like the kids? Was the teacher too strict? She had wanted to invite herself to dinner. She had books for Karen, she said. She had a box of paints. She wanted to come over that night. "Tonight's not good," Valerie had said.

"Isn't there anyone in your class you like?"

"Amy," said Karen. "Jane."

"Well, whenever you want to invite them over you can," Valerie said. She looked across the table at Roy. He seemed more relaxed. Things could be all right. Karen was already less disruptive at home. Maybe she could make some friends, maybe she could be socialized the way the psychologist had said, transformed into a daughter despite herself.

Karen had been in kindergarten nearly a month when Mrs. DeCamp called. Karen was having tantrums. She couldn't make friends.

"What about Amy?" Valerie said.

"Amy?" said Mrs. DeCamp. "There's no Amy in my classroom."

"What about Jane?"

"Mrs. Hayes."

Mrs. DeCamp cleared her throat. She told Valerie Karen kept to herself. She kept drawing these paper dolls with clumsy genitals, drawings Mrs. DeCamp had to confiscate before they confused the other children. Karen hit the other children. She used the words "damn" and "shit."

"But why I'm really calling," Mrs. DeCamp said, pausing, "is that Karen keeps walking out of class."

Valerie felt suddenly dizzy. "She does?" she said. "Where does she go?"

"Don't be silly," said Mrs. DeCamp. "I catch her before she's halfway onto the playground."

"I'll take care of it," Valerie said.

She hadn't the foggiest idea how to take care of such a thing. She didn't want to do one single thing that might make Karen dislike school enough to start balking about going. She had to be discreet.

That night she was leafing through a *Parents* magazine when she came across the answer. Sleep hypnosis. You could tell a drowsy child that he wasn't going to wet the bed anymore and the suggestion would implant as firmly as if a hypnotist had given it. You could make a child think behaving was his own idea and not yours.

Valerie put down the magazine. Karen was already in bed, burrowed sleepily under the soft blue coverlet. Valerie bent toward Karen. "You want to stay in the classroom," she whispered. Karen's lids fluttered open. She looked at Valerie with real interest. "You stay in school," Valerie whispered again, stroking Karen's small pulsing lids shut.

The hypnotism didn't work. Valerie got a call from Mrs. DeCamp two days later and then again the following week. Karen kept trying to walk off. Karen had hit another student. Karen had taken her wax carton of milk and poured it into the lap of another student.

The more Valerie tried to tame her, the wilder Karen seemed. At home she hurled her dinner plate to the floor. Her nightmares increased. In desperation Valerie began bringing Karen to Lee's, but even at Lee's Karen seemed worse. When Valerie came to get her, Karen was filthy dirty, zooming around and around in furious circles, and although Lee shrugged it off as play, Valerie was alarmed.

She and Roy went to conference after conference with the teacher, with psychologists, but no one seemed to make any difference. Valerie and Roy kept Karen in at night. They tried rewarding her with toys when she was good; for one week Valerie even gave her baby tranquilizers, which seemed to make Karen edgier. She began to have prickles of doubt about ever having adopted, and although she could never come right out and ask Roy, she wondered if he was sorry they had adopted, if secretly he blamed her for not being able to conceive.

The truth was that Roy didn't blame anyone but himself. He should have insisted they find a baby; he should have convinced Valerie a childless life was still one worth living. He shouldn't have given in to love.

He hated feeling like a bad father, but he couldn't discipline Karen any more than Valerie seemed to be able to. When he was most furious, he made her go to her room. Exhausted, he'd slump in the living room, thinking about when he had first courted Valerie, how the two of them used to go and rent movies, bringing four back to his apartment, but by the end of the evening they hadn't watched a single frame. They hadn't seen a thing but each other.

There was never a single sound from Karen's room. When he went to check on her, she was coloring on her bed or leafing through a picture book Lee had given her, making up her own words to the story. When she saw him, she fiercely turned away.

He couldn't help his frustration. He couldn't help the way his stomach clenched as soon as he approached the house. He began to wake up early just so he could have some silence. He kept out of Karen's way simply because he couldn't bear the way she seemed to stare through him, and he began to get angry about it. What was so terrible about him that a little girl would seem to hate him this way? What was so unappetizing about his hugs? He got into bed and burrowed against Valerie, who was so still and quiet, it bothered him. "You there?" he said, propping himself on one elbow. She was staring into the darkness, listening to Karen kicking her bedroom closet, the thud like a heartbeat through the wall. "Val?" he said. She didn't turn toward him. He floated a hand down her breast and she moved away. "I'm just too knotted up," she told him.

"You want to talk?" he said.

She shook her head.

"No? Not even to me?" He stroked her stomach lightly.

"Not even to you," she said. Stricken, he took his hand away.

He lay in bed until almost three, and every time one of the fluorescent numbers clicked ahead into the next, he didn't think, This is a new day. Instead, he thought, Time is running out.

He was gone when Valerie woke up. Uneasy, she hustled Karen off to school and then went to Roy's office.

His secretary told Valerie he hadn't wanted to be disturbed, but she went into his office anyway. He was sleeping on his office couch, his mouth soft and open. She crouched beside him, kissing his cheek. He blinked up at her.

"I missed you this morning," she said.

"Did you? You don't seem to that much anymore."

She sat on the edge of the couch. "Yes, I do," she said.

He lifted himself up, ruffling his hair. And when he turned to her, his face was beaten. "What are we going to do?" he said.

Valerie looked for help where she could find it. She began reading every child care book she could find, but none of them ever seemed to quite apply to Karen. She cornered mothers with kids in the restaurant, but the mothers always seemed vaguely insulted when

Valerie asked them if their kids ever had tantrums. The parents at the PTA meetings she and Roy now dutifully attended looked at Valerie with slight hostility. Karen had hit some of their own children. They acted as if Karen's behavior were her fault, as if there were something she should be doing, but no matter how she asked, no one could tell her what that was.

"I'm not to blame," Valerie cried in the car. Roy kept one arm about her as he drove to pick up Karen from Lee's. "Of course you're not," he insisted. "Neither of us is."

Lee was calm and unruffled. In the living room, Karen was curled onto a chair. "Come on, honey," Valerie said to Karen, but Karen wouldn't move. "Honey," Valerie said, near tears again. "I want to stay here," Karen said roughly. She wasn't in the nice clean pajamas Valerie had sent over with her. She had on one of Lee's T-shirts that said "I'd Rather Be Sailing," and as far as she knew Lee hadn't sailed once in her whole life. It was past ten and she had six chocolate cookies in her lap. Of course a child wouldn't want to leave a home like that. Of course a child would gravitate toward a place like that the first chance she could. She studied Lee as if she had never seen her before. Lee was also wolfing cookies. She was barefoot even though everyone knew there were splinters in wood floors, and on Lee's dusty floor there were also stray glasses, a coffee spoon, and God knew what else. Valerie straightened. She began to think that maybe Lee was the one who was at fault, that maybe Lee wasn't such a good influence on her child, that maybe it had been a mistake to have been so grateful for her sitting.

Valerie determined to switch Karen's alliance. She had expected things to come too naturally; she hadn't tried hard enough. Well, she could be as spontaneous as Lee, as surprising, only she wouldn't be giving her daughter cookies at eleven at night. She wouldn't let her walk in the night.

One evening she hustled Karen into the car. "It's a surprise!" she said. She drove ten miles, past Dairy Queen stands and shopping malls, Karen tense beside her. "Lean back, now," she told her, gently lowering her against the seat, but as soon as she released her hold, Karen sprang forward again. "Guess where we're going?" she said brightly.

"To Lee's?" Karen said.

"No, not to Lee's," Valerie said crossly. "We don't always have to

go to Lee's. There are lots of other things in this life than Lee's."
Karen sank onto her seat.

Karen perked up when she saw the green-and-yellow neon in front
of the roller rink. "What is it, what is it?" she said, and Valerie smiled.
"You'll see," she said. She parked in front of the neon sign and helped
Karen out.

Inside, Karen was even more dazzled. She cocked her head at the
sound of the skates. She loved the flashing lighted board that
announced LADIES CHOICE or MEXICAN HAT DANCE. Amazed, she held on
to the wood banister and watched the skaters. Valerie paid for two
pairs of skates, but Karen was so excited holding the small white
leather skates that at first she didn't want to let go of them for
Valerie to slip them on her feet. She clung to Valerie's hand while
they skated. "This is fun!" she shouted over the tinny piped-in music.

They stayed for three hours. "More," Karen cried, even though she
could hardly keep her balance any longer. She lagged at the banister.
As soon as the roller skates were off her feet she wobbled, taking
Valerie's hand. "We'll do this lots more," Valerie said, squeezing
Karen's fingers.

Valerie thought she had won her over, at least a little. The rest of
the evening Karen played quietly, and when Roy came home she
raced to meet him. "I roller-skated!" she shouted. "Well, *we* skated,"
Valerie said, kissing Roy. "And how did we do?" Roy said, beaming. "I
didn't fall down once!" said Karen. She skated for him, in her bare
socks, pale yellow anklets with blue violets on the cuffs. Her hair
looked shiny and clean, and for once it wasn't in her eyes. When
Valerie touched her she didn't pull back.

Valerie couldn't stop Lee from dropping by the house, undoing all
her good work. She told her it wasn't a good time, but Lee ignored
her. She told her to call first, but Lee never did. Sometimes she
brought Andy, whose face was always a strange mixture of delight at
being with her and annoyance at having to be at his sister's. "Come
on," he said, tugging at Lee. But Lee was hard to remove. She took
Karen into the backyard and crouched down with her and pointed
out constellations in the sky.

"It's too light. She can't see them," Andy said.

"Yes, I can," Karen said. "There's the Big Dipper." She scribbled
fingers in the blue sky.

"You've got a good imagination," Andy said.

"The stars are there," Lee said. "Whether you see them or not, they're there." She looked at Karen. "Wish on a star."

"Yeah, well, we gotta get going," Andy said.

Lee bounded up. "Okay, toots," she said, kissing him, taking Karen by the hand.

Valerie saw how irritated Andy was with Lee when she insisted on staying longer than he wanted. He was a little irritated with Valerie, too, though. He came over some nights and sat in the kitchen with Roy and Valerie, all three of them sipping on glasses of table wine. He noticed how Roy never complained about Karen, how instead he'd just get silent. He'd look out the window into the distance as if there were something there of interest. Valerie, though, never stopped complaining. One night after Lee had refused to see a movie with him because she wanted to bake a surprise cake for Karen, he hinted that maybe Valerie shouldn't go out. "A kid needs her mother," he said.

Valerie's gaze sharpened. "It's not my fault those two are in love with each other. So don't stick around here so much. Go someplace alone with Lee."

"She talks about Karen all the time," Andy said. "It's like Karen's with us even when she's not."

"Lee," Valerie snorted. More and more she was angry with Lee. She somehow blamed her. She was determined to get other sitters, to change them so Karen wouldn't have time to form an allegiance, but the first new one she tried, a junior high school girl who showed up with curlers in her hair, was nearly in tears when they came home, and behind her Karen was crying, too, standing in the midst of a pool of milk.

She vented her anger the best she could. She sniped at Lee for coming to work ten minutes late or for leaving early. At work, on a day so hot no one had the energy to set the red-checkered cloths on the tables, never mind cook, she made Lee make soup. "You've been here long enough to know how to make something," she said. She hadn't really cared one way or another whether there was soup or not, but she left Lee alone in the kitchen, afraid her soft heart would ruin everything. "Valerie?" Lee, face flushed, called her in. "Taste this," she commanded. Valerie peered into a pot. "It's cold," Lee said. "Blueberry soup." Valerie dipped in a spoon. The soup was cool and light and delicious. "You know," Lee said, "I wouldn't mind doing some cooking here."

"I bet you wouldn't," said Valerie.

Andy knew Lee loved Karen, and sometimes he thought she loved him, too. She was always telling him so in his daydreams, always agreeing to marriage and a house, and kids, and a life that was going to start any minute. Awake, though, she got upset when he mentioned marriage, and the only thing she'd say about it was that she needed more time. All right. But he would use that time to his advantage. He would expose her to weddings so happy they would make her heart shatter with longing. He would be so funny and kind and loving that she couldn't help but melt. All he had to do was wait for Lee to catch up with his plans. All he had to do was catch her at every wrong turn and bring her back to him. When she snapped at him, he told her jokes. When she was silent, he let her be.

And he did more than daydream. He began saving money in a special bank account. He began taking the long way to work, stopping in the suburban neighborhoods to look at the houses, and every time he spotted one with a "For Sale" sign on it, he imagined Lee inside it.

He knew how dependent on her Karen was, but he hadn't realized it might be the other way around until one day, when Valerie and Roy whisked Karen off to the ocean. "We all need a vacation," Valerie said. "My folks have a place on the Cape. It'll be great," she insisted.

Lee didn't know what to do with herself. She missed Karen. Restless, unanchored, wired with resentment, she waitressed at the restaurant, slamming down wrong orders, adding up the tallies wrong, sometimes in the restaurant's favor, sometimes in the customer's. By midafternoon she was in the kitchen, badgering one of the cooks to let her help. Cutting carrots into thin curls, making flowers out of radishes, or simply stirring a silky sauce, made her relax. She cooked soups so cool and beautiful, she sometimes saw the customers studying their plates before they put a spoon into it. At home, unable to sleep, she stood in front of her stove and made lemon pies, dark meaty soups, and custards she never had the appetite to eat.

At night she walked alone. Exhausted, lonely, she settled into Jim's old jacket and walked. Just like old times, she thought ruefully, digging her hands into the pockets. She thought about Jim for a minute, and then, without intending to, she suddenly thought about her own daughter. Joanna, the newspaper had printed her name. If she had thought she had a right to name her, she wouldn't have named her that. Her daughter wouldn't remember her the way Karen remembered her mother; her daughter had Jim. She wouldn't need her. She was surprised at how much worse a thought like that made her feel. She turned back home.

Everything seemed suddenly to fray her nerves. She was now grateful for Andy's calls, for the way he would whisk her off to a movie or out to dinner at a moment's notice. One weekend he took her to the state fair. She had a good time. She held his hand, she kissed him, and if she bought fifty dollars' worth of soft plastic souvenirs and plush toys, if she bought a T-shirt sized for a five-year-old, he said nothing. For Lee he bought a small globe with sparkles inside it. "I give you the world," he told her.

Valerie and Roy and Karen were back within the week, but Lee didn't feel less restless until Valerie walked into the restaurant, sunburned under a white piqué dress, her hair shored back with a white headband decorated with shells.

"Well, was it wonderful?" Lee demanded.

"Sure it was," Valerie said. She examined one of the fruit mousses Lee was preparing. She didn't want to tell Lee that Karen had stormed and sulked and refused to go near the ocean, that her own mother had never stopped criticizing the way she and Roy were with Karen. "If a child's bad, the parents make it that way," she pronounced. Roy and she baked on a beach littered with soda pop bottles and college kids on the make. The vacation hadn't done one thing to bring anyone any closer. There was no air-conditioning in the cottage, and no one slept at night under the blanketing whine of the mosquitoes and Karen's nightmares, which rang out in the still beachy air. As soon as Valerie saw home, all she wanted to do was be alone to walk through her restaurant and supervise things and not have to think about a cranky husband and a recalcitrant child. If Lee wanted to watch Karen nights, if Karen wanted Lee, Valerie was suddenly too tired to protest.

Karen had a plastic bag full of sand and shells that Valerie had collected for her. She had a soft rubber shark that squeaked when you pressed it, which Roy had bought for her. She had accepted the gifts but had shown no interest in either the shells or the shark, not until Valerie took her over to Lee's. Karen excitedly packed her toys.

"Well, better late than never," Roy said, but Valerie just sighed. Why didn't people belong to the ones who tried to love them?

After Roy and Valerie had driven away, Lee and Karen jiggled the bag full of shells and put the rubber shark in a bathtub full of water. For a moment she imagined Roy's car hurtling down a dark road, Valerie pressed against a loosening door. But, no, she didn't want them killed. Maybe they would run off to a second honeymoon and both get amnesia, and she could take Karen. There was a sudden, fleeting image of her own daughter, a faceless girl she could have passed on the street and not known as her own. She bent down to kiss Karen, and she was flooded with so much longing that she abruptly started to cry.

She shifted Karen off her lap and almost immediately felt empty. Alarmed, Karen stood up, faintly shivering. Lee swiped one hand across her running nose. "It's all right," Lee said. "I'll be right back, darlin'," she said. She left Karen trailing fingers into the soapy bathwater, and she went to the telephone in the kitchen. She pulled out the receiver, stretching the tangle of cord so she could still see Karen. Five years old, she thought. Five years. She dialed Information for Maryland. "Jim Archer," she said.

"Archer," the operator said. "Here it is: 555-8914."

Lee stiffened. "That's 555-8914," the operator repeated.

For a moment she was crashing into time. How could he still be at the same number, at the same house? In a kind of hypnosis she dialed the number, and then a small voice answered. "Hello?" Lee, stunned, gripped the phone. Another voice, older, more resonant, wove in the background, a woman's. "Honey, say 'Hold on, please,' remember, honey—"

"I have a red truck," the voice said matter-of-factly to Lee. "I have two whole dolls. And I want a gerbil."

"Hello?" a woman said. "Sugar, don't touch that." Her voice took on an adult tone again. "Hello, I'm sorry." She was polite and cheerful. Lee slumped against the counter.

"Is Jim Archer there?" Lee said. Her voice sounded as if it were punched full of holes.

"He sure is," she said. "Who's calling, please?"

Lee crashed down the phone. Sick, she felt sick. She turned toward the sink. She could fill it with water. She could douse her head into it. She was about to twist the spigot when she saw Karen, silhouetted in the door, dangling the dripping shark from her hand, her eyes luminous with tears. "I thought you left!" she cried.

Lee moved toward Karen, crouching down, drawing Karen against her. "I'm right here," she said. Karen wound her two hands so tightly around Lee's neck that for a moment she felt completely lost, and it was only when she felt a tremor moving inside her heart that she knew it must be breaking.

"I thought I was alone!" Karen said, crying a little harder. Lee stroked her hair, a headful of dark strands, not blond, not fair like her own—like her daughter's.

"Would I do that?" Lee said, and tilted Karen's chin so she could see her. Then she tickled Karen behind her ears, waiting until her face bloomed into a smile, until she could study her and study her and never for one single moment ever believe she had been crying.

They were driving to the aquarium, and already Valerie and Karen were fighting. Karen kept trying to undo her seat belt. "You and Daddy don't have yours on," she accused.

"We're adults. We're ready to die. You're not," Roy said, turning the wheel. Valerie flashed him a look.

"I hate this seat belt," Karen said, pouting.

"What do you think we'll see at the aquarium?" Valerie coaxed, brightening her voice. "Monkeys? Rocket ships?"

"They have tiger fish," Roy said. "Imagine that. Do you think they roar?"

Karen, in the back seat, unclipped her belt. She slid over to the window. The houses blurred past her.

"Andy tells me he's thinking of going out to California for a vacation. He wants to take Lee with him."

"I don't know why she doesn't just marry him," Valerie said. "My brother's a doll. I'd even marry him."

Karen looked up. "I want to visit Lee," she said.

Valerie shut her eyes. "Not today, peaches," she said.

"Today," Karen said.

"But, baby, we're going to the aquarium!" Roy said, twisting around. "Look what you did," he said, and briskly clipped her back into her belt, tightening it so she couldn't move.

They left the aquarium a little over an hour after they had arrived.

Karen had started kicking another little boy near her, until Valerie had yanked her by her arm. "That's it," she said furiously. "We're going home." She half dragged Karen out the door. "No more tiger fish, no clown fish," she said. "You understand what that means, no clown fish?" Karen slapped one hand along the wall.

The whole drive home Karen clamored for Lee. "It's too late, we're going home," Roy said. Karen kicked at the seat. "It isn't," she said.

"Don't kick the seat," Roy said.

"The way you've behaved, you'll be lucky if you see her by next month, Lady Jane," Valerie said. "I'm sick of this. I really am. I do everything and this is the thanks I get."

Karen's mouth snapped shut. She edged toward the window, squeezing her eyes shut so the colors blurred the world into another place. When the car passed Lee's block, she stiffened. She tried to catch Roy's eyes in the rearview mirror, but he was looking straight ahead. He swerved into the turn toward home. She didn't move until Roy had parked the car back in front of the house.

"Into the house until supper," Valerie said. She was going to make something easy, something adult. Pasta and clam sauce. Karen, she thought meanly, could just eat the pasta plain or with butter. Or she could stay in her room and sulk until she was hungry enough for a peanut-butter sandwich. She strode into the kitchen and surveyed the open cupboard of food. Cilantro, she thought, and reached for the oblong green can.

Roy, face set, grabbed the paper from the porch and headed for the bedroom. He sprawled on the bed, his shoes hanging over the clean spread, and flipped through the entertainment section. He felt like seeing a movie, but not with Karen or with Valerie.

Neither one of them saw Karen getting her jacket, stepping lightly onto the front porch, and walking purposefully down the street. It wasn't until nearly ten minutes later, when Valerie began making a tomato sauce out of guilt, that she thought to call Karen, and by that time Karen was nearly halfway to Lee's.

She knew the way. She had walked it with Lee in nights so black she had to count her steps just to know where a curb was. Lee had told her it was Indian walking, that they were scouts staking out their territory. "Sight isn't the only way you know something," Lee told her. She had shown her how to know which direction a car was coming from just by the sound. She had taught her to find the gas station just by the smell of the gas. "You use all your senses, even the invisible ones," Lee said. "Like sometimes you just *feel* someone's behind you." Karen started. She thought Lee meant the ghost or the way she sometimes smelled her mother's perfume or heard her boots. She thought maybe Lee could tell her how to turn around so quickly her mother might still be there.

She hadn't liked the aquarium. She hadn't wanted to tell Valerie or Roy, but she had been afraid of the fish. Their mouths suctioning up against the glass, their white eyes staring at her, were like nightmares. "Look at this," Valerie kept saying, edging Karen closer to the tank with the weight of her body. Roy pretended he didn't care when she wouldn't go up close to the baby shark tank, but she felt him watching her. Valerie kissed too hard, the way her mother's friends had when her mother had asked them to. Her touch was angry. She jerked on Karen's jersey; she smoothed Karen's hair right down to the bone of scalp. Valerie and Roy punished her all the time. She waited for them to get tired of it, to send her home, to stop insisting they were her parents. They wouldn't let her hang up the pictures she had drawn of her mother. They wouldn't let her talk about her. Behave, they said. Behave. She banged her feet across the wood floor; she threw a spoon so hard that her mother could hear and trail it clear across the country.

Karen recognized the street by the sound of the cars. There up ahead was the stop sign. Lee had made her practice stopping in front of the sign. Look all ways, she had said. Cars don't have eyes. You do. Karen widened her eyes. Two cars passed, whizzing so fast she heard a smear of music, and then she saw Lee, standing at the far end of the road, resting on a rake, talking to Andy.

She looked in back of her to check traffic. Two cars were coming, and she stopped, patient, the way Lee had told her to. She was rocking on the heels of her red sneakers when she saw a third car coming toward her, a flash of red skidding to a stop so sudden, she bounced from the curb.

She could see Valerie's head poking out of the front window, and Valerie suddenly jerked open the front door, hinging out her legs. "Karen!" Valerie shouted. The sound made Lee start. She set down the rake and was suddenly striding toward Karen, trying to cross the busy street. Lee waved her arms at Karen.

Panicked, Karen looked back at Lee, and then she began running into the street. In front of her Lee was zigzagging through traffic toward her. In back of her she saw Valerie, her face as pale and white as a slice of moon, and for a moment it seemed as if Valerie were running toward Lee and not toward her at all.

She didn't see the car. Her blood was coursing through her like electric current. A car horn sang in her ear. Valerie made a sudden lunge, and Karen bolted back, turning toward Lee, slamming into the sudden path of a blue sedan that arced her up into the air, and the whole time she could hear her own breath, like the heady rush of wind from the back of a motorcycle.

Valerie had refused to leave the hospital. She kept asking every nurse who walked by if there had been some mistake about her daughter. She kept trying to go into the room where they had brought Karen, even after the nurse told her that Karen's body had already been removed.

Valerie nudged Roy's hands from her, circling the waiting room, sitting down on one of the turquoise plastic chairs and then rising up again every time a doctor approached. "Come on, baby," Roy said. "Come on. Please." She looked at him blankly and then sat down on one of the chairs again.

She couldn't quite remember. Details kept shifting, jumbling in sequence. She remembered the car, how it had fishtailed to a stop with a scream of tires. She remembered the driver, a weeping middle-aged woman in a bow-blouse suit, who braced her body against the hood of her car as if she were an ornament. She remembered being frozen, too, encased in a kind of force field. She kept thinking, If I don't move, nothing more will happen. She remembered Karen hitting the pavement in a spasm of blood, and then she remembered Karen limp in Lee's arms, a bright spreading star of crimson on Lee's white shirt. When the ambulance came, the driver had put a hand on Lee's shoulder, crouching down, whispering, as intimate and shocking as a slap. Valerie moved through the force field. She grabbed on to the sleeve of the attendant. His limp black hair skidded into his face when he looked up at her. "My little girl," Valerie said, the only words she knew, and the attendant stood up, pivoting from Lee, fading her into the background, and this time the arms he touched were Valerie's.

She remembered Roy. His shirt had been pasted to his back. His hair and face had been so damp with sweat that he looked as though he had stepped from a shower, and when she had touched him, he had shaken beneath her fingers. Andy had been crying. His face was puffy with tears she hadn't seen since he had been kicked off Little League when he was twelve. She hadn't wanted them to touch Karen. She kept telling them that everyone knew you weren't supposed to move people after an accident. "That rule's for everyone but us," one of the attendants told Valerie, crouching over her daughter like a shroud. They wouldn't let her ride in the ambulance until she threatened to sue them, and the whole ride there she kept one hand on Karen, in a way Karen never would have permitted if she had been aware. "I'm here," Valerie said.

She didn't remember the others arriving, only that they had somehow always been here, always been crying, too, it seemed. Lee slumped against Andy. Valerie looked at him, and he carefully extricated himself from Lee and went to his sister, crouching before her. "Hey," he said.

"I can't leave," she said.

"Sure you can. You can leave with me."

"No, I can't," she said, but then he was lifting her up, her weight braced against his arm. She wasn't aware of moving, but the hospital was trailing past her, one room seeming to blend right into the next until they were at the back emergency doors, and for a moment Valerie was pinned in place. "It's all right," Andy said, and pushed at the door, leading her into the cold night. "There's a million stars out," Valerie said in amazement. "Oh, God, it's a clear night." She twisted in Andy's grip, turning around a little, stumbling against Roy and Lee, and as soon as she saw the starry stain of blood, rusted on Lee's white blouse, she remembered everything all over again.

"Get her away," Valerie said, her voice hard and shiny.

"Valerie," said Lee.

"Get her away from me," Valerie said. She began shaking, trying to wrench from Andy's grip.

"It's all right," Andy said. He soothed Valerie back around so she was facing the night. "Let's just get you home first," said Andy. He let her walk on ahead by herself, and then he turned to Lee, who had her arms bundled about her as if she were freezing.

Awkwardly he rubbed her forearms. "Here. Take the keys. Get a cab and go to my place. I'll be there as soon as I can." Baffled, she stepped back from him. "I'm supposed to go?" she said.

"No, just for a minute," he said. "Just a minute. Just so I can tend to my sister and Roy. She's in a state. And I have to make sure they aren't alone in the house. I have to make calls."

"I can't be there?"

"Lee—she's in shock. Every time she looks at you, it upsets her." He smoothed back her hair. "Give it time."

Lee started to cry. She turned to look back at Valerie, who deliberately shut her eyes. Lee abruptly took the keys from Andy, but when he bent toward her she moved from him so that all he was touching was air.

He worried about her the whole drive home. Flushed with guilt and grief, he made the turns toward Valerie's home. He knew how much she had loved Karen, but Valerie was his sister, Valerie was the mother. And he had told her to go to his place. He knew if she went home, she'd be surrounded by Karen's pictures on her refrigerator, by the toys she kept for her. His place, at least, would be full of him. He looked at his watch. The first call he'd make would be to her.

He drove Valerie and Roy home in silence. He saw Valerie flinch when the car pulled into the driveway. There was a tricycle in the front yard, a muddied blue ball by the side. The dining room table was set for three. He made them come into the kitchen and sit around Valerie's huge oak table while he made the calls. He called Lee first, feeling a flicker of fear when she didn't pick up. Then he called everyone he knew. He told them the same thing, but every time he said it, it didn't feel any truer. He called Roy's parents, he called his own, and when his mother answered he burst into tears.

Roy stood up. "Excuse me a minute," he said, and walked out of the room.

When the first knock came, the first people, for a moment Andy kept thinking it might be Lee. He waited until there were at least a dozen people in the house. Waitresses, cooks, friends, all of them orbiting edgily around the kitchen. Someone had brought a platter of fruit, still encased in crinkled paper. Someone else had brought a bag of groceries and was chopping in the corner. He walked over to

Valerie, who was sitting perfectly still, her hands folded schoolgirl style in her lap.

"I'm going now," he told Valerie, bending to kiss her hair.

"I know," she said.

"You let me take care of the details, all right?"

"Yeah."

"You call any time of night," he said. "I'll be here first thing in the morning." He looked at her. "You want me to stay?"

"No. You go." She frowned. "Roy hasn't come out of the bedroom all evening."

"You want me to go get him?"

"No. Let him be alone."

He nodded and then Marielle, one of the cooks at the restaurant, came over and promptly burst into tears. "Oh, honey," she wept, and rocked Valerie into an embrace.

He drove past Lee's apartment on the way to his, peering up at her dark windows. When he got to his house he rang the bell, half hoping Lee might answer the door. Instead, though, he jiggled the key into the lock himself. He entered an apartment so dark, it made him feel helpless. He didn't realize Lee was there until he started to walk toward the phone, and then he heard her, crying in the bathroom. "Lee?" he said.

She was in the bathtub, her arms about her knees, her face so swollen it seemed as if flesh had been puttied on. As soon as he saw her, he felt wounded. "Come on," he said. He bent and lifted her up into the one clean towel he had, and then he led her, as if she were blind, to the bedroom, her wet feet making prints on the dark wood floor. "Okay now," he said, and lowered her to his bed and stretched out beside her, stroking her hair, her face, the hollows just under her chin. "Talk to me," he said, but she kept choking. The shoulders of his shirt were wet with her tears. "Just get it out," he said, but no matter how much he coaxed, she couldn't seem to tell him anything at all.

He felt like a voyager between two planets. The first thing he did when he got up was go see his sister. There were always people in the house. Valerie cried nonstop, talking incoherently about Karen, blaming Karen's wild mother, blaming the adoption agency and herself, and almost always blaming Lee. "She lured her," Valerie said. She looked up at Andy.

"She didn't lure her," he said. "We were talking, planning a vacation."

"Hah," said Valerie. "Lee go on a vacation with you."

"Val," he said.

"Shut up," she said. "Don't tell me. You're blind."

"Come on. Let's go sit on the porch. It's cooler."

"Karen was running to *me*, Andy."

"I know," he said. "I know she was."

He was exhausted most of the time and constantly worried. He didn't like the way Lee was grieving, as terribly and as hard as his sister. He'd get to Lee's house and she'd be wobbling on her feet. "I can't sleep when you aren't here," she whispered. She listed toward him, and as soon as her head rested against his shoulder, she seemed already to be dreaming. He put her to bed, and as long as he was aside her she slept, but all he had to do was get up to get water and she would bolt upright, alarmed.

He wasn't used to her needing him so much. "Talk to me," he said. "You have to talk about it." But every time he even started to probe, she wrenched from him. "I loved her," Lee said. "And I thought Valerie was my best friend."

"You've got to give her some time."

Lee faced him. Her skin was so pale it seemed to shimmer. "What about me?" she said.

"Well, it's different," he said. "She wasn't your little girl."

Lee flinched. She bent to scoop up her sweater from the dusty floor, tugging it onto her arms.

"Where're you going?" he said.

She didn't look at him. "What are you doing?" he said. She shoved up the sleeves of her sweater. "You're right," she said, crying. "She wasn't." And then, abruptly, she walked out his door.

Roy had refused to hold any sort of service or funeral. Karen was to be cremated, and as far as he was concerned the place could keep her ashes. He didn't want to be there, and he didn't want Valerie to be there, either. The day of Karen's cremation he set the alarm for five in the morning. In a morning white with fog, they threw on jackets and got in the car, so that by the time the sun was burning off the haze, they were out of the state altogether. All they did that day was drive, the radio bebopping Top 40 hits, the two of them switching off driving every few hours. Neither one of them spoke or pointed out sights or did anything but look straight ahead. They stopped at Howard Johnson's to use the bathrooms and to buy cans of Coke they didn't really drink, and when they passed families with kids Valerie would avert her face. It wasn't until the sun was setting that he turned around and started the drive back again, taking his time, gauging the trip so that they wouldn't be back until the next afternoon altogether.

He knew it was different with Valerie, but Karen was burned out of him. All he cared about now was what he had always cared about. Valerie. He had all these plans. What else was there to do with the time but make plans? He shaped a future for them. He was moving her to California, to stay with his parents, who had a house right on the beach. The salt air could sting memory away. They'd both have enough time to find new jobs, create lives. He could sell the restaurant and use the money to start up a new one if that was what Valerie wanted. He had closed the place for a month, but he could reopen it, let it run itself for a while, and give her time to decide. The best thing about California was the fact that there were no seasons. He wouldn't have to shore up against any other fall. He wouldn't have to avoid looking at a leaf burnished with color for the way it would make him sick. No, there'd be one long, endless, dazzling summer. A marking of time that was completely in place.

He took care of his wife. Every night he lay with her resting against his shoulders, and every time she told him what a bad mother she had been, he hushed her. "Listen," he murmured. He told her bedtime stories about the lives they were going to be leading. He talked to her the way he had talked to Karen, paring down his language, softening his tone. "We can start a whole new restaurant," he told her. "We can call it East Coast California. You like that? Or maybe just California East. We'll serve bagels. We'll import waitresses from New York who'll be so rude they'll charm the customers." Valerie half smiled. "We'll both tan," he promised. "We'll get a large rangy dog and make it wear a red bandanna about its neck." She smiled again. "A blue bandanna," she said. "I like blue." She trailed two fingers along the side of his face, as tender as if his skin were glass. The stories seemed to calm her, and when he caught sight of her face, she looked almost as if she believed him, and eventually she would fall asleep.

Every time Lee called Valerie, Valerie would hang up on her. She was in bed with Andy one evening when he told her that Valerie and Roy were planning on moving. "They need the change," he said.

"Oh, no," Lee said. She moved closer to him, wrapping one arm about his hip. He hated himself for it, for almost basking every time she clung to him. He recognized the grief in her need, but sometimes, too, he told himself he recognized something else, something quite different.

"They're selling the restaurant," he said.

Lee got out of bed, tossing the coverlet over Andy.

"Hey, they're not selling it right now," Andy said.

Lee was pulling eggs out of the refrigerator, a mixing bowl from under the sink. Andy simply sat on one of Lee's chairs and watched her bake. She was a good cook. He could already recognize the things on Valerie's menu that were hers just by tasting them. There was always some mysterious ingredient he couldn't pinpoint. He rested his chin on the edge of the chair. She had a dot of flour on her chin. "Lemon upside-down cake," she said.

"What's the secret ingredient?" he said, but she was pushing the cake tins into the oven, and even after the cake was frosted and cooling under a bonnet of waxed paper, when they were both back in bed, she wouldn't tell him.

Lee took the cake to Valerie's the next day, before even one car was in front of the door. Lee rang the bell, but when Valerie saw Lee, her face shut in upon itself. Lee held out the cake pan awkwardly, keeping her arms stretched until finally Valerie opened the door.

"Andy told me you're leaving next week," Lee said. "Don't go. Don't do it."

Valerie stepped back toward the house.

"Andy'll give me your address," Lee said.

"I guess Andy will give you whatever you want," Valerie said. She wrapped her hair about her hand, knotting it.

"I'm going to write you," Lee said. "I don't care what you say. I'm going to keep writing and one of these days you'll write me back. I know it."

"There's the phone," Valerie said, but there was no sound. "You were my first real friend," Lee said. Valerie stood perfectly still for a moment. "Don't you believe me?" Lee cried, and then Valerie quietly took the cake.

"Don't throw the cake out," Lee said. "Please. Eat it. It has six eggs in it." Valerie looked down at the cake in her hands and then, turning, finally shut the door.

They left before the house was even sold. Andy had hired an agent to take care of things. Lee felt as if there were a fissure in time. All Lee could think about was her father wandering happily with her through rooms other people had lived in. Perfect for a child, he used to say, pushing Lee forward with a touch so gentle that even now, remembering, it made her yearn.

Lee began going back to work. The restaurant had been sold to an accountant, who wanted it only as a tax shelter. He showed up one day with Andy, following Andy so gingerly into the kitchen that it seemed as if he had done something wrong. He was young and sloppy, and he kept shrugging. "Meet the new owner," Andy said, "Hank Malorian." Lee stopped stirring a sauce. The waitresses clumped together. "Nothing's going to change," Hank said. He had kept the original name. He didn't fire or hire one new person. "The head chef, he's in charge now," Hank said, pointing to Rico, a twenty-four-year-old Spanish expatriate who had already published a cookbook on greens. Hank told them he had no intention of ever coming to the restaurant at all, because the embarrassing truth was that he really preferred to eat at home. He made his hands a semicircle. "I know investments. You guys know restaurants."

Nothing changed, but everything changed. The old customers kept coming, but new ones, having read about Karen in the papers, came, too, out of curiosity at first and then because they liked the food. Lee couldn't risk standing idle for one single moment, so she began doing more than waitressing. Whenever she could she busied herself cooking. Reckless, she threw herself into projects, lulled by the rhythms of the kitchen, never really thinking if a recipe might work. Some of them did, enough so that all Rico had to do was take a taste and want it on the menu. "You take risks," he told her, tasting the roasted red pepper soup she had made. "Keep on surprising me like that and I'll make you second chef. How'd you like that? A *career*, not just a job." She flushed with pleasure.

"What's in this?" he asked her, but when she shrugged he became annoyed. "Memory. That's all recipes are. And if you don't remember, you won't ever be able to have this delicious dish again. And neither will anyone else. You start remembering. That's part of your job description."

She remembered. At five o'clock she couldn't go outside the kitchen because every time the door opened, it would remind her. She would almost swear she saw a small dark head. She walked past Valerie's house, and although there was a new blue station wagon parked neatly in the drive, she expected the front door to slap open any minute, for Valerie to run across the lawn and embrace her.

She remembered the accident, taking it apart second by second. If she had not been raking, would Karen be alive? If she had run faster, if she had shouted louder. She kept thinking about this thing she had once read in one of Jim's science books. Something about the new physics. Something about probable universes. Every event had several probable outcomes, and every one of those outcomes could somehow be occurring somewhere in space and time. Karen, she thought. A probable Karen sidestepping a car to fling herself, hot and damp and churning with emotion, into Lee's embrace. A probable Karen growing up close to Lee. A probable Valerie staying the best of friends. A probable Lee who was anything but what she was—miserable and lost and seeming to fade from life.

Every day she felt herself growing smaller, more compact. She needed less air to breathe. She had to remind herself to eat, and even then, after a few forkfuls, she was stuffed. Her jeans bagged so that she dug a new hole in the belt she used to cinch them with. Her skin seemed translucent, as if you could see the heartbeat beneath it. Sometimes now, when Andy touched her, she couldn't even feel him. "You all right?" he whispered, concerned. She rolled in his arms when he made love to her, but she didn't feel herself participating. "I'm fine," she said, but she was helpless, traveling away from him, so fast that even if he had tried to, he couldn't have managed to stop her.

It hurt her even to look at Andy. Already she saw shadowy images of other women at his side, women from a probable universe who deserved him, women who didn't belong to their memories. She should have turned away from him the first time he had thought he could rescue her, pulling her from the heavy blank white of a storm.

She didn't know what had happened. It was impossible, but

suddenly she didn't see Karen anywhere. When other children came into the restaurant, they didn't remind her of Karen. When she passed a school yard, she wasn't drawn to every crop of dark hair jumping rope, to every tomboy scuttling on hands and knees. Instead she suddenly saw a world full of blond little girls, of shy little voices talking about gerbils. Instead she saw her daughter.

She lay awake at night and thought about her. Joanna. She remembered the voice, as high and thin as a wire. She wished she had held her when she had been born—she never would have left her then. She would have known her daughter's scent, the texture of her skin and the blue of her eyes. If she had given herself two seconds with her baby daughter, she never would have been able to escape.

Now when she made desserts in the restaurant, they weren't for Karen anymore, they were for Joanna. She made cupcakes in the shapes of clowns; she put extra powdered sugar in the frosting. Karen hadn't been hers, but Joanna was. If they were together, she could hold her in her arms and feel another heart beating up against hers. If they were together, she could look into those eyes and see back into a past that connected them both. And a future. She lightened.

She began dreaming about Joanna. She hadn't left the hospital at all. She had gone home with her baby and with Jim. She and the baby had piled into the car and driven to see her father, and as soon as he saw Lee holding her baby, he had burst into tears. He had pushed past Janet to welcome them into his home. She sometimes dreamed about Joanna's room in Jim's house. She never saw Jim, but she saw herself sitting on the edge of a small white bed, next to a small child, and she was singing. When she woke up she was so weak with longing, she couldn't get up from the bed. Lying there, she thought about Joanna, and then she realized she couldn't remember what she had been singing in the dream. She didn't know any real songs, she couldn't remember any from Claire, and she knew she had never sung to Karen. And that afternoon she went to the library and took out a children's record. She played it late at night, humming along, memorizing, and when she went to bed she lay there singing "I Went to the Animal Fair" and "The Ash Grove," her low clear voice soothed over her like a blanket, lulling her to sleep.

She began to hum and sing the songs more and more.

"What are you singing?" Andy said, amused. "I swear I hear 'Bah Bah Black Sheep.'"

"It's just something I remember," she told him.

She began to wear her memories like a weight. She still loved cooking, but somehow it became muddied. She'd see a child's fingerprints in the pie she was making; she'd hear a child's laugh just to the right of the stove, a presence calling her so strongly, it hurt her. She stopped what she was doing and pressed her hands about her head. "You don't look like you feel so hot," one of the other cooks told her. "Why don't you go home. I'll cover for you."

"Thanks," Lee said. She started walking home, thinking it might clear her head, but every block there suddenly seemed to be a new travel agency started up. She kept spotting people carrying suitcases or speaking in East Coast accents. A little girl in a cherry-red coat skipped alongside her tall blond mother.

That night, when she saw Andy, she instantly began crying. He rolled her in his arms. "Let me see that pretty face," he said. He gently swiped at her tears. "Tell me what's wrong."

She lifted her chin, snuffling. Her tears were pooling against his T-shirt.

"Did something happen at the restaurant?" He tickled her under her chin. "You want me to go beat up the new owner?"

She half smiled and shook her head. To amuse her he started humming the parts of "The Ash Grove" he remembered her singing. She laughed a little, and then she sat up, studying him. "Do you think I'm a bad person?" she said finally.

He grinned. "Absolutely," he said. "The most evil I've ever met." He kissed strands of her hair. "What's this about, Lee?"

"I don't know. I'm just a little blue," she said, lowering her gaze from his. She lay against him, heartbeat to heartbeat, and she wanted to ask him, What happened to people if they decided to suddenly reappear after years of disappearance? She wanted to know if leaving your baby was a crime you could be put in jail for, if coming back for her was equally criminal. She had a million terrifying questions she wanted to ask, a million terrifying things she wanted to tell him, but no matter how much she wanted to, she couldn't. How could she trust someone she had been lying to for so long, how could she ever think he might ever forgive her?

Andy owned stacks of law books, but instead she went to the library. She wouldn't bring any of the books to the tables but instead stood in the aisles, balancing one heavy text after another, trying to find out if she were still legally her daughter's mother. She read through forty different custody cases, ending up more confused than when she began. She was afraid to call a lawyer. She didn't know who knew Andy and who didn't, who might have known she was Andy's girlfriend, who might casually ask Andy how come she was so interested in custody and abandoning mothers all of a sudden.

The more she thought about Joanna, the more she began thinking about her father and about Jim, too, and the more she thought, the more real they became to her, as if they were hurtling through time toward her. Had they waited at train stations, thinking she might be coming home? Did they ever do the same things out of habit, like a ritual, the way she set out cookies at four for Karen, thinking, Somehow this must be a mistake, this must not be the way the afternoon was going to end, turning into silence, solidifying into an evening so endless it was all you could do to get through it. Did her daughter ever feel a kind of odd nameless yearning toward a picture of a woman everyone said was her mother?

When she thought of Jim, a sudden river of grief and pity swelled within her. She kept remembering his sad, slow face, the face she had helped to create. The only way she could ever give him back those years was to tell him about her half of them.

It terrified her. She lay awake at night thinking what might happen if she went back, what might be the scenario. Sometimes she saw herself walking up to her father's door, and then abruptly her father would strike her, just as if she had been seventeen. Sometimes she'd see Jim bolting the door against her, or else he'd stare at her uncomprehending, as if he had been looking for her so long, he no longer knew who she was at all. Sometimes she saw Joanna running to her and sometimes running away. But the thing was, once she saw herself holding her daughter, she couldn't think of one single event past that.

It made her tired. She'd sit down to dinner with Andy, and it seemed to her as if there were always a ghost or two insistently dining with them.

"Hey, you don't have to keep getting up. You're not playing waitress with me," Andy told her. She laughed. "Oh, it's fine," she said. She couldn't tell him she kept getting up because of the way her past wouldn't let her present continue.

It was too hard. She was too weak and cowardly to barge back into lives she had once left for good. She had Andy. She had a job. A home. And then she'd think of Karen, staring at a motorcycle that looked like her mother's, and she'd think of her own daughter, a girl she had never once looked at, a girl who had nothing more of Lee than photos, and then she'd know there was nothing else to do but to go.

The next evening, right after work, she stopped at a travel agency. It was half-empty. A woman with black hair severely pulled back with a rhinestone clip nodded at Lee. "Where to?" she said.

"Baltimore," Lee said. "No. No. Philadelphia first. Then a flight on to Baltimore."

The woman's head dipped. She pecked out something on a computer and squinted at it.

"Round trip?" the woman said.

Lee was silent for a moment. The air suddenly seemed to have weight. Anything could happen. "One way," Lee blurted.

She had three weeks before she left, but already she felt herself traveling back through time. The past shimmered and expanded before her, crowding out her present. She could be walking by the maple trees out front, and all she would smell was the lilacs and the wisteria that were growing in the Baltimore backyard she remembered. She couldn't help but get lost because if she didn't look really closely the street signs now bore names like Eutaw Place and Hughs Avenue instead of Miffland and University and Oakes.

If anyone had asked her, if she had been able to talk about it at all, she would have said it was a relief. It was easier to wear your past like sudden new blinders, easier not to see too clearly just what it was that might not be waiting for you if you came back, because then leaving might wound you so much, you might never be able to continue.

Andy came over to cook her dinner, and the whole time he was cutting vegetables she sat dreaming on a chair in the other room, half hearing the conversation he was making. When she sat down to eat, she toyed at the salmon he had made, she stared out the window.

"Do you want to tell me what's going on?" Andy said. "Don't make me ask what's wrong fifty times."

"Nothing's wrong," she said.

"Do you think that helps either of us?"

She set down her fork, angled on the plate, a signal she had learned to recognize when she was waitressing, a sign that the meal was finished.

"I have to go away," she said finally, not looking at him.

"Away? Why?" he said.

She looked down at her plate. Already she was traveling. She concentrated on the hum of the plane beneath her.

"Are you coming back?"

"I don't know."

"Can I come with you?"

"No," she said.

"I don't believe this!" he said. "Why are you going? Aren't you going to tell me?" He waited, and when she was still silent he turned away from her.

"What's happened to us?" he said desperately. "You still care about me. I know you do." He stroked her hair, and as soon as she felt his hands, she couldn't help herself, she didn't care how much it was going to hurt later when she remembered, she leaned against him. "I do," she said.

"So what is it?" he cried. "What's going on?"

"Look, I—" She stumbled. Every time she looked up and saw his face, she felt something crumbling. "Don't you think I love you?" she said finally.

"Then why are you going?" he said.

She looked down at her hands. "I have to go," she said. "I have to take care of something. It just can't wait."

"What? What something?"

"Please," Lee said. He looked at her, completely baffled. "Lee—" Then he stopped. He traced one finger along her chin.

"Okay, you don't have to tell me. But whatever it is, it doesn't matter," he said. "Believe me, it doesn't. We'll work it out together."

Lee felt herself tottering at the edge of something dangerous. She could reach out her hand and touch his face. She could wrap herself about him and he'd hold her and rock her and love her and never ever ask her one single question she didn't want to answer, and if she could let it go at that, they could be happy. She could learn to look the other way every time she saw a small blond child. She could learn not to look at a map too closely or a crowd scene on the news. One more step and she might never be able to get back. She looked at Andy. She smelled the lime after-shave he sometimes used. The kitchen fell into a focus so dazzling, she felt dizzy. Exhausted, she rested her head against Andy's shoulder.

"Don't go," he whispered. An image flickered in her mind. Karen standing in her kitchen holding a dripping plastic shark. "I thought you had gone!" she had cried. And then, in that moment, it didn't matter how much she was going to miss Andy, how much it was going to hurt. It mattered only that she find her father and Jim and her daughter again, it mattered only that she somehow fix things so she could stop running, so she would never again be in this position, where someone was having to beg her and beg her not to go.

"I'm sorry," she told him, her voice a whisper.

"Well then," Andy said, pained. He resettled on his chair, and as soon as he moved away from her, she felt him becoming dimmer. "I guess, then, I have to go now, too."

The week before she left, Andy turned icy with civility. He had thought she was just angry, that she wasn't really going to leave. Even when he saw the suitcase, he still had thought it was just acting out. Cases could be unpacked, after all, tickets returned. When he caught her shivering by the window, her palms pressed against the chilly glass, he sometimes would try to take her shoulders. "I guess you think I'm going to ask you where the hell you're going, but I'm not," he said. Something flickered in her face, a look he recognized from false witnesses in his courtroom.

He couldn't quite bring himself to ignore her, because every evening he thought might be his last with her, which terrified him, but he never for a moment thought it might be terrifying her as well. He began missing her, sometimes the most when she was right there beside him. They ate long silent dinners in good restaurants, where he insisted she order desserts she barely touched. They sat numb in movie theaters, a small bucket of greasy popcorn uneaten between them. Around them couples whispered and laughed too loudly or got up during the second plot point. They sat perfectly still until the closing credits were over. Sometimes they were the last people in the theater, and when they got up neither one of them could remember much about what had gone on on the screen, and then he took her home.

He never went home himself, though. He parked the car a block away from her house, willing himself to stay awake, to make sure she wasn't leaving. Once, not more than ten minutes after he had seen her enter her house, he saw her leave it again. She was burrowing into her leather jacket, and he bolted out of the car, ready to follow her. She was halfway down the street when she turned abruptly, watching him. Her eyes were luminous. Her hair showered down her back. "I'm just walking," she said stiffly. He was so humiliated he backed away from her, nodding curtly. Then he took the car, but he went to an all-night supermarket. There were only four or five other people in there, two couples and a young woman dressed all in black who kept giving him sharp, hopeful stares. He was methodical, grabbing a steel cart, pushing it down each and every aisle, and never taking one single item from one single shelf. It took him only twenty minutes to peruse the entire market, and then he replaced the cart carefully and walked outside again. He couldn't go back to Lee's, not that evening, so instead he went back to the courtroom and in the silence looked through cases. There were laws, things made sense. People who lied were punished.

The night before Lee was to leave, he came home drunk. He had performed a wedding just that day, to a couple so in love they had kissed through the whole ceremony. They had been so oblivious that they hadn't seen the stricken look on his face. Lee could smell the alcohol, she saw it reeling in his walk as he came toward her. His face was tight and miserable and angry, and for one instant, it was all she could do to not touch him, to not give up or take him with her. Instead she flattened herself along the wall.

"I'm not going to be around when you get back," he said.

"Come on, sit down," she said.

"If you get back."

She led him into the bathroom and hinged his legs down so he was sitting on the closed lid of the toilet. She drew him a bath. "Was I wrong to think we cared about each other?" he said. "Tell me. Was I wrong?" She couldn't bear to look at him. She couldn't risk being pulled back. She twisted, turning off the spigots, and started to undo his shirt. "Come on," she said. "Please." She refused to get in it with him, but she sat beside him while he soaked, and neither one of them looked at each other. He began splashing water into his face, so violently that she began to know he was crying. That night they slept naked in his bed, and although the bed was very small, they didn't touch, and in the morning, when Andy woke up, his heart drowning within him, Lee was gone.

She almost turned around at least five times. She was suddenly paralyzed with fear that she was on a fool's mission, that she might never see her daughter. It had been years. She had heard a woman's voice on the phone, joking with Joanna, soothing. What kind of person had she been that she could just leave—and what kind of person was she that she could just come back? Maybe she'd just watch Joanna at a distance, make sure she was all right. Maybe she could talk to Jim in private, tell him that all she wanted was for her daughter to know that her mother was in the world.

She might never see her daughter. She might never see Jim. And she might never see Andy again. She should have told him the truth the day she had met him. She should have walked away from him the day she had first seen him. She boarded the plane to Philadelphia and her father, already missing Andy so much that she stumbled. She was so unsettled, the flight attendant asked her if she wanted an aspirin.

~11~

As soon as the bus from the plane pulled into the Philadelphia station, Lee jumped to her feet, crash-diving the contents of her purse onto the floor. She jammed everything back in and then stood quickly, moving amid the current of people to the outside, and then she was completely disoriented. The city looked familiar, yet something was vaguely wrong. The names on the signs seemed foreign. The air smelled burned.

"Taxi!" she called to a Checker cab prowling toward her. She got in and gave the driver the address she had looked up in the library two days before. Frank's address. The cabbie was an old man, burrowed into a plaid cap, and hung from the rearview mirror was a huge green crucifix with a weeping Jesus entwined around it. "That road," she told the cabdriver, but when he rounded the curve, the high school she and Jim had attended was gone. In its place was a brick apartment complex. "When did this happen?" Lee asked the cabdriver. "Wasn't there a high school here?"

"Nope," the driver said. "Never."

"But there was," Lee insisted. "I ought to know, I went there long enough."

"I'm telling you never," the driver said, and rounded the corner again. "You think I just started driving a cab yesterday?"

"But I remember it," Lee said. "You're wrong."

"Lady," he said, his voice an edge.

"Okay, fine, forget it," she said, trying to keep her own voice calm. She made him drop her off at the end of the block. She felt seasick.

Her legs kept buckling. Mosquitoes whined in the shimmery heat. At the far end of the block a small boy was riding a red tricycle around and around in dusty circles. When she passed, the boy looked up.

What was the worst that might happen? Frank could smash the door in her face. He could weep and embrace her. Or Janet could answer. Or another woman. That thought made her ridiculously hopeful.

There it was: 409. A large white colonial springing from the midst of a carefully manicured lawn. Hedges framed the yard, and there was a casual sprinkling of yellow and blue four-o'clocks. The flagstone was chipping a little.

Lee measured her steps up to the glass front door. Her reflection blurred back at her. Her hand hovered in midair, fairly floating on the air. And then she rang the door.

She could hear steps. "Hang on a sec," a voice said, and then the door opened and there was Janet, looking exactly the same as the day Lee had left. Her hair was wet from the shower, dripping into points across her dress.

Lee stepped back. "It's Lee," she said.

"Lee?" Janet said. She leaned forward, peering into Lee's face, starting to raise one hand before she lowered it again, dropping it against one hip. "Jesus," she said, and then all the soft curves of Janet's face grew suddenly rigid, and she drew herself up.

"Well," Janet said finally. She studied Lee. "You look like hell," she said coldly.

"I've been traveling," Lee said.

Janet shook her head. "That sounds about right," she said. She looked out past Lee, toward the end of the block. "So what kept you?" she said quietly.

"Could I please see my father?" Lee said.

Janet snapped Lee back into her focus. "I ought to slam this door right in your little face," Janet said.

"I can wait someplace else," said Lee.

Janet lifted up one hand. "Wait all you want," she said. "It won't do any good. If you had cared enough to keep in touch, you could have known. You could have saved yourself the trip."

Lee stared at her. "Known what?" she said.

Janet rubbed at her forehead. "Frank died," she said. "Last year." The sunlight was so bright, Lee could see individual blades of grass.

She could see the diamond wedding band on Janet's finger, the lean line of shoulder poking up through the blue shirt.

"Did you hear what I said? Or do you still not care?"

Stunned, Lee blinked up at Janet. "I always cared," Lee said, and burst into ragged tears.

Janet didn't move toward her. Instead she opened the door and stood back. "You come in," she said. "If I keep this door open, it'll bring the flies and the neighbors both, and I can't say which is worse."

She let Lee in, but she kept her body distanced. She led Lee into the living room, and right away Lee noticed that she didn't recognize one single thing in it. Every piece of furniture she had ever sat on or stumbled against or leaned upon was gone. The new pieces were sharp and angular, as like Frank and unlike Janet as she could imagine. There was a Chinese black enamel desk. A black leather sofa. A gray canvas chair and track lighting. On one side of the room was a large white porcelain poodle. On the mantel was a studio portrait of Frank and Janet, but as far as Lee could see that was the only picture in the house. Lee sank down against the leather. It cooled her bare legs.

Janet sat down opposite her on the canvas chair. "Heart attack," she said. "Doctor gave him a clean bill of health and two days later he was showing a house and—well, that was that." She shut her eyes, stroking the bridge of her nose.

"When you ran off with Jim, it did something to him," Janet said. "He got so *angry*. So hurt he couldn't discuss it. Who did you think you were, a couple of wild kids running off like that? What the hell did you ever see in Jim anyway? He was like a big baked potato. No personality."

"He had personality," Lee whispered.

"Oh, really? Is that why you left him?" Janet flopped her hands into her lap. "Oh, hell. Frank would have come around, I think. But when you ran off again, you didn't run to him, did you. It was like losing you twice."

"He never made me feel like he was losing me," Lee said.

"He was so furious with you," said Janet. "And he couldn't *stand* Jim. Thought Jim had ruined your life, and his right along with it. After a while he insisted he had washed his hands of you. Jim used to send us pictures of the baby, little locks of hair, booties. Frank would toss everything out into the trash, but then he'd go out later and dig it all out again." She shook her head. "That little girl was so pretty. I would have liked to have a granddaughter running all around the house, but Frank didn't want any reminders. I think he was terrified your daughter would look just like you. It was the only thing we really argued about. Sometimes in secret I'd buy a little present, a little dress or a soft toy, and write a card with both our names scribbled in. The only reason I never sent it is I knew how furious Frank would be, and the truth was he mattered more to me than any granddaughter, so I ended up returning everything or giving it to Goodwill." She looked at Lee. "That matter to you any, that you have a daughter?"

"He never answered the cards I sent him from Baltimore."

Janet shook her head, exasperated. "You think he didn't love you, is that it?" She stood up and moved heavily to the Chinese enamel desk. She bent and pulled something out and then turned back to Lee. "You want the truth? I was the one who stopped loving you. But only after you left, only when I saw what it did to him. I loved you when you were around. And really, why I did is God's mystery to me. You were this spindly mean little girl, and every time I moved to so much as touch you, you pulled away as if I had suggested we eat the cat down the street. Then you got wild." Janet sat down opposite Lee again. "We could have been pals," she said. "We could have sat up nights having heart-to-hearts about boys and school and life in general. You know, I was dying to take you shopping. Dying to buy you outfits for school, for dating, for whatever you wanted. Dying to take you to the best hairdresser in town with me."

"I didn't want a haircut," Lee said.

"Maybe that was the problem." Janet slapped a packet in her hand. She stopped talking. "Here," she said. "Take this. Frank saved it for you."

Lee took the packet. Inside was a bankbook. She looked up at Janet. "It's yours," Janet said. Lee fingered the bankbook, then opened it tentatively. There was ten thousand dollars in it. Quietly she shut the book.

"No one could have touched that money while Frank was alive, but then he died and I could have used that ten thousand," Janet said. "You were declared legally dead." When she saw Lee start, Janet half smiled. "Surprise," she said. "Anyway, God knows I had some bills. I could have used a trip to Europe after Frank died."

Janet stood up. "I lied before. I did care about you once, but it was never really love. It was secondhand. I loved you because Frank wanted it that way. And I saved this goddamned bankbook because Frank would have," she said. "So take it, then I don't have to have one single thing left to do with you. I don't have to even think about you."

She moved to the desk. "I'll write down where he's buried. You can go there if you like." She gave Lee a sharp look, then stood up, smoothing down her skirt. "Well, I have things to attend to," she said. The light from the window suddenly caught and flickered in Janet's earrings, the same small diamonds Lee's father had courted her with. She wondered if Janet ever took them off, if all she had to do was touch them and feel Frank's fingers gently tracing her lobes. "You can use the phone to call yourself a cab," Janet said.

"I want to walk some," Lee said, and Janet nodded.

"I'll walk you to the door," she said. She wrote something on a scrap of paper and handed it, folded, to Lee. Then she opened the door, blinking at the sun. She waited until Lee was at the end of the flagstone. "As far as I'm concerned, you're still gone," she called out, her voice pulling. "To me, you never came back."

"I did come back!" Lee cried.

Janet shut the door.

Lee couldn't remember how long she walked. She wasn't sure of the direction, but when she got to a street she hailed a cab back to the airport. She'd never come back here. She crumpled the piece of paper. She didn't need to see his grave to remember him. All she'd have to do was shut her eyes and she'd see him. All she'd have to do was think his name.

Lee spent the rest of her week in a Philadelphia hotel, and the whole time all she did was cry. She wouldn't allow the maids in to clean her room or give her fresh towels. She kept going over and over in her mind what she might have said to Frank, how he might have looked, how it might have felt to hold him. He might have forgiven her everything the moment he saw her. If only she had made this trip just a year ago, or two years ago, or any time other than right now, when all that was left her was some strange hotel room and her grief.

At night she dreamed of her father. She was standing with him in the middle of a house, a shell really, just one huge empty room with a door at the end. There was no furniture in it except a big oak clock, ticking so loudly she could hardly hear Frank. He was older, in a soft blue suit, and he was holding up blueprints for her to see, pointing things out to her, smiling. "And this will always be your room," he told her, showing her the biggest square on the paper. "Blue, your favorite color," he told her. "When do you want to move in?" he said.

She looked around her anxiously. The ticking boomed in her ears, and she put her hands over them. "Today," she said. "I can move in today."

He grinned. "That's my girl," he said.

She leaned forward to hear him over the ticking. "Come on, pussycat," he said, "I'll show you." He took her elbow and led her to the door at the far end. "Ta-da!" He beamed as he opened the door. The room was filled with thousands and thousands of broken clocks.

"Frank!" she cried, but when she turned to him the room was empty again. The clocks were gone. And then she bolted up out of bed, turning on the TV, swinging open the cheap fiberglass curtains, switching on every single light in the room. She was drenched with sweat. She stood against the wall, panting, drowning in panic. And then she grabbed at the phone.

She remembered the number by heart. She punched down the keys, and then it rang, once, twice, and a recording stuttered on. "I'm sorry," a male computer voice said noncommittally, "but the number you dialed has been disconnected."

Lee's bones filled with ice. She was pressing the receiver so deeply into her cheek, she'd later have a bruise there. Her hand shook. It was the right number. She knew it. She had dialed it enough times. People didn't just pack up in the night and leave without a forwarding number—not unless they were her. Not unless something so terrible had happened, you might want to disappear. Joanna, she thought, and then she forced her hands to unclench. She forced herself to dial the O with her thumb, tensed for the operator. "There's some problem on the line. Will you dial it for me?" she said.

The operator sighed, but she dialed it, and Lee leaned forward into each ring. Please, she thought. Oh, please. The line rang and rang, seven times. It was late. People were sleeping. And then suddenly it caught. "Yes?" Jim said in a low, sleepy voice.

Lee started to cry with relief. She cupped one hand over the receiver. "Who is this?" Jim said, and then Lee gently hung up the phone. She lay across the hotel bed and closed her eyes and cried some more. She thought about that voice, and thought about Joanna, and fleeting across her mind, too, she saw Karen, running across a newly tarred road toward her. And then she got up and steadily began to pack.

She left the hotel the next day, arriving in Baltimore while it was still morning. She tried to imagine what her daughter looked like, but all that kept coming into her mind was Karen—and then herself, seven years old, in second grade, wearing a yellow quilted jumper over a purple blouse, her wild hair unraveling from careful braids.

As soon as she saw the house, she felt catapulted back in time. She was seventeen again, her life wrapped about her like a tight itchy sweater she couldn't remove. She was angry at Jim again, angry at Janet and at her own stubborn self.

The front yard was empty when she got to it. It confused her. She quietly made her way to the backyard. A bright red swing set was planted in the damp grass. Marigolds and four-o'clocks bloomed by the side of the house. On the back walk was a large red ball festooned with white stars. She didn't touch it.

She came back around front. She couldn't just climb the stairs and jauntily ring the bell. She couldn't rap on the window or toss small stones the way she used to when she was dating Jim. Jesus. Jim. She couldn't imagine anything stranger than seeing him. She felt dizzy with fear. She stood sideways on the flagstone, paralyzed.

The front door suddenly opened. A woman was backing out, rushing, a heavy black leather purse slung across one shoulder. She was in a nurse's uniform, with those awful white crepe shoes, the white stockings that paled your legs bloodless. She finished locking the door and peered anxiously down at a large red Mickey Mouse watch banding her wrist. She had bright shiny red hair and bangs so long that Lee could hardly see her eyes. Someone in the house must be sick, Lee thought, starting to panic.

"Jim," Lee said. Startled, the woman with the red hair looked up at Lee. All that crazy motion suddenly stilled. "Is Jim here?" Lee repeated, her mouth dry.

"He's at work." The woman seemed frozen to the steps. "Who are you?"

"Andrea Banrett," Lee said, backing away onto the street. "I . . . I used to go to school with him."

"Andrea," the woman repeated. She gave Lee a hard long look, then abruptly pulled herself from the steps. She strode toward the car. "I'll tell my husband you were by," she said. She jammed the keys into the car, idling, staring at Lee, not pulling out of the drive until Lee started walking away from the house.

Lee was halfway down the block when the sedan drove by. It felt as if the car slowed as it passed her, but she kept her head bowed, almost as if she were praying.

As soon as the car was out of sight, Lee circled back to the house, her heart bumping fitfully inside of her. Husband. Jim was married. He had a wife who sat down to dinner with him nights, who rubbed his back and might have been calling Lee's daughter hers for years. Lee stood on the steps of the house, fingering the wrought-iron railing, picking at the rusted pieces with her fingers. She felt a sudden queasy stab of fright. She looked up at the top of the screen door. Once, when Jim was studying late at night, he had wired a makeshift alarm to keep intruders away. "You have to feel like your home is safe," he told her. When he knew the baby was coming, she had had to talk him out of bars on the windows. She ran her fingers along the top of the door. The wire was still there.

She rang the bell, hoping for a sitter, but no one answered. It was past three. Her daughter would be out of school. Her daughter could be anywhere. She glanced at the house next door. The drive was empty; the house looked dark. She remembered the woman who lived there, Maureen, a nosy neighbor who had taken to Jim as though he were her own son, who had joked with Lee and invited her shopping, until finally Lee's refusals had dampened her enthusiasm.

She could come back here, but she didn't want to have to face Jim's wife again, to see that sharp, sudden look on her face again. She wanted to find Jim and explain. And she wanted her daughter.

There were local pharmacies. She could get a phone directory and a roll of quarters. She could call until she reached him, and in reaching him she'd reach her daughter. She thought of the woman suddenly. Jim had always told her he hated short hair on women. He had liked wrapping hers about his hand as though he were smoothing a skein of wool.

She remembered where the library was. They had a directory. She could sit down and write out names, and no one would bother her. She refused to think any further. On the way to the library, she kept seeing children. Every small face made her jolt. Any one of the little girls might be her own.

There were over forty pharmacies listed in the Yellow Pages. In despair Lee scribbled ten numbers at random. She'd disguise her voice, make those calls, and then come back and make ten more, and no matter who answered she'd hang up as soon as she knew he was or wasn't there. She needed to see him in person.

In the end it took her thirty-four quarters before she found Jim. The druggists she spoke to were always annoyed that she didn't have a prescription to call in. "There's no Jim here," voice after voice told her.

Perfunctorily she called Labber Pharmacy. "Yes," a clipped young voice said. "Jim Archer," Lee said. "Hang on," said the voice, and Lee slammed down the phone, so exhausted she had almost forgotten which number it was she had just dialed.

She didn't recognize the name of the pharmacy. It was on the far end of town, too far away from the house for Jim to walk it. She cabbed over, but she made the driver let her off more than three blocks away. "Jesus, lady. Spend the extra fifty cents," he told her. "I can get you right to the door." She fit the fare into his hand and got out.

The heat slammed against her. It was weather where anything could happen. The sidewalk shimmered before her. She took her time walking toward the drugstore, but as soon as she stepped on the black pad by the door, the door swung open. The pharmacy had mahogany shelves and a large center area that seemed devoted to cosmetics. A woman in a red dress was leaning toward a small mirror, gingerly dabbing pink cream into her cheeks. In the back was an old-fashioned soda counter. Her heart raced, ramming up against her ribs. She propped one hand along the smooth wood for balance. In the back a little girl was sipping ice cream, twirling on a chair. She had light brown hair, and Lee felt herself unraveling. "Anna," a woman said, and daubed the girl's face with a napkin. And then there, in the back, was Jim.

She saw him before he saw her. He had on an open white smock coat over a blue shirt, and a tie and jeans. He looked the same as the day she had left him. Her mouth moved, soundless. He was leaning across the counter, talking earnestly to an old woman, pointing to something on the back of a bottle. His hair was very blond. His face looked older, and she suddenly felt sick with nerves. Her shirt was pasted along her back. She braced her hands along the wall, and when he looked up and saw her, she took a step back, as if the force of his stare were too much for her, as if all she might want to do was get on the highway again. She pushed forward, trying to keep her voice steady, jamming the words up out of her.

"Hello, Jim," she said.

Lila had already left Joanna off with Maureen and had been rushing to get to work when she noticed the blond woman in the front yard. Another boring survey taker, she thought, or worse, a Jehovah's Witness trying to trick her into talking about Jesus. It wasn't until Lila got a good look at her that she felt a slam of fear.

She waited until the woman had walked off, and then she drove to the pay phone by the Thrift-T-Mart and called Jim. "Honey, I'm swamped. Let me call you later," he said. She wanted to tell him she loved him, but it sounded so corny and flat that she skipped right over it, blurting, "Andrea Banrett was by. She said she went to school with you."

"Andrea?" he said. "I don't know any Andrea."

She wanted to tell him Andrea was blond. She wanted to unload the details so he could shape them into any other story than the one that was forming in her mind. Lots of women were blond. He knew lots of his customers by their first names. Lots of them called him by name, too. Lots gave a friendly honk of their horns when they drove past him on the road or stopped to chat in town.

She wasn't kidding one single person but herself. She was almost sure the woman was Lee. Nursing had trained her to be observant, to recognize detail, to remember. And even if she hadn't seen all those photos, she would have been able to shape a person from Jim's descriptions. And the worst of it was that after all this time she wasn't sure what Jim would do with a ghost who had suddenly sprung back to life again, and she wasn't sure what she would do, either, and most of all, she didn't think she wanted to find out.

Reality shift. It was a phrase Jim remembered from high school, when he had sat behind some of the boys who did drugs. It was when everything seemed suddenly to tremble and then shift, when alternate universes seemed possible, and it felt as if you were hovering between the two.

Jim saw Lee standing in front of him, and everything transformed except for her. The air seemed suddenly solid. It seemed to be moving, spinning lazily about him. Lee was unsmiling and very still. It was as if time had traveled back, as if he were seeing her again, during that first heartbreaking instant, when she was the long tall blonde illuminated on the highway, so mesmerizingly lovely that he hadn't been able to think of anything but getting her in his car beside him.

"Lee?" He moved toward her, coming out from behind the counter, passing the old woman who still held the pill bottle in her hand. The whole time he couldn't quite believe it was really she. He resisted blinking, as if that split second could make her disappear again. In a kind of heady daze he moved toward the corner where she was. He leaned forward and then clasped her bare arms in his hands. The feel of her warm skin was a shock to him.

"Don't cry," she told him.

"You're alive," he said in wonder. He couldn't stop touching her. Her hair. Her back. The slope of her hips. His smile kept changing shape.

"You're all right."

"I'm fine."

He held her for a moment, so tightly he swore he could feel her heart beating through him. She peeled herself apart from him, sweating faintly. "What happened?" he said. "Lee. What happened, Lee? Where were you?" He gestured blindly. "All this time," he said. "Where've you been? My God."

She swayed on her feet. "Wisconsin," she said finally.

"Wisconsin?" He wet his lips. "You were in Wisconsin?"

"Jim—there's too many people here to talk."

He looked around. "I don't care." He stared back at her. "I can't let you just walk out, meet up with you later. I can't do that." He put his hand on the side of her face.

"What happened to you?"

"I left," she said. "Once I started, I couldn't stop leaving."

He frowned. "You just left?"

"It's complicated," she said.

"You never said one thing to me," he said in amazement. "I never had a chance to talk you out of it." He looked back at the counter. The other pharmacist was leaning over the counter toward a young woman, his face so close to hers they seemed to be sharing a secret. Jim looked at Lee. "How could you leave us? How could you leave your baby?"

"It wasn't just the baby."

Something moved in his face. "What?" he said. "What? Why couldn't you even let me know you were alive?"

She was looking at the floor, her hair half covering her face. "I didn't feel alive," she said.

He gripped her shoulder, his face flashing. "People leave all the time, but they keep in touch. Didn't you love us at all?" He shivered involuntarily. "You know what I went through? You understand?"

"Please," Lee whispered.

"I loved you. I would have done anything for you."

"Don't," Lee said. "You don't have to do this now."

"I was a *suspect*, Lee. Couldn't you have at least sent me a postcard? 'Jim, I'm all right. Not coming home. Don't wait up. Lee.' Just to let me know I wasn't crazy, just so I could stop reading every god-damned newspaper in the goddamned country looking for you, worrying. Couldn't you have done that?"

Her head lifted. "I'm sorry," she said, putting one hand on his arm, but this time he whipped around, stalking from the pharmacy, banging out the front doors into the bright hazy sun. Panting, she struggled to keep up.

She clipped her fingers to his sleeve. He stopped short and faced her. "Do you know what I did? Do you know how I lived, what I went through?" he said.

"No, I don't know," she said.

"Where were you, Lee?" he cried. "The hospital didn't fuck up. You weren't kidnapped. And you told me it wasn't just the baby. It was *me*. You took out *our* money and you left on your *own*. I thought maybe you were just scared, that you'd come back. I used to think if only I could see you, I could convince you to come home to me." She tried to take his hand, and he struck it from him. "I *mourned* you, Lee."

She couldn't look at him. "I couldn't," she said. "I was afraid—I couldn't think about it."

"*I* thought about it," he said stiffly. "All the time, every god-damned moment. It's a wonder I didn't implode. And then one day while I was thinking about you, I met someone else, I fell in love. That's right. You think it couldn't happen? Stupid Jim, who'd want him when you didn't." He slapped his hands together. "Dissolved. That was our marriage. Like it never happened. You were declared dead. I remarried. I started a new life that has nothing to do with you." He began walking again, and then stopped abruptly.

"You look exactly the same," he said, pained.

She was pinned to her patch of sidewalk, and then instantly he was upon her, shouting, "Where are you going?"

"Going?" she said, astonished. "Do you see me going?"

He shook her. "Are you going away again?" he demanded. "Are you going to disappear?"

"I came here to see you!" she cried. "I'm sorry, I'm sorry, I just want to make things right."

He stared at her, stupefied. "Make things right?" he said. "Are you crazy? What do you take me for?"

"Please, can't we just sit down somewhere," Lee said. She looked around, searching out a coffee shop, a cafe, a bench where she could get her bearings; but he whipped her back around toward him again.

"What did you come back for?" he interrupted. "Are you in trouble? That must be it. Trouble. You think you and me, we'll just get into a souped-up hot rod and drive, is that it? You think you'll stay just long enough for me to get used to you and then go off again?"

"No," she said. Inside of her, a speck of fear took hold.

"You need money? More of my money?"

Lee stepped back from him. "No," she said. "No. I want to see Joanna."

"Joanna," he said suddenly, amazed. "Why, you're just a photograph in an old album to her. Little Red Riding Hood has more reality than you do." He blinked. "And anyway, she thinks you're dead."

She flinched. "Are you going to let me see her?"

"I don't want you around my family," he said.

Lee pulled out a piece of paper and a stub of pencil and with a tremble of fingers scribbled her hotel number. She fit it into Jim's pocket. "You can find me here," she said. "Please. I'm not going to be around your wife. I just want to be around my daughter. I have a right to see her."

"You have no right. You gave her up the moment she was born."

"She's my daughter," Lee said.

"Really?" Jim said. "How do you figure that?" He turned from her to push back into the pharmacy, where it was familiar, where he had some control. "According to the law, you don't even exist," he said. Just before the door swung shut again, he realized he still really didn't know why she had left. He didn't know whether she intended to do anything more with Joanna than see her. He turned back to Lee, his head reeling, but although he looked and looked, she was nowhere to be seen.

He left work shortly after that, and the whole drive home he was rigid with rage and longing and fear. He drove the way he had when he was seventeen, wild with need, his heart smashing against his ribs, his breath ragged. He kept waiting for an accident to happen. He kept angling the car toward every slick and dangerous weave of the road. He kept his body braced against the sticky leather seat, arms stretched, legs so starchy they made his whole body ache. He banged the horn at a car that took a millisecond too long to make a right turn. He beeped so many times at a woman crossing the street that she began deliberately to take her time, stopping to delicately scratch her ankle, all the while giving him a smug, sly grin.

It seemed imperative to get back to Lila fast. He had to keep slamming Lee out of his mind with chips of memories about his wife, image fragments of Lila so vivid they didn't leave room for anything else. He remembered how as simple a gesture as her hand placed on the small of his back could stir him, how every time he saw a poster advertising Bermuda he was caught in a tangle of fear, relief, and absolute gratitude. He had no doubt that she had saved him.

He parked sloppily outside the house. He wasn't halfway to the walk and he could hear their new dog barking. He stepped through the door. The house was an assault. Lila was racing toward him, in a stained white T-shirt and frayed too big jeans, her hair shored back with a child's cheap red plastic headband. She stuffed the shirt into her jeans and flashed him a grin. "I got home late," she said. "I'm sorry. Maureen took Joanna to see a movie. I thought you and me could have a real grown-up romantic dinner out, but I need half an hour."

"Joanna's gone?"

"Just to the movies, I told you." Flustered, she tugged the band from her hair, scrutinizing the plastic teeth. She began to bite at a thumbnail.

"Stop that," he said. "It's disgusting."

Surprised, she put her hand down. "You all right?" she said.

"I'm hungry."

"I just need half an hour."

"Fine, so I'll just walk the dog."

"He was just out," Lila said. "And it's hot."

"Dogs don't know time from shit," Jim said, and clapped his hands for the dog.

She planted her hands on her hips and scowled at him. "What's wrong with you?" she said. "Why are you sniping at me like that? Do you want to hit the dog while you're at it?"

"Nothing's wrong," he snapped. "And I'm not sniping."

"Fine, you're not sniping," she said. "I'm going to shower."

It *was* hot outside. He had to walk ahead of the dog and pull him. The dog's name was Fisher, a wheaten terrier they had just bought for Joanna's birthday because her year had been so rough. Jim was practically racing, trying to wear down his anger, and Fisher's doggy ramblings annoyed him. The dog snuffled in some hedges, and he yanked at the leash. The dog glared at him accusingly, took three lazy paces, and began snuffling again. Jim yanked him forward, almost dragging him across the ground. He gave one final tug and the dog suddenly pitched forward, vomiting on someone's petunias.

They ate dinner at a small Italian restaurant they both liked. Lila was in a new red silk dress and silver earrings, and every time she leaned forward he caught a drift of roses. He hated himself. He loved Lila. She had spent enough time worrying over Lee; she didn't need to anymore. He could handle whatever had to be handled. He stroked her hand on the tablecloth. "Gee, you look pretty," he told her, but, helpless, he thought suddenly of Lee, her blond river of hair he could no longer touch.

Lila picked at her lamb. "It's funny, that woman coming by. Andrea," she said. "I told her you were at work."

Jim pronged a string bean and studied it.

"Did she find you?"

"No, I don't think so," Jim said.

"Really?" Lila stopped eating.

"Really," Jim said, and put down his fork. "This place is famous for their desserts," he informed her. "Let's eat ourselves sick."

"I don't know if I'm hungry for dessert."

"I'll get a menu," said Jim, lifting his finger like a flag.

Lila knew Jim wasn't sleeping. She heard him wandering around. Or she'd wake and find him standing over her bed, his face so terrible it frightened her to see it.

"Bad dream," he said. He was angry and edgy. He got into bed beside her.

"I'm right here," she told him. He sat slowly on the bed beside her, pulling her up against him, rocking her. "Shh," he said. "It's okay."

He didn't eat the dinners she prepared for him. He studied her and he studied Joanna, and he watched the phone, and every time it rang he jumped up to grab it.

She was going to confront him. She planned to pick up Joanna from school and drop her with Maureen and then sit down with Jim. Wordsworth Elementary was only two blocks from the house, but she still got there a little late. She parked the car and started walking around the back, where the kids were streaming out. The crossing guards, little girls with white belts strapped across bright plaid and flowery dresses, were making a string of smaller children stop before a crosswalk on a perfectly empty street. They had those poor little kids marching just like little Nazis.

Joanna was always supposed to wait at the back. Even from here Lila could see her, in a red corduroy dress, rocking on her heels. Joanna used to have lots of friends. She had been inseparable from her friend Denny, but ever since she had been skipped ahead a grade, she was almost always alone. When Lila asked about Denny, Joanna just shrugged. "She's a baby," she announced, but her face was miserable. The few times Joanna was with another child, it was always someone who was as ostracized as she now seemed to be. Just last week she had brought home a girl named Sandy who had waddled into the house in a fizz of crinolines, her hair artificially brightened into an icy gold. There was Merilyn, who was so overweight Lila could hear her gasp when she walked. Joanna didn't seem very happy with these girls. She played school or read aloud to them or played with her Barbie doll, and when one or the other of these girls left, summoned by the honking of her mother's car horn out front, Joanna didn't even look up to see them leave her.

Lila waved to Joanna. Maybe on the way home she'd stop at Hit-Or-Miss and let her pick out a new dress.

Joanna, leaning against the chain-link fence, saw Lila edging toward her. Resigned, she pulled herself from the fence. She had a note in her pocket from the teacher, but before she had even left the school she had gone into the girls' room and read it in the stall. Another conference.

Last year, when the teacher told her she was being skipped ahead into third grade, she had been so excited she could barely wait for summer to pass. She had insisted on getting to school her first day nearly half an hour before the janitor. For the first time in her life, she wasn't bored. She could open a math book and be wonderfully puzzled by formulas and equations. She could open up a science book and find pictures of stars and moons and planets. She loved school, but it didn't take her very long to see that there seemed to be something wrong with loving it. Denny began to avoid her. "You think you're so *big*," Denny accused, and even though Joanna was baffled, Denny ended up being best friends with Trina O'Shea, who wasn't even in the first reading group, who still couldn't add without using her fingers like an abacus. The two girls linked arms. They whispered every time they saw Joanna. She tried to make friends in her new grade, but she was so much smaller than the other kids. The teacher put her right in the front row. Worse, when she announced to the class that Joanna had been skipped ahead, instead of admiration, the class groaned. Her excitement with learning only irritated the class. Every time she raised her hand, stretching it up, waggling it frantically into the air, Rosie Gordon who sat behind her would whistle loudly through her nose. When she went to the blackboard Billy Shearer would throw spitballs at her. She got good at hiding her report card from the other kids. She lied easily when Rosie asked her in a scornful voice if she got all A's again. "No," she said, trying to be equally scornful. She didn't mention the A minus. Jo-A-na, they called her. They didn't choose her for a partner in gym even though Jim had shown her how to hit a baseball in the backyard, even though Maureen had taught her tennis. She didn't understand it. She was too ashamed to tell her parents, who treated her report card as if it were a trophy.

She kept trying to make new friends. She invited girls over, but they seldom came. Once Rosie approached her, and for a flash second Joanna actually had hope. "So what day is it?" Rosie asked. "Thursday," said Joanna, and then Rosie had screamed, "Wrong!" and gripped the edge of Joanna's skirt and flung it up high to her waist. "It's Dress-up Day!" Rosie cawed. "Dress-up Day!" And all the other girls had giggled at the flash and ruffle of Joanna's white panties, at her burning face.

She gave book reports on books no one else had ever heard of, let alone could read. A High Wind in Jamaica. The Secret Garden. The other kids were giving oral reports on books like Lad, a Dog, and they gave her fishy stares when she recited, their faces turned hard and angry.

Her only ally was the teacher, a young lanky woman named Miss Tibbs, who had long frizzy black hair and always wore short skirts. She kept clapping Joanna on the back. She gave her special books and special lessons, but when she mentioned that maybe Joanna could be skipped ahead again, Joanna began to get headaches so terrible she sometimes spent afternoons lying on a white table in the nurse's office with a cool cloth on her head.

She was lonely. She began purposefully to fail, to have more and more headaches. She began biting her nails with a vengeance. Miss Tibbs sent a note home saying Joanna was clearing her throat every five minutes.

She began to retreat more and more into what her father called "the zone." She could mesmerize herself so that she didn't see the spitballs flying toward her. She didn't hear the other girls whispering about a pajama party she wasn't invited to, the other girls asking her if she ever combed her hair. And she didn't have to hear her parents' concern.

Lila honked the horn. She parked by the curb, idling the motor, and then, suddenly, she saw the same blond woman who had come to the house, crouched down by the fence, fingers hooked through the wire rungs, staring over at a corner. She was better groomed than the first time Lila had seen her. She was in a short red dress and black heels, her blond hair piled into a ponytail. Lila watched the blond woman unhinge her legs. She was focusing wildly, her gaze stuttering from small face to small face. "Mom!" cried Joanna. The woman looked toward Joanna, frowning, and then she spotted Lila, and abruptly she looked back at Joanna, her face flooding with color. "Hey!" Lila called, and began striding toward the woman. She bolted in the other direction. "Wait!" Lila called. She knew that face. She remembered the photo Jim had shown her. "Lee!" she suddenly called out, stunned by her own audacity. The woman looked at her for a moment, alarmed, and then kept walking.

"Who was that?" Joanna said.

Lila yanked open the car door. "No one," she said firmly. "Just some crazy lady. If you see her again, you stay away from her." She pulled the car into gear. "So," she said, trying to be cheerful. "How was school?"

"Fine," said Joanna, turning her face from the school.

Lila was furious with Jim. She waited until Joanna was in bed and then she strode into the living room. He was sitting in the rocker, leafing through the newspaper, and when he heard her he looked up. "When were you going to tell me?" she said quietly.

"Tell you what?" he said.

She felt her anger spreading through her body, rising like steam. "About Lee," Lila said, a hollow wave of nausea washing through her. No, it's not Lee, he could say. Lee is dead. You must be imagining things. "She was on our front *lawn*. She was at the *school yard*."

"Lila," he said.

"I know it's Lee."

He sat up straighter. "I didn't want you upset," he said finally.

Her heart bumped. "Are you crazy?" she said. "What happened? What does she want?" Lila slumped onto the couch, pulling at the tufts of fabric the dog had chewed out.

She angled her body so he'd look at her, but instead, head lowered, he got up and moved to her, cupping her head in his hands.

"Why'd she come back?" Lila said.

He was silent for a moment. "I don't know exactly. She says she wants to see Joanna."

"See her?" Lila stood up. "What else?"

Jim looked suddenly weary. He rocked Lila. "She's not seeing anyone," he said.

Every time Jim thought of Lee, she suddenly appeared. He would be talking to a doctor on the phone in the pharmacy, and suddenly

he'd think: Lee. And there she'd be, curled around a stool at the soda
fountain, sipping something frosty and dark from a parfait glass. Or
he'd be walking over to the school to fetch his daughter and he'd see
some tiger lilies growing wild in the scrubby grass and he'd remember
how Lee had loved them. When he got to the school there would be
Lee, walking away from him, the bottom of her dress floating up in
the wind, like a wave. Once, he saw her sitting on one of the
child-size swings, staring up at the sky, barely moving in the empty
school yard. She hadn't seen him, but he had stood there until she had
gotten up and walked out of the yard.

He didn't know how, but the world had stopped being ordinary.
The air crackled with possibility. If he had seen the March Hare lope
into his pharmacy, he wouldn't have been surprised. Memory floated
on every surface, rising up over the present, obliterating it until he'd
feel himself metamorphosing, nine years back, the old Jim again, an
old life starting up again. He'd remind himself that she hadn't come
back for him, her face lit up when she saw Joanna, not him—and
he . . . well, hadn't he stopped waiting the day he had married Lila? He
told himself it was just the past, these flickerings of the old desire, as
keen and yearning as the day he had met Lee, and as impossible.

He struggled for balance. He didn't want her around, but when she
wasn't he somehow missed her. He ate himself up worrying how she
might go to his house. She might confront Lila, she might somehow
win his daughter, who, despite all the hugs and attention he and Lila
showered her with, still sometimes seemed starved for affection. He
didn't want Lee out of his sight, and he began to encourage her to
come to the pharmacy, where he could at least watch her, where he
could torture himself in the bargain. Oh, how he hated her. He loved
her. He felt nothing and everything and a supreme, overriding anger.

"Let me have time with Joanna," she asked him. "I won't tell her
who I am. Not until she's used to me."

"No," he said. "I don't think that's good. And I don't want you
disturbing Lila."

"Lila," Lee said. She thought of that woman, her red hair flashing,
her eyes dark. "Have I been to the house since the first time? Have I
called her? I haven't even walked by the house." She lied about that.
She didn't tell him how some nights when she couldn't sleep she
walked silently down her old street, and every time she stepped over
a roller skate or a toy, she'd have to stop and touch it, wondering if it

belonged to her daughter. She'd look at her old house and imagine the life going on in it. She didn't feel anything toward Jim except a sad regret, but she wondered, if she had stayed, would she? If she had given it the time Jim had begged for?

"She loves Joanna," he said.

Lee stiffened. "So do I," she said.

"Hah. You love her. What do you know about love?"

Lee felt herself collapsing. "I know something," she said.

"You don't even know her," Jim said. "Did you sit up with her when she was screaming with an ear infection? Did you help her learn to read or listen to her cry or patch up her scrapes?" He dug his hands in his pockets. "We're a *family*, Lee."

"I know." Lee heaved a breath. "Look, what do you want me to do? Just tell me and I'll do it."

"You think you can just flash in here and confuse Joanna and then flash out again?" Jim demanded.

"Nobody's flashing anywhere," Lee said. "Come on. Sit down with me someplace, Jim. Let's just talk. Come on. I'll tell you whatever you want to know."

"The truth?" he said. "No bullshit?"

"The truth," Lee said.

They walked over to a nearby park and sat on a bench, and almost as soon as she was settled, she started to talk. He spent two hours with her, talking about the past, about why she had left, about what she had been doing, and the whole time he only half believed what she told him. "That didn't happen," he kept interrupting her. He kept watching her eyes to see when she didn't meet his gaze; he kept her mouth in sight to see what it wasn't telling. It seemed to him that she remembered everything wrong, that she had left on a complete false-hood about him. "How was I stopping you from doing anything?" he demanded. "Didn't I tell you to go back to school? I never stopped you."

She looked at him. "Yes, you did."

"You wanted the baby."

She shook her head, but when she told him about the two failed abortion attempts, he stood up, pacing. "I don't believe this," he said. "This conversation isn't really happening, is it? We still could have worked things out," he insisted. "If you had let yourself, you would have loved me so much you never would have left." He roughly brushed his hair from his face. "Don't you think that's true?" he said.

"I don't know," Lee said. "It's like we're talking about a different person now—" She saw him flinch, and then she quickly touched his shoulder. "I know, though, that if you had been able to find me, you would have been able to convince me to come home."

"That's love," he said. "You can't tell me it isn't."

"You know what else?" Lee said. "If I had seen Joanna for one moment, I never would have been able to stay away."

His mind reeled. He kept reimagining his daughter's birth. All he had had to do was gently tilt Lee's face toward the baby's when she was born. All he had had to do was sit by her hospital bed with the baby so that they were the first two things she would have seen. None of this would have happened.

"Why did you come back now?" he said.

"I had time to work things out," Lee said.

"Great. It took you nine years to work things out." He stood up to leave and then sat back down again. "How did that happen? What do you do in Madison?"

He kept asking her questions about her past without him. He thought she'd tell him about nights so lonely that she'd go to all-night supermarkets just to have some company. He thought she'd tell him about food stamps and typing jobs and clothing picked from Kmart. A little regret, a little need, all snowballing, leading her back to him. But instead she told him about finding her first friend, finding a job she could do well, a man whom she used to see. Everything she revealed ended up somehow hurting him, and then he was instantly sorry she had told him anything at all.

"What's she like?" Lee said quietly.

He knew she meant Joanna, but he suddenly felt mean and small, as if his heart had atrophied to the size of a peach pit. "She's a nurse," he said. "And she's wonderful." Lee blinked, surprised at how such a thing could nick at her and hurt. She wondered suddenly what he and Lila talked about at night, if he brought her flowers, if he loved her one-tenth of how much he had loved Lee when she was just seventeen and absolutely impervious to anybody's love, especially his. Lee shook off the image. She had no right to care.

"We could be the same person, we're so close," Jim said.

Lee leaned forward so that they were almost touching. "Are you going to let me see Joanna?" she said.

"No," he said.

"I'm not going to blurt out to her that I'm her mother," Lee said. "I just want to get to know her, give her time to like me a little first." She touched Jim's sleeve. "I know how to act with kids."

"Really?" he said. "How?"

She was suddenly silent. "What?" he said, but she just shook her head. "Look," she said finally. "What's to stop me from just going to see her myself?"

"Abandonment's a crime, isn't it?" he said coldly. He felt like a fool. He'd never call the police.

"I'm going to see her," Lee said.

He waited, he kept watch, but she didn't call the house or show up. She stayed away from the school, and she came to the pharmacy a few times, when she knew Joanna would be at school. She came, he thought, to see him. She sat at the old cherrywood counter like a work of art. He could look up from his work and see pieces of her, a prism of shining hair, a section of her blue dress, refracted among the aisles of shampoo or a sudden rush of customers. Sometimes, when he was counting pills, he was so concentrated on her that he would give a customer three pills too much or twelve too little.

If she couldn't see Joanna, she could have news about her. She asked Jim about Joanna as a baby, about Joanna in kindergarten, about every period of her life except what was going on now. And she asked him for photos.

"You weren't around for the real thing, what makes you think photos'll do it?" he said. He was determined not to bring her one thing, and that morning, when he dressed, he riffled through the photos for a moment. He used to have all these pictures of Lee. Lee in a light summer dress, her hair skating down her back. Lee pregnant, looking thin and frightened, her arms around her blooming belly. He had kept those photos hidden away in a shoebox in the attic because he didn't want to upset Lila, and, too, he didn't need to upset himself, to keep pulling open that wound. He hadn't looked at them in years, but now suddenly he climbed up to the attic and plundered through the debris. He couldn't find the box at first. He had to plow through some old skirts of Lila's, some toys of Joanna's she refused to let anyone throw out because she "was saving them for her own children." When he found the box he felt something unraveling in his stomach. He opened the lid and stared at the first photo, Lee sitting in cut-off denim shorts and a T-shirt on their porch, smiling up at him lopsidedly. She looked so young, like the teenage daughters of some of the families on the block. Like a memory. He closed the box and shoved it back under Lila's skirts.

He thought he'd just bring a few pictures, because he was so angry, because he'd show her how he had had a family, how she was no longer a part of it. He picked the ones with Lila in them, with Maureen or his mother, with all the women Joanna knew and loved.

"My pride and joys," he said, handing her the pictures. She looked at the shots. They seemed like the photos of a stranger. The small baby face turned toward the camera could have belonged to the woman in front of her at the Shop Rite yesterday. The toddler in overalls and a flowered hat could have been the neighbor's, not hers. Only the recent photos gave her some comfort. She could at least recognize her daughter in them. She could recognize Lila and Jim.

She tried to listen to what Jim was telling her about each picture, but the more information he gave her, the more confused she became.

"Mrs. Mannama took that shot," he said, holding up a picture of Joanna, recognizable in a paper pilgrim collar.

"Who?" said Lee.

"The mother of one of her schoolmates."

"Oh," Lee said. She tried to imagine it. She had never once noticed the school the whole time she had lived here. She couldn't remember even driving past it. School. An image flashed. Karen carrying a cardboard hand she had made in kindergarten. She felt something wrenching inside of her. "Well, look at you," she said, showing Jim a photo of himself in a tuxedo, Lila in a gown. "Big night," she said.

He looked at the photo thoughtfully. "Yes, it was," he said, but he didn't tell her how.

It wasn't until Jim was nearly through the pictures that Lee decided to steal some. All of them of her daughter. One from each year. She waited until he went to attend to a customer, a woman who wanted to know if her itching salve might work on her cat. And then she quietly slipped a few photos into her purse. And when he came back toward the counter, she gave him an open, innocent smile.

She wouldn't look at the pictures until she got to her hotel. She spread them across the white chenille spread, her hands trembling. Jim had told her what each picture was, but here in her hotel she couldn't remember. She got up and got the small nail scissors she had bought on a whim, a ridiculous buy since she bit her nails to the quick. She carefully scissored out all the other women, Lila in a red bathing suit, that nosy Maureen in a flowery housedress no one wore anymore, Jim's mother, who had never once met Lee. She threw all those faces in the basket and then ferreted through the pictures of her daughter again, the jagged edges catching against her skin. She lifted up a black-and-white picture of a baby on a blue blanket, surrounded by lawn. Where had Jim said this was? She turned the print over, hoping for a faint scrawl, a way to place the image in time. The back of the picture was blank. She lifted up another picture. More recognizable. Joanna, her long hair in knotty pigtails, dressed as a cowgirl. Halloween, Lee decided. She could show this picture to people and say, "This is my daughter at Halloween. This is her cowgirl outfit. Look, we both have long hair." It seemed such a stingy thing to have so little to say about a life.

The next day she walked over to the pharmacy around four, seating herself at the counter and ordering hot chocolate. She didn't get up to try to talk to him. She sat quietly reading from a paperback she had in her purse, until it was almost closing time, and then she approached him. "Let me take you to dinner," she said.

"My wife's cooking dinner," he said.

"I just want to see Joanna," Lee said.

"Not tonight," he said, and ushered her outside, leaving her standing there on the sidewalk. He kept his neck so rigid that he couldn't have turned around to look at her even if he had wanted to.

He knew Lila was worried about Joanna. "Tell her to leave," Lila said. "She doesn't deserve to see Joanna. She'll only confuse her."

"I know how Lee is," he said. "She'll be leaving soon."

He didn't tell her that he was worried, too. Every time he saw her walk into the pharmacy, he thought he should go to the phone and call a good lawyer, get a restraining order. And then he thought about Joanna, and then he thought about what damage a journalist could do, covering a simple custody case, digging a little deeper, and rediscovering that whole weird disappearance years ago, back when Jim was a suspect.

He didn't know what to do, didn't have a clue what was the right thing to do, for Joanna or anybody.

One day, when Lila had to work, he picked up Joanna after school and brought her to the store. "Can't she stay with Maureen?"

he said. He didn't want to tell Lila that sometimes Lee was there.

"Maureen's got a cold," Lila said.

The whole ride in the car, Joanna kept looking at houses. "Why don't we move?" she said. She found the schools, pointing them out to him. "That would be a nice school," she insisted. "Look at the kids! They look great!"

"You go to a nice school," he said, but Joanna pressed her face to the window, straining wistfully around to see the kids streaming into a sunny courtyard.

He parked the car in back of the store. Joanna straggled into the pharmacy, and as soon as he was in the door he saw Lee, sitting on a stool, and as soon as she saw Joanna she bolted off her stool and began smoothing down her dress, straightening her hair.

"Hello," she said. Joanna looked up, cautious.

Jim tried to orchestrate, to make things seem casual, almost normal. "Well, want to read in the back?"

"My name is Lee," Lee said suddenly.

"Joanna."

"I know," Lee said.

"You do? How?"

Jim put one hand on Lee's shoulder.

"Magic," Lee said.

He could see a line at the pharmacy, too much for the assistant to handle. He looked toward the counter again. "I'll watch her," Lee said. "We'll stay right here." She touched his arm. "Right in sight. It's okay." She pressed at his shoulder. "Please. We won't talk about anything but the weather."

He hesitated. "Can you read?" Joanna said to Lee.

"All right," he said.

It was nearly impossible to concentrate. He spent half the time watching them. Lee and Joanna were both at the ice-cream counter, poring over one of Joanna's books. The two of them ignored him. He kept expecting something sudden to happen. Lee bolting out with Joanna. Lila walking in, off her shift early, thinking to surprise her husband and daughter. He miscounted theophylline tablets and had to start again. He heard a customer's question about over-the-counter cough syrup and found himself handing her a bottle of Maalox.

He couldn't wait for closing time. Usually he liked to linger a little, straighten up, survey what he considered his kingdom. Tonight,

though, he rushed through the last bits of paperwork. He locked up
the restricted drugs so clumsily that any addict could have had them.

"Well," he said, approaching Lee and Joanna, "ready to go,
pumpkin-head?"

"Can Lee come to dinner?" Joanna said. Flushed, she turned to Lee.
"We're having spaghetti and cake," she promised. "*Chocolate* cake."

"Not tonight, honey," he said.

Joanna looked up at Lee. "Another time," Joanna said with a
queenly air.

"Another time soon," Lee said.

He had just gone into the shower, just for a minute, and when he
came out Joanna was telling Lila about Lee. "She knew the books I
know," Joanna said. "I wish I had hair like hers."

Lila looked as if she had been struck. She seemed to lengthen along
the refrigerator, bracing against it as if for balance. "Who's Lee?" she
said haltingly.

"She's just a lady who was in the pharmacy."

Jim put one hand on Lila's shoulder.

"I liked her," Joanna said.

In bed, they talked. "What are we going to do?" Lila said.

"We're going to have to tell her," Jim said.

Lila sat up, bunching the covers about her. "You think it's good for
a kid to know her mother walked out the day she was born? You
think that's a pretty thing to hear?"

"No, I don't think that's good," Jim said. "But it's the truth."

"And what if she leaves?" Lila said. She lowered herself back down
against the pillows. "What if she wants Joanna?"

"I won't let her take Joanna," Jim said.

"Can't we wait to tell her, let her be a kid a little longer?" She
looped her arms about Jim.

"All right," he said. "For a little longer."

Jim hated himself, but every time he began his drive home, he
ended up going to Lee's hotel. The road suddenly switched right
when he was driving on it. His hands on the wheel swerved left
instinctively. Seeing her hotel, he thought he might as well go in,
might as well try to convince her to leave, convince her to let them

all alone. And then, for a moment, sitting in the car, the motor idling, he imagined her disappearing again, as seamlessly as she had at first. He'd start panicking. He'd rush inside, his resolve wavering. She looked fresh and lovely; she was always happy to see him.

One night she made him soup on her hot plate. He took the bowl and tasted it. "Whose is this?" he said. "This is delicious."

"It's mine," she said, laughing. "I cook now."

"You?" He remembered half-frozen TV dinners because Lee hadn't turned the stove up high enough, peas served in the water they were boiled in. "How did this happen?"

"Lots of things happened you don't know about," she said.

"You live alone in Madison?"

She nodded.

"No gentlemen callers?" He fumbled a grin.

"One," she said. She sat on the edge of the bed.

"Still?"

"I don't know."

He sipped the soup, studying her. "I feel like I'm supposed to say 'Now you know what it feels like, being left.'"

"I know what it feels like," she said. Andy flashed in her mind, and she felt suddenly undone. She looked up at Jim's sad, serious face. "I made a mess of things, didn't I?"

"What are you going to do?" he said.

"I don't know," Lee said.

"What does that mean, 'I don't know'?" Jim's stomach churned inside of him. He put down the soup and stared at it. There was something green and flaky dusting the top, making a swirling pattern. "Are you staying or leaving?" He felt suddenly sick. "Do you have a lawyer, Lee?"

Startled, she put down her own soup mug. "No," she said. "Do you?"

He picked at the chenille spread on her bed. "What happened to us, Lee?" he said suddenly. "Sometimes, when I was looking for you so hard, I used to rack my brains trying to think of the one thing to say that might bring you back. I don't know what I would have done if I had actually found you, what I would have said. I just kept thinking of us at home, happy."

"I used to worry that you'd find me," Lee said slowly. "Every time I saw a blond head, I'd freeze." She frowned. "You just wanted so much. But there was nothing there that I could give you."

"Oh, yes, there was," he said.

He looked at Lee's phone. He suddenly wanted to call Lila, wanting to hear her voice, speeding across the wires to him, reconnecting.

"What do you want with Joanna?" he said.

"She's my daughter," Lee said. She washed one hand over her face. "It's not too late for us to know each other, is it?"

"She knows her mother."

"She has to know!" she cried. "What if I went to a lawyer? What if I wanted some kind of custody?"

"Custody," Jim said, suddenly angry. "What are you talking about, custody? You can be put in jail. That's what you can do."

Lee took his empty soup bowl and brought it into the bathroom sink. He heard the rush of water, and when she came out her eyes looked red. "You think I'm not in jail now?" she said quietly.

Lila couldn't relax until Joanna was home. She didn't want to tell her own daughter to shut up, but it was difficult hearing her talk about Lee. It was worse when Jim began to be late. It didn't take that long to close up the pharmacy. There were no emergencies he needed to stay open to handle, no problems with closing up. He had always joked with her that she was lucky she was marrying a pharmacist and not a doctor. He had clientele, not patients, and they never called at one in the morning because they couldn't breathe. He blamed his lateness on the buses, or sometimes he said he had to talk to the assistant about some matter or other. And once he told her he had been to dinner with Lee. He said it so matter-of-factly that it stunned her. "I need to find out what she's planning to do," he said.

Lila rubbed her hand through her hair. It felt suddenly flat in her hand, vaguely greasy and boring. "She's a criminal," Lila said.

"I just need to get things straight," he told her.

She tried to be busy, to carry on her life as if she didn't care. She pretended she didn't see him looking at an old photo of Lee or studying her with such pain that she had to go into the kitchen and busy herself so she wouldn't cry. When he didn't touch her in bed, she pretended he was just tired. And when he did reach for her, with a touch that felt almost desperate to her, she pretended there wasn't another woman right there in bed with them, rolling in between them as easily as air. When he came in the house she was watching a movie on the TV or so engrossed in a book that she wouldn't rise up to meet him. "Hey," he said, bending to kiss her. She always held her breath. She didn't want to smell Lee.

One night he came home at three. She was sitting on the chintz chair by the light, a magazine in her lap, her face drawn, and as soon as she saw him she felt a swoon of nausea loosening her pride. He stood by the door. "I would have called, but I was arguing." He looked exhausted.

"Why can't you get a lawyer to argue?" Lila said.

"You want Joanna in court? You want lawyers?"

"Are you going to leave me?" she said. She was instantly ashamed. He sat on the edge of her chair. He lifted up a ribbon of her hair. "Come on. Don't be silly."

"Are you?" she said. "Are you still in love with Lee?"

"No," he said. "And I'm not going to leave you."

Lila tried to tell herself that things would work out. She was married to Jim. He loved her. She tried to imagine herself in Jim's position and decided she could never forgive someone who had disappeared like that. Second chances were for the movies. It didn't make her feel any better.

She tried to lose herself in work, but everything seemed to remind her of what she might be losing. She walked into a patient's room, a twenty-five-year-old woman getting her nose done, to find a man nuzzling in the bed with her. She spotted a man wandering the halls, his coat bundled in his arms. She wouldn't have even noticed him except he was humming the same lullaby she sang to Joanna at night. The man seemed to walk faster, and when he whipped about a corner she saw a small blue bootie.

The pay phones reminded her that Lee could be calling Jim. The terrible hospital food jarred an image of Lee eating lunch in a hotel room or, worse, dining with Jim. Get hold of yourself, Lila's mother used to warn her, but Lila couldn't seem to find a grip. She kept trying to recall herself back when she had felt in control, back when she had been simply Lila, a woman in love with a profession and not a person, a woman whose worst dreams didn't earthquake into reality. She wanted to go back in time, before she had ever stood poised at the threshold of Jim's room, half in the harsh hospital bright, half in the soothing dark. Lila didn't know whom to turn to for advice. She didn't want anyone at work to know, and when she called home, weeping, her mother told her to smarten up, to go out and get herself the best lawyer in town. "I'll pay for it," she told Lila.

"It hasn't come to that stage yet," Lila said.

"Oh, please," her mother said. "That's what they all say."

Lila's father was no better. Slowly, deliberately, he told her to go out and buy a backless dress. "A dress?" Lila said, mystified. "Yeah, and wear heels," her father said. "Bright red, as high as you can walk on them." He advised her to throw dinner parties, to serve the kinds of foods men liked. "Men foods?" Lila said, baffled. "What are men foods?"

"You know," her father said, talking to her as patiently as if she were five years old. "No fancy icings. Those crescent cookies. The kind your mother makes. You listen to her, she'll give you the recipe."

Her mother, on the other line, sighed. "Get a lawyer, honey," she said.

Lila didn't get a lawyer. She walked around with emotion surging inside of her, struggling to keep her shell cool and efficient and intact.

Every time she looked at Joanna, the child seemed to be dimming right in front of her. She reached for the hand Joanna tugged away. She kept touching Joanna's hair, her smooth skin, the hem of whatever dress she had on, and everything she touched felt somehow different. It chilled her. She began coming to school early so she could whisk Joanna away before Lee had a chance to see her.

She thought up reasons why Joanna couldn't go to the pharmacy to see Jim. She kept remembering a spate of newspaper stories and magazine articles all about women taking kids into this kind of underground railroad, never to be found again. These kids were raised in trailer parks or high rises, in ranches so far west they weren't even on any map you might find. All Lee would need was a fast car and a box of hair dye and scissors for Joanna. Lila began checking up on Joanna, calling the school so many times that Joanna's teacher finally requested that Lila come in for a conference if she had such doubts about the school.

"No, no, it isn't that," Lila said. "I'm just a worrier."

Still, Lila couldn't help it. She found excuses to call, excuses to take a break and drive like a maniac down to the school just so she could make sure Joanna was all right and that Lee wasn't there. She saw Joanna's panicked face when she drove up, she saw the other children giggle. And when Joanna came home, she wouldn't talk to Lila.

Her thinking began to change. She sometimes imagined herself taking Joanna into hiding herself. She'd have to make up a story. She'd have to say she was the mother. She believed that was true. She had been such a fool. She had never even thought to press Jim about adopting Joanna.

She ended up walking into a legal aid clinic two cities away from her own. She was still in her nurse's uniform, so she kept her blue raincoat buttoned to her throat. She gave them a fake name and began asking questions. Could a mother who had abandoned her child reclaim her? The lawyer who was listening looked younger than Lila. She had long black hair clamped back with silver, but she wore an expensive dark suit and polished high-heeled shoes.

"Well," she said to Lila. "It isn't likely, but judges do favor the mothers."

"They do?" Lila said. She stood up. The room tilted, and Lila braced one hand along the table.

"Are you all right?" the lawyer said, and Lila nodded.

She paid fifty dollars for the advice.

In the end she confided only to Maureen, who had always been her ally. The two women sat out in Maureen's yard, and Lila would finally break down, crying in her hands, sluicing the tears from her face until the top of her blouse was damp.

"It's just the pull of the past," Maureen soothed. "And there's nothing to do about it."

She made Lila come inside. She gave her a cool, clean cloth and ice-cold lemonade and sat with her, rubbing the back of her neck. "Don't you worry," she told her. "Jim's no fool."

Maureen, though, had her doubts about that. The whole thing made her furious. She waited until Lila was out of the house one morning to barge over to Jim's. He grinned when he saw her.

"You're making a big mistake," she told him.

"Oh, yeah? About what?"

"I'm talking about Lee," Maureen said. "I hear she's back."

He shifted uneasily. "No one's making any mistake."

"They had better not," she said coolly.

He picked up his coffee cup. "Is this your business?" he said.

"Gee, it sure seems like it, doesn't it?" Maureen said, and walked out of his house.

~~12~~

Every city had highways. Nights after Jim left, nights when the hotel room seemed more the residence of a runaway than a grown woman, Lee tumbled outside, Jim's leather jacket hugged over her shoulders. The night felt clean and cool, and already stars prickled the sky with light. She began striding, pumping her arms, trying to deepen her breathing into a kind of calm. The cars swerved lazily away from her. She walked so briskly, sweat banded her back. Her palms were clammy and her hair suddenly hurt, as if each strand had a nerve pulsing within it. She pushed on, walking determinedly along the shoulder of the road. She must have walked an hour and a half, but she didn't feel better. The churning in her mind hadn't slowed one single bit. Instead she felt sick and panicky, and for the first time that she could remember, the endless strip of road gave her no pleasure. The highway seemed like nothing more than the highway. She dead-stopped, the night crowding in upon her. Cars whizzed and blurred past her, and she caught a brief smear of song from a car radio, the first trembling bars from a falsely written love song she had never much liked. She stood there, alone and trapped in the hardness of the night, and every direction she looked toward seemed like one where she had already been. She was suddenly shivering and so defeated that it was all she could do not to sink down onto the cold road and not ever move anywhere again.

The walk back seemed to take forever, and by the time she reached the hotel her whole body felt boneless. She trudged up to her silent room, clicking on the TV almost immediately. There was already a movie on, some kind of science-fiction film about a man who did his murdering with the help of a time machine. She drew a bath. Maybe she'd make herself tea on the hot plate. Maybe she'd read some of the book she had bought. She'd take a bath and act as though she had a normal life that anyone might want to live.

As soon as she got into the tub, she felt impatient. She pulled herself out, wrapping a towel about her, wandering back into the main room. Flopping on the bed, she searched for the phone. She started to ring Jim's number, wanting something familiar, then she thought of Lila, lifting up the phone, maybe laughing, saying something to Jim, expecting the voice on the phone to be a friend, or the hospital, or anybody but Lee. Lee hung up.

She picked up the phone again, hesitated, and then dialed Andy. He always picked up the phone. He always said you never knew who might be on the other end. His line rang eighteen times, and as soon as he picked up she hung up. She lay prone on the bed, and then she suddenly felt so alone, it seemed she might disappear if she didn't make contact. Abruptly she dialed again.

"Yes," he said, his voice edgy.

"Andy," she said. She had a sudden fleeting image of Andy, driving in the night, a crumpled map beside him. She was a point on paper, a destination circled in red.

"I wanted to let you know I'm okay."

There was a clip of silence.

"Good," he said finally. "That's good."

Static fizzed and popped on the line.

"You want me to ask you where you are?" he said.

"Baltimore," Lee said.

"You want to tell me why?"

She felt the words moving up in her throat, lodging. And then she heard music, low and soft in the background. Voices threaded together.

"Who's there?" she said.

"Listen, I'm happy to hear from you," Andy said.

"Who's cooking at the restaurant? You still go?"

"They didn't hire anyone new yet." He cleared his throat. "I guess you expect I'm going to try to figure out why you left, that I'm going to pry, but I'm not."

"You can if you want," Lee said. She put her arms about her body, holding on tight. "Do you want to?"

"Are you coming home?"

"I don't know," she said. The music in the background seemed to get louder. She heard the clink of glasses.

"Oh." Something rustled in the background. "Listen," he said, "I have some people here."

"Oh," said Lee. "All right." People. Was that one, or a couple, or a long, lovely woman who might sit so close beside him they might share the same breath of air? Her throat knotted. She could hear him breathing on the other end. "I'm not lying to you," she said.

"Everyone says that," he told her.

"Andy—" She wanted to ask him what he would do if she appeared in his court telling him what she had done, asking custody of her daughter. He had once told her that he believed everyone deserved a fair shake, murderers, petty thieves, even child molesters, but she had been in his courtroom one day when a twenty-year-old drug dealer came in. He had been caught selling speed to sixth-graders. She had seen it herself, how Andy's face had shut down, as if a layer of varnish were solidifying his features. She knew before the dealer opened his mouth, before the lawyer or Andy said one word, that Andy had made his mind up, that the sentence was going to be as tough as he could get away with and still be just.

"I really have to go," he said, his voice hardening. "I'm telling you so you don't think I'm cutting you off."

"Okay," Lee said. She kept the receiver cupped against her ear. She didn't think he'd really hang up. They used to have phone conversations that lasted two hours simply because every time she said her good-bye, he would think of something else he had to tell her.

The click came. The connection broke. Lee kept her stubborn hold on the line. She kept listening, almost as if he were still somehow talking to her, a secret language that any moment would reveal itself to her. She missed him.

She didn't go to a lawyer. One night she turned on the TV in the middle of an advertisement. "Landers and Landers, Attorneys at Law," the TV intoned. "When a good friend just isn't enough." The number flashed: 1-800-555-WINN. Lee copied it down. She didn't know about a good friend being enough or not because right now she didn't have one.

She kept the number in the top drawer of her night table. She had an intuitive fear of lawyers. She wasn't sure how to declare yourself alive again, and she worried about how the law could bend, how she could be left without a daughter at all or, worse, somehow punished for having left her in the first place. Jim hadn't called a lawyer, either, and although she wasn't quite sure why, she was grateful and silent about it, and she began to think that maybe she could convince Jim to let her have her daughter some of the time.

Jim never actually came out and said Yes, you can see Joanna, but when Lee showed up at the pharmacy, and on the odd occasion that Joanna was there, he didn't actively stop her, either.

Every day Lee showered and dressed as carefully as if she were going out on a date, making sure everything was pressed and buttoned and tied, brushing her hair as best she could. She walked to the pharmacy and waited for her daughter. It was always a kind of giddy relief to see her.

Joanna always looked at her suspiciously. She was shy, slow to warm. She hung about Jim, watching Lee out of the corner of her eye. Lee always casually brought out a book, something with large colored photographs of the moon or of exotic animals. She held the book at an angle so wherever Joanna was she could be drawn to it.

It sometimes tore Jim up to watch his daughter with Lee. Joanna became feverish. It was almost as if Lee were peeling her, pulling back the stubborn silence, the bunched-up anger, all of it layer by layer, until Joanna reemerged, new and shining. Joanna switched on, scrambling to study the book Lee had. The two of them would bend their heads together and talk excitedly. Joanna had told Jim that Lee didn't call her "smartie-pants" or "braino" the way the kids at school did. Lee didn't encourage her patronizingly the way the teacher did. Lee seemed as excited as she was by the graphs and charts and photographs, as new to Lee as Joanna herself was. And when it was time to go home, both of them looked at Jim with such raw gratitude that he could hardly speak. "I'll be here tomorrow," Joanna told Lee.

"No, puss," Jim said. "Remember? Tomorrow your mom's taking you shopping for shoes."

Joanna blinked at Lee. "Wanna come?" she said.

"Oh, I can't," Lee said quickly. Joanna kept looking at her. "I have to go to the dentist."

"The dentist." Joanna frowned. "I'd cancel."

Jim gave her a gentle push toward the back. "And I'd go get my coat if I were you, miss. Time to go."

She slipped off the stool and walked away from them, slow and graceful, turning around once to see if they were still watching her, which, of course, they were.

"I made a big mistake," Lee said abruptly to Jim.

"She did fine without you," Jim said.

Lee buttoned her jacket thoughtfully. "I can't bear living in the hotel anymore," she said.

"When I think of you, I think of hotels," Jim said.

"Don't think that anymore," Lee said. "Maybe I should just rent a place for a while. Maybe I should get a job."

Lee looked beyond him, at Joanna, who was bounding back toward them, carrying her book by the open cover.

"You know what you're doing?" Jim said.

"Maybe for the first time in my life," Lee said.

Lee went to the Keystone Bank and opened up an account for herself with the money her father had left her, and every morning she got the paper and scouted jobs and apartments. She psyched herself up to like the city. She told herself it wasn't the same place that she had so willingly fled. Every Sunday she cut out the city calendar from the paper and stuck it to her refrigerator with magnets. She tried to tick off the things she might like to do that week. She could go to the museum. There was a waterfront so new and gleaming and rebuilt that she bet she wouldn't recognize it. She repeated to herself like a mantra: Baltimore isn't the worst possible place a person could live. She had once thought you could learn to love a person, and she had been wrong, but maybe you really could learn to love a place, maybe if that love was finite, if it was only for as long as you needed to be there.

She looked for a job. She was positive she could find work as a cook somewhere, but in two weeks' search she found only two positions open, one for an experienced Cajun cook and one for a pastry chef, and she was neither. She walked the streets in her one suit, a navy blue wool with a skirt that was a little too short, a navy silk blouse that had a stain on one sleeve. This is for Joanna, she told herself, sipping in air before she entered yet another strange restaurant. She refused to talk to anyone but the manager. "You should see the soups

I make," she said. "You should see what I do to a piece of fish. Try me out. Two weeks, I guarantee I'll increase your business."

"Business is busy enough," one manager told Lee curtly.

In the end she got a job waitressing, with a promise of some cooking. It was just a hole in the wall, a basic continental restaurant called Trax's, where on a busy night she'd be lucky to get weekly carfare in her tips. She didn't care. The place seemed full of customers, and she didn't have to wear any uniform other than her own clean clothes. It could work out. The manager who hired her was a young brisk woman with a spiky punk haircut. Her name was Georgia Ranter, and she told Lee that managing a restaurant wasn't her real life at all. "I'm a drummer for the Sick Potatoes," she said. "You know that song, 'Grandma's Syringes'? It played in all the dance clubs? That was us." She nodded at Lee encouragingly. "So what are you *really* into?"

"I'm a cook," Lee said.

Georgia was silent. The light left her face, like a dimming candle. "Right," she said, disappointed. She handed Lee an application. "Fill 'er up."

Lee looked at the application. Name. Social Security number. Address. Homing devices, anchoring you to a life.

"What?" Georgia asked Lee, peering over her shoulder.

"Nothing," Lee said. Her hands felt shaky. It's now or never, her father used to say to her when she couldn't make up her mind. She remembered that the never part always used to scare her, a word as final and lonely as a locked empty room. Her heart hammered, but she picked up the pen and wrote carefully: Lee Archer. 053-46-9855. Oh, God, she thought. Her face was flushed, and for a moment she was afraid to look up at Georgia.

"That wasn't so terrible, was it?" Georgia said, taking the form from Lee's startled fingers.

It wasn't so terrible, but it was strange. And as soon as the paper left Lee's hand, she felt something change. Everything suddenly seemed inevitable, speeding forward. She was starting work in just two days, and then the very first realtor she contacted took one look at Lee and announced she had the perfect apartment for her. "Come on, let's go take a look right now," the woman said. "If you like it, you can move in tomorrow." She wasn't much older than Lee, but already her hair was white, and she kept frisking one hand through it.

"We can walk to it," she said.

"Tomorrow—" Lee felt slightly dazed.

The apartment was filled with light and windows and polished wood floors that echoed as they walked across them. There was one big bedroom and a small side room that might be perfect for a small girl. Lee wandered through, following the realtor, listening to her spiel about moldings and character and extra closets, the same speech she had heard Frank give so many times that she could have recited it by heart herself. She turned from the realtor, who was gesturing at the baseboards, and in the hazy dusty light sprinkling in from the kitchen window, Lee thought, for just a moment, she saw her father.

"Look at the size of that closet!" the realtor said.

Lee blinked. The light sifted and settled and was just light again. "I'll take it," she said.

She bought a couch and a table and chairs and a bed small enough so a little girl wouldn't feel lost in it. She ran to the corner store and bought two cans of pink paint so pale it might seem like a wash on the wall. She wrapped her hair up and put on the transistor radio she had carried with her all the way from her Atlanta days, a radio that still worked, and that tiny back room was the room she painted first.

She put a vase of flowers in the pink room. Every day before she went to work, she dusted the room. Every night when she came into the house, she imagined what it might be like to have a child in it, if only for a little while.

She was always flushed when she came into the pharmacy. "You should see the chairs I found," she told Jim.

"Chairs!" he said, amazed. "The whole time we lived together, you never even wanted to buy a set of cups that matched. We never would have even had wastebaskets if I hadn't gone out and bought them myself."

"Well, things are different now," Lee said.

He didn't know if he believed her. Every time she pulled something out of her purse, he half expected to see a train schedule, a set of tickets.

"Come and see," Lee begged him. "You and Joanna."

"I don't know," Jim said.

"What could a visit hurt?" Lee said. "Think of it as supervised visitation. An hour."

"I don't think so."

"Aren't you curious to see the chairs?" Lee said, smiling. "I even have a set of silverware. Jim, a whole set."

"Look, I don't know."

"Come on, Jim. A half hour."

He dug his hands into his pockets. "I must be out of my bloody mind," he said.

"It was the chairs that did it, wasn't it," Lee said.

He'd never tell her, but it really was the chairs. He could imagine her living a life on the road, in hotel rooms or cheap sublets cluttered with somebody else's furniture. He could imagine her in any kind of transient life without him in it, but if he thought of her in a home, in a place that made sense, he thought of her in his past, with him.

So the next afternoon, on his lunch hour, he and Joanna walked over to Lee's for lunch. She didn't live in such a bad neighborhood, and the apartment building looked fairly well kept up. Still, when he saw her name on the buzzer, he flinched. "I want to press it," Joanna said, stabbing a finger on the bell.

Lee met them both at the door, jittery with nerves, in a clean white shirt and blue jeans and sneakers. "I was afraid you'd change your mind," she said.

He led Joanna in. He didn't expect the wood floors Lee had buffed and polished herself, rubbing so strenuously that she had worn through the knees of her jeans. He was surprised by the clean white walls Lee had painted, the single framed print above a black couch. The place was clean and bright and inviting. The kitchen table had a fruit-printed cloth on it and a blue plate of cupcakes.

"Go on," Lee said, grinning at him. "You're dying to see if I really do have a set of dishes that match."

"I am not," he said, but he walked to the cupboards. Inside, neatly stacked, were dinner and salad plates, some soup bowls and cups, all in the same deep blue. On the stove was a heavy cast-iron set of cookware. Amazed, he turned to her. "What have you become?" he said.

Joanna was hunched over the table, eyeing the chocolate cupcakes Lee had made. "You can have as many as you want," Lee told her.

"Can I have five?" Joanna said.

"As many as you want is two," Jim said.

Lee showed them the rest of the apartment, leading to the pink room, watching Joanna as she stepped inside. "Whose room is this?" Joanna said.

"You like it?" Lee asked her, and Joanna, mouth full of cupcake, nodded.

"It's a guest room," Jim said.

"Sort of," Lee said.

Joanna sat on the small pink bed, looking around, getting so comfortable that Jim suddenly straightened. "We'd better get back," he said. "Come on, peach."

Lee walked them both to the door. She waited until Joanna had bounded outside before she touched Jim's sleeve.

"Thank you," Lee said.

He stepped back. "It's not for you," he told her. "I just don't want to have to ever tell her that I refused to let her know her mother."

Lee looked at him. "Can she ever visit by herself?"

Jim looked past her, into her apartment. "Are you going to try to take her?" he said.

Flustered, Lee dug her hands into her pockets. "What a way to say it," she said. "*Take* her. You think I'd force her to be with me if she didn't want to?"

"I wouldn't try."

"I just want her to know who I am," Lee said.

"I thought you were going to wait on that."

"So I changed my mind," she said, suddenly miserable. "What do I have to do to show you I'm serious? I rented this place. I work a job. I'm *here*, for God's sake. Why can't I be a part of her life? How long are we going to fight about this? What's best for her—what's best for us.... Listen, she's going to have to know sometime. She *knows* me already. She *likes* me. You can see that. And when she's older, you think she'll forgive either one of us for not telling her?"

Jim had a fleeting image of Joanna at nineteen, angrily slamming out of the house.

"If you don't tell her, I will."

"No," he said. "Don't do that." He looked over at Joanna, who was polishing off another cupcake, littering the sidewalk with crumbs. When she saw them watching her, she started walking firmly away.

" 'Bye, Lee!" she called. " 'Bye, Daddy! 'Bye, everybody in the whole wide world!"

"I'll tell her," Jim said. "But let me tell her alone."

They went for a ride. To get ice cream, Jim said. They all rode on the front seat, Joanna between him and Lila, Lila vaguely tapping out some rhythm on her knee.

Jim pulled into the first Dairy Queen he saw, buying them all scoops in a cup. "You know what?" he said. "I think we should eat these by this really pretty wooded road I know."

Joanna blinked. "How come?" she said.

"A pretty view helps digestion," Lila said, taking her dish of vanilla.

"I'm eating mine now," Joanna said, but she twirled her white plastic spoon around once and then looked across Lila at the road.

It took him only ten minutes to drive to the road and park, but it seemed to take him a hundred more to get up the nerve to tell Joanna. He took slow, tasteless bites of his own chocolate ice cream. "Isn't this pretty?" he said, watching Joanna, who was taking careful licks of ice cream; Lila, who nibbled uncomfortably. They ate in silence, and when Joanna had almost finished he turned to her.

"Joanna," he said suddenly. "Do you remember all the photographs I showed you of your mother?"

Joanna nodded.

"Remember I told you that she had had to go away, that she was coming back?"

"And then she died," said Joanna.

Jim felt a flicker of pain. "Well, no," he said. "That's what we thought. When a person isn't heard from or seen in a very long time, they're considered dead." Joanna stopped eating. She looked at Lila. Lila carefully napkined off the wet dot of ice cream on Joanna's nose.

"You go on with your life. That's why I married Lila. I love her. And she loves you." He nodded at Joanna encouragingly.

"More than anything," Lila said.

"What's wrong?" Joanna said suddenly. "Why are you both looking at me like that? Don't you feel good?"

"Honey," he said. His voice seemed to be drying even as he spoke, cracking into dust. "Your mother didn't die."

"She's alive?"

A knot lodged in his throat. Jim said, "I spent years trying to find her, and now she's found us."

Joanna stared. "Found us? My mother's here?"

Jim nodded. Lila looked at him above Joanna's head, her eyes swimming.

"Where is she?"

"Well," he said, "well, Lee's your mother, honey."

Joanna was silent for a moment. "I don't believe you," she said.

"You see how she loves you, how she comes to see you."

"I still don't believe you. She *likes* me, but she doesn't love me. And anyway, she never said she was my mother. Did she tell you that?" Joanna asked Lila.

"Well, honey, she told your father."

"We thought it would be better if we told you."

Joanna bit down on her lower lip. "Why didn't she ever find me before? What took her so long?"

Jim stroked her hair. "She was having a hard time."

"What hard time?"

"Honey, sometimes life is really hard for people," Jim said.

"But she knew I was alive, right? She knew where we were." Joanna looked at Jim.

"I don't know. I just know she found us now."

"Was she still away on business?" Joanna said. "All that time? You couldn't find her through her business?"

"Baby," Jim said.

Joanna looked down at her ice cream. "I can't finish this," she said abruptly. He took the dripping dish from her and pitched it into the garbage bag he kept in the car.

"Don't you want to talk a little about it?" Lila said.

She shook her head. For a moment she remembered how, when she was really little, she had played dolls with her mother's photographs. No one had ever asked her where her mother was; everyone had assumed that was now Lila, including her. "What happens now?" she said. She thought of Amy Mandoza in her class—Amy, who had two sets of parents, who spent Christmas in Aspen with her mother and stepfather and the rest of the year here with her father and her stepmother. Amy hated Aspen. She came back one time with a broken leg because her stepfather had insisted a big girl like her didn't need to baby around the bunny slope any longer. "Do I have to go live with her sometimes?" she said.

"Things don't have to change one single bit," Jim said. "You don't have to do anything you don't want to do."

"What do you want me to do?"

"I want you to know how very much Lila and I love you."

He waited for her to say something, but she was frowning. She stared down into her lap.

He drove her home in silence, and only when they walked into the house did he see how red her eyes still were. Lila looked at Jim with a little flicker of alarm. He shook his head. "Wash up for bed now," he said to Joanna. He watched her walk on her coltish legs, clapping her hands for the dog, and then he turned to Lila.

Lila folded down onto the couch. She picked at the tufts of fabric on the arms, staring down at the rug, not looking at him, until he couldn't stand it any longer. He had to go and crouch down beside her.

"You think we did wrong?" he said.

She continued to study the carpet. "I hate Lee," she said.

Joanna wouldn't talk. No matter how gently Lila or Jim brought up the subject of Lee, Joanna tuned them out so expertly it sometimes took them minutes to realize she wasn't listening, she was in the zone.

She didn't ask about Lee, and she refused to go to the pharmacy. The only person she trusted was the dog, and even he sometimes bolted from her to chase squirrels or to flirt with the neighbor's toy poodle. She spent two hours one Saturday looking for the photograph albums of herself as a baby. There were a million shots. She was lying in a drizzle of sunlight. She was rocking on a chair. There were pictures of her with Jim and with Maureen and Lila. There were shots of her as a newborn, but there wasn't one single shot of her with Lee. She piled the pictures back into the album pages and shut it, stuffing it into the bottom of the closet.

She kept thinking about her mother. At school, during recess, when the other girls were walking around and around the small oval playground excitedly whispering confidences, Joanna walked alone, imagining her mother leaving her. She had never really thought of it before. She had always imagined her mother had been away on business like Beth Kitany's mother, who traveled to Europe, but why would someone go away from a baby that little? Had she been such an ugly baby that her mother couldn't possibly want her? Had she hurt Lee so much being born that Lee couldn't stand to look at her?

In class she was distracted. More than once the teacher reminded her to put on her thinking cap. She lay in bed at night and every single thing she used to think about her mother felt just like a slap in the face. Her mother hadn't had to go someplace on business, someplace so exotic she hadn't been able to write or call or remember her family. She had chosen to leave. Her mother hadn't died. She had been a plane ride away, and she hadn't thought to call her own daughter. Until now, and Joanna didn't even know why. Maybe she was dying and trying to kiss up to God. Joanna drew the bedclothes up to her chin. Which was worse, she thought, to finally see your mother after all these years and find out she was dying or not to ever see her at all?

She bolted out of bed, padding barefoot into Jim and Lila's bedroom. She shook him. Bleary-eyed, he struggled up. "What is it?" he said, alarmed. Beside him Lila stirred.

"Is Lee dying?" Joanna whispered.

He wiped one hand over his face. "Dying? No, of course not. Why?"

She was silent for a moment. Her eyes looked luminous. "Can I sleep in the bed with you?" she said.

He looked at her for a moment, then patted the bed. "Come on, baby," he said. She got in, burrowed against him, against Lila, who murmured drowsily, who half roused herself to look at them both. "What's going on?" she said.

"It's nothing," he said. He wrapped one arm about Lila, drawing her close. With the other arm he held his daughter. "It's all right, pumpkin," he said, but long after both Lila and Joanna were asleep, his eyes remained open.

Lee didn't tell Jim how as soon as he had said he was going to tell Joanna himself, she had felt as if she were being eaten alive with terror. She didn't say how she had paced her apartment, finally taking down all her books and dusting and alphabetizing them, getting down on her hands and knees and scrubbing the same kitchen floor she had scoured the day before. She rewashed her new dishes, she showered, and then, her hair still wet, she started walking so she wouldn't hear the deafening silence of the telephone, so she could keep the fear at bay. She walked so far that she didn't recognize the neighborhoods. She didn't recognize her own reflection in the store windows. She might have been one of the ghosts who suddenly seemed to be whispering frantically in her ears, and although she strained and strained, she couldn't pick up one single word they were saying to her, only sounds that made her whole body ache with yearning.

That night, when it was too late for anyone to call, for anyone to come by, Lee couldn't sleep. She made herself herbal tea, but as soon as it was poured she couldn't bring herself to take even one small sip. She ran a bath halfway before she knew there wasn't any way she could sit in it for more than two seconds without losing her mind. She turned on the radio and then turned it off, and then she began pacing the apartment, shadowed by the same whispering she had heard when she was walking. The apartment settled in the night, as lonely as if no one in the world had ever stayed there or ever would again.

She walked past the room that was Joanna's. Joanna's bed had one stuffed animal on it, a new blue elephant she had bought the other day. Lee pulled back the brand-new pink floral spread. She had gone to three different department stores before she found the rose-sprigged coverlet, before she noticed the matching pure cotton sheets, all edged with soft pink lace that the saleslady assured her had come all the way from France. She traced a hand down the sheet and a sudden, sweet new smell of baby powder floated up, the smell of a young girl. It was a still, warm night, but a breeze ruffled the coverlet. If you listened, you could hear stars starting to break through the night sky. Very, very slowly, Lee sat down on the bed and lay across it, and as soon as she did, the space beside her on the bed seemed suddenly warmer. Heart beating, she took one of the pillows and hooped an arm around it, bringing it close, and she was so overcome by the way the pillow fit beside her, like a small, compact girl, that she would have wept if she could have allowed herself to. She shut her eyes, the pillow moved with her, and then something suddenly let go and she realized just how tired she really was. Her breathing evened out; she rolled toward dreams, and around her the air was so blue and heavy, the night so quiet, that for a moment all around her seemed to be miracles, just waiting to happen.

Lee showed up at the pharmacy every single day for two weeks, hopeful and expectant, but Joanna never came. "You must have told her wrong," Lee said. "Maybe you frightened her. I want to talk to her."

"Absolutely not," Jim said. "She's upset enough."

"Try and stop me," Lee said.

She kept insisting. She would have gone to the house right that second if Jim hadn't stopped her. "All right," he said, flushed. "You're so anxious to talk to her, talk to her, but in my house. With me there."

"Not in the same room," Lee said. "She won't hear me if you're there."

He sighed. "All right, but if she doesn't want to see you, I'm not making her."

"You won't have to make her," Lee said. "I know it."

Lila wasn't thrilled about Lee coming over. "Why does she have to come here?" she demanded.

"You want her to approach Joanna at the school?" he said. "You want her talking to Joanna without either one of us being nearby? We'll be here. We can control things."

Lila was silent for a moment. "Sure," she said.

The day Lee was supposed to come over, Lila had spent the morning vacuuming up dog hair, even attempting to hold the dog down so she could vacuum him a little, too. She instantly regretted never having made Jim move out of the house he had lived in with Lee. She regretted never having painted or fixed up the place more; they hadn't even bought new furniture. She put their wedding picture on the TV in the living room. She thought about cooking elaborate snacks and then decided not to cook at all, not to make Lee any more at home than necessary.

That day Lee had woken up at six in the morning, too jazzed up to sleep. She showered and washed her hair, even though she had washed it the night before. She put on two different outfits before ending up in jeans and sneakers. And then, right before she left for Jim's, she sat on Joanna's bed for a minute, her hands splayed across the French spread. Please, she thought.

She was at Jim's by noon. Jim came to the door, Joanna and her dog behind him. When she saw Lee, she stiffened. "Lila's in the kitchen," Jim said.

"I haven't seen you in a while," Lee said to Joanna.

Joanna turned and walked back into the house.

"Well," Jim said. Lee could hear Lila's voice in the kitchen, low and soothing, and then Joanna reappeared holding Lila's hand.

"Lee just wants to talk to you, honey," Jim said.

Joanna looked up at Lila. "We'll be right in the backyard," Lila said. She nodded curtly at Lee.

Joanna stood perfectly still. After Jim and Lila left the room, for one moment Lee thought she was going to bolt, but instead Joanna sat on the farthest chair she could find. The dog settled at her feet, so friendly-faced that for a minute Lee considered talking to him.

Lee lowered herself onto the couch. "Did your father tell you?"

Joanna nodded.

"Well, what do you think?"

She seemed to be dreaming, half there. "Well?" Lee said. Joanna ruffled the dog's fur.

Joanna looked at her. "I thought you were dead," she said.

"Do I look dead?" Lee said.

"If I had a baby, I wouldn't have left her."

Lee twined her fingers together. She wanted to say "How do you know what you'll do, what you'll feel, how you'll be, at nineteen? How can you know that one day you might be so terrified that the only thing that seems safe might just be an open road?" Instead she composed herself. "Then you're stronger than I was." She leaned back against the soft cushions of the couch, suddenly exhausted.

"I started thinking about you all the time. I wanted to know you," said Lee.

"You don't know me."

"I know, but I *want* to." She flopped her hand in her lap. "Listen, I know it's weird. It's odd for me, too. But we can take it slow, as slow as you like. Maybe you could come out to my apartment some afternoon. Just you and me. Would you like that?"

Joanna studied her. "No," she said.

Lee wet her lips. "We could bake cookies," she said. "I have books you might like."

"No," said Joanna.

"Well, you can think about it. Maybe decide later."

Heated, Joanna stood up. There was no air in the room. The light seemed to be dimming. "I said *no*," she said, her voice rising, heaving into a shout. "What's wrong with you? Don't you understand English?" And then she ran from the room, the dog barking after her.

Joanna hurtled out of the house, slamming the back door behind her. She tore past Lila and Jim, who stood up from their lawn chairs. She was too fast for them. "Joanna!" Lila cried, but Joanna no longer heard her. She ran blindly, into Maureen's yard, toward Maureen's always open back door.

"I knew it," said Lila. Jim stood up, putting one hand on Lila's shoulder. Then he turned and walked into the house, his face set with anger.

He was going to shout her from his house, tell her that enough was enough. Anyone could see that Joanna didn't want to go with her. He stormed into the living room, his head lifting in fury, and there, in a corner of sunlight, was Lee, crying helplessly, hunched over. His anger deflated and he felt suddenly weakened.

Lee was crying so hard that she was shaking. Her face was damp and flushed. Even when they were seventeen he had never been able to look at her without wanting to take care of her. Abruptly he touched her, felt the sudden heat of her skin, and then he leaned her toward him, as easily as if she were made of paper. Gratefully she dropped against him and he closed his arms about her with a sigh. "I was pregnant with her in this house," Lee cried. "I lived here!"

Outside, waiting, Lila, too, began to cry. She swabbed helplessly at her face and then stood up, brushing off the seat of her skirt. Enough was enough. She was going to walk into her house and tell Lee to leave, and then she was going to walk into Maureen's and tell her daughter to come home where she belonged.

Lila didn't see them at first. They were in the shadows by the window, Jim rocking Lee, talking to her in a voice so low, it made her frightened. "Jim," she said, and then, startled, Jim and Lee released. Lee looked merely surprised, but Jim's face was a map of confused yearning that made something inside of Lila start to chip and break apart.

"I'd better go," Lee said, her voice raw. She scooped up her purse, nodding briefly at Jim. "Thanks," she said to Lila. "I guess it didn't go so well today."

"I guess it didn't," Lila said coldly.

Lee leaned along the wall, deflated, swiping at her runny nose. She straightened, resigned, and pulled her coat closed about her. When she walked to the door, she kept her head down, not looking at either Jim or Lila.

Jim followed her to the door, and then he stood there, at the entrance, just watching Lee walk down the flagstone walk away from him, back out into the street, and when he finally turned back toward Lila she was stiff with anger.

She turned before he could reach her and stormed into the kitchen. She crashed dirty dishes into the sink, flooding them with water.

He fiddled with the edge of the dish towel. "I'm sorry it was rough for you," he said finally.

"Not too rough for you, though, was it," Lila said sharply.

"What are you talking about?"

"You like having her here," Lila said. "It's unfinished business for the Archers all around, now, isn't it?" She stopped doing the dishes and turned to face him.

"What's wrong with you?" Jim said. "Can't I even comfort her without your thinking something's going on?"

"Something *is* going on," she said acidly. "You've never forgotten her, have you, never given up hope."

"Do you see me running after her?"

"You're running in place."

"Don't tell me how I feel," he shouted. "I know how I feel."

Lila splashed soapy hands up from the water. "How?" she cried.

Joanna was feeling better. Maureen had taken one look at her and taken her right down into the family room downstairs. She didn't ask Joanna one single question about what was going on or why. Instead she simply turned up her favorite record, an old Elvis Presley album, so loud the dog scampered back upstairs. "Not a Presley fan, huh," she said. "Okay, now *scream*," she advised. "Go on, get it out."

When Joanna remained paralyzed, Maureen started screaming herself, carrying on until Joanna joined her. As soon as Joanna screamed, she felt the anger dissolve, and with it she suddenly wanted to go home.

She was barely in her own yard when she heard the shouting. They must have been yelling before, sound insulated by Elvis. She felt suddenly frightened, but she made her way into the house, following the sound, right at the edge of the living room, where her parents were fighting. Frozen, she heard them.

"You didn't agree to it for Joanna, it was for you!" Lila cried.

"Fine," Jim said, his face drawn. "This is just goddamned fine." He slammed out the front door. Lila turned her head away, crossing her arms over her chest. As soon as she heard the noise of the car starting up, she whipped around, moving so fast that she didn't even see Joanna, crouching like a wild animal, pressed so closely against the wall she might as well have been invisible.

Joanna retreated more and more. She would take the dog and sit in the backyard and stare into space. She didn't hear the arguments in the house anymore or the silences at dinner. She didn't hear the phone when Lee called, asking to speak to her, and when Jim or Lila tried to speak to her about it she found she could shut out their sounds. She could watch them, their mouths moving silently, and she could imagine they were simply asking her what she wanted for dinner, what she wanted packed in her school lunch. She was lost in daydream. She was in the stars. She was swimming at Cape Cod, the water lapping against her legs.

The house began to feel hopeless. Every morning, before her shift started, Lila gardened. The squash was coming in now, the few carrots the rabbits hadn't gotten were full grown. She pulled them up so fiercely that she sometimes scratched her fingers. Jim began coming home for lunch, trying to catch Lila in the half hour before she left for work, but it seemed that no matter how he gauged it she was always leaving or already gone.

They were polite about each other. At night, in bed, they lay together as if they had never kissed or held each other or made love. In the living room the dog whined and dreamed. And in the other room, even though it was past midnight, they could hear Joanna rustling, clicking her light on and off, six times, a ritual every night now, before the house quieted and then quickened into sleep.

Lee knew how badly things had gone at Jim's. He hadn't come by to see her almost all week, and she had been too nervous to go to the pharmacy, too afraid he might tell her to forget ever seeing Joanna. She didn't know what to do anymore. She could threaten with a lawyer all she wanted, but how could she even think of taking custody of a child who hated her?

Every night Lee called Jim's, hoping Joanna might answer. And every evening she hung up, defeated. She was stunned that her daughter had so little interest in her.

She kept thinking, What might Joanna have been like if I had raised her? Would she be more adventurous, running out into the road so many times that she'd have to be tethered into a baby leash? Would she like to cook alongside me, the two of us freckled with flour? Joanna didn't even look like her. But if Lee had raised her, at least her mannerisms would have been the same, wouldn't they? She wouldn't stand so stiffly like Lila.

When she could stand it no longer, when another Sunday had passed, Lee went to the pharmacy. When Jim saw her, he came out from behind the counter.

"It went terribly, didn't it," she said to Jim.

"She won't talk about it," he told her. "She won't talk about anything." He looked suddenly exhausted.

"She'll be all right," Lee faltered.

Jim glanced back at the counter. A woman was experimentally daubing a lipstick shade across her hand even though there were signs all over the place about not testing the cosmetics. He looked at Lee. "Joanna's not coming by here today."

"Oh." She clumsily put her hands into her pockets. "Maybe I'll have some tea."

"You look terrible," he said.

"You too," Lee said.

She sat at the red Formica counter sipping sugary tea, and suddenly she wished for tea leaves, for someone beside her who might tip over the cup and read them. She didn't care what they'd tell her. It would be enough to know you had possibilities. She twisted her spoon in the cup, creating a small whirlpool, but the only thing at the bottom of her cup was porcelain. Abruptly she got up and left.

It began to scare her. She lay awake in the bed, holding up one of the snapshots of Joanna she had stolen, and thought over and over: She's my daughter. We should know each other. She wondered why she had felt more of a connection with Joanna before she had actually met her, why now her own daughter made her feel as if she were living on a planet a million miles away. She fretted her hands over her head. An image flashed: Karen in one of her T-shirts, whirling about the room, arms outstretched into propellers. Lee shut her eyes. The only memory she had of her daughter was in being pregnant and giving birth, but she had turned her face away when they had tried to bring the baby to her. She had refused to touch her. She got up. She riffled her purse for a crumpled snapshot. Valerie had taken the picture. Lee was swinging Karen up into the air, the two of them laughing. She looked at that picture, and she could swear she felt the Wisconsin wind; she could hear Karen's laugh belling out, feel her fingers wrapped tightly about her. She remembered the moment surrounding that photo, knew what had happened before and after the picture had been taken. Her longing was so sharp, she felt suddenly sickened by it. She slid down to the rug, folding over to her knees, rocking, giving herself comfort.

The next day Lee walked into the pharmacy, looking for Jim, wanting company. "I'll get him," the other pharmacist said, going to the back. She heard him calling Jim. "Someone's here for you," he sang. Jim came out, his face expectant, hopeful, and she saw, stunned, how he faded right there before her. "I thought you were Lila," he said.

"You want to get some coffee?" she said.

He shook his head. "I'm sorry," she said suddenly, and he nodded. "Another time," he said helplessly.

She told herself that you couldn't always make things happen, that sometimes they took time, and all that mattered was if you had at least laid down the groundwork. The thought soothed her when she noticed another new day on her calendar, when she felt the seasons changing around her.

She filled her time the best she could. She waitressed, itching to be in the kitchen. There was only one cook, a young woman named Elaine, and like most of Georgia's staff Elaine considered herself something other than a cook. Elaine was an actress, always muttering lines as she stirred and chopped. Lee could see her practicing facial expressions, flashing her hands. Elaine was sloppy and hot-tempered and so careless a cook that it hurt Lee to serve the food she prepared. Elaine didn't like anyone watching her, because it disturbed her concentration learning her lines, but Lee could take one look at her dishes and know what they needed, and sometimes, when the chef wasn't looking, she made the additions. A dusting of basil. A few chopped chives. A few times Lee got into trouble. The customers sent compliments to Elaine about the extra cheese now on the pasta, about the cream suddenly spread across some soup. "It was my idea," Lee said, but instead of being pleased, Georgia was annoyed. "Cream and cheese cost money. Customers don't know the difference unless you educate their palate, and at a restaurant like Trax's it's better palates get so drunk on expensive drinks that you could feed them tire rubber and they'd all think it was delicious." She gave Lee a warning. "I could fire you," she said.

"No, please. I need this job."

"Then do it," Georgia suggested.

She did it. People drifted in, ordering burgers and fries and an occasional pasta dish that required nothing more strenuous than a sauce over packaged noodles. They ordered coffee after coffee, staying at tables so long they felt they owned them. Lee now moved so silently that the other waitresses began calling her the invisible woman.

She worked as long as she could just so she wouldn't have to spend any more time by herself in her apartment than she had to. On weekends she left her place as soon as she could, planning activities as relentlessly as a scout leader. She spent half an afternoon at the zoo, wandering purposefully past the somnolent-looking monkeys, the furiously pacing tigers, but she was drawn to the night zoo, to the familiar rustlings of the bats. She was drawn to the white polar bears, lolling in a landscape so frozen it reminded her of a Wisconsin winter. "How many places have you lived in?" Jim had asked her once. "One," Lee had said, and it was the truth.

She visited and revisited every single park and museum and sight there was to see in Baltimore, until the thought of getting on another bus filled her with despair.

She began pointing out sunsets to herself. She reminded herself what a good kitchen she had, that a house didn't have to be lonely if you were working with peace and pleasure inside of it. So right from work she began stopping at the all-night supermarket, buying whatever was fresh and then coming home and experimenting. Lee stirred and chopped until she calmed, floating on, unthinking. She made more than enough food for a dinner party, but she didn't know one single person who might be willing to come. She froze all the food, not throwing it out until the freezer was so crammed that she needed to make new space.

Lila and Jim were fighting again. "Let's settle it once and for all," Lila said. Her face was pursed and white.

"What do you want me to do?" Jim shouted. "You want me to call a lawyer, you want Joanna in court? You want that?"

Joanna was listening from behind her closed door, and for the first time in her life she couldn't seem to enter the zone. She couldn't shut out the sounds, and it terrified her. Panicked, she walked to the edge of the room, by the windows. She shut her eyes, trying to concentrate, but her parents' arguing pinned her in the present. She heard her own name, bitter, accusing, as sharp as a curse. *Joanna.*

Joanna rummaged in her bureau drawer and took her blue sweater and an extra pair of jeans and stuffed them into her school knapsack. She wanted the dog, but he was somewhere else in the house. She couldn't risk calling him, couldn't risk his barking. She tightened the knapsack, pulled open her window, and climbed lightly to the ground.

It was just past six o'clock, dinnertime. Cars had already pulled into drives. Kids had already been called inside to suppers. Soon there wouldn't be enough real light left to do much of anything. She looked at the row of houses and then bent her head and walked right out of the neighborhood.

She didn't go very far. As soon as she saw the highway stretching out, the brush of wind from the cars, she felt helpless. Abruptly she turned from it and began steadfastly to walk deeper into the suburban streets.

She didn't know where to go, and none of the houses looked very friendly to her. Instead she circled back to the house. The car was still in the drive, the lights blazing. Lila was still shouting at her father, so loudly that she wondered why the police didn't come. She knew these fights. They'd go on until midnight, and in the morning her parents would be tightly polite. They wouldn't look her in the eye. They wouldn't touch.

She wandered back over toward the school. She remembered how she used to love school, how excited she got just from seeing the flagpole out front. Now the flag was off the pole. The windows were black with night. That day in school the music teacher had brightly lined up all ten girls in the class and asked the boys to line up behind whatever girl they liked, and it hadn't taken more than three minutes for Joanna to realize no one was standing behind her. There was a sudden boom of thunder. Shoulders hunched, she walked past as if the school were nothing more than an apparition.

Jim's voice, when he called Lee, was hoarse with fear. "I'll look," she said. "I'll look everywhere." She rushed outside, stunned, directionless. She kept thinking about Karen running from Valerie, running desperate and glad to her. Lee ran, jaggedly cutting across lawns, but the only thing in the road coming toward her was a crumpled red Macy's bag.

Jim called the police, but almost immediately he started looking. "You wait here," he told Lila. "In case she comes back." He called for the dog. "Maybe he can find her."

Lila was so upset, it suddenly made him afraid. He gripped at her sleeve. "You'll be here, won't you?" He wouldn't let go of her until she had nodded.

He didn't care what kind of a fool he was, he rang every single bell in the neighborhood, asking if Joanna might be there. "Is something wrong?" person after person asked, and all they had to do was look into Jim's face to know how bad a thing it was. He kept thinking how someone could disappear so easily from your life, you might wonder if your memory of them had been a lie. He thought of Joanna. He thought suddenly of Lila. They had been fighting almost until midnight last night, hushed angry whispers so as not to wake Joanna. Lila had finally bolted away from him, flinging open the front door in fury, in nightgown and bare feet, white legs flashing in the dark. "I've had enough," she had told him. She had made it to the dewy front lawn, her nightgown fluttering behind her, before he had grabbed her. "Where are you going?" he cried, pulling at her, so panicked he could barely breathe. "Come back inside. Please. I'll sleep on the couch. Just come inside." He had pleaded and pleaded until his voice was raw, and she had finally, reluctantly, come inside. And although he had made himself a bed on the couch, he had lain still only until he felt she must be sleeping, and then he had gotten up and stood by the bedroom door, just watching her sleep, just making sure she was still there.

In the backseat, Fisher sprawled out and panted. It was nearly midnight, so late the lights in the houses were off. He was on the street with the purple house when the dog spotted a cat and began to bark. Fisher was crazy, not calming until the cat fled. Jim searched for lights, for people he could ask.

He wouldn't give up for the night. He kept circling the routes Joanna might know. It started to pour. Sheets of water drenched the windshield. He parked by the school and called her name. He went by the supermarket where she said all the older kids hung out. "One more time," he said. He was soaking from running in and out of the car. The vinyl upholstery was slick with water.

He was driving on their street, but he had no intention of stopping, not without Joanna.

"Oh, my God," Jim said.

By Maureen's front door, face hidden, was a small familiar figure. He jammed on the brakes, knocking the dog forward. He flung open his door, running so fast into the wet street that he fell, tearing open the knee of his pants. He stumbled to her. Shivering, soaking wet, she lifted her small face up to him.

"No one was home," Joanna cried.

They walked across the yard in the rain. He could hear his breathing. He could hear Joanna's beside him. He wouldn't let go of her hand. He banged on the door. Almost instantly Lila opened it, her face filling with Joanna, filling then with him. "I love you," he said, and burst into tears, and then her arms were around him.

Terrified, Lee called Jim's house, but when Lila answered she hung up. You fool, she told herself. You idiot. She stalked from one end of her apartment to the other, all the while thinking of all the dangers that could befall a child, and then she grabbed her jacket.

By the time she got to Jim's, it had stopped pouring. Panting, she ran up the walk and rang the bell.

There was commotion. She could hear voices.

The door opened. Jim's body hid the house from her. He came outside, shutting the door behind him. "She's home," he said. "She's fine."

Lee felt herself collapsing with relief.

"I found her at Maureen's."

"Thank God," Lee said, moving toward the door. Jim pushed her hand from the doorknob.

"Don't you understand, she doesn't want you!" Jim said sharply.

"She's upset," Lee said.

"Of course she's upset. We're all upset."

"What can I do?" Lee said. "Just tell me—"

He stared at her as if he suddenly didn't know her. "What should you do?" he said. "I can't believe you. What should you do—you should stay away from us for a while."

"Stay away? You think she ran away because of me?"

Jim was silent for a minute. "She ran away because of the situation."

"I can't stay away. Not now," Lee said.

"*I* want you to stay away."

Lee shook her head. "No," she said. "You don't."

He looked at her as if she were already very far away. "I love my daughter. I love Lila. It took me a very long time to love my life again. And now you come back and you make me remember you all over again. And things that had stopped hurting years ago—all of a sudden, they hurt again."

"I never wanted that," Lee said. "I wanted to make peace—I wanted—"

"You can't do that!" Jim said, astonished. "What do you want from any of us?" He suddenly straightened. "Please," he said. "Stay away for a while." He opened the front door, the door that Lee herself had stormed out of countless clear nights to walk and walk and follow the highway, the door Lee had once had the key to, only this time he was the one closing the door. She was the one standing helplessly out in the night, feeling as if she were searching for something that wouldn't ever be found.

Almost immediately Joanna came down with bronchitis. She was out of school for two weeks. Every day Lila tended her own wounds by doing nothing more than tending Joanna's. She gave her sponge baths with imported perfumed soaps. She was no cook, but she made her daughter soup from scratch, painstakingly following recipes she clipped from the papers. She put two kinds of antibiotics in bright paper cups. She disguised the cough syrups in shakes she made in the blender. She filled the bathroom with steam and brought Joanna into it. "Breathe deep," she said. "It'll clear your lungs." She fixed up the bathroom with big white towels and a pitcher of clear lemonade, and she sat in there with Joanna. She could hardly breathe in there herself, but she stayed so through the steam Joanna might see her.

She didn't think about why Joanna had run away that night or why she had come back. She was simply grateful that she had. Jim couldn't stop looking at Joanna. And, too, Lila felt him looking at her. He called her ten times a day. He came home every afternoon to have lunch with the two of them. Sometimes they all napped together, too, and he would wrap Lila up in his arms, holding her as tightly and as gratefully as he held Joanna. He was home every evening, with flowers for her, with toys for Joanna, even once a rubber bone for the dog, who was ridiculously pleased.

Jim thought about Lila all the time now. He was working late at the pharmacy when he suddenly missed Lila so much, he had to see her. He drove to the hospital, asking the nurses where she was. He found her in the cafeteria, sipping coffee, and when she saw him her face bloomed into a smile. "Hey," he said, taking her hand.

"Hey yourself," she said.

"You know what?" he said.

She shrugged, happy.

"Will you marry me?"

"You? I'd have to be crazy."

"No, I mean again. A big wedding, flowers, honeymoon."

She was silent for a moment. "Lee's not coming, is she?"

"Not this time," he said, and kissed her until she smiled again.

A week later Joanna went back to school, and for the first time in his life Jim was glad his daughter had the zone. It protected her. She came home and stared dreamily out the windows, and he didn't disturb her because she seemed so content. When Lila came to get her at school, Joanna would be sitting contentedly on the ground, oblivious of everything, and sometimes Lila would have to honk the horn.

Joanna herself didn't realize how deeply she had been in the zone until she came out of it, suddenly, abruptly, right in the middle of arithmetic. Suddenly she noticed everything was different. There was a new boy in the class who was French, and everyone was trying to mimic his accent. She had been so nonreactive in the zone that teasing her had become boring. Even the wildest of the kids gave up because

Joanna no longer showed any emotion, even when you threw a spitball at her.

It was nearing the end of the year. She was behind in long division, but when she went to the board and floundered not one single person laughed, not even when the teacher got exasperated and told her she wasn't trying, instead when Joanna sat back down, Rosamund Phillips, who used to shoot spitballs at her, felt sorry and twisted around and showed Joanna how to do the problem. And later, during reading, no one groaned when she stood up and announced that the book she had read was *Oliver Twist* by Charles Dickens. On the playground, while the girls formed groups and walked around and around or jumped rope, while the boys played punch ball, they seemed to have tired of jumping on Joanna. No one knew anything had gone on with her other than a lengthy flu. No one asked how she was feeling, but no one asked her anything different from what they might ask anyone else. She walked around by herself, and when she got down and drew a clumsy hopscotch, she was startled that two other girls joined her.

Lee thought about Joanna, but she didn't try to see her. She slept in Joanna's bed, flooded with dreams about Wisconsin and a smaller, younger child than Joanna, a dark-haired scrubby child who had a temperament so rough she might as well have been Lee's daughter.

Lee seemed to swim up toward consciousness, shocked at the suddenness of morning and light. On automatic, she then rushed herself awake. The pink walls were smudged by her handprints as she pulled herself along toward the shower. The wood floor was starting to mottle from the way she dripped from the shower to the kitchen.

She was late to work, and another waitress was already gloomily taking an order from one of Lee's tables. Lee didn't feel the clothes on her body. She barely stepped on the ground. The air brushed past. I was supposed to come alive again here, she thought, so how come I feel so dead?

She didn't go back to the pharmacy, but she wasn't going to leave, either, no matter what Jim said. She walked a lot around the city, toward all the places where she thought Joanna might be: roller rinks, bowling alleys, malls. Once she walked past Jim's house at night, silently standing for a moment in front of it until she felt like a prowler.

At home she sat in the pink room and tried to think about what to do, and then after a while, restless, she'd go into the kitchen and bake bread. She experimented with different flours, with different rising times and yeasts, and she spent a lot of time punching down the dough, forcing her fist into it. She set the dough in a large new blue bowl. The pink room had the best radiators, the kind of strong heat she thought a child could use, so she let her bread dough rise in there. She sat and read until she could finish with the bread.

She was sleeping in the pink room one day, and when she woke up she suddenly felt a scent sharp in her nose. It wasn't the warm sleepy smell of a daughter. It was wheat or cinnamon raisin. It was sourdough. She woke up, sniffing, wanting toast, and she got up and prowled toward the kitchen. It was such a simple thing to ask for, and such an easy thing to get for herself, that for the first time in a long while, she felt comforted.

Without Jim, without Joanna, her days were numbing. She didn't really have friends at the diner. Most of the waitresses were busy hustling for their tips, and most were students, as different from Lee as if she had come from Mars. She tried sometimes to meet people in movie lines or at the supermarket, but they just gave her odd stares. When Friday came around she began to get a feeling in the pit of her stomach. Two days were suddenly too long to get through alone. She once blurted out an invitation to a waiter she kind of liked. "Would you like to see a movie?"

He grinned at her. "Can my girlfriend come, too?" he said. When she blushed he laughed it off. "Hey, I'm flattered," he told her. Lee didn't tell him that she was so tired of going solo that even a threesome would suit her.

"Hey, you need me this weekend, I can be here," she told Georgia.

"Jesus, get a life," Georgia said.

One night Lee simply began dialing. First Jim, who didn't pick up the phone. Then Andy, whose machine clicked on, but at least he didn't have a "we" on his tape, at least he was still living alone. She called California Information for Valerie, all the time thinking of how when she had first met Valerie, Valerie would ask her to movies, to dinner, and she had refused to go. "It's unlisted," the operator told Lee politely.

Lee dialed. She called Madison weather and listened to the recording warn of an impending heat wave. She called Madison time. She tried to get Valerie's number one more time, and then, half-asleep, something flickered across her memory. When she was a little girl Claire had once told her that mothers had a special kind of telepathy. "If you're ever in trouble, why, I'll know it," Claire had told her. She had told her lots of things. Dreams could be prophetic. The right one would come along and she would know it. You could whisper to the dead at night and they would hear. Lee sank onto the bed, crossing her arms over her head. Claire had been wrong. She blinked up at the ceiling. "Karen," she whispered. Nothing happened. Nothing moved in the room, there was no sudden chill wind. She got up and called the recording for Madison weather, and then, abruptly, she called the restaurant in Madison, she called Rico.

"Lee," Rico said, his voice warming with surprise. "We all miss you."

"You do?" she said, startled. "So you haven't hired another new cook?"

"Why would I do that?" he said.

"Good," Lee said, pleased. "That's good." She sighed.

"You're not leaving us permanently, are you?" he said.

"Why, you'd hire me again?" Lee said.

"Are you kidding? I still remember your blueberry soup," he said. "Come on, what're you doing out there, a Madison girl like you. Come home."

When she hung up the phone she suddenly thought of the blueberry soup. She could smell the sweet cream in it. She could feel the restaurant's heavy wood stirring spoon. Her hands flexed, expectant, and closed on the surprise of air.

Lee hadn't seen Joanna in over a month. She went to work and went to movies and cooked at home and told herself that for now that was a life, that any minute things would change. It worked until one afternoon when a mother came into the restaurant with her daughter, the two of them dressed alike and laughing, and then something in Lee snapped. She couldn't wait any longer. She couldn't be patient. "I don't feel well," she told Georgia. "I gotta go home." Georgia frowned at Lee for a moment and then saw the expression on her face. "Go," she said, waving one hand.

Lee half ran to Joanna's school. It was just noon. Kids would be out on the playground, one class after the other. If she timed it right, she could see her daughter.

By the time she reached the school, the playground was emptying of kids. Little kids, kindergarten it looked like. Twin lines. Panting, her hair pasted to her forehead, Lee hooked her fingers into the dirty wire rungs of the fencing, when suddenly another group of kids came out, and there, tagging at the end, was Joanna. Lee pushed against the fencing. Kids were whirling and speeding, breaking up into groups, but Joanna was walking around aimlessly, her hands buried in the pockets of her dress. Look up, Lee thought. Look up. Joanna arched her neck, squinting, lifting her gaze gradually across the horizon and then to Lee. Lee hesitantly lifted one trembling hand. Joanna froze. For a split second she seemed to be wavering in place, the air seemed to be warming around Lee, and then, suddenly, Joanna bolted away, skidding past a jump-rope game, nearly knocking into one of the jumpers.

"Joanna!" Lee cried, but Joanna was running from her, right to the other side of the school, and now a teacher standing at the far end of the playground noticed Lee and began striding toward her. Lee abruptly peeled herself from the wire fence. "Miss!" the teacher called, waving her long arms angrily, but Lee broke into a run.

She ran for nearly six blocks, her pocketbook swinging wildly, her hair whipped back. She ran and ran, thinking of nothing but the sound of her own breath, until she stumbled on a pebble and pitched forward onto the pavement, tearing a hole in her stockings and skinning both knees red. Exhausted, out of breath, she slowly got to her feet and began to walk, ignoring the glances of the people she passed. The whole way home she replayed Joanna racing from her. She went into her apartment, and suddenly the polished floors looked old and musty to her, suddenly even the kitchen seemed small and uninviting. She had no one to call, no one to give comfort, so she sat in her living room, coiled tight as a spring and waiting, and when the phone rang she picked it up automatically.

"You know how upset she is?" Jim said. "Can't you just let things be for a while?"

"Jim," Lee said.

"No, that's all I'm going to say," he said, and hung up.

Let things be, she thought. But things were neither here nor there.

She was settled nowhere. She belonged to no one. She felt herself suddenly chipping apart.

She waited a week, and then another. She roamed restlessly through Baltimore, always thinking she might see Joanna, things might progress, but although the streets were filled with children she never once saw her daughter.

One day she was waiting on a man and his daughter in the restaurant, and she suddenly smiled at the girl's red sweater. "You know, my daughter loves red, too," she said.

"Isn't that nice!" the man said, and later when she cleared his table she found a ten-dollar tip.

Her daughter began to be a story she found herself telling people. "She's smart as a whip," Lee told one customer. "Oh, you should see how well she does in school!" Lee said. "Really?" the woman said. "What school does she go to? My niece has that wonderful Mrs. Sands at the Whittamore." Lee knew the school, but she realized she had no idea who her daughter's teacher was. The woman was rattling about SRA and learning centers and Lee suddenly felt frightened because she didn't know those things, either, things any mother would know about her child. She picked up the woman's bill, folding it around the money, and then whisked up the woman's half-empty glass of iced tea. "I'll just get you a refill," she said. "On the house."

She took her time. Sometimes customers got so edgy that they called for another waitress or they just left. But when she came back with a new iced tea, the woman was still there. "You must be very proud," the woman said. "Who takes care of her while you're working?"

"She lives full-time with her father," Lee said. The woman gave a sympathetic cluck.

"Well, she's still your daughter," the woman said.

"It's just for now," Lee said. She gathered up a dirty cup and saucer and turned back toward the kitchen. As soon as Lee had said "just for now," it had sounded just like the words "happily ever after." Fairy-tale words, words you wanted to believe in, but you knew, after all, that nothing was that simple, because even heroines were not always willing participants, and sometimes what seemed most like reality had as much substance as a spell.

That evening, when she got off her shift, long after kids had cleared from the suburban streets and gone in to supper or schoolwork or just a night of TV, Lee stood in the dark across the street from Jim's house. The lights were on in the living room. She thought, I could just walk up to the porch and ring the bell. I could say "Listen, we have to talk, we have to settle this, you have to hear me." Her breathing was so loud, she was stunned they didn't come out and confront her. She saw something moving in the bushes in the front, out of the corner of her eye, and, dazed by her own daring, moved close enough to see it was Joanna, her small shoulders heaving. Lee had a strange sick feeling, as if time were opening up for her. Whether she was supposed to be here or not, she couldn't just stand by while her daughter cried in the bushes alone. She took a step. And then, abruptly, the front door whined open, freezing her in place, and there was Lila, in a long white cotton nightgown and bare feet. "Honey," Lila said. She stepped out onto the porch. She walked onto the dewy grass and moved exactly to the place where Joanna was, and then Joanna jumped out, her body still shaking, but with glee, and then, face shining, she threw herself into Lila's arms.

"Look what Fisher dug up," Lila called toward the house, laughing.

Lee stepped back farther into the darkness. The door slapped open and Jim came out. "There's my wild babies," Jim said. He stepped off the porch onto the front lawn. He nuzzled Lila's neck; he stroked back Joanna's hair.

"Can I sleep in your bed again tonight?" Joanna said. Lila looked across at Jim. "Our bed is your bed," she said.

Joanna, arms and legs like elastic, ran around the lawn, in and out between Jim and Lila, looking up at both of them every time she made a full circle, marking her place.

"Who wants cocoa?" Lila said, and then Joanna stopped running and took Lila's hand, pulling her close. She didn't let go the whole lazy walk up the stairs, she kept hold as Jim opened up the screen door. "Ladies," Jim said gallantly, ushering them back inside where it was warm and well lit, where Lee could hear a few chords of music before the door shut again on the house, the very same house she had run from, lifetimes ago.

Lee stood outside, and even though it was a warm night she was shivering. She couldn't see one single thing through the front window; she couldn't hear any sound. She could imagine them sipping cocoa at the same kitchen table she and Jim had bought; she could imagine them all curled up in the same bed she herself had once slept in, Joanna, warm and sleepy and safe, sandwiched in the middle. She moved closer, and then quickly, one by one, all the lights snapped out; the house grew dark and silent, and she felt a hurt so sudden and powerful, it caused her physical pain.

In the distance she heard a car. If it was a police car, if they saw her standing here half-hidden in the shadows, they might think she was a prowler, or a Peeping Tom. They might take her for a suspect personality, wondering over a life that didn't belong to her.

Lee started to walk. How could she have ever believed she could make things right? She had left a life she was too scared to love, to try and make peace with another, and she had never managed to live fully in either, so why did it surprise her now that it still all felt like running away?

She was walking down the same paths she used to take, following the exact same highways, feeling the same whiz and rush of the cars past her. From the first moment she had set foot in Baltimore she hadn't liked it, she hadn't felt at home, and the truth was that no matter how much she had tried, no matter how much she had kept waiting and waiting, she couldn't seem to like it now, either. She couldn't seem to feel at home. Suddenly she thought about Madison. She remembered a winter night so cold that a snow angel she had made had frozen solid in the ground. She remembered a bat hanging on her good winter coat like a fur collar and how Andy had helped her free it back into the night, where it belonged.

A car honked at her. She knew these roads. And she knew there was no longer any reason for her to keep walking them. She turned toward the main road and, exhausted, unthinking, started back to her apartment, where she would sleep, deep and dreamless, until morning.

She was at Keystone Bank ten minutes after it opened. She had eight thousand dollars left from her father. "I want to take everything out," she said. The teller raised her brows. "You want it in cash?" she said.

"I want to put it in another account," Lee said. "A trust fund." She scribbled a name on the paper. "And this is who it's to belong to."

She set it up so she didn't need to tell Jim or Lila anything at all. The money would sit there gathering interest, a secret that would reveal itself to Joanna when she turned sixteen, wild enough to get into the backs of cars with boys, but with money enough so she could climb on out again.

When Lee walked into the pharmacy, Jim immediately came toward her. "Hello, stranger," he said.

"I thought it would be better." She smiled uncertainly.

"It was. Thank you." Jim said.

"Listen, I—I'm going back to Madison."

He straightened. "You're leaving?"

Lee rubbed at her arm. "Joanna turned out wonderful."

Jim looked at her. "Are you going to call a lawyer?" he said quietly.

"No lawyers," she said. "No more disappearing. I just want to stay in touch. See what happens. I need to stay in touch."

"It might take a long time with her, you know," Jim said. "It might never happen."

"And it might. You won't fight it, will you?"

He shook his head. "What are you going to do in Madison?"

She shrugged. "Undeclare myself dead," she said. "Start living a life."

"Haven't you been doing that?" he said.

"You're being kind," she said. "That's nice."

He watched her. She was still the loveliest woman he had ever seen, and already he could feel himself missing her. He reached forward and touched her shoulder.

"It's so funny," Lee said. "You've got this life—a wife, a kid—"

"Hey. You didn't want it," Jim said.

"I know," Lee said. She looked around the pharmacy. "You, a pharmacist. Me, a chef. What do you think, if we had met now, would it have worked?"

Jim's face wavered. He thought of Lila, the night they had found Joanna, how she had slept in his arms, Joanna sandwiched between them. He thought of the wedding they were planning. "What good does it do to ask questions like that?" he said finally.

Inside the house he had always loved, his wife was probably reading, the daughter he had thought would bind Lee and him together was probably drawing, sprawled across the kitchen floor he himself had scrubbed that morning. Lee moved, and he felt a pull of desire. He remembered Lee at nineteen, the slope of her belly, the lift of her breasts. He remembered when she had started to show with Joanna, how he'd wait until she was asleep and then gently lay his head against her belly and talk to the baby, his wife's belly a conduit between them. He would tell it how things were going to be, and not one thing he had told his child or himself had even remotely come true. He had all manner of memories, and every one of them was ragged from remembering.

She wasn't looking at him. "I have to close up," he told her. "Why don't you come by in the morning?"

She nodded. "I want to say good-bye to Joanna." He nodded.

"You want me to wait for you to finish?" she said.

"No, you go on," he said.

He heard her leaving, the soft sudden pull of the door. If he looked up, he would see her through the window. A flash of blonde hair. That long striding walk of hers. He sat on the stool.

He was so quiet when he came in the house that Lila asked him if something was wrong. He wrapped his arms about her, swaying her against him. "Don't be silly," he said.

"Lee's leaving," he said. "She's going back to Madison."

Lila pulled apart from him.

"She wants to say good-bye to Joanna. I said okay."

"This will never be over," Lila said.

Jim kissed the pale skin at the base of her shoulders. "No," he said, "but it'll be different now. It'll work out." He folded her toward him, and then suddenly, at that moment, there wasn't anything that he felt he had ever wanted except for her, and there she was.

Lee was half an hour early. She had walked from the apartment, carrying a bag full of things she wanted to give her daughter, and she had ended up walking so quickly that she had misjudged her time. She was rounding the corner when she saw Jim and Lila, standing in the yard, kissing, and with an odd pang she remembered herself at seventeen, kissing Jim, feeling he was every escape she had ever wanted.

She waited until they had pulled apart, and then she lifted her hand awkwardly. "Hi," she said.

Lee was sitting on the floor of Joanna's room, watching Joanna brush her bride doll's short chop of dark hair. Joanna refused to look at her. She refused to speak, and every time Lee moved so much as an inch closer, Joanna flinched three more inches away.

"I'm going away," Lee said. "But not because of you."

Joanna kept brushing her doll's hair, not looking up.

Lee unfurled the map she had. "Look," she said. "It's Wisconsin. It's where I'll be." Joanna kept brushing, but Lee stood up. She grabbed some tacks on the dresser and carefully pinned the map onto the bulletin board. "See this red tack? That's where I live. That's where you can find me. I'm not going anywhere. And Joanna—" Joanna continued to brush, her eyes down. "Joanna, I wrote a phone number right on the map. It's a restaurant but they'll know where to find me." Lee felt her voice rushing faster and faster, speeding away from her. She felt as if any moment she might burst into tears. "And I wrote you a letter. It just explains things better than I've been able to. Maybe you'll want to read it."

She looked desperately around the room. "Joanna," she said, and this time Joanna looked up at her with a gaze so closed and stony that it made Lee feel as if she had been struck. "Here," Lee said. She fumbled for the tack. "You'll always know where I am now. Always. That's a promise. You call me and I'll come."

Joanna stopped brushing, her eyes on Lee. "Is that a true story?" she said.

"No," Lee said quietly. "It's not a story at all."

Lee crouched down beside Joanna. As soon as Lee bent down, Joanna stiffened. She grabbed at the hairbrush again and jerked her eyes down. Lee was so close, she could hear the light and spark of electricity as Joanna furiously brushed her bride doll's hair. She could see her daughter's hand tremble; she swore she could hear her daughter's closed fist of a heart loosen just a beat. Gently Lee reached up one hand and slowly, carefully, as if she were reaching for something as fragile and breakable as a dream, she touched Joanna's hair, and although Joanna didn't take her eyes from her doll, she didn't jerk her head away from Lee's hand. She didn't move away, not for a very long time.

When she left Joanna's room, Joanna, head down, was still furiously brushing the doll's hair. Lee saw Lila folding clothes in one of the rooms and stopped. Lila looked up, awkward. "Thank you," Lee said, and slowly walked past.

Jim was at the front door, waiting for her.

"She's all right," Lee said.

"What about you?" he said. "You don't look so good."

She shrugged. "As soon as I have one, I'll give you my address and phone number. I'm going to get a place big enough for visits."

"It's funny, isn't it," Jim said. "All these years, and now I'll always know where you are. I can pick up the phone and call you."

She leaned toward him and kissed him, so gently that he was startled when she pulled away. "No," she said. "It's not funny at all." She studied his face. "What should I say? I'll see you?"

He half smiled at her.

"Okay. I'll see you, Jim Archer."

"I'll see you, Lee Archer."

He touched her face, just for a moment, and then she stepped down from the porch and was gone.

Joanna hadn't said one thing about Lee's leaving. Jim walked into her room and saw with a small shock the map hanging on her bulletin board, but Joanna herself wasn't looking at it at all. He saw a sealed envelope on the dresser. Joanna's name was written in Lee's handwriting. "You all right, puss?" he said, stroking her hair. He crouched down beside her. "You know how much we love you?" he said. She continued to brush her doll's hair.

And when later Jim glanced out the window and saw her digging in the dark dirt by the rosebushes, Fisher's favorite bone-burying spot, he didn't call out to her. He didn't remind her to be careful of what she might one day miss. He waited until she had buried the map and letter deep in the earth, until she had come back inside. For a moment he thought of digging out the letter, of saving it for a time when she might one day want it, or of reading it himself, finding out what Lee's words to her daughter were; but then Joanna was beside him, smelling of the earth and the heat, and instead he simply placed one hand on her head.

That night Lila made a special chocolate cake, she bought a special book of fairy tales for Joanna, and she acted as if it were an everyday occurrence. The three of them sat at the table, and after dessert Jim insisted they all go out to a double feature and after that for ice cream, until they were too exhausted to do anything but sleep.

The morning Lee left Jim got up early and opened the pharmacy at six. He wanted company, but people were used to the opening hour of seven. They could look in all they wanted, but no one would come in. He finally made himself a chocolate milkshake and sat at the fountain stirring it with a straw for almost twenty minutes before he realized how little he liked chocolate shakes.

Every hour he looked at the clock he could see Lee doing something else, only now he knew she was really doing it. At ten she'd be on the plane. By twelve she'd be in Madison. And by six he'd be home with his wife and his daughter. He'd take all of them out to a dinner and a double feature. They'd all stay up late. Later and later, until distance and time had blurred him and Lee apart again into seemingly separate and connected lives.

Lee, who had always been good at leaving, arrived at the flight gate so late, she nearly missed her plane altogether. She raced toward the closing gate door, stumbled past an aisle of irritated passengers to find her seat.

She sat by herself, in the back of the plane, staring out at the sky, trying to catch her breath. She had a picture of Joanna stuck in her wallet, beside the one of Karen. She had a small bag of airport postcards that she thought she'd send to her as soon as she was home. She had already sent one to Andy, of the Baltimore skyline thawing toward spring. She had said she was coming home for good, that she wanted to see him and hoped he wanted to see her, too. She had sent a card to Rico to tell him she wanted her job back, that she could now bake breads so delicious that just one bite could cure loneliness or a fearful heart or even the slightest need to keep secrets.

She wished she had the Want ads with her. This time, whatever apartment she found was going to be home. She'd need something big, something with a back room she could now fix up into something a small girl might want to stay in, although maybe the only small girl in it might be that of a ghost she had loved—and even so, there was an odd kind of comfort in that. Who knew what kind of life this daughter of hers was going to have and what part Lee might get to play in it? Lee would send her birthday gifts every year, and cards and letters, with her return address so Joanna could send them back unopened if she wanted to. But Lee wouldn't intrude with a call. Maybe there would be nothing but silence, maybe all Joanna'd ever want was Jim and Lila, but maybe, when Joanna hit the natural rebellion of puberty, or even later, when she was seventeen or eighteen, or nineteen like Lee had been that day she had disappeared, maybe then some of Lee's genes would storm out of her and beg to be recognized and healed. Joanna might be stealing makeup and junk jewelry from Woolworth's, and as soon as she got them out of the store she wouldn't remember why she had wanted them in the first place. She might be falling so deeply in love with a boy so wild and fresh that running off with him might seem like a good idea. And maybe then, right before she decided not to (she had Jim's genes in her, too, after all), she'd suddenly remember something similar about Lee—like a fragment of a story. She'd feel a shock, a connection. And maybe by then Joanna would want to know her. Maybe she'd have all the questions finally ready for Lee, questions Lee would have stopped running from a long, long time ago.

Lee looked out of the plane. Below her were houses and a rickrack of roads and highways and people who might have once been looking for her, counting on a reward, trying to force her back to her life.

"The captain has turned on the seat belt sign," a voice said.

In ten more minutes she'd be back in Wisconsin. Lee clapped her arms about her body. She listened to the rustlings around her. A man dressed completely in black gave a loud, bored yawn. There was a young girl, her red hair cut into a bristling rooster cut, fiddling for something in a huge black leather purse. Lee leaned against her seat, her heart bumping so crazily that she pressed her arms against her chest to still it. Suddenly she wanted always to remember the way she was feeling. She wanted always to remember the plane, the scratchy voice of the flight attendant, the scuffs on her shoes. Lee's breath stitched up; she felt a sudden new exhilarating flicker of fear.

She felt herself lifting up, becoming lighter and lighter, even as the plane began edging into its descent. Outside, nearly invisible in the pale wash of sky, there was already a full white moon, slowly rising. Small distant stars were already growing brighter and brighter until eventually lovers or children or dreamers would catch sight of them and make their wishes. Lee rested her cheek against the plane window and looked down at the ribbon of runway that was speeding up to meet her. The plane hummed and dipped and lowered, and then slowly, finally, headed her home.